PRAISE FOR JAKE TAPPER'S
THE DEVIL MAY DANCE

"The gears of this thriller move expertly and fast... The seriousness of this book never gets in the way of the breathless fun. Tapper obviously enjoyed sourcing it, writing it, and using can-you-top-this gamesmanship from start to finish. Just when you think he's pulled the biggest rabbit out of his hat, he turns out to have been hiding something bigger... Tapper humanizes Sinatra as a victim of forces he never understood and as one of the least objectionable members of the Rat Pack... He also makes Margaret a wonderful role model for the many people who will enjoy this buoyant book."

—Janet Maslin, *New York Times*

"Jake Tapper's deep inside knowledge of power, greed, and politics fuels this riveting page-turner. Warning: Don't start this book late at night unless you have no plans the next day." —Harlan Coben

"A wickedly fun, adrenaline-fueled page-turner about Hollywood power and corruption. From page one, I was sold. Get ready to get lost in the suspense of this story. —Shonda Rhimes

"Tapper's excellent sequel to *The Hellfire Club* opens with a highly effective tease... Tapper makes good use of the rich source material." —*Publishers Weekly* (starred review)

"Frank Sinatra, Robert Kennedy, and Charlie Marder—you can't lose with this combination of characters in *The Devil May Dance*. Jake Tapper explores the thin lines between politics, pop culture, and crime, and the story is always gripping, accurate, and right on target when it comes to underlining that the past is prologue and politics are always played for keeps."   —Michael Connelly

"Sinatra is the most intriguing and fully developed of the book's famous characters, but Tapper deftly sketches all of them…Rich in research, packed with pop culture and historical detail. The book is set six decades ago, but neither politics nor show business has changed as much as we might hope. Tapper connects the dots, but he does it with a light hand that doesn't slow down the Marders' adventures."   —Colette Bancroft, *Tampa Bay Times*

"One helluva mystery—bursting with early '60s luminarios from Bobby Kennedy to Frank Sinatra and his swinging gang. Tapper effortlessly blends a journalist's sharp eye with a storyteller's keen sense of suspense: The result is as bracing as the bourbon the book's Rat Packers knock back and as fizzy as the champagne the Hollywood stars swig. Raise a glass."   —Gillian Flynn

"Hugely entertaining…a thoroughly involving story, and Tapper is clearly having a great time re-creating Tinseltown in the Swinging Sixties."   —David Pitt, *Booklist*

THE DEVIL MAY DANCE

THE DEVIL MAY DANCE

A NOVEL

JAKE TAPPER

BACK BAY BOOKS

Little, Brown and Company

New York   Boston   London

For Alice and Jack
I love you the most

———

Copyright © 2021 by Jake Tapper

Back Bay Books / Little, Brown and Company
Hachette Book Group
1290 Avenue of the Americas, New York, NY 10104
littlebrown.com

Originally published in hardcover by Little, Brown and Company, May 2021
First Back Bay Books trade paperback edition, May 2022

Back Bay Books is an imprint of Little, Brown and Company, a division of Hachette Book Group, Inc. The Back Bay Books name and logo are trademarks of Hachette Book Group, Inc.

The publisher is not responsible for websites (or their content) that are not owned by the publisher.

The Hachette Speakers Bureau provides a wide range of authors for speaking events. To find out more, go to hachettespeakersbureau.com or call (866) 376-6591.

ISBN 9780316530231 (hardcover) / 9780316530248 (paperback)
LCCN 2020947376

Printing 1, 2022

LSC-C

Trouble just seems to come my way—
unbidden, unwelcome, unneeded.

—Frank Sinatra, 1971

THE DEVIL MAY DANCE

CHAPTER ONE

GLENDALE, CALIFORNIA

January 1962

Frank Sinatra handed the congressman the bottle of Jack Daniel's.

"These places give me the heebie-jeebies," Sinatra said, looking around the graveyard. "What about you, Charlie?"

Congressman Charlie Marder paused as he surveyed the small group circling the makeshift bar: stacks of paper cups and whiskey on top of a marble crypt.

"Sure," Charlie said. "I mean, who likes graveyards?"

"Graverobbers," said Peter Lawford. A young woman laughed. Her friend, who was a model or actress of some kind, rolled her eyes. They'd joined up somewhere along the way.

"How about maggots?" added Dean Martin in his rich baritone, prompting *Eww*s from the ladies. Earlier, Charlie had asked his wife, Margaret, if she'd caught the girls' names. "Betty and Veronica," she'd replied. "Or might as well be."

The Rat Pack—which tonight included Sinatra, Martin, Lawford, Sammy Davis Jr., and Shirley MacLaine—and their assorted hangers-on had come to Forest Lawn Memorial Park not to mourn the dead but to rage against death, to celebrate, to drink and be merry. Just a couple of hours earlier, at Puccini—the restaurant Sinatra co-owned with Lawford—they had received word that an old acquaintance, Salvatore Lucania (better known as mobster

Charles "Lucky" Luciano), had dropped dead of a heart attack in Naples. It put them in a reflective mood. The news was especially disconcerting because they'd gathered at the restaurant to toast the memory of innovative TV comic Ernie Kovacs, who'd been killed in a car accident two weeks earlier.

It had been pouring the night of Kovacs's crash, but the skies were clear now. At this moment, before dawn, the heavens twinkled with scattered stars, and the lush grass of Forest Lawn Memorial Park glistened with dew.

"Fill 'er up, Smoky!" said Sinatra to Sammy Davis Jr., using the nickname that was a nod to his four-pack-a-day habit. Sinatra placed his empty glass on the marble crypt in front of Davis, who was holding the bottle of Jack Daniel's at that moment.

As Davis poured the whiskey, ash from his cigarette drifted onto the rim of Sinatra's glass. Davis glanced over to see if Sinatra had noticed, then quickly dusted it off. "Clark Gable's over there," Sammy said to no one in particular, gesturing up a hill.

"Where?" asked Betty. "I don't see anyone."

"He's been dead for two years, ya quin," snarled Sinatra.

"Now, Pope," cautioned Martin.

"Unless I'm mistaken," said Margaret, "wife number five arranged to have Gable buried next to wife number three."

"Interred," said Charlie.

Sinatra rolled his eyes. He'd turned forty-six last month and what once might have played as impish now registered as old-man cranky. The sharp light from the streetlamp near them emphasized the crags in his weathered face, the scar on his neck, the onset of sagging jowls.

"Learn to read a room," Margaret jokingly advised Charlie.

"Frankly, my dear, I don't give a damn," he replied.

"Classy broad, that Kay Gable," Davis said about Gable's fifth and final wife.

"She gave birth to their kid at the same hospital where Clark croaked weeks before," Martin recalled.

"Look at the memory on Daig," said Sinatra.

"Ring-a-ding-ding," said Martin, grabbing the bottle of Jack and taking a swig. "Who wants another?"

"I do." MacLaine, elfin-looking in her pixie cut and bright red lipstick, raised a hand. "Why would she want her husband to be buried next to another woman?"

"*Interred,*" Lawford drawled.

"Carole Lombard was the love of his life," explained Davis. "Kay knew that."

"Too bright," Sinatra growled. He was glaring at a streetlamp that cast a punishing white light, washing them all out so it was almost as if they were in a grainy black-and-white talkie, Frank reduced to Ol' Gray Eyes. "Pucci, give me your piece."

"Fat" Tony Pucci, Chicago mobster Sam Giancana's gigantic bodyguard, had a face that looked like it'd been whacked with an oar. Pucci glanced at Giancana, a buddy of Sinatra's whose presence none dared question. The mobster nodded his assent, the light reflecting off his thick glasses, and Pucci reached underneath his jacket and pulled out what looked to Charlie to be a Colt Python .357 Magnum with a four-inch barrel and a nickel finish.

Sinatra, cigarette dangling from his lips, grabbed the piece, aimed it at the streetlamp, squinted, and fired. He missed, and the bullet pinged off the metal of the pole. He fired again. Another miss.

Giancana snorted. He would not have missed.

Charlie scanned the area to see if anyone had heard the shots, but no one was around for miles, it seemed.

Margaret remembered reading about Sinatra getting arrested after he and Ava Gardner took his Smith and Wesson .38s and shot out streetlamps and storefront windows in the small town of Indio, California.

"Apparently he was a better shot in Indio that night," Charlie whispered to her, sharing the same thought.

No one cracked wise about Sinatra's poor aim. This was the Pope, as he was known; they kept quiet. After missing a third shot, Sinatra calmly handed the gun back to Fat Tony.

"You do it," Sinatra said to the bodyguard. "Jack Daniel's keeps moving the target."

"Wobble-wobble," said Martin.

Fat Tony aimed and fired, and the bulb exploded, dropping a cloak of gray upon them all.

"How's your bird, Pope?" Martin asked, a Rat Pack inquiry about the status of a fellow traveler's penis or, more broadly, his happiness in that arena. The others held their breath. Above them hung a half-moon, about which Sinatra started to sing:

Something, something, man in the moon
something, something, baboon,
something, something swoon...

Everyone exhaled; the wind had blown his dark mood away with the clouds. Lawford led the pack in a charge up the hill as Martin sang a song mocking the very young girlfriend of Sinatra's rival Elvis Presley. *"Are you lonesome tonight?"* he crooned. *"Are you horny tonight? Have you reached puberty yet, my dear girl?"*

Sinatra cackled. He'd hosted the television special *Welcome Home, Elvis* after Presley's discharge from the army, but Sinatra made no secret of the fact that he found most rock and roll deplorable; he thought the music was written and performed by cretinous goons, and Presley was the gooniest of them all.

Charlie and Margaret walked slowly, bringing up the rear. Margaret sighed, seeming annoyed.

"Stop pretending that this isn't a little cool," Charlie said, indicating the scene—they were hanging with icons of the zeit-geist, boozing in a celebrity graveyard in the middle of the night.

"Ring-a-ding-ding," said Margaret dryly.

The crack of a gunshot echoed across the grass. It took Charlie and Margaret a moment to make out what was going on: Davis was firing Fat Tony's gun at a grave. Or, more precisely, at the sculpted angel on top of a crypt.

"What th—" said Margaret, poking Charlie in the ribs.

"I think 'Who the' is more like it," Lawford said to Margaret. "Doyle, the guy buried there, was a producer who screwed Sammy back when he was touring the country on the Chitlin' Circuit with his dad and uncle."

Charlie looked at the crypt. He didn't recognize the name.

Davis yelled, "Son of a bitch!" as he fired off another round. The angel's head exploded.

"There ya go, Smoky!" Martin cheered. He ashed his cigarette on a freshly dug grave, then took a swig from a paper cup.

"I'm not done yet," Davis said, pulling the trigger once more. The blast hit the cherub in the crotch, shattering the statue. One of the pieces of concrete clipped Charlie.

"Oof," he said, grabbing his shoulder.

"Honey!" Margaret cried.

"I'm fine," he said, rubbing the bruise.

"Oh, man," Davis said. "I am so, so sorry."

Davis was soused but clearly concerned. He made his way precariously toward Charlie, wobbly and contrite. The singer was a wee man, not even five foot five, all bone and sinew, maybe ninety pounds dressed for winter.

"It's nothing," Charlie said.

"Yumpin' Yiminy, now it's a clambake!" yelled Sinatra. "More booze!" Another bottle materialized as the pack continued its run through the cemetery, minus Giancana and Fat Tony, who'd turned to walk back to their car. Charlie and Margaret stayed in place, leaning on a thick, slightly cracked tombstone.

"Irish exit," Charlie said, motioning toward the departing mobsters.

"Not sure they're Irish, honey. Did it tear your shirt?"

Charlie lifted his hand, revealing a small hole in his suit jacket. "That might have been there before," he lied.

She poked her finger into the hole. "You're bleeding," she said. She held her finger up to capture whatever light she could steal from the moon. "We should go back to the car, see if we need to take you to a hospital."

"Oh, c'mon," said Charlie, who still had shrapnel in his chest from World War II. "I'm fine."

His shoulder might be fine, but Margaret knew that Charlie was not. He slept poorly and drank too much and worked too many hours. He often lost his temper over trivial things, and she worried about how to deal with it. Eighteen years earlier, Charlie had experienced the horrors of war, fighting the Krauts in France after D-Day, and in the past few years Margaret was often reminded of the army's slogan that "every man has his breaking point." She was constantly looking for ways to prevent Charlie from reaching his. Whatever the doctors were labeling it, combat exhaustion or combat neurosis or battle fatigue, Margaret knew it would be with him forever. Beyond that, his life in Congress, where he'd been for almost a decade now, was infinitely frustrating—accomplishing anything good required Sisyphean efforts, while ethical compromises were everywhere. And at some point along the way, Charlie found that the constant fundraising and glad-handing to stay in office for his New York constituents had begun to eclipse the work itself.

Ahead, the members of the Rat Pack and their hangers-on were oblivious to the Marders' concerns; they were soaked in bourbon, singing, laughing, and loudly gossiping about ghosts as they stumbled around the graveyard. Charlie and Margaret could make out pieces of their conversations.

There goes Wallace Beery.
He won an Oscar too, Frank!
Remember he and a couple mobsters beat that guy to death at the Troc?
Suzan Ball.
Lucille's cousin.
Twenty-one?
Cancer.
Bit parts. Aladdin and His Lamp.
Here's the Garden of Memory.
Some reverence, folks, Bogie is over there.

Bogart, Sinatra's hero, was credited with coining the term *Rat Pack* to describe an altogether different group of friends, but both the term and Bogie's beloved Lauren Bacall had been posthumously co-opted by his protégé Sinatra.

Charlie and Margaret headed back, and the snatches of conversation soon grew too distant for them to hear. They made their way over the hills on narrow paved roads to the parking lot. Earlier, Margaret, the ever-prepared former Girl Scout, had stashed the small first-aid kit she brought with her on all family excursions in the trunk of their rented white 1962 Impala convertible.

"We're missing all the fun," Charlie said as a gunshot followed by the pop of an exploding light bulb cracked in the distance. "I'm really fine, honey."

"Sure sounds like fun," Margaret said as she held out her hand for the keys. Charlie reluctantly produced them.

She inserted the key and opened the trunk while Charlie looked to the hills, where the echoes of crooning and guffaws sounded almost like local wildlife. Then Margaret screamed.

From the gauzy illumination of a distant streetlamp, Charlie saw the shape in the trunk, a big shape.

It was a body.

Charlie stepped closer. He recognized the face, as did Margaret, who turned away. He looked with horror at the woman that they'd last seen days before and that he'd seen quite a bit of in the past few weeks.

Her eyes were two bloody caverns; they must have been shot out. There was some brain and bone residue in the trunk but not enough to suggest she had been shot there. Her mouth was agape, her jaw helplessly, horrifically slack.

Charlie and Margaret stood frozen until the sudden arrival of the Rat Pack, who apparently had raced over in response to Margaret's shriek.

Sinatra looked into the trunk.

"Charlie," he said. "Just what the hell have you done?"

CHAPTER TWO

NEW YORK CITY

One month earlier—December 1961

The Marders' phone did not usually ring at five in the morning, but Charlie had been up, staring at the ceiling, so he picked it up right away.

It was his father, Winston Marder. "Call my lawyer, Alistair Crutchfield. Then go to my house, get my diabetes medicine, and bring it to me. I'm in the Tombs."

"You're what?"

"It's a nickname for the federal—"

"I know what the Tombs are!"

"Good, then I don't need to give you directions." The line went dead.

Charlie dressed quietly so as not to wake Margaret. She'd gone to sleep before him last night; these days, she regularly turned in before he did. Charlie's nights were consumed with meetings, fundraisers, drinks with aides and consultants. He'd been in Congress for roughly eight years now, providing constituent services, pressing the flesh at street fairs and parties for local big shots, helping veterans, pushing for the Civil Rights Acts of 1957 and 1960 and, less successfully, the Equal Pay Act for women. Charlie did whatever he could to stay viable as an Eisenhower/Rockefeller Republican in an increasingly Democratic Manhattan.

He tiptoed down the steps of their Greenwich Village brownstone and quickly hailed a cab to the Manhattan House of Detention, called the Tombs because the original structure, built in 1838, had resembled an ancient Egyptian mausoleum. The prison had been torn down and rebuilt twice since then, but the nickname stuck, as did its reputation for unrivaled wretchedness.

Two hours later Charlie was wedged into a small booth deep in the bowels of the facility looking through a thick pane of glass at his freshly arrested father.

"This place is infested with cockroaches and rats," Winston Marder barked into his end of the telephone. "My cellmate weighs around eight hundred pounds and was pinched for molesting children. How do you *think* I'm doing?"

"But what did they charge you with?" Charlie asked.

"Some nonsense about consorting with known criminals. You can blame the playboy in the White House and his prick brother," his father said, apparently by way of explanation. "A particularly specious charge to level against an attorney, as Alistair will prove. I'm sure they'll cast it as part of *Bobby's* crusade against organized crime."

By his inflection, Winston conveyed his contempt for the attorney general. Charlie wondered if there was any truth to the charges but didn't ask; the walls probably had ears.

"But why aren't they offering bail?" Charlie asked.

"Some nonsense about me being a flight risk," Winston said. "Where's Alistair? Didn't you call him?"

"He's in Washington, he's coming back on the first train."

Winston grunted, a guttural note of dissatisfaction.

Winston Marder had a predilection for dark rooms and evening hours, so it had been years since Charlie had seen his father in such harsh light. What he saw under the fluorescent bulbs was dismaying. Winston's skin looked almost greenish. The bags under his eyes appeared inflated and underlined. He was sixty-five but looked eighty, and his voice was shaky.

To the outside world, Winston was a savvy fixer and New York power broker who had worked his way up from a Brooklyn tenement to a four-story Upper East Side residence by making the right friends and the right deals. A Teddy Roosevelt Republican, he'd fought on the western front during the Great War and was wounded in the Second Battle of the Somme. Winston had a hand in every political pot he could reach. Seeking distraction after his wife's death, he'd worked hard with his friend Governor Rockefeller to deliver the Empire State to Nixon in 1960, only to see that slick Jack Kennedy and his bootlegger father snatch it away.

The double blow of his wife's death three years before and the election-night loss seemed to defeat Winston. Charlie's father now often failed to show up for lunch dates at the Harvard Club—something that would once have been as unthinkable as putting ice in his whiskey—and Charlie frequently paid unannounced visits to his home to check on him. His dad initially would seem as sharp as the knuckle-duster trench knife he'd brought back from the war, but after a few drinks he'd sometimes repeat himself or descend into non sequiturs. Now, looking at his father through a cloudy, scratched glass window in the tiny room that stank of filth and mildew, Charlie worried that the trauma of the arrest had accelerated Winston's decline.

There was a rap on the steel door, and Charlie turned to see a guard and a man he guessed was an associate sent by Crutchfield. The young man—closely cropped blond hair, air of noblesse oblige—dripped with disdain for his surroundings. Winston gave the slightest nod to acknowledge their arrival, then lowered his head and whispered urgently into the receiver: "Find out what Bobby wants and give it to him."

Charlie looked at his father, waiting for more, but the guard grabbed Charlie under his arm and roughly pulled him out of the seat so the young lawyer could take his place.

CHAPTER THREE

NEW YORK CITY

December 1961

Charlie couldn't wait to breathe the cold air outside after the stench and claustrophobia of the Tombs. A brutal wind ripped his coat open; a winter storm had rolled onto Manhattan Island, pelting the city with freezing rain. He looked left and right for a neon sign. He needed a bar.

Ah. Across the street: the Last Shot.

It was 9:40 a.m.

The day drinking had started when his shell shock—a constant state of restless anxiety—had returned in full force, around the time of his fortieth birthday. So far he'd done a decent job of hiding it. Pushing away thoughts of what would happen if Margaret found out was as much a part of his routine as the mouthwash and chewing gum.

He had gone from nearly daily to assuredly daily drinking earlier that year, after a tough election. Forced into a brutal contest for his House seat against a young Democratic city councilman, Charlie reluctantly hired an Albany consultant with legendarily fungible morality, a man who made promises to local labor unions that Charlie learned about only after he'd won. Some union goons came calling with a list of demands Charlie couldn't possibly accommodate, and they made it clear they were backed by friends in Chicago whose manners weren't so genteel. They had delivered the union vote for Charlie Marder and now it was time for Charlie to deliver for them.

Charlie kept all this stress from Margaret, said nothing about the fire that burned inside him that only booze could quell. But now, before he could even step off the curb and cross Canal for that breakfast bourbon, a black Chrysler Imperial pulled up. On the passenger side, a man with white hair and a bullfrog neck that swallowed his chin rolled down his window and flashed his ID.

"Addington White, Department of Justice," he said. "Hop in."

Charlie hesitated, looking longingly at the entrance to the bar, then ruefully did as he was told. He guessed that the driver and the man in the back seat were also with the Justice Department. Based on their washed-out faces and similar builds, he assumed they were once-trim veterans now growing soft due to too much time behind their desks.

Charlie focused on his breathing, which sometimes helped him overcome the agitation in his soul until he was able to get his hands on the means to drown it. Back in France, fighting the Krauts, he'd learned to jam his anxieties and emotions into some faraway corner of his mind. He tried to do this now; he needed to channel all his energy toward figuring out a way to extricate his father.

The agents were quiet. Then White said, "We'll be there in a few short minutes, Congressman."

"There?" Charlie said. "Am I under arrest?"

"No, no," White said. "Nothing like that."

"And you're taking me..." Charlie said.

"To a meeting," White said.

"Do I need to call my lawyer?" Charlie asked. "My wife?" He looked at his watch; at this hour Margaret would have dropped Lucy, seven, off at elementary school and would likely be at a playground with Dwight, five. He probably wouldn't be able to reach her on the phone until after lunch. He and his wife had moved back to his Manhattan congressional district after an insanely crazed first year in Congress, during which both he and Margaret had been enveloped in a vast conspiracy. Charlie now spent his weeks in DC and traveled home from the capital on the weekends and during congressional breaks, as was the case now.

"No," said White. "The attorney general wants to see you."

"Well, great." Charlie wasn't sure which made him angrier, being shanghaied by the Feds or missing his morning appointment with Jack Daniel's. The sight of his father—stooped in his prison grays, undereye bags so big they could hide contraband, hands shaking—had hollowed him.

"Find out what Bobby wants," his father had said, "and give it to him." What Attorney General Kennedy wanted, Charlie could not yet fathom.

Winston Marder hated Ambassador Joseph Kennedy and, by association, his sons Jack and Bobby with the intensity of the hellfire that the Allies had unleashed on Dresden. Charlie, for his part, had gotten along with the Democratic princes, an attitude born of both hope and necessity.

Charlie had campaigned, unenthusiastically, for Nixon. But when he lived in DC, before he and Margaret started their family, he had enjoyed having then Senator Kennedy and, more important, his wife, Jackie, as neighbors. And he respected Robert Kennedy's brute force of intellect and ambition, even if he didn't trust him; they had spent some time together due to Charlie's work on a House Armed Services Oversight subcommittee as well as socially. He told Margaret he thought Robert the sharpest of the Kennedys, and she'd pointedly asked how he could be so sure without having met any of the Kennedy sisters. Touché—he'd admitted, and not for the first time in their nearly seventeen-year marriage, that she was right.

Margaret had been eagerly anticipating Dwight starting kindergarten so she could return to her work in clinical research as a postdoc in zoology at Brooklyn College, specifically studying equine behavior. She'd always found animals easier to understand than humans; they were so refreshingly straightforward and real. Lately, reading *Runaway Bunny* or watching animated shorts featuring Daffy Duck and Porky Pig or arranging the stuffed bears on her children's beds, she felt she was going out of her mind.

The car pulled over on the east side of Fifth Avenue in front of St. Patrick's Cathedral. Charlie and his Justice Department sentries removed their hats as they walked through the massive, intricately carved bronze doors and into the sanctuary. Charlie heard the choir rehearsing for Christmas and winced.

Wahr Mensch und wahrer Gott,
hilft uns aus allem Leide,
rettet von Sünd und Tod

The last time he'd heard German, he'd been in France, listening to defeated prisoners of war. He could understand the lyrics: "True man and true God / It helps us from all trouble / Saves us from sin and death."

Sin and death. Charlie's already foul mood darkened. He needed that drink.

Addington White guided Charlie past men, women, and children in winter coats lighting candles. In the distance, lit brightly, was the main sanctuary, which contained the crypts of past archbishops. An organ of nine thousand pipes filled the chamber with the kind of music that always unsettled Charlie, calling to mind Lon Chaney unmasked in *Phantom of the Opera*. He followed his escorts down the main aisle, passing dozens of empty darkened wooden pews and a white marble baptistery, a place of purification where worshippers were absolved of their sins.

White patted Charlie's shoulder, less a friendly gesture than a way to guide him down a pew, at the end of which, next to a white marble column, was a familiar silhouette: a nest of hair, a beaky nose, and an overbite. The man's elbows rested on his knees, his head hung low, and his unruly bangs flopped forward; it was hard to tell if he was deep in prayer or lost in thought.

Charlie eased himself next to the man. "I hope I'm not interrupting you, Mr. Attorney General."

Kennedy raised his head and forced a smile. "Hello, Charlie," he said. The attorney general reached down into the briefcase next to his feet and withdrew what appeared to be a sandwich wrapped in tinfoil. Dispensing with any further pleasantries, looking toward the altar rather than at Charlie, Kennedy spoke quietly. "I'm sure you're concerned about your father." He peeled back the tinfoil and took a bite. To Charlie, whose olfactory gifts were a constant curse, the smell of fried egg was unmistakable.

"I'm not quite clear what the charges are," Charlie said. "How can an attorney get in trouble for consorting with known criminals if the alleged criminals are clients?"

"I'm not certain how steeped you are in organized crime, but Sam Giancana is, one, a murderous thug and, two, not one of your father's clients. And we're not talking just consorting—there is evidence of conspiracy."

Charlie knew who Giancana was, of course, primarily because two years ago, Robert Kennedy himself, as Democratic counsel on the Senate committee investigating labor racketeering, had chastised the mobster for laughing while invoking his Fifth Amendment right against self-incrimination.

"I thought only little girls giggled, Mr. Giancana," Kennedy had said.

The choir abruptly began rehearsing another song, "Hark! The Herald Angels Sing," startling both men. Kennedy chuckled; Charlie, whose heart had been pounding since his father called him that morning, exhaled. What did Kennedy want? But voicing that rage would only hurt his father. He tried to relax and listen to the choir. He held no cards.

"He's an old man," Charlie said. "It doesn't make any sense. Does Rockefeller know?"

"I'm sure there's very little that goes on in New York that the governor is unaware of," Kennedy said dryly. "This is very simple, really. We need help combating organized crime, help that your father is refusing to provide. Information."

Kennedy took another bite of his sandwich. Chewed slowly. Swallowed. The casual arrogance drove Charlie mad. And meanwhile, his father, his poor sad dad, was in a dank cell downtown.

The attorney general was as ruthless as he was effective. He'd been an aide and loyal friend to Senator Joe McCarthy through the years of McCarthy's witch hunts right up until the senator was censured. Then it was as if his time as chief Democratic counsel on the McCarthy Committee had never happened. Afterward, as chief counsel of the Senate Labor Rackets Committee in the late 1950s, Kennedy pursued Teamsters boss Jimmy Hoffa by starting with the suspect and then proceeding to find the crime. Kennedy ran his brother's 1960 presidential campaign with the same single-mindedness; Democratic primary rival Senator Hubert Humphrey once expressed outrage over "that young, emotional, juvenile Bobby" paying off local West Virginia pols with "wild abandon." Humphrey was hardly the only suspicious Democrat; the entire civil rights community, including and especially Martin Luther King Jr., eyed the Kennedy brood warily.

Liberal wariness hadn't slowed the Kennedys' sprint to power, and they now had the levers of government to use as they saw fit. Charlie had never fully trusted the younger Kennedy, who had Charlie and his dad in his sights.

"We need information," Kennedy said. He took another bite and this time seemed to chew even more slowly.

Excruciating. And yet Charlie had to remain silent. He hadn't been aware that his father was in contact with Giancana, though such an allegation was not a surprise; his dad had spent decades overcoming previously insurmountable hurdles. Often that required knowing some unsavory characters. He knew that his father occasionally had to communicate with members of the Five Families, not to have anyone rubbed out but to guarantee the availability of union labor.

"I'm trying to figure out how I can help, but I'm drawing a blank," Charlie said. "I don't know anything about my father's relationship with Giancana. I didn't even know he had one." He wondered if the attorney general knew that the Teamsters had also been visiting Charlie in New York, had been leaning on him for almost a year.

"Did you ever hear of a man called Mooney?" Kennedy asked. "Or Momo?"

"No," said Charlie, thinking about it. "No Mooney. No Momo." Why did mobsters always have such moronic nicknames? "I'm guessing you've seized my dad's files and haven't found anything."

"Nothing yet," said Kennedy.

"Who's Momo?" Charlie asked. "Who's Mooney?"

"Aliases," Kennedy said. "Giancana."

"*Hail the son of righteousness!*" the choir sang. "*Light and life to all He brings.*" The lyrics were about Jesus; Charlie couldn't help but wonder if the Kennedy brothers thought of themselves as the sons of righteousness. There was certainly nothing virtuous about their father, the would-be appeaser of Hitler. From the pew behind them, Addington White gave Kennedy a manila envelope. The attorney general opened it and handed some papers to Charlie.

"A transcript from a wiretap this week," Kennedy explained. "Giancana and Johnny Rosselli, the Mob's man in Hollywood."

In the dim light of the nave, Charlie read:

ROSSELLI: You ask Winston?

GIANCANA: I leave messages with his secretary.

ROSSELLI: Christ, he doesn't call you back? What the sainted [expletive deleted]—

"I don't know what any of this is about," Charlie said. "Keep reading," said Kennedy.

GIANCANA: What happened with Frank?

ROSSELLI: We talked. I said, "Frankie, can I ask one question?" He says, "Johnny, I took Sam's name and wrote it down and told Bobby Kennedy, 'This is my buddy. This is my buddy. This is what I want you to know, Bob.'"

GIANCANA: Well, I don't know who the [expletive deleted] he's talking to. Maybe one of these days he will actually do what he promised.

ROSSELLI: He says he wrote your name down.

GIANCANA: Well, one minute he tells me this and the next minute he tells me that. The last time I talked to him was at the hotel in Florida and he said, "Don't worry about it, if I can't talk to the old man, I'm going to talk to *the* man." One minute he says he talked to Robert and the next minute he says he hasn't talked to him. It's a lot of [expletive deleted]. Why lie to me?

ROSSELLI: If he can't deliver, I want him to tell me, "John, the load's too heavy."

GIANCANA: When he says he's gonna do a guy a little favor, I don't give a [expletive deleted] how long it takes, he's got to give you a little favor.

The transcript ended there. Charlie handed the papers back to Kennedy.

"I don't know what they're talking about either," Kennedy said. "I don't know what favor Giancana wants regarding me or my father or my brother. No one ever brought any of this up to me."

"Who's Frank?" Charlie said.

"Sinatra," Kennedy said. He reached into his briefcase and withdrew another transcript.

FORMOSA: Let's show 'em. Let's show those asshole Hollywood fruitcakes that they can't get away with it as if nothing's happened. Let's hit Sinatra. Or I could whack out a couple of those other guys, Lawford and that Martin, and I could take the coon and put his other eye out.

GIANCANA: No, I've got other plans for them.

"Who's Formosa?" Charlie asked.

"Just another one of these thugs," Kennedy said. "You know the kind, they got 'em in New York too."

Charlie looked at him again, trying to read his face. Did he know about the union toughs? He saw no indication one way or the other in Kennedy's eyes.

The carol drew to a close, and the church was briefly, dramatically silent save for the hushed stirrings of worshippers lighting candles and finding seats. Charlie looked around; no one seemed to recognize him or his famous pew mate.

"Sinatra thinks the president is going to stay with him when we go out to California in March," Kennedy said quietly. "He's been on the president's case about it ever since the inauguration. Apparently, he's had all this work done at his Rancho Mirage estate prepping for a visit. Whole place wired for sound. A press filing room. He's even building a helipad."

Charlie had to smile at the excess. "You don't want the president to stay there?" Throughout the 1960 election, Sinatra and the Rat Pack had gone all in for Kennedy, and the campaign had been only too happy to capitalize on the fame, the glamour, the money. Sinatra had even rerecorded his Oscar-winning song "High Hopes," written by Sinatra songmeister Jimmy Van Heusen, with new lyrics:

> *Everyone is voting for Jack*
> *'Cause he's got what all the rest lack*
> *Everyone wants to back—Jack*
> *Jack is on the right track!*

As if reading Charlie's mind, Kennedy shrugged. "When I started at Justice, an agent asked me how he could be expected to go after Mob bosses when my brother's most famous supporter is *paisans* with a bunch of them. I took his point. Unfortunately, the FBI doesn't have any evidence supporting the rumors that Frank is mobbed up, but now he shows up in this wiretap."

Charlie, encouraged by Kennedy's willingness to confide in him, ventured a question. "What docs Hoover say?" he asked. "Why don't you ask the FBI to investigate Sinatra?"

Kennedy considered his answer. Finally, he said, "The FBI has been looking into it, but in all honesty, it's not a priority for them.

It's not as if Sinatra and the Rat Pack are actually robbing five casinos in one night, right?"

"I would imagine not," said Charlie.

Kennedy sighed; he clearly wasn't telling Charlie everything he had on the subject of Hoover, who'd been running a rogue fiefdom for years. "I really would prefer to have my own intelligence sources, the way Eisenhower once did," he said. "You ever hear anything about that, Congressman?"

Charlie froze. He had never spoken of his secret work for Eisenhower, which started back in '54. "Ike's Platoon," as its members referred to themselves. Or as they once had; with Ike's retirement, the group largely disbanded.

"Don't think so," Charlie lied.

Suddenly, breaking the choir's silence, a lone treble voice rose above the murmuring.

Once in royal David's city
Stood a lowly cattle shed,
Where a mother laid her baby
In a manger for his bed

"We know a lot of folks in Hollywood," Kennedy said. "Sinatra's working on a picture now for United Artists. It's about a soldier who goes into politics, like my brother. Like you."

"Your brother was a sailor, I believe. I might've heard that somewhere," said Charlie sarcastically, given the vast amounts of PT-109 folklore to which the nation had been subjected—campaign tie clips, a bestselling book, a newspaper serialization in the *Herald Tribune*, a TV dramatization, yet another heroic retelling in *Reader's Digest*, and there was much more to come. A Hollywood studio was currently casting for the feature film of the story—would the lead be played by Warren Beatty? Peter Fonda? The White House would get final approval; Charlie hoped to God that wasn't what Kennedy was referring to.

"It's called *The Manchurian Candidate,*" Kennedy continued. "I don't really care for the project as it's been explained to me. Sinatra called to talk to the president before accepting."

"Right," said Charlie, still thoroughly confused.

"You're about to enter an election year, so congressional recesses are going to be long," Kennedy said. "The head of the studio is a friend, Arthur Krim. What if you became a consultant to the picture? For the next month or so, you can help coach them all in how to walk and talk like soldiers. You can cozy up to Frank and see how legit these rumored Mob ties are. Befriend him. Let me know everything you learn. Everything."

Charlie knew he'd be well out of his element among the Holly-wood set. "And after I do that, you'll make your decision about your brother's visit," he said.

"Yes," Kennedy said.

"So if I figure out what this favor is that Giancana asked of Frank, you'll resolve this situation with my father?"

"We announce the LA trip next month, February latest," Kennedy said, ignoring the question. "You won't have much time."

"Absolutely," Charlie said, hating that he was acquiescing to what was essentially extortion. Nearly a decade in Congress could turn any would-be James Dean into Sal Mineo.

"This stays between us, Charlie," Kennedy said. "Addington here will be your point of contact. Don't trust phones."

"Copy," Charlie said. "And maybe then—"

"No quid pro quos, Charlie," Kennedy said, anticipating Charlie's next question.

Charlie nodded. His dad was in a cell and he had to get him out. He had no choice. He would do whatever Kennedy told him to do.

CHAPTER FOUR

HOLLYWOOD, CALIFORNIA

December 1961

One minute she was missing her children and the next she was lusting for the wiry crooner with the icy blue eyes. Sinatra, whose ballads had once driven schoolgirls to shriek and even faint, was no longer a skinny kid but rather a middle-aged man with an expanding waist and a matching chip on his shoulder. But his charisma was unmistakable—and Margaret stared as he sauntered across the movie set, stepping over cables and around equipment, bringing with him an atmosphere of excitement and, yes, sex. She felt guilty for being there. *The kids are fine with their grandmother,* she thought, grateful that her mother, Catherine, had flown from Ohio to New York to take care of Lucy and Dwight. Catherine had been staying with Margaret's sister, who was in the midst of a family crisis that made Margaret's problems seem trifling by comparison—Margaret's teenage niece, who'd always been some-what troubled, had run away from home.

She mulled over all that, then resumed drooling over Sinatra. In this particular scene, Major Bennett Marco—played by Sinatra—was sweating. Standing at attention, ramrod straight, unblinking, but with a sheen on his forehead and upper lip that betrayed his nerves. Next to him, in front of the gathered crowd, Senator John Yerkes Iselin, played by James Gregory, glanced sideways at Marco, trying to assess his stability. Marco looked ready to hit him.

"You have something to say, soldier?"

"*Cut!*" John Frankenheimer, lanky and intense, sprang from his canvas director's chair and shot an exasperated look at his crew. The actors broke character and exhaled.

"What was wrong with that?" Major Marco had lost his military poise and become once again Frank Sinatra, irritated and impatient.

"The boom was in the frame," Frankenheimer said.

"Sorry!" yelled Joe Edmondson, the soundman.

"Let's take ten," Frankenheimer said. Sinatra glared at him, then looked around the set for a cigarette.

The set—a Senate hearing room—sat in the corner of an immense soundstage that housed various other sets for the film. In one section, the set designer had constructed a train car. In another, the first floor of a house. In the middle of it all stood the Spring Lake Hotel lobby, where a poster promised FUN WITH HYDRANGEAS. Dozens of lights hung from thick chains. Construction workers, crew members, makeup artists, caterers, executives, and others heard Frankenheimer's announcement and began buzzing.

"Whatever happened to those wireless mikes you were working on?" Frankenheimer asked Edmondson. "These booms will be the death of me."

"Still working on them. Last prototype was too staticky."

The director shook his head. "It's 1961, for the love of God. We're still using technology from *Birth of a Nation*." Frankenheimer turned to Charlie. The director had initially seemed irritated to have the congressman and his wife foisted upon him. But after Margaret praised his earlier television work on *Playhouse 90*, and Charlie proclaimed *The Young Savages* the best film of the year, Frankenheimer warmed right up.

"Does this feel right to you, Congressman? Would an army major get in the face of a senator like that?"

"Soldiers tend to defer to people in power," said Charlie. "Especially those in the civilian command structure. But if he's desperate enough, maybe."

Charlie and Margaret had flown to Los Angeles on the Justice Department's dime, dropped off their belongings at the Miramar Hotel in Santa Monica, and gone to the set. The studio had told Frankenheimer to use Charlie as a resource for any question that was military or political. Margaret's decision to accompany Charlie was explained to Frankenheimer as a fringe benefit for him because of her keen academic eye for detail and her ability to advise Angela Lansbury on the behavior of congressional spouses. Oh, the stories Margaret could tell—of the voice-of-God television anchor with breath like a warthog and hands like a squid, the strutting cowboy-booted senator who shrank from confrontation as if he'd been gelded, the 2 Corinthians–quoting reverend who seemed personally to cotton more to Sodom and Gomorrah. Margaret had seen it all—in power, out of power, shiny new thing, old hat, all the highs and lows. Charlie had been stunned that she'd insisted on joining him with the kids still so young and needy, but she had convinced him that she might come in handy. Plus she could meet some movie stars and get a little time in the sun. The truth was she was worried about Charlie and his drinking and his having to fend for himself three thousand miles from home.

"Of course, Marco's in something of a manic state," Margaret noted. "He wouldn't be thinking clearly."

"Yes, the manic state conveyed so subtly by coating my face with petroleum jelly," Sinatra said.

More than two decades of fame and fortune had done little to smooth the rough edges of Sinatra's New Jersey origins; there was a combative arrogance to him that reminded Charlie of his dad. Since arriving in Los Angeles, he hadn't heard from Addington White, didn't know if his father had been moved to a less harsh prison or how he was doing. He hadn't felt so disconnected from his father since the war, and given the precarious state in which he'd last seen him, a hum of anxiety was his constant companion.

Sinatra grabbed a towel off the shoulder of a production assistant and rubbed the Vaseline off his face. His makeup guy, a short old man whom Sinatra called "Brownie," scurried quickly to his boss's side and offered him a Chesterfield cigarette, the kind the singer helped advertise—*Man-Size Satisfaction; Clean, Smooth, Fresh!*—and a light. Sinatra inhaled deeply, then turned to the director. "I'll be in my dressing room when you get your act together here." He stalked off the set, Brownie following in his wake. As Sinatra walked by an attractive young woman presumably from the wardrobe department—she was carrying three dry-cleaned Chinese army uniforms—he said, "Hiya, doll." She blushed.

Frankenheimer rolled his eyes. "He's gifted, but he never has more than one good take in him," he said dryly. "It's usually the first one."

The director reached into his pocket, dug out a pack of Pall Malls, and offered cigarettes to Charlie and Margaret. Smoothly, his lighter appeared in his other hand and he offered them his flame.

Frankenheimer was ascendant. He'd been labeled "television's boy genius for 1954," and in 1957, convinced movies were where an artist could take risks, he directed *The Young Stranger,* a film that everyone pretended to have seen but no one had. Four years later, in 1961, the transition to film was complete with the release of his critically acclaimed "thinking man's crime drama," *The Young Savages*, starring an uncharacteristically restrained Burt Lancaster. Executives saw promise in his craftsmanship and his ability to direct films that could make audiences think while earning studios buckets of money. The wunderkind's bloodshot eyes and bloated face indicated that he might be equally precocious in his noncinematic pursuits.

Margaret discreetly looked around to make sure no one could hear them.

"Oh, this is hardly a secret," Frankenheimer said. "Frank himself told me he's a performer more than an actor."

"Whatever it is, it was good enough to get an Oscar," Margaret said.

Some hammering from the corner of the studio reminded Frankenheimer. "Tomorrow we're shooting the scene on the train," he said.

"The shell-shock scene," Margaret said, helpfully reminding Charlie, who was looking blankly at the director. "Marco is blinking, unsteady, hands shaking so much he can't light a cigarette." Charlie was glad Margaret was there. She seemed to have memorized the entire script already.

"Have you seen a lot of that among your fellow vets?" Frankenheimer asked.

"I've seen battle fatigue manifest itself in all sorts of ways," Charlie said. "The scenes I read with the nightmares rang truer. To me, at any rate."

"Do you think it works for the train scene?" Frankenheimer asked. "We need a quick way to telegraph he's having a rough go of it."

Charlie stroked his chin. "Sure," he said. "It's not just standard battle fatigue that Marco has, right? It's the brainwash thing."

"But what would read as more, you know, standard for a veteran?"

"I've been married to a veteran for sixteen years, since Charlie got back from France, and I've met a ton of veterans since then," Margaret said. "Washington is lined with them. But those are the ones who came back and instead of healing were determined to keep working, keep moving, never stopping, never slowing down, no time to think, no time to let the mind wander. The whole goal is to keep running, to hide it, to pretend there's nothing wrong."

Charlie looked at his wife, who returned his gaze with earnestness. Was she talking about him? Of course she was.

"I have yet to see any veterans in DC with the shakes, with outward signs of pain," Charlie said. "They—we—put one foot in front of the other like everyone else."

"I agree with that," Margaret said. "One foot, then one foot, then one foot, never stopping, because were they to stop, they might feel something they couldn't stand."

Frankenheimer was listening intently.

"So maybe Marco has the shakes or maybe he drinks a lot more than he knows is healthy, just grabs it and downs it all the time when no one's looking, but never enough to stumble or embarrass himself. He drinks the perfect amount so he's somewhere between numb and bumbling, smooth as China silk," Margaret added, and Charlie knew that she knew.

"Ready?" United Artists PR honcho Manny Fontaine asked Charlie and Margaret.

Margaret nodded and Charlie shrugged and Fontaine knocked briskly on Sinatra's dressing-room door, then rested an ear against it to detect signs of movement. He grimaced slightly in Charlie's direction and gaily called out: "Knock-knock!"

Fontaine was slick and handsome and young—late twenties, early thirties—and it would be easy to conclude he was just another mindlessly ambitious studio drone, preternaturally optimistic and cheery. But in the two days since Fontaine had picked them up at Los Angeles International Airport, Charlie and Margaret had come to appreciate the wit he deployed like a surgeon with a scalpel. He was deferential to stars and directors and executives, but it was always with a wink in his inside jacket pocket; he clearly knew how silly it all was. "Just a movie," he would say under his breath, "just some popcorn." Fontaine further tried to bond with Charlie as a fellow veteran; he claimed to have served in Korea with the Eighth Army Ranger Company. Charlie knew those Rangers. They were small Special Forces units expert in what was called "irregular warfare"—tough, nasty stuff.

Sinatra's dressing-room door cracked open to reveal Brownie.

"Why, hello, Mr., um, Brownie," Fontaine said. "I told Mr. Sinatra yesterday that we had hired Congressman Marder here to serve as a consultant on the film, purely as a resource if Mr. Sinatra wants to get more background for his role. Charlie's a war hero. Fought in France. Just wanted to make a cursory introduction, won't take more than thirty seconds."

Brownie remained silent, turning his head toward the room behind him. Charlie remembered a similar maneuver by his father's assistant, blocking and guarding his dad's study door when Charlie was in high school and needed money, permission, a signature on a report card. Echoing that past, Brownie made a regretful expression, then he shook his head no.

"Completely understandable, sorry for bothering you!" Fontaine said brightly. "Tell Mr. Sinatra we are happy to set up another time for him to meet the congressman, at his pleasure and convenience!" Brownie closed the door firmly. Fontaine, unfazed, turned to Charlie and Margaret, arms outstretched, and shooed them back down the hall.

"That went about as well as I thought it would," he said, walking quickly.

Margaret was never one to suffer fools or rude behavior, even if the offender was one of America's biggest stars. "I thought you'd set up this time for Charlie to meet him?"

"I did," Fontaine said with the rueful smile of someone who knew the routine. "Don't worry about it; we'll figure something out." He was already heading toward an exit, waving over his shoulder. "Promise."

Margaret took Charlie's hand. He looked at her grimly; he'd never be able to help his father if he didn't get close enough to Sinatra to learn something that Kennedy and White would find helpful.

"Well, there go our 'High Hopes,'" Margaret said, trying to get a smile out of him.

"Well, let's 'Ac-Cent-Tchu-Ate the Positive,'" Charlie responded, smiling. "At least we're here."

Surrounded by the film crew busily preparing for the next day's shoot, Charlie and Margaret weren't quite sure where to stand or what to do. They spotted Frankenheimer deep in discussion with the set designer and several workers next to the faux train car, which looked as though it had been cut in half lengthwise. This was where Sinatra's Marco would have trouble lighting his cigarette and meet his love interest, played by Janet Leigh. Images of a landscape were projected onto a giant screen outside the train window so it looked as if the train were moving.

"How much footage?" Frankenheimer asked the set designer.

"Twenty minutes," he said, "about."

Frankenheimer ran a hand through his mussed hair. "That's it?" He sighed. "Just make sure we don't have them speed by the same water tower five times. This isn't Bugs Bunny."

"Gotcha."

Charlie and Margaret sat down on a nearby bench near the door to a hallway. "I guess we just sit?" he said.

"What did Cagney say?" Margaret replied. "'They pay me for the waiting, I throw the acting in for free.'"

From somewhere down the hall came a horrifying high-pitched shriek.

"Sweet Jesus, what in the hell?" Charlie asked as Margaret rushed toward the scream. Before she could make it far, however, a wheeled Madagascar cage was pushed around the corner. Inside perched a plump white bird with a long fleshy wattle.

The bird regarded Margaret with cold black eyes, then opened its beak to form a giant black diamond and let out another piercing scream, the loudest that Margaret, in all her years in zoology, had ever heard. It sounded almost like an air-raid siren, a warning for the town populace to run and hide.

Cast and crew on the set behind her filled the air with curses and complaints, but Margaret relished the moment.

The slender woman pushing the cage smiled mischievously. Her dark brown hair was in a tight bun, and she wore large-framed glasses, but underneath the professional exterior she exuded charisma. "It's a special delivery for Mr. Frankenheimer," she said.

"Margaret, this is Symone LeGrue," Frankenheimer said. "My bird girl."

"Bird handler," LeGrue corrected him.

Though her zoological expertise was restricted to animals with four legs, Margaret had become a gifted amateur ornithologist over the years. "Wait," she said. "I know this breed of bird. It's from somewhere in the Caribbean, right?"

"Yes!" said LeGrue excitedly.

"A white, a white—" It was right on the tip of Margaret's tongue. "Darn it."

"A white bellbird," LeGrue said.

"Right!" said Margaret. "From the Guianas! I just read about them in *Birds of the Caribbean*!"

"Robert Porter Allen, my hero!" said LeGrue.

"Sainted savior of the spoonbill," said Margaret.

Charlie joined the group and listened intently, impressed, although he had zero idea what the two were talking about.

"Symone brought me all the sparrows and canaries for *Birdman of Alcatraz*," Frankenheimer said. "Comes out this summer."

"Right, looking forward," said Charlie. "Love Lancaster."

"But there are no birds in *Manchurian Candidate*," Margaret noted. "Not in the screenplay we got."

Frankenheimer shrugged. "The garden-club scene, I told Symone we were playing around with different ways to make it extra-weird. She said she had a spectacularly strange bird to show me, one that American audiences had never seen before."

"You look familiar," LeGrue said to Margaret. "Are you in animal training?"

"I wouldn't call the canaries and sparrows you brought us particularly trained, Symone," Frankenheimer joked. "I gotta finish up here. You can bring that to my dressing room, Evans will show you the way." He pointed to a young woman with a broad smile.

"I'm a zoologist," Margaret told Symone. "Margaret Marder. I do some teaching at Barnard. You're a bird trainer?"

"My team does all animals, but I'm mainly birds," LeGrue said. "Right now we're doing the new Hitchcock up in San Francisco. It's nuts."

Fontaine reappeared, looking noticeably less relaxed than he had a few moments earlier. He approached them, ashen-faced.

"Manny, you look as though you've seen a ghost," Margaret said.

"The police are here. One of our actors on a different picture was found dead this morning."

"Oh my God, no," said Charlie. "Who was it?"

Fontaine seemed almost out of breath. "Chris Powell. He was a boxer in the Elvis flick *Kid Galahad* they're shooting next door."

"Did you know him well?" Margaret asked.

"What happened?" asked LeGrue.

"I don't know yet. I knew him a bit. He was trouble, that kid. He and Sinatra got into it a few times. Fighting over a dame. This isn't going to be good for anyone."

CHAPTER FIVE

BEVERLY HILLS, CALIFORNIA

December 1961

Flashbulbs popped as the custom-made red Ghia L6.4 approached the Daisy, a drinking club on North Rodeo Drive—private, but no secret to the photographers and reporters who scavenged nightly for scoops they could sell to the tabloids. Dusk was beginning to settle on Beverly Hills, exaggerating the artificial bursts of light.

"These goddamn shutterbugs are everywhere, like mosquitoes," snarled Peter Lawford from the front passenger seat as his driver eased his way through the swarm. The car was one of only twenty-six built; a few had been gifted to Rat Packers for the free publicity. Margaret and Charlie exchanged a glance in the back seat—once again, DC and normal life seemed a long way away.

"Take us around the block," Lawford instructed the driver. "Let me get myself together." He pulled down the visor, peered at himself in the tiny mirror, took out a comb, and began tending to his thick brown locks. Charlie had noticed that Lawford seemed limited in the use of his right arm and hand, a disability he hid rather well by making pronounced and dramatic gestures with his left.

Charlie had phoned Lawford a week ago after Attorney General Kennedy, the actor's brother-in-law, had assured him that Lawford would help Charlie and Margaret insinuate themselves into the Rat Pack. Lawford, a bridge between the two worlds ever since his marriage to Patricia Kennedy—who came between Jack and Bobby in birth order—was only too happy to assist. He'd joined them at the Miramar for brunch last Sunday, and this was their second outing.

The brunch had been fun enough. Lawford spoke with a clipped British accent and seemed on the surface to be the embodiment of class and erudition, a real-life version of Dashiell Hammett's Nick Charles, whom Lawford played on the NBC TV series. In actuality he was, Margaret thought, probably about half as bright. He was, however, full of gossip about both Hollywood and Washington, and seemed a good entrée to Sinatra.

As the driver rounded the block, the voice of a radio newsman filled the car.

...Castro's admission that he is a Marxist-Leninist. President Kennedy vowed the U.S. would never accept any government not chosen through free and fair elections. In local news, police say they have no leads in the death of actor Chris Powell, whose corpse was found earlier this week in a room at the Santa Monica Hotel. Powell's role in the Elvis Presley film Kid Galahad *will be recast, United Artists says. In sports—*

"When we get out of the car, these bloodsuckers are going to bombard me with questions about Powell," Lawford said.

"Did you know him?" Charlie asked. "I heard he and Frank fought about a girl."

"It's seldom truly about the girl," Lawford said.

The car circled back to the entrance of the club and Lawford turned on his beaming white smile, hopped out of the car, helped Margaret out, and waved to the throng.

"One over here, Peter!" shouted a squat gray photographer. He resembled a toad, warts and all, topped by an obvious toupee. "Any comment on Powell?"

"Hi, Joey!" Lawford said, ignoring the question. "Say hi to Congressman Charlie Marder and his wife, Margaret. Charlie's in town advising on Frank's new picture. Charlie, this is Joey Tarantula," he said, pronouncing it "Tah-ran-*too*-la."

Tarantula snapped photographs of the three while shouting out a steady stream of questions, an accumulation of tabloid filler and innuendo: "Cops say it looks like a Mob hit. And what's this I heard about Powell and Frank fighting over a girl?" Lawford ignored it all. "Thanks, Joey!" Lawford said, guiding Charlie and Margaret to the Daisy. The doorman nodded at Lawford and waved them in.

The Daisy, which had opened earlier that year, was the first private bar and dance club in the Greater Los Angeles area, a place for the rich and famous to drink and carouse without having to worry about gossip columnists or riffraff. The building took up a quarter of a city block, and membership was offered to a select group of Hollywood stars and power players as well as a few attractive, aspiring (and willing) young men and women carefully chosen and brought in by talent scouts.

A cocktail waitress rushed to them, took their drink orders, and practically sprinted to the bar. In the large main room of the club, oak-paneled and filled with a smog of cigarette smoke, were a well-stocked bar and a dozen small tables. At one of these, an aging Charles Boyer flirted with a barely adult Natalie Wood. Debbie Reynolds sat with a coterie of admirers; Kim Novak and Jayne Mansfield were at adjacent tables, each with an older man, each acting as if the other weren't present. Standing at the bar, Tony Curtis slapped Troy Donahue on the back; near them, Sandra Dee was knee-deep in a drink that didn't look so wholesome.

The waitress returned with bourbon rocks for Lawford and Charlie and a daiquiri for Margaret.

"This is a preposterous number of fabulous people," Margaret said, taking a swig of her drink.

"Where else can they go on a Saturday night?" Lawford replied.

While overwhelmed by the sheer number of celebrities, Margaret was surprised at how much tinier they appeared in person. Liz Taylor was so short she almost resembled an elf, and walking in, Margaret had towered over several leading men. Also surprising were Rock Hudson's drinking companions. They weren't exactly the nubile young starlets Margaret might have expected; the strapping heartthrob, a vision of all-American swinging bachelorhood, had surrounded himself with four slim, handsome—even pretty—young men.

A framed photograph hung on either side of the doorway. One was an image of Sinatra punching a photographer in the nose, and the other showed Dean Martin holding a finger to his lips, an instruction: *Shh.*

"Our crew's in the back," Lawford said, pointing. Live jazz played in one of the rooms; the Daisy had so many, it was hard to keep track. Charlie recognized the tune: "Pfrancing," from *Someday My Prince Will Come.* He polished off his bourbon in one gulp and began to lose himself in the tempo and the strutting trumpet solo, which sounded to him like a man crying.

"It's like Miles Davis himself is here," Margaret said. She was trying to keep cool, but she had her hand on his arm, and he could tell she was a bit thrilled. They followed Lawford through the crowd of stars, ogling in every direction and catching snippets of gossip:

> *So there was Rock in a mink, looking as fabulous as you might imagine, and the studio sent the goddamn pic to every paper from here to Piscataway like it was a joke, like ha-ha-ha, look at the he-man in the mink. If they only knew!*
> *Ed Sullivan is boycotting anyone who goes on Paar. That's just the reality of it.*
> *No, no, no, you're drunk,* West Side Story *is gonna end the year number one,* Guns of Navarone *two.*

Nuremberg *and* Tiffany's *won't be in the top ten. They didn't make*
any money. They were just for awards.
As the journalists might say, Chris Powell couldn't be reached for
comment.

All of it reminded Margaret of when she and Charlie had first arrived in Washington, DC, in 1954. She'd seen then how stunningly,
pathetically human the boldface names actually were—Senator
Jack Kennedy hobbling around with his wretched back, Vice President Nixon as insecure as Othello. Margaret would read about a
seemingly omnipotent committee chairman, witness him banging
his gavel and throwing his weight around, only to meet him later at
a cocktail party and see he was nothing more than a sack of neuroses
with clever writers and a good poker face. Stalwart moralists were
in truth libidinous bed-hoppers; Christian wives were beehived
roundheels; iron-jawed anti-Communist crusaders were terrified of
even a lightly critical editorial. Public images were as fragile as
they were phony, Margaret had concluded, so it wasn't surprising
to find that the silver screen's wholesome girls next door and pillars
of manhood were, in reality, lascivious, desperate, drunk, sad.

They walked past a billiards room, where none other than Paul
Newman was lining up a shot. Another, darker room was packed
with couches and love seats. Finally, they took a right into yet
another room, this one even smokier than the others. Congregated
around a card table, perched on high leather stools, were Sinatra,
Dean Martin, Sammy Davis Jr. and his young blond wife, May
Britt, Shirley MacLaine, and two men wearing sunglasses and
nondescript suits whom neither Charlie nor Margaret recognized.
One was tan and good-looking with thick black eyebrows and a
movie-star smirk; the other was pale and squat.

"Brother-in-Lawford!" Dean Martin called out, looking up from
shuffling the cards. "Who are your friends?"

Lawford had been distracted by a curvy cigarette girl, but he turned back to the pack. "They're working on Frank's picture," he said. "Consultants. Congressman Charlie Marder and his wife, Margaret."

Sinatra looked up from the table as the new arrivals sat down. "Congressman." He nodded pleasantly. Then to Margaret: "Madame." She suppressed a grin. Then, to no one in particular and less pleasantly, he barked: "Can we change the music to something that swings? Enough jazz! I'd even listen to Dago sing 'Volare' instead of this."

"Call the papers! Frank's willing to listen to someone else sing!" Martin quipped.

Sinatra smiled as Martin dealt the cards clockwise around the table: Sinatra, Davis, Britt, MacLaine, Lawford, and the two silent men. He skipped Charlie and Margaret.

Charlie noticed, of course. He couldn't put his finger on why, but he got an unwelcoming feeling from Martin.

"You're not dealing in the congressman and his missus?" Lawford asked him.

Martin paused. "We've never had three broads in one game before," he observed.

"As long as they know the rules," Sinatra said. He turned to Margaret. "You know the rules, right, dollface?"

Margaret loathed Marilyn Monroe's breathless dumb-blonde persona, but she did a devastatingly accurate impression of it, as she demonstrated now: "The eights are crazy, right, daddy?"

Everyone laughed except Sinatra, who stared at Margaret for a moment and then looked down at the card table as he lit a cigarette. "Poor Marilyn," he said, and shrugged.

The brief acknowledgment of Monroe's downward spiral reminded Charlie of the way all good people sometimes followed words of sympathy with a shrug. The shrug conveyed a resignation, an understanding that humanity was fragile and life could be brutal. And in Sinatra's case, Charlie thought, given that he'd treated Monroe as if she were just another piece of leftover cheesecake, perhaps his shrug also suggested that not just life but, yeah, maybe he himself could be brutal.

Sinatra's blue-eyed stare had not signaled anything so psychologically complicated to Margaret; quite the contrary. His cool look had washed a warm wave over her. Thin and blond with bewitching hazel eyes, Margaret constantly had to fend off the inquiring gazes of congressmen at dinners; lawyers and CEOs at fundraisers; policemen and construction workers and shopkeepers in Manhattan and Washington. She was not one to be easily charmed by power and charisma. When she'd encountered Sinatra on set, he was just a grump, but here he was in his glory, as confident as a matador, and she felt it. In a flash of his eyes, she fancied that she could see his temper and passion and the heart Ava Gardner had broken into a thousand pieces. Margaret found her own heart quickening its pace, and she glanced around the table to make sure no one could tell.

"Tell me, Congressman," Martin said, looking at his cards, "don't you have, like, laws and stuff to write? Something to do besides sit around drinking with a couple of crooners and their pals?" He smiled at Charlie, though there was definitely nothing friendly about the question.

"I felt it was my sworn duty to answer the call of your movie studio," Charlie said. "And anyway, we're on recess for another month."

"Politics is just a lot of acting," Margaret said. "I told Charlie he could learn a thing or two from the best. I'm a big fan of Mr. Sinatra—of all of you, actually—and we needed a little sun."

"Honestly, Dino, what's got your shorts in a bunch?" MacLaine asked. "It's not as if we couldn't stand to have someone hoist up our average IQ."

Martin elbowed Sinatra and whispered in his ear. Sinatra turned. In the next room, a tall, handsome man with a jutting jaw and red hair was pressing the flesh like a city council candidate. He was dressed fashionably but obviously without the benefit of a movie star's salary—thin maroon tie, shiny dark blue suit that didn't quite fit, shoes that tried too hard. A bargain-basement Rat Packer.

"Detective Ellroy Meehan," Lawford said to Charlie and Margaret. "He's like the Showbiz Cop."

"Here because of Chris Powell?" Margaret asked.

"Presumably," said Lawford. "Want to meet him?"

"If I could," said Charlie.

Lawford nodded.

"We'll keep an eye on your wife, Congressman," Martin said. "Frank will, at any rate." Everyone laughed.

Lawford sauntered over to the policeman; Charlie followed. Rock Hudson thumbed the lapel of the young man beside him. No one was being even the slightest bit discreet; all inhibitions were gone. Gregory Peck was downing bourbons; buxom aspiring starlets were hanging on Robert Mitchum's every word as he told them about being on a Savannah, Georgia, chain gang as a teenager. The punch line was that was why they were now shooting *Cape Fear* in California instead of on location in Savannah, a town Mitchum had hated ever since then. In the middle of this explosion of stars, Detective Meehan was making short work of a vodka tonic as he chatted up Tuesday Weld, who was wearing a tight blue dress and appeared eager to exit the conversation.

Meehan must have sensed someone more famous in his vicinity because, like a remora sensing a shark, he turned to find its source: Lawford.

"Peter!" he said. The two alpha-dogged each other, grasping each other's hands with vise-grip aggression, pushing each other back and forth as if working a two-man crosscut saw.

"Detective, this is Congressman Charlie Marder from New York," Lawford said. "He's here working on Frank's *Manchurian* film, advising. He's both a vet and an old Washington hand."

Meehan smiled and patted Charlie on the shoulder. "Welcome to Tinseltown," he said. He took a gulp from his drink. "Oh, Peter," he said, "you know I've landed the Powell case."

"No, I didn't. Awful. We haven't heard much about the circumstances. Suicide?"

"Unless he shot himself in the eyes, both of them, then no, I don't think it was a suicide," Meehan said. "Classic Cosa Nostra. Make the corpse unpresentable for viewing. Old-world greaseball stuff. Frank might know something about it from his days in Hoboken." Meehan laughed and squeezed Lawford's shoulder; he shook it off slowly but with unmistakable distaste. "Speaking of Frank, didn't he and Powell have a beef about some skirt? Lola something?" Meehan asked.

"I don't know anything about that," Lawford said unconvincingly. "You'd have to ask the man himself."

"Oh, I will," Meehan said, staring toward the back room where Sinatra sat.

At that very moment, Sinatra was ranting about gossip columnist Louella Parsons, who had devoted an entire chapter to him in her new memoir, *Tell It to Louella*.

"She calls me 'mixed up,'" he told his fellow Rat Packers and Margaret, rage simmering. "She said I go by the 'law of the jungle.' I mean, what in the hell is she talking about? That stupid fucking quin doesn't know me." He drained his glass of whiskey, and a waitress materialized instantly with another.

"Francis, she wrote nice things too," said MacLaine. "Compliments about your charm and your talent and how you're willing to do anything for friends. Yes, there was some nasty stuff, but what do you want? She and Nancy are like sisters." Sinatra and his first wife, Nancy, had divorced in 1951 after twelve years of marriage. They had three kids: Nancy, twenty-one, Frank Jr., seventeen, and Tina, thirteen.

"There's also, if you'll permit me, my captain, quite a lot of praise for you as a father," Davis offered. "As I understand it, that is. I would never peruse such garbage."

"Honestly, who even reads a book by a gossip columnist?" asked Martin. "She's been on our drop-dead list forever." Martin then began to belt out as if he were onstage:

She's the worst
She's a Vegas has-been
She's accursed
She's Joey Bishop's foreskin

But Sinatra was immune to Martin's charms at the moment. "She's a cunt," he spat.

Margaret flinched, then glanced at Britt and MacLaine, who subtly rolled their eyes at each other. Martin lightly patted Sinatra on the shoulder as if consoling him. Margaret looked around the table, but everyone avoided eye contact with her, even—maybe especially—the women.

Charlie was making his way back to his wife when he felt a tug on his arm. He turned around to see Manny Fontaine. "Hey, pal!" the United Artists PR flack said, wobbling. He was solidly in the bag. Charlie looked at his watch—it was just after eight p.m.

"Hey there, Manny."

"Don't tell anyone, but it looks like Chris Powell was a Mob hit." Charlie could smell the gin oozing out of the man as he leaned closer. Manny's face was alight with ghoulish enthusiasm. "Shot through the eyes. Both of them! *Blang! Blang!*"

"I heard that as well," Charlie said, wishing he could extricate himself from the conversation.

"Well, this is no good for Frank or for the studio. Frank's rival rubbed out by the Mob!"

Charlie was skeptical of that theory. "Because they were competing for a girl?"

"Competing for Lola now, competing for parts in pictures in a few years, maybe? Powell was a comer."

"So the Mob had him killed on Frank's behalf? You really think that?"

"Oh no, no, no, no, no, no," Fontaine said. Suddenly a sober expression came across his face and he lowered his voice. "I don't know, stranger things have happened. You know how they got Frank out of his first contract with Tommy Dorsey?"

"I'd heard rumors."

"More than rumors," Fontaine said, pushing a beefy thumb into Charlie's lapel for emphasis. "Yes, Powell was in *Kid Galahad*, that stupid Elvis boxing movie, but he was a good actor. There was talk of him playing Frank's younger brother in *Come Blow Your Horn*. You know, the Neil Simon play. You seen it? Anyway, Frank didn't want Powell in the picture. Fought it. Maybe felt threatened by his looks and talent?" Fontaine shrugged. "Guess he won't have that problem anymore."

"Good Lord," Lawford said under his breath to MacLaine when he returned to the table and found Sinatra ranting. "Who brought up Louella?"

"Handsome Johnny," MacLaine said, motioning toward one of

the two anonymous men at the other end of the table. "Said his girlfriend was reading it to find out more about Hollywood. It was like dropping a match in the Strait of Hormuz."

"He has every reason to be upset," Britt offered, also speaking in the hushed tone they had all adopted as if to avoid waking a sleeping baby. "Parsons goes into detail about everything, him leaving Nancy for Ava, the troubles he had with his voice in the fifties. Lot of dirty laundry. And she trashes a number of his performances."

"That's a pity," said Lawford.

Sinatra continued his diatribe. Martin and Davis nodded along with his assessment of the gossip columnist and tried to convince him to forget about her. Charlie, returning to the table, tried to make sense of it all.

"She's a nasty old cooze, Frank, just forget about her," Martin was saying.

"Her latest column was nice, Pope," said Davis. "She interviewed Janet Leigh, who gushed about how happy she was that you cast her in *Manchurian*, how you're a great neighbor to her and Tony out in Rancho Mirage."

"Who are those men at the end of the table, anyway?" Charlie quietly asked Lawford.

He shrugged. "Friends of Frank's." He didn't seem to want to say any more.

Lawford took a swig of bourbon. "I read the book. There was a lot in there about Frank having successfully launched the greatest comeback in the history of showbiz. I wish he wouldn't focus so much on the negative."

"Why does he care?" Margaret asked. The passion and presence she'd seen in Sinatra just minutes before had morphed into something else: spite. He was a downed power line, writhing spasmodically. Out of control and best avoided.

"Honestly, I think what's really pissing him off is Parsons's crack about him losing his hair," Lawford said.

"What was that?" Sinatra asked Lawford.

"Just talking about that cunty book, Frank," Lawford said.

"*Cunty* is right," Sinatra agreed, venom in his voice. The word echoed past their group, stopping conversations at other tables. The room got a little quieter.

"Well, you know what they say," Margaret said, taking a sip of Charlie's bourbon, "ask not what your cunty can do for you."

Silence.

Followed by Sinatra's face breaking into a smile, like an eggshell that'd been delicately tapped. A full grin. Teeth. Then Sinatra laughed and everyone exhaled and laughed along with him.

"Congressman, this one is a keeper," Sinatra said, pointing at Margaret. "C'mon! Let's get some swinging music going in here!" He raised his glass and held it up to Margaret.

From the speakers came a rapid race of trumpets and trombones, soon interrupted by Sinatra's voice singing an old Mexican song from the 1930s that he'd covered in May and released on *Swing Along with Me* in June.

> *Granada, I'm falling under your spell*
> *And if you could speak, what a fascinating tale you would tell...*

Martin patted Sinatra on the shoulder and the two toasted each other.

"You're the belle of the ball, Betsy," Charlie whispered to Margaret, placing his hand on the small of her back.

"Or at least Best Supporting Actress," she said. Charlie knew how much she loathed that particular word Frank had used. She'd deployed it anyway—to break the tension, to help the cause. But she'd hated doing it. She felt like a sellout.

And not for the first time. Margaret had put her career on hold to have Lucy and Dwight and she still beat herself up over it, resenting how her focus was now on dirty dishes and diapers instead of scholarship and the chance to gain recognition. Sensing her frustration, Charlie often told her he was eager to have her return to work full-time as soon as she wanted. She never said it, but she did wonder how sincere he was being.

After the momentary introspection, Margaret dived back into the sea of revelry, where neither the Sinatra songs nor the drinking ever stopped. Soon she and Charlie were dealt into the game. MacLaine mentioned how much she was looking forward to seeing the fellas in *Sergeants 3*, which was to hit theaters soon.

"That's the one that's based on *Gunga Din* but takes place in the Old West," Margaret explained to Charlie.

"You're not a big fan of pictures, Congressman?" asked Sinatra.

"Don't get to go to the theater as much as I'd like," Charlie said. "With work and the kids. We used to go every Saturday night. We're fans of everyone here."

"Really?" asked Martin incredulously. Then he leaned forward with a challenge: "Name your favorite film starring each one of us."

Charlie sat up in his seat as everyone eyed him curiously. He loved being underestimated, though it seldom happened anymore.

"I liked you in *Rio Bravo*," Charlie told Martin.

"I liked how they cast you against type, made you a lazy drunk," Margaret added. This elicited guffaws from everyone, including Martin. "Good to see you branch out."

"Sammy was great as Sportin' Life in *Porgy and Bess*," Charlie continued, going around the table. "May, I loved you in *The Hunters*. Obviously, Shirley was mesmerizing in *The Apartment*, and I liked Peter best in *The Thin Man*, but I know that was TV, so he was also stellar in *Exodus*."

Charlie waved toward the serious-looking men to his left. "I don't know who these two gentlemen are but I suspect they don't care to be captured on film much."

The men grinned. They sure didn't.

"As for Mr. Sinatra," Charlie said, "he's giving a great performance in *The Manchurian Candidate* right now, but until that one's released, I gotta say *The Man with the Golden Arm*. I know it's probably trendier in this town to go with the role that won him the Oscar, but Frankie Machine still haunts me." Charlie took a couple of swigs from his glass of bourbon, finishing it, while everyone stayed quiet. "If I'm still thinking about a performance years after I saw the picture, then the artist did something right."

"See, politicians know plenty about what we do," Sinatra said. "When I talk to TP, all he wants to hear is Hollywood gossip."

"TP?" asked Margaret.

"The president," Lawford explained.

They drank. And drank. Margaret was increasingly reminded of her 1940s fieldwork observing chimpanzees in the Belgian Congo. The monkeys were tribal, wild, focused on mating and alpha status, and the Rat Packers' antics increasingly resembled the chimps' as the night proceeded. Margaret whispered the observation to Charlie, who laughed heartily when Dean Martin coincidentally underlined her point with an operatic solo that recalled nothing so much as a primate's pant-hoot.

It was maybe an hour later when Britt nudged MacLaine and gestured toward something behind her. MacLaine looked, then turned back to May and mimed sticking her finger down her throat in an exaggerated expression of nausea.

Margaret peered over her shoulder and saw an obese man in his fifties escorting a voluptuous curly-haired blond girl who couldn't have been out of her teens to a table. His hands slid all over her—hips, legs, abdomen—as soon as they sat down. The room they were in was too dark for Margaret to see the girl's facial expression.

"Yuck," said Margaret. Charlie, focused on his cards, looked up at his wife, then back at his three aces.

"That's Itchy Meyer, with MGM," MacLaine said. "Total masher."

"Who's the skirt?" asked Sinatra.

"Dunno, I can't really see her face that well," said Britt.

"DC is a whole town of Itchy Meyers," said Margaret. "Senator Itchy Meyer, Congressman Itchy Meyer..."

"President Itchy Meyer," whispered Charlie.

Margaret squinted at the young woman again. "Jesus," she said under her breath. "Violet," Margaret said, walking toward her. "Violet!" she shouted.

The young woman looked around to see who was calling her name.

"How does your wife know her name?" Martin asked Charlie.

Charlie was too stunned to speak at first. "That's her sister's daughter, our niece Violet," he finally said. "She ran away from home six months ago."

CHAPTER SIX

BEVERLY HILLS, CALIFORNIA

December 1961

Margaret's relief at seeing her runaway niece vanished quickly. Violet was glassy-eyed and looked as if she barely understood that someone, let alone her aunt, was approaching.

"Violet?" Margaret said. "Violet!"

No response. Violet looked around the room, past Margaret. *She must be stoned*, Margaret thought. *On pills or something.*

"Hi there," Margaret said, extending a hand to introduce herself to Itchy Meyer, hoping to break the strange spell. He shot her a dirty look and then stood, took Violet's hand, and briskly ushered her out of the club. Margaret was stunned. She called after her niece but was ignored as they walked out the door. She scrambled to catch her, but by the time she got through the crowd and made her way outside, they had vanished.

"What happened?" Britt asked Margaret when she returned, shoulders slumped in defeat.

MacLaine arched a perfectly penciled eyebrow as she examined the cards in her hand. "Here's a guess," she said. "He realized you might hasten her escape from his greasy paws, so he made up an excuse to vamoose."

"He didn't even bother acknowledging me," Margaret said. "Out the door like Chuck Yeager."

"She isn't even eighteen yet, is she?" asked MacLaine.

"She isn't even seventeen," said Margaret.

"Not even seventeen and she's got a figure like that!" Martin said under his breath. Charlie looked at Margaret, who thankfully didn't seem to have heard over the din of the busy social club.

Britt batted Martin's arm lightly with the back of her hand. "They're worried about their niece, guys," she said. "You can't see the forest for the trees."

"I can't see the forest for her fun-bags," said Martin. Margaret heard this time and made a face of disgust.

"The good news is it doesn't look like she's skipping meals," said Lawford.

"*Peter,*" scolded MacLaine.

Charlie thought about objecting to Lawford's comment, albeit against his better judgment—after a decade in Washington, DC, he had calluses on his tongue from biting it so much. But before he could say a word, he heard a familiar drawl.

"Hello, Francis" came the voice.

Charlie and Margaret turned and saw a tall, craggy-faced man. John Wayne.

"Duke," said Sinatra uneasily from across the table.

"Haven't seen you since that night at the Moulin Rouge," Wayne said.

"Oy," said Davis.

Lawford leaned closer to Charlie and said quietly, "They almost came to blows that night."

"What about?" asked Charlie.

"Albert Maltz."

About a year and a half before, Charlie remembered, Sinatra had hired screenwriter Maltz, one of the Hollywood Ten who'd been jailed for refusing to tell Congress whether he'd ever been a member of the Communist Party. Sinatra wanted him to write his picture about Private Eddie Slovik, a soldier whom the U.S. Army had court-martialed and executed for desertion at the end of World War II. But veterans' groups and John Wayne protested the hiring of the Commie, and Wayne, an outspoken Republican, quickly dragged "Sinatra crony" Senator Kennedy into the controversy. The Kennedys leaned on Sinatra to scrub the project, which he did.

"The month after Frank had to fire Maltz," Lawford continued, "Frank and Wayne went at it at a charity event."

"An actual fight?" Charlie asked, surprised because he'd never heard of the altercation and, frankly, because Wayne was so much bigger than Sinatra.

"No, no," Lawford said. "Christ, Wayne would kill him. They were just in each other's face. Wayne asked him if he wanted to step outside. Frank said yes, but Lord Almighty, we all knew he didn't. So we got in there and separated them before anything could happen." Lawford emptied his glass. "Then of course later that night, Frank roughed up a parking-lot attendant."

"I just wanted to tell ya that I hope there's no hard feelings," Wayne was saying. "My guy didn't win, and yours did. I think he's too liberal but I wish him the best."

Sinatra shrugged and flashed a brief, insincere grin. "Thanks, Marion."

"Now, there's no reason to get cute, Frank," Wayne growled.

"There was no reason for you to open your stupid mouth about Maltz!" Sinatra said, his cheeks flushing.

"Yeah, well, I was asked what I thought about your hiring that Commie. I said my opinion didn't matter much, they should ask Kennedy, your buddy who's now running the country," Wayne said, lighting a cigarette. "It's true, though, I do have this weird thing about Communists and radical liberals. I don't know what it is." He took a drag. "Maybe it's the treason?"

"Last time I checked, we had a Bill of Rights in this country," Sinatra snapped.

"Look, Frank, the radicals were taking over our business," Wayne said. "They were starting to control who could do the writing. They were preaching about the beauty of Communism, for the love of Christ. Your amigos over in Cuba, that's the way they want to live, fine, they can destroy their own country, but that's not the way we do it here."

Charlie stole a glance at the two silent men at the end of the table. They remained in their seats but were clearly on alert, carefully watching the six-foot-four cowboy challenging their *paisan*.

"Maltz wasn't preaching," Sinatra said. "He was telling an American story. He's pro-America."

"He was glorifying a deserter."

"You have no idea whether Slovik was going to be glorified. You're still defending the goddamn blacklist and fucking McCarthy." Sinatra rose to his feet and planted his hands on the poker table. Lawford, Davis, and Martin looked at one another and then stood too. Martin put his arm around Sinatra and tried to guide him to the back of the room. Lawford approached Wayne.

"If Frank wants to come outside and settle this like a man, I'm happy to oblige," Wayne said to him. "And don't bring your friends from Chicago," he added, nodding toward the glowering duo who'd been observing the exchange. "We settle this mano a mano, with fists, not guns."

Charlie and Margaret had both assumed cooler heads would prevail but before they knew what was happening, they were swept up in a tide as Wayne, Sinatra, and the rest of the Rat Pack all barreled through the crowd and out onto the dark street. Paparazzi quickly realized they were about to hit a major payday.

As the two men squared off, streetlights cast an air of menace. Flashbulbs burst, tomorrow's headlines and bonuses practically visible on the journalists' eager faces. Wayne and Sinatra stood a few feet apart, surrounded by a circle of onlookers. Dean Martin, swaying slightly, was trying to convince Sinatra to let it go, while Lawford had stationed himself next to Wayne. The other Rat Packers joined the waitstaff in trying to block the view of the photographers.

Charlie wanted to make himself useful, but he didn't know how. He spotted the two thugs lurking behind Sinatra with uneasy looks on their faces. Martin was advising his friend not to fight in front of a crowd of reporters with a man who could clearly kick his ass, but Sinatra had been in fights before, had once even been arrested for punching *New York Daily Mirror* columnist Lee Mortimer.

Separated from her husband in the chaos, Margaret found herself jostled and pushed until a woman lightly grabbed her wrist. "Just stick with me, honey." She was in her late forties, slightly plump, and pretty, with a cigarette hanging out of her mouth and a reporter's notebook in her hand. She wore too much lipstick, and it was too orange, though Margaret gave her credit for picking a shade that matched her hair, which was as bright as a pumpkin.

Martin was so close to Sinatra, they looked as if they were slow-dancing. Wayne pushed Lawford away gently once, then more aggressively. That's when Charlie wiggled through the crowd and got between the two men. Charlie was a few inches shorter than Wayne but probably outweighed him, mostly with muscle. He smiled at the actor and shook his hand, thinking on his feet.

"Congressman Charlie Marder of New York," he said. "I'm out here helping on *Manchurian Candidate* and we just can't have Frank banged up."

Wayne looked at him warily as Charlie extended the handshake longer than was normal. Charlie rubbed his chin with his left hand and kept the hand over his mouth so no one could read his lips as he leaned in to Wayne's ear. "I was with the First Battalion, One Hundred Seventy-Fifth Infantry," Charlie said quietly. "Landed at

Omaha Beach. Before we shipped out to kill Krauts, we went to Fort Benning, where we learned how to kill with our bare hands. The way you fight in movies, you wouldn't last a second in combat. In real life, it's rabid-dog stuff."

Wayne tried to pull away, but Charlie held on to his hand.

"In combat, you can't be squeamish about using your teeth to rip off an ear or tear out a windpipe. Testicles, kidneys, temples, noses, Adam's apples—anything." He stared into Wayne's eyes and saw sheer panic. "Now, I'm going to continue to act as if this is friendly," Charlie said, "and you're doing me—an actual veteran—a favor by getting the fuck out of here." Charlie lowered his left hand. "Okay, Mr. Wayne?" he said loudly. "Thanks so much. You're a pal." He let go of Wayne's hand.

Wayne looked around at the crowd and the photographers. And then, almost as quickly as the situation had ignited, it was defused. Wayne disappeared into the night. Charlie glanced at Sinatra, who breathed a sigh of relief and winked at him before being escorted to his car. Within seconds, all that remained were spectators with nothing to see.

Margaret got a little thrill seeing Charlie adapt himself so well to the alpha-dog environment, but the woman who'd rescued her seemed disappointed that the fight had broken up before it even began.

"Aw, that's a shame," she said.

"Why?" asked Margaret as the crowd began to dissipate.

"I'm with *Hollywood Nightlife*—I'm Charlotte Goode," the woman said, handing Margaret a business card.

CHARLOTTE GOODE

REPORTER AND PHOTOGRAPHER

HOLLYWOOD NIGHTLIFE

6299 HOLLYWOOD BLVD

SCOOPS 4-8760

"I'm—"

"Margaret Marder, wife of the congressman who's approaching us now," Goode said.

"Well, that was weird," Charlie said, visibly relieved as he approached his wife.

"What magic words did you use to save Frank's life?" Goode asked.

"I'm sorry, we haven't been introduced," said Charlie.

"This is Charlotte Goode. She's a reporter," Margaret said. She turned to Goode. "Why don't we buy you a drink? You can educate us." Someone who knew Hollywood as well as Goode might be able to help her track down Violet, Margaret thought, unable to shake how lost her niece had seemed.

"I'm not going to talk to any reporters, honey," Charlie said.

"Oh, we're off the record, Congressman," said Goode, dropping her cigarette to the pavement and crushing the butt. "But given that your ride just left without you, why don't I run you both back to your hotel? I'll give you a little tour of the Hollywood you don't hear much about."

"'They don't worship money here, they worship death,'" Goode said. "That's Faulkner, the patron saint of writers who come here to have our hearts broken." She lit a cigarette with one hand and used the other to steer her beat-up blue Chevy Bel Air. Margaret had unsuccessfully tried to brush aside the fast-food wrappers that littered the front seat before giving up to focus on gripping the interior door handle. Charlotte took an abrupt and unsignaled turn onto Santa Monica Boulevard, prompting a cacophony of horns.

Margaret glanced over her shoulder to see Charlie grimacing, both hands braced against the back of her seat. She offered him a small smile of encouragement.

"So where are we headed?" Margaret asked.

"The site of a whacking," Goode said with a grin, cigarette dangling from the corner of her mouth as she took a wide left.

"Whose?" asked Charlie.

"Bugsy Siegel," she said. "Syndicate sent him here in the 1930s. He took over the rackets, got dope coming in from Mexico, and muscled in on the Screen Extras Guild. Big power there."

"In the Screen Extras Guild? How does that work?" asked Charlie.

"Say you want a crowded street in ancient Athens for your movie," Goode said, "or a packed coliseum. How much money do you lose if all the extras call in sick one day?"

"I remember seeing photos of Siegel popping up with Gable and Grant and the like," Margaret recalled.

"Oh, sure, he was legit pals with a bunch of these folks—Jean Harlow was godmother to his daughter!" Goode said. "Then the studios started blocking those photos and censoring news of those friendships."

"How did they block it?" Charlie asked.

"Traded it for dishier scoops," she said. "Someone else gets human-sacrificed into my lava, but the news gods are appeased. Win-win."

"Not for whoever ends up on the cover," Charlie observed.

"Yes, not for them," Goode agreed. "But so shall ye reap."

She applied the brakes with more enthusiasm than Charlie would have recommended, and he lurched forward in his seat. Goode put the car in park and gestured with her cigarette across Margaret's lap toward a white Spanish Colonial mansion, the mud-colored tiles on the roof barely visible behind a forest of palm trees. "This is Virginia Hill's house, where Bugsy was killed in '47."

She put her car back in drive and negotiated a rapid U-turn. Charlie was flung across the back seat and swallowed down a wave of nausea.

"Just a few blocks away from here is where Johnny Stompanato was killed." Stompanato, a World War II veteran, had been an enforcer for Mob boss Mickey Cohen and an abusive beau of Lana Turner until her fourteen-year-old daughter stabbed him in what was eventually ruled justifiable homicide.

"Where *is* Mickey Cohen these days?" Margaret wondered.

"Prison," said Charlie. "Just a few months ago."

"Alcatraz," added Goode. The streets around them were changing from lush opulence to dingier commercial fare.

"For tax evasion, I assume?" Margaret asked.

"Of course," said Goode.

"People lie," Charlie said. "Numbers don't."

"Isn't it odd that mobsters are just, y'know, hanging out with these big stars?" Margaret asked, fishing.

"Handsome Johnny even got a producing credit on a few pictures!" Goode said.

"Who?" asked Margaret.

"Johnny Rosselli," Goode said. "Indicted with the head of the Theatrical Stage Employees Union. Racketeering. He was with you guys tonight!"

"Who?" Charlie asked.

"'Handsome' Johnny Rosselli and Wassy Handelman," Goode said. "They were the two thugs with Frank tonight. Handsome and Harry Cohn at Columbia are thick as thieves. Also tight with Giancana, of course. But then, everyone's friends with Momo."

"Momo?" asked Margaret.

"Giancana," Charlie said.

"Momo has tons of friends," Goode said.

"Like Sinatra?" asked Margaret.

"Sinatra," said Goode. "Dino..."

"How connected is Frank, really?" Margaret blurted out, looking at Charlie to gauge his reaction. She couldn't tell in the darkness of the car, but Charlie was surprised and a bit pleased. Why not just ask? Charlie's careers in academia and politics required finesse and diplomacy, but Margaret was a scientist. She pursued facts, and she thought the dances around obtaining them were nonsense. Even if she did make a fine dancer.

"That's a complicated question," Goode said. "I mean, take the world of nightclubs that he grew up in. Can't really make it without some shadiness, whether the artist knows it or not. Then, of course, for about a decade he's been a two-percent owner in the Sands."

"Bugsy built the whole town," Charlie noted.

"Precisely," Goode said. "So nothing too crazy there. The real juiciness happened in Cuba in '47!"

"What happened in Cuba in '47?" Margaret asked.

"I am constantly amazed at how effectively he had this buried," Goode said, shaking her head. "This is why he punched Lee Mortimer in the nose, because of the big Cuba exposé."

She looked at Margaret, who shrugged.

"So 1947 was before *Revolución cubana*, obviously. Sinatra was with Tommy Dorsey's band. He flew to Havana with a buddy from Hoboken who just *happened* to be Al Capone's cousin. They checked in at the Hotel Nacional and later that night were photographed eating and drinking with various known members of the Mob, including Lucky Luciano."

"Wow," said Charlie. "But maybe they just ran into them?"

"No way, José," Goode said. "Luciano got out of prison but was banned from the U.S., so he called for all the bosses across the country to meet him in Havana to make him *capo di tutti capi*, the boss of bosses. Lansky, Costello, Three Finger Brown, and on and on."

"Handsome Johnny and Wassy were drinking and gambling with us," Margaret observed. "By that measure, someone could raise suspicions about Charlie and me."

"Hm," Goode grunted as she swerved out of her lane to pass a poky Nash spewing exhaust. "That's pretty much what Frank said. 'It was all just a coincidence, right place, wrong time, took me a couple days to realize what was going on, didn't wanna be rude or ungracious to the fellas buying me drinks.' More to it than that, of course. When Frank was trying to get out of his contract with Dorsey, Lucky spotted him about fifty Gs. So Frank's trip to Havana was a way of paying him back—sing for his friends, drink with them, carouse; mobsters like celebrities as much as any of us do. That's what Lucky says, anyway. There was also a rumor that Frank brought a suitcase full of unmarked bills for him. But who knows—hey, that's my house!" Goode pointed out Margaret's window to a nondescript two-story home that sat behind a line of palm trees. She'd been driving east on Sunset for a while now. "I'm in the basement. I rent from a nice family. Hospital executive and his wife, two kids."

"*Hollywood Nightlife* must put you in touch with all sorts of characters," said Margaret, thinking about Violet.

"You wouldn't believe me if I told you," she replied. "Think about all the young things who flock to this town desperate for a speck of stardust. Then add a whole bunch of unscrupulous gangsters and the *goniffs* who run Hollywood—fat old men with insatiable appetites."

"What can you tell me about Itchy Meyer?" Margaret said. "I saw him at the Daisy with my niece Violet, who ran away from home earlier this year."

"Ugh," Goode said. "He's grotesque. He's the perfect example of how power works in this town. He's got millions of dollars and a government and law enforcement structure built around protecting the industry rather than the girls."

"Do you think you might be able to help us track down my niece?" Margaret asked, unable to keep the rising fear out of her voice.

Goode shrugged. "I could try," she said. "Tomorrow when I'm sober, call me and give me all the particulars."

She paused to light yet another cigarette, then said, a bit too casually, "Say, what do you think about Chris Powell getting whacked? Do you buy that it was over gambling debts? Folks I know say he wasn't really known for big bets, though he played the horses."

"Um, I'm not sure," Charlie said.

"We never met him," Margaret added, put off by Goode changing the subject.

"I know he and Frank almost got into a jam about a broad, but I doubt that had anything to do with this," Goode said. "Frank doesn't have rivals killed—he just ruins their careers. Or ices 'em out. Like he did with Lawford after he heard he'd taken Ava to dinner. Then, of course, Lawford married a Kennedy, and Frank forgave him 'cause he loves Jack. And the rest is history."

"Meehan told me and Lawford that Powell's eyes had been shot out," Charlie said. "Some Mob thing so you can't have an open casket."

"I mean, over gambling debts?" Goode said. "Kill the golden goose and chop off its head? Doesn't make sense."

"None of it makes sense, right?" said Margaret. "Killing Bugsy Siegel—"

"Doesn't matter anyway," Goode said. "By the time Detective Meehan is done with it, the whole job will be blamed on a hobo the cops shanghai hopping a freighter in Bakersfield. That's his job, Meehan, to clean it all up."

With the famous Hollywood sign looming above them, Goode pulled over to the side of Canyon Lake Drive, essentially deserted at this time of night, and cut the engine.

"Have you ever seen it up close?" she asked, nodding up at the sign. She opened her door and Charlie and Margaret followed her out. Surrounded by mountains, desert, and mansions, they felt like they were in a new world, a place where riches were being amassed and anything was possible. The moon lit the sign better than a Hollywood stage manager could have dreamed, and it was easy to feel the mysterious allure of the city around them as they gazed up at it.

"Ever hear of Peg Entwistle?" Goode asked, taking a deep drag on her Lucky Strike.

"I don't think so," Charlie said.

"Broadway actress, came out here in the 1920s," Goode said. "Gifted. It was said she inspired Bette Davis to go into theater. Costarred with Bogie. Cast in a picture called *Thirteen Women*. But it did no box office, and RKO and Selznick tossed her. Rumor has it she had to resort to nudie pictures. Anyway, long story long, she took a dive off the *H* of that sign up there."

"How terrible," Margaret said.

Goode's voice had lost its usual hard-bitten tone, and she almost seemed to be talking to herself. "Left a note. 'I am afraid. I am a coward. I am sorry for everything. If I had done this a long time ago, it would have saved a lot of pain. P.E.'"

How odd and how sad that Charlotte memorized a suicide note, Margaret thought. A police siren cried in the distance. Goode shook her head as if to remind herself of where she was, took a last drag of her cigarette, then stubbed it out with her foot.

"It's a rough town," she said with a shrug, her tough exterior restored.

"It's not any nicer in Washington," Margaret said.

"No, I know," Goode agreed. "We have Sinatra, you have Kennedy."

"Oh, jeez," Charlie said. "Let's not get into that—Margaret has faith in her boy in the White House."

"You do?" Goode asked.

"He added a women's rights plank to the New Frontier,"

Margaret said. "He's appointed women to high-ranking posts. President's Commission on the Status of Women, chaired by Eleanor Roosevelt!"

"It's all crap," Goode said. "He's like all the rest of them. He's a pig."

Margaret started to protest, but Goode's face took on an angry expression. "Your worldview bears little resemblance to the real worlds of women like me and Peg Entwistle, all of us trying to make a living," she said.

Margaret was stunned by the sudden shift in Goode's mood, all her tour-guide bonhomie replaced by a barely contained rage. Within minutes she was driving them back home, an aggressive silence filling her junker. The night took an even worse turn when they got back to the hotel and the receptionist alerted Charlie that the Justice Department had left an urgent message: his father had had a heart attack.

CHAPTER SEVEN

LAS VEGAS, NEVADA

December 1961

"Zippedy-zoo-bah-zee-bah," Dean Martin sang. *"Zabbety-zoo-bah-zee-bah boom."*

"Scat," said Sinatra.

"That's indeed what I'm doing, pally," Martin said. "Scat."

"No, I mean *scat* like 'get outta here, that sounds horrible,'" said Sinatra, prompting an explosion of laughter from the crowd watching the show in the Copa Room of the Sands Hotel.

It might have been just a random Monday night in December, but every night in Vegas was New Year's Eve. At a table near the back of the room, Congressman Isaiah Street raised his eyebrows and polished off his scotch.

"What white folks find entertaining never ceases to amaze," he said to Charlie and Margaret.

To thank Charlie for keeping John Wayne from stomping him, Sinatra had invited the Marders to take in a Rat Pack show. Charlie had then invited Street, a decorated Tuskegee Airman, Chicago Democrat, and one of only five Black members of Congress. He had been Charlie's closest friend since 1954, when they'd met in Ike's Platoon. So when Charlie called needing to talk, Street hopped on a plane. He discussed sensitive matters in person only, assuming, probably correctly, that J. Edgar Hoover had tapped the phones of every Black man with power.

"That's Rosselli over there," said Margaret, pointing out the handsome mobster. He chose that very moment to casually pinch the rear of a passing Copa Girl. Her face initially expressed shock, then Pavlovian deference.

"Who's he with?" Street asked, craning his neck as Rosselli pulled out a chair at a table near the stage. "Is that Momo?"

"Sure looks like him from here," Charlie said. He pushed his chair back from their tiny square table (dinner and two-drink minimum, $5.95 per person, not a room for people without some means). "I'm going to go over there and check it out."

"You sure that's a good idea?" Margaret asked.

"No, but I suspect a middle-aged white guy will blend better at this stag party than either of you."

"Point, Charlie," said Street.

"*What is this thing called love?*" Sinatra sang. Onstage, he and Martin slouched on stools, drinks in hand.

"Frank, if *you* don't know, then we're all in trouble," Martin quipped. Then, in a singsongy voice: "*Did you ever see a Jew-jitsu?*"

"I did," Sinatra responded, raising his hand.

Davis, who had considered himself a Jew since the 1950s and had formally converted earlier this year, ran onto the stage in mock offense.

"Be fair!" Davis barked at Martin as Sinatra pretended to hold him back. "Would you like it if I came onstage and asked, '*Did you ever see a Wop-cicle?*'" The audience ate it all up like the free breakfast buffet.

Charlie tried to saunter through the dimly lit room, filled to its maximum four-hundred-person capacity, but there was not a lot of room for sauntering. The crowd was clustered in groups of four, the tables inches from one another and set out in ten long rows. The

Copa Girls followed the rules of the highway, moving on the right, passing on the left, yielding when necessary.

He approached Rosselli's table. The mobster was leaning back in his seat expansively, a cigar in one hand and a highball in the other. Onstage Dean Martin protested Davis's arm on his shoulder, saying, "I'll go out and I'll drink with ya, I'll pick cotton with ya, I'll go to shul with ya, but don't touch me," again to uproarious laughter from the room. Charlie got a good look at the people at the table: handsome Rosselli, ferrety Giancana, and an attractive dark-haired woman who was maybe twenty-five. He returned to Isaiah and Margaret, the only two people in the room who didn't look delighted by what was happening onstage.

"Rosselli, Giancana, and a lady I haven't seen before," Charlie reported.

"I called a friend at LAPD about Powell's murder," Street said. "An eyewitness saw a car with Illinois plates speed away from the hotel, guys with fedoras inside. But the cops are wary. They've seen the LA Mob pull this move before, replacing plates and wearing costumes to implicate Momo and the Chicago syndicate."

"So the theory is it's the boss of the LA crime family—what's his name?" Charlie asked.

"Frank 'One Eye' DeSimone," said Street.

"Right, so One Eye is trying to frame Momo for killing a Sinatra rival?" Charlie asked. "But why?"

Street shrugged. "Maybe One Eye is losing control of his territory—maybe he wants to show some muscle." He turned to Margaret. "I told Charlie earlier over drinks, before you joined us, I tried visiting Winston at the Tombs, but they wouldn't let me see him."

"Why not?"

"They claimed he was in the infirmary and too ill to have visitors. I phoned Governor Rockefeller, but he wouldn't take my call."

Charlie's heart sank as he again imagined his once indomitable father alone and hopeless. "We need to get something to the AG about—" He gestured toward Sinatra, who was in the midst of the intro to "Luck Be a Lady."

"They won't even let Charlie talk to him on the phone," Margaret said.

"They really seem to relish being bastards, the Kennedys," Charlie said. "The good news is, the prison doctors told me they don't think it was a heart attack after all."

"If it wasn't a heart attack, then what was it?" Street asked.

"I don't know; they don't know," Charlie said. "Nothing life-threatening, they don't think. They also ruled out a stroke. But he isn't talking." They all sat sadly at the table.

"Why is he at the Tombs anyway—isn't that a city jail?" Street asked.

"Feds have a wing," Charlie said. "And the AG gets a lot of leeway."

"I'm amazed it's stayed under wraps," Street said.

"Not really in anyone's interest to have it out there," Margaret said. "Kennedy doesn't want to be seen as punishing political enemies, and Winston doesn't want the public humiliation."

"Might be the only thing they've ever agreed on," Charlie said.

"*Luck, let a gentleman see…*" Every time Sinatra began a new verse, he was interrupted by a slurred quip from Martin.

"Does Dean pretend to be drunk or is he actually drunk?" Street asked.

"Both," said Charlie. As if on cue, Sinatra turned to the audience, cocked his head toward Martin, and mimed knocking back a drink. More laughter from the adoring crowd.

"I just had a bowl of bourbon and some crackers," Martin protested.

A young cocktail waitress breezed past them, drawing wolf whistles from a tableful of old men to Margaret's right. She frowned, thinking of Violet. Her sister had been ecstatic to hear that her daughter was alive, less so when she heard the details of Itchy Meyer and Violet's stupefied state. Margaret had promised she would find her and save her.

"It's too bad the presence of Momo and Handsome Johnny here tonight isn't enough for the AG," Street said.

"I wish we were anywhere close to finding out what the favor was," said Charlie. "Momo's ask."

"And how are you planning to go about that?" Street asked.

"We're working on it," Margaret said, snapping back to attention. "Charlie stopped John Wayne from rearranging Frank's face, so he likes us now. We're hoping we'll get an invite to Sinatra's place in Rancho Mirage, hang out at the pool, let the liquor flow."

"Loose lips sink ships," said Charlie.

"You know, I might have an in with these guys too," Street said.

Davis was starting to walk off the stage; Sinatra and Martin were singing "Boys' Night Out," arms around each other's shoulders, swaying jokily.

"*Hey there, mister, build a fence 'round your sister, it's the boys' night out,*" the two sang.

"Better keep smiling, Sammy, so everybody knows where you are," Sinatra said. Riotous laughter.

Suddenly, Street seemed irritated; Margaret asked him why. They were speaking in hushed voices, but a woman at an adjacent table turned around and shot them a peevish look. "Ssshh!" she said.

"That whole Stepin Fetchit routine they have Sammy doing, it's bullshit," said Street, lowering his voice even more. "I hate that they make him do that Buckwheat schtick. Especially after everything Sammy's been through."

"Been through?" asked Margaret.

"That flat nose he has," Street said. "That's from all the beatings he took during basic at Fort Warren."

Charlie shook his head in disgust. He couldn't imagine what it must have been like for Black soldiers before Truman integrated the military. Or after, for that matter.

"One time, a bunch of privates covered him with white paint, wrote *nigger* on his chest, *coon* on his forehead," Street said. "He could have gotten them court-martialed, but he wouldn't give up their names."

"Jesus," said Charlie.

"How do you know all this?" Margaret asked.

"I met him at a bar back in Chicago, I think around '51," Street recalled. "This was before I met Renee, so don't ask me why I was out drinking, Margaret!"

Margaret batted Street's arm lightly as the woman at the adjacent table glared at them again. Street returned her look with stony indifference, and she turned away, flustered.

"He was touring with his dad and uncle, the Will Mastin Trio," Street said. "They were performing at Chez Paree, and I recognized him from articles in the *Chicago Defender*—that's the Black paper. You should get a subscription, Margaret. Langston Hughes writes a column for them."

"I will," she said, blushing. Street was always trying to appeal to Margaret as a fellow progressive, which embarrassed her establishment Republican husband, as did Street's oft-stated belief that she had at least twenty-five IQ points on her lesser half.

"Okay, okay," said Charlie. "Back to when you met Sammy Davis?"

"It wasn't anything cinematic," Street said. "After the show, he was sitting at the bar by himself; I don't think anyone else recognized him. I bought him a drink, and we traded war stories. I fought Jerry in Europe, he fought yokels in Wyoming. Special Services, entertaining the troops. The way he said it, he was trying to warm the hearts of racist NCOs, trying to make them, at the very least, appreciate his talent. Seems like that's become a mission for him." Street shook his head. "An odd cat. But a good man."

Street took another sip of scotch. Charlie caught the eye of a Copa Girl and did a whirl with his finger—another round of drinks. Onstage, Dean Martin began singing "White Christmas," prompting more yuks when he alluded to Davis's hue. From there, he segued into a Rat Pack Noel medley. Margaret turned to the subject preoccupying her, her niece, hoping that Street might have some ideas on how to track her down. He didn't, but he promised he would think about it.

It was after one a.m. when a familiar face appeared behind Street. The short, wiry man squeezed Street's shoulders affectionately.

"Sammy!" said Street, standing to hug the singer.

"I saw you from the stage," Davis said, grabbing a seat.

"All the way back here?" asked Charlie, surprised.

"You wouldn't understand, my friend," Davis said, patting Street on the back. "Not a lot of our kind can afford these Vegas shows. And I've been following this cat's career for quite some time now!"

"Well, thank you, Brother Davis!" said Street with a smile. A waitress appeared, unbidden, with a drink for Davis. He took it and lit a new cigarette from the one still burning.

"*You*, sir," Davis said, pointing to Charlie, "you, sir, are a mensch for helping Frank avoid that ass-stomping!"

"What exactly did you say, Charlie?" Street asked.

"Get this, man," Davis said. "Charlie whispered to Wayne all the ways he knows to kill a man with his bare hands." Davis started laughing uncontrollably. "By the time Charlie mentioned testicles, Gunga Din was Gunga gone, baby."

Charlie was stunned. "How do you all know that?" he asked. "I only told Margaret."

"And you certainly didn't go into such exquisite detail," Margaret observed.

"Oh, grapevine, baby," Davis said. "Wayne told people. He thinks you're psychotic, my man!" Davis and Street were both laughing now. Davis patted Charlie's arm. "This is great. It's why Frank loves you. It's why you're here!" He raised a glass and they all toasted Charlie's terrifying Davy Crockett. "To the Alamo!" they cried. *Clink-clink.*

"Is May here tonight?" Margaret asked.

"No, she's home with the baby," said Davis. "I'm flying back in a few hours. I promised her I'd take Christmas and New Year's off."

"Yes, congrats on the wedding, Sammy," Street said. "I read it was going to be last September, then I saw it was delayed a few months. She got jitters?"

Davis swiveled around dramatically to see if anyone was listening; he always moved with broad determination, as if a camera were recording every gesture.

"The old man, President Kennedy's dad, made a specific request that I not get married before the election," Davis confided. "The election was tight, and Jack was so publicly associated with our gang, he was worried about a backlash if I married May before the vote. Frank asked me to hold off, so I did. And I was rewarded by being blackballed from the inaugural gala. Pun intended."

"You were blackballed?" Charlie asked incredulously. The Streets had brought the Marders to the event, which was held at the National Armory, hosted by Sinatra, and featured Gene Kelly, Milton Berle, Jimmy Durante, Tony Curtis, Janet Leigh, Laurence Olivier, and Bette Davis, among other stars.

"Nat King Cole and Sidney Poitier performed," Margaret recalled.

"Maria Cole and Juanita Poitier ain't white," Davis noted. "This is, of course, *entre nous*. Frank would be furious if he found out I told you all this."

"See, that really gets me," Street said. "Why do you put up with that from Frank?"

"From Frank?" Davis said. "That wasn't from Frank. That was from the president, man. Or, more accurately, from his dad—*el padrino*, the Ambassador."

"Okay, but Frank delivered the message, and he's the one making all those darkie jokes onstage," Street said. "You're up there saying, '*Okay, Massuh Dean, Massuh Frank!*'"

Charlie knew that Street, like Jackie Robinson, hid his righteous anger behind a polite veneer. Rarely, and only in discreet settings, would he express outrage at the indignities he suffered as a Black man in the United States of America. Charlie had never heard Street talk like this in public. He suspected his friend had imbibed a bit much, as had they all. Charlie tensed, unsure of how Davis would react.

The singer took a long drag on his cigarette and exhaled slowly.

"We're just having fun out there, man," Davis finally said. "I make jokes about them too. The audience loves it. You need to understand something about Frank. He took me under his wing. I was living in Harlem, my family was on welfare. We were just a hoofing act! Frank saw us and hired us for his show, paid us twelve hundred and fifty dollars a week. All the money in the world. Frank would come out, open up, sing a couple songs. He'd say things like 'I want you to keep an eye on the little cat in the middle.' He'd say, 'You watch him, he burns the stage out!'"

"Really?" Margaret said. She'd never heard any of this before.

"Absolutely, my friend!" Davis said. "Frank's the one who got the theater to hire us. More than that, Frank insisted—insisted—that we all got paid the same. The white acts and the colored acts.

Then he pretended it was a surprise to him. 'Glad we're working together, Sam,'" Davis said, doing a spot-on impression.

"His orchestras had to be integrated, he said. He forced the Copa to seat me," Davis continued. "He's the one who got the Sunset Strip desegregated. Before him, I couldn't sing here; I couldn't sleep here." Davis leaned in and lightly poked Street's chest. "Listen, Congressman: This cat has done more for civil rights than all your Kennedys put together."

Street threw his hands up in surrender and smiled ear to ear. "Don't get me started on those motherfuckers!"

By two thirty a.m., Margaret was barely able to stay awake; she said her good nights to the men, and about an hour later Davis headed to the airport to catch a flight back to Los Angeles on the single-engine plane of Jimmy Van Heusen, Sinatra's friend and songwriter. With lyricist Sammy Cahn, Van Heusen had won the Best Original Song Oscar two years before for "High Hopes" from the film *A Hole in the Head*, and two years before that for "All the Way" from *The Joker Is Wild*, both of which starred Sinatra. There was a lot of buzz that he might get nominated and win again this year for another Sinatra ballad, "The Devil May Dance" from *El Cid*. Van Heusen, Davis confided, was also a major supplier of party girls for Sinatra's fiestas. The girls' provenance was never completely clear but that didn't matter to the guys who pawed them.

At four a.m., Charlie and Street realized they were both nodding off midconversation.

"We oughta…" said Charlie, failing to finish his sentence.

"Yeah," said Street, yawning.

"I'm hitting the latrine," said Charlie. "Call me for breakfast."

Street grunted and walked to the elevator bank. Charlie staggered into the restroom, relieved himself, and splashed water on his face. He was having difficulty not walking into walls. Then he

found himself at the elevator bank and realized he had been waiting for a few minutes. He probably should press the Up button, he
concluded, too drunk to feel sheepish.

Someone approached him, then Charlie was in the elevator, then
he was in Sinatra's suite sitting on a couch with a drink in his hand.
He was unsure how he'd gotten there.

Charlie looked around the room, a deluxe suite with a television
and a hi-fi. Sinatra sat at a giant card table with Momo, Handsome
Johnny, and some other toughs; Dino stood at the bar. There were
some women too, including the raven-haired knockout who'd been
sitting with Giancana at the show.

"Looks like Sleeping Beauty is awake," Martin quipped.

"I only had to kiss him five times," Sinatra said, prompting
obedient chuckles.

"Wow, Vegas drinking is a whole different order of business,"
Charlie said, rubbing his head. He stood. "Aspirin?"

"Give him an aspirin, Dago," Sinatra said.

"Sure," Martin said. He handed two white pills and a cocktail to
Charlie. "And a little hair o' the proverbial canine. Come on, why
don't you play a hand or two?"

Charlie was dimly aware he was past the point of good judgment,
but he downed the aspirin, then made his way unsteadily to the
poker table and sat down.

Giancana extended a meaty right hand. "Sam Hill," he said, his
eyes at once menacing and dull. Charlie was too drunk to care what
the man called himself.

"I think you know Handsome Johnny and Wassy Handelman,"
Sinatra said.

"We weren't formally introduced," Charlie said, nodding to the
two men he'd seen at the Daisy. "I think you know my father,"
Charlie said to Giancana. "Winston Marder?"

Giancana didn't look up as Sinatra dealt him two cards.

"Rings a bell," Giancana said. He had a high voice. Girlish.

"Say, speaking of rings," Sinatra growled, "where's that ring I gave you, Momo?"

"In your mother's wazoo," Giancana said.

"Ah, come on, Momo, why you gotta bring his sainted mother into it?" Martin asked.

"Seriously, that was a nice ring," Sinatra said.

"What's this?" asked Charlie.

"Star sapphire pinkie ring Frank had made for Sam," said Martin.

The dark-haired woman appeared at the table, and Sinatra looked up at her appreciatively. "Let me smell your hair, Judy," Sinatra said.

"Smell your own hair, Frank," said Judy.

"Yeah, Frankie, want me to take it off and hand it to you?" Giancana asked.

Sinatra waved at him dismissively and offered a tight smile; he looked like he was making a great deal of effort not to show how angry he was. Something in the way the Chairman of the Board had crudely flirted with Judy reminded Charlie of something, but he wasn't sure what, something about his dad from long ago...but the memory was hazy and just out of reach. The people of questionable character around the table also evoked Winston, a man who, like Sinatra, had risen high above the streets he'd come from, who dined with senators and foreign leaders but never lost touch with the rougher men who muscled control of businesses and unions, who made things happen and made problems and people disappear.

Why would Sinatra consort with the likes of these thugs? Charlie wondered. But he knew they could be charming and, at times, fun. Charlie remembered the allure and style of some of the gangsters his father knew—Siegel and Lansky, Luciano and Frank Costello. Charlie had a fond memory of Three Finger Brown—aka Tommy

Lucchese—plucking a quarter out of his ear when he was a boy. Being a sociopath didn't necessarily mean an absence of charisma; in fact, it often seemed to require it.

His father. His thoughts snapped back to the task at hand. He needed to find out what favor Momo wanted from Sinatra. It wasn't like he could just ask. He had no desire to join the long list of those who had gotten on the wrong side of the men in this room. He had to think. Although, stewed as he was, thinking was nearly impossible.

"You know, Congressman, we have mutual friends," Giancana said, studying his cards.

Charlie was unsure what to say. "Okay," he finally said. "I'm glad." He wondered if Giancana knew about his problems back in New York, how the union thugs, after helping Charlie secure re-election votes, were now asking Charlie to lean on a U.S. attorney to take it easy on one of their associates, to drop the charges. Could he have known that?

As if in response to the confused look on Charlie's face, Rosselli jumped in: "So we're all friends here."

"Is that right, Charlie?" asked Martin.

"I, uh—" Charlie stammered. "I have a good relationship with some of the local unions."

"They backed you last time," Rosselli said. "Without them, you wouldn't be here. Without them next time around, you're done."

"Um," said Charlie, "they were helpful."

"It's good to have friends," Giancana said. He looked up at Charlie, but his eyes were dead. "But it's not nice to forget that." He held eye contact for a few more seconds.

Even in his state of inebriation, Charlie recognized that the Mob boss was threatening to end his political career and maybe also his life. But his thoughts were interrupted by a pang of nausea so strong that he rose abruptly and, to the mild and unconvincing protests of the group, waved good night and ran to the elevator. He got out on his floor, rushed into his suite, passing a sleeping Margaret, and reached the bathroom with seconds to spare. After his stomach had emptied itself, Charlie collapsed onto the hotel bed, wondering who was in more trouble, Winston or his son.

CHAPTER EIGHT

LAS VEGAS, NEVADA

December 1961

Sinatra stood above the shallow end of the pool at the Sands and observed the lovely Judy as she made her way up the steps and over to a chaise, twisting her dark wet hair into a ponytail, leaving a trail of drops that quickly evaporated on the concrete.

Charlie looked at his watch—almost noon. The relentless sun and dry desert air hit him like a blast from an A-bomb. Margaret, hungover and baking in the heat, released a sigh. With this crew, cocktails began at breakfast, and the rest of the day was all just a long surf on a buzzy wave. Dean Martin was passed out on a chaise, snoring.

Most of the gang was there, in the latest and most fashionable bathing suits: Martin, Sinatra, Davis, and, fluttering around them like butterflies, a coterie of women, including Judy, whose attention Sinatra was desperately trying to catch. Someone said that Lawford was back east with his wife and the rest of the Kennedy clan; Charlie and Margaret would soon be returning briefly to New York City to spend Christmas with their children, even though they had made little progress in their quest.

"A pretty girl is like a melody," Sinatra crooned, then shook his hips like a burlesque dancer: *"Boom chicka-boom."*

Judy ignored him and reached for her towel.

Sinatra displayed a mock pout—he was accustomed to a little resistance. "Come on, baby, let's have a little kiss and hug, a little rock and roll! It's been a long dry spell for me!" His confidence made that an unlikely story, and not for the first time, Charlie marveled at the blithe presumption of the man—whether or not the world truly was his oyster, he would grab it and attempt to shuck it any chance he got.

"A long dry spell? I doubt that," Judy said as she settled down next to Margaret and picked up a copy of *Hollywood Nightlife* with a sad Liz Taylor on the cover, making a convincing show of bored disdain.

Sinatra turned to Charlie, who was sitting at a nearby table under an umbrella reading William Lederer's *A Nation of Sheep*. "What would you say, Charlie, if I told you that this little broad with the cold German blood has broken my heart? And not just once, but many times!"

"That would surprise me, Frank," said Charlie, since Sinatra could easily have had a hundred other women fall at his feet. Judy rolled her eyes and turned a page in the scandal sheet.

Sinatra took a seat at Charlie's table and drummed his fingers on the dimpled glass tabletop. Charlie obediently closed his book. The great man demanded attention.

"You know, Judy, you're really stupid," Sinatra finally said.

"Well, thanks a bunch," Judy said.

"I mean it. You're beautiful and you're bright, but you're so square. You don't know how to take advantage of the opportunities you're being offered. You don't walk through any of those open doors." An angry note had entered Sinatra's voice, a neediness that bordered on hostility. Sinatra's playfulness was turning belligerent. Margaret threw Charlie a look above the pages of *Franny and Zooey*, but he didn't respond to it for fear Sinatra might see.

The singer lit a cigarette and then pointed it, clamped between two fingers, in Judy's direction. "Sometimes you remind me of a silly schoolgirl." He must have realized he was getting overheated because he paused, found a smile that almost looked sincere. "Come on, baby. Swing a little. You only live once."

Judy lit a cigarette and walked away, presumably to the ladies' room. Sinatra gave an uncomfortable chuckle and turned to Charlie for some masculine commiseration, but Charlie looked steadily at his book until the moment passed. Sinatra, clearly searching for a graceful exit from his failed pursuit, picked up a random newspaper and snapped it open.

"Holy shit," he said.

"What?" Charlie asked.

"The Ambassador had a stroke," Sinatra said.

"Which ambassador?"

"Kennedy," Sinatra said in a daze, handing the newspaper to Charlie.

> West Palm Beach, Fla. (AP)—President Kennedy's father, Joseph P. Kennedy, suffered a stroke at his Palm Beach home today and was rushed to St. Mary's Hospital.
>
> The 73-year-old former ambassador to England is reportedly in serious condition. The elder Kennedy and his wife arrived here December 11 to start the Christmas holidays at their home.

"Christ, what time is it?" Sinatra asked.

"Almost three back east," Martin said.

"Oh, maybe that's why Peter called," Britt said. "He left a message last night."

"Shit, he left me a message too," said Sinatra. He rushed off to return the call. The pool had been cordoned off for Sinatra and his party, and he swiftly pushed past the rope and onlookers by the stairs to the elevator.

"That's nice that he's so concerned," said Margaret to Charlie.

"The ambassador's his in with the family," observed May quietly.

Judy reappeared and Margaret looked at her, her giant black sunglasses reflecting the sun above them, her skin flawless and tight. Youth and the assuredness that came from having experienced no consequences of anything, she thought, not even gravity.

Charlie, too, regarded the young Judy, though less lofty thoughts ran through his head. He'd been perfectly content as a faithful spouse in a marriage built on family, but he could also see clearly that the Rat Packers had fun. Amoral, vacuous, meaningless, exploitative—sure. And? Was this virility not what America embraced? Charlie wanted a drink, and luckily enough, there was a bar at the other end of the pool. Martin was heading toward it.

"Want an orange juice or anything, ladies?" Charlie asked, standing. "Coffee? Lemonade?"

"Oh, that's nice of you, Charlie, I'll take a lemonade," Margaret said.

"Me too," said May.

"Mimosa, thanks," said Judy, as if a congressman fetching her a drink were an everyday occurrence.

"Hey there, Charlie," Martin said as Charlie joined him at the bar. "How's your bird?"

"Hey, Dean," Charlie said. "Um, I guess it's good. How's yours?"

"Not so good," Martin said. "And forget the bird, I gotta find that monkey."

"Monkey?"

"The one that beat on my head and shit in my mouth," Martin said. It was a hangover joke he'd clearly made before. Sporting only his red bathing suit, sunglasses, and a deep tan, Martin turned toward the pool and leaned back against the bar. He was surprisingly fit.

"Ah, look at the talent here!" he said, surveying the bevy of attractive young women—Copa Girls, dancers, models, actresses, and some, like Judy, whose occupations weren't clear. "Next time your wife turns in early, you should sample the local wares. Vegas is a confectionery—it's a chocolatier, a patisserie." He nudged Charlie's ribs with his elbow in case his words had somehow been too subtle. "Go ahead, buddy, bite yourself off some marzipan!"

"I'm good," Charlie said. "Thanks." He reminded himself that he had a job to do and couldn't afford to alienate anyone.

Martin took off his sunglasses and squinted at Margaret. "You have two kids, you said? It doesn't show." His gaze remained on Margaret. "I'm sure things are different from the rabbit days when you first got together, though, right?" He slapped Charlie on the back.

"Your scotch, sir," said the barkeeper. Martin reached back without looking and waited for the drink to be placed in his hand. He rattled the ice in his glass, swallowed half its contents, then stood a little straighter and adopted a sterner tone, as if speaking to a recalcitrant child. "You're a man, Charlie, and you are perfectly entitled to behave as a man does, taking what you want and what you need."

Charlie contemplated this. Truth be told, it was no different from how powerful men in Washington and New York City behaved.

"And speaking of what you need," Martin continued, "pardon my French, but just why the fuck are you out here? None of it makes much sense to me. I'm not a fan of politics, but it seems fishy for a Republican congressman to take leave from his job to work on a picture and hang around with an actor who likes Democrats. Goldwater send you? Nixon?"

Charlie laughed. "I thought you weren't a fan of politics."

"I read the papers," Martin said, smiling.

"If they wanted intel," Charlie said, "they'd send a pro, or at least someone who could hold his liquor. Margaret needed a break from the New York winter and two little kids, so when the studio asked me to come out here, we jumped at the chance. Sunshine, movie stars…"

"Mmm-hmm," said Martin skeptically.

"Scotch," bellowed a voice. It was Rosselli, approaching the bar from the hotel lobby with another man. In his brightly colored Hawaiian shirt and bathing trunks, Rosselli looked like a handsome aging celebrity, and Charlie had a hard time reconciling what he knew about the mobster's brutal reputation with the gregarious charmer before him.

"Frank's in a state," Rosselli informed them. "Calling the White House, trying to get through to Kennedy." Rosselli massaged his forehead with a beefy thumb and forefinger. He pointed to his friend. "This is Bob," he said.

"Bob Maheu," said the man. He was bald and in his forties with a sad expression and a lumpy body, a bag of potatoes compared with the glamorous gangsters and stars at the pool. Charlie knew the name but he couldn't remember how.

"So what's your connection to these fine gentlemen?" Margaret asked Judy.

"Oh, Frank and I have known each other for a long time. And he introduced me to Sam." She spoke with the casual assurance of someone who assumed her life's details were well known.

"Sam?"

"Sam Hill, the distinguished older gentleman who hangs around here?"

Margaret didn't see anyone by that description, only a pool full of young women splashing rather showily, careful to keep their hair dry and their assets on full display. They had an appreciative audience among the men who lounged nearby, most of whom barely bothered to conceal their interest.

"Who are all these other girls?" Margaret said, waving toward the pool.

"Oh, I don't know them," Judy said. "I guess they're just here for the show and the sun and the company."

Margaret pulled down her sunglasses to get a better look at the young women, all of them with dimpled cheeks, flawless skin. "What do they do?" she asked. The women in Las Vegas, the nontourists, seemed to do whatever they needed to do to survive—from Copa Girl to cocktail waitress to burlesque dancer to bed-hopper, with various levels of clientele. She didn't know why she was judging the women this way. It was unlike her. Judy was silent, which made Margaret nervous.

Judy looked at Margaret as if noticing her for the first time. "You're the congressman's wife?"

"I'm a zoologist, but yes, I'm also his wife."

"So you're a zoologist but you married a congressman and now you're hanging with the Rat Pack in Vegas?"

"Charlie and I met at Columbia University," Margaret said. "He fought in Europe and then came back and we got married. Congress didn't happen until almost a decade later."

"We're all just on a journey," Judy said.

"Part of me looks at these...these girls, like lambs with the wolves around the pool, and I worry," Margaret said. "Maybe it's just the mom in me."

"Those girls don't need some housewife to protect them," Judy said. "They're fine. We're fine."

Among Rosselli's insatiable appetites was a hunger for Hollywood gossip, and after his first sip of scotch, he began peppering Martin with questions about Natalie Wood.

"I mean, did you see *West Side Story*? Did you see *Splendor in the Grass*?" he exulted. "She's an angel! And that figure—"

"You're in luck, Johnny," Martin said. "She and Bob Wagner are splitsville. Happy to introduce you if you'd like."

"How old is she now? Maybe twenty-two?" Rosselli asked.

"Old enough," said Martin with a leer that was quickly growing tiresome to Charlie. "I saw her on a date maybe two months ago with Chris Powell, that kid who died."

"Oh yeah, poor guy," said Rosselli. "And hello there, pretty lady," he said appreciatively as the bikini-clad Judy made her way to the bar.

She ignored him and ordered a screwdriver. "I thought you were going to bring me a drink," she said to Charlie.

"I always knew I liked you, Judy," said Martin, and once again Charlie observed the power she held over these men by simply ignoring them. Judy settled herself comfortably on a barstool and waited for her drink.

"What was the story with Powell?" Charlie asked. "I heard he and Frank were fighting over a girl."

"Lola," said Judy.

"Frank doesn't really care about any of these dames," Martin said. "Not since Judy here broke his heart."

"I'm telling you," Rosselli said, laughing. "Did you see the shit he pulled with Lauren Bacall?"

"You two are worse than a couple of eighth-grade girls," Judy said, prompting a chuckle from Maheu, whom Charlie had almost forgotten.

"What *do* you think happened to Powell?" Charlie asked, even though he also wanted to hear about the shit Sinatra pulled with Lauren Bacall.

"Dunno," said Martin. "Didn't know him well. Did you, Johnny?"

"I saw him a few times in LA at poker," said Rosselli. "Had a tell like Durante's nose."

"Did he owe anyone money?" Charlie asked.

"Not that I know of," said Rosselli. "And anyway, I never heard of anyone getting whacked for not paying. Maybe a broken leg, sure. Like when Harpo and Chico asked me to get money from Jack La Rue. But in this case...doesn't make sense."

The sun beat down on them. Maheu guzzled his screwdriver and ordered another. A foot-long iguana scampered at the edge of the pool.

"I need to go back in," Judy said. "Jesus, it's like we're ten feet from the sun."

"Is Sam coming down?" Rosselli asked Judy.

"Here he is now," she replied, waving toward the stairs where Giancana, wearing a tan linen suit, was making an entrance.

"Momo!" Martin shouted. He polished off his drink and motioned for another. "Swing over to this tree and join your fellow chimpanzees."

Giancana smiled, walked over to the bar, and shook the hands of the men. He patted Judy affectionately on the back and then—subtly, though not so subtly that Charlie didn't notice—on the rear.

"I heard Elvis is PO'd they have to reshoot a bunch of scenes from his boxing picture," Martin said.

"'Cause of Powell?" Charlie asked.

"Who's that?" asked Giancana.

"That dead actor," said Judy. "From the hotel."

"Ah, right," said Giancana. Then, to the bartender: "Scotch rocks."

"I heard he tried to get help for his gambling problem," said Judy. "Some sort of new therapy. From the guy who wrote that Dianetics book a few years ago? He has a church now. Science—no, Scientology, I think it's called."

"Oh, right," said Martin. "I've heard about that. Gloria dabbles, I think."

"Gloria?" asked Charlie.

"Swanson," said Martin.

"That broad ain't been right since Joe Kennedy stopped shlonging her," observed Giancana.

"What's this?" asked Charlie.

"When the Ambassador was out here making Tom Mix cowboy pictures before the war, he and Swanson had a thing," Maheu said. Charlie studied his face; he was pretty sure he had never seen him before, though Maheu's blandness rendered the lack of recognition unreliable. How did he know him?

"Also Marlene Dietrich," said Judy.

"Yeah but he really boned Swan-song," said Giancana, who had an odd habit of messing up names.

"Swanson," Maheu corrected him.

"Whatever," said Giancana. "He set up Gloria Productions for her. She was a partner, and he billed everything to the company, including gifts he bought her, real estate, minks, whatever. Gloria Productions lost millions, and when she found out and confronted him, he announced he was no longer part of the company and vamoosed back east."

"She's really never recovered," Martin observed. "Add yet another broken soul to the roster. No wonder she's seeking help from that wack job, what's his name, L. Ron..."

"Hubbard," said Maheu. "L. Ron Hubbard."

"Maybe the Ambassador's bill is coming due," Rosselli said.

"What do you mean?" asked Judy.

"The Ambassador had a stroke," Maheu said.

"You didn't hear?" asked Rosselli. "That's why Frank ran off, to call the president."

Judy's face flushed and she seemed genuinely shocked. She put her hand to her chest as if she needed to stabilize herself. "That's so horrible!" she finally said, on the verge of tears. She ran off herself.

"This one's sad, and Frank's mad," said Giancana. He shook his head, disgusted with both of them, though Charlie wasn't sure why. In fact, the only thing Charlie knew right then was that soon he and Margaret would be back in New York City with their kids and he knew even less about Sinatra than he'd thought he did, which didn't bode well for anyone.

CHAPTER NINE

LOS ANGELES, CALIFORNIA

January 1962

"What sorcery is this?" asked Margaret, leaning over the steering wheel of her rented white Chevy Impala and pointing toward the sky. She and Charlie had just returned to Los Angeles after a month in New York City with Lucy and Dwight, and the last thing she'd expected to see here was snow.

"Holy cannoli," said her passenger, Sheryl Ann Gold, née Bernstein. A former intern in Charlie's congressional office, she'd moved to Los Angeles a few years ago and now swore she'd never set foot in DC again as long as she lived. Margaret spared a glance at the younger woman, grateful for an old friend in an unfamiliar city. "It can't be."

But it was. For the first time in thirty years, it was snowing in Los Angeles. More precisely, it was snowing, sleeting, hailing, and raining all at once. Bewildered locals stood with their mouths agape, staring at the heavens. Children had begun to dance and run around their front lawns; even some adults got in on the act. Margaret had picked up Sheryl Ann at her Santa Monica apartment, and as they drove east, the snow fell more heavily, covering the city like a thin layer of sea foam. Margaret steered the car cautiously, passing blocks of indistinguishable, recently built one-story homes. Sheryl Ann turned up the radio.

Giesler's estate is worth eight hundred thousand dollars, most of which will be controlled by his widow in two separate trust funds, his will indicates. The colorful attorney represented a number of clients from the worlds of Hollywood and organized crime, getting both Charlie Chaplin and Errol Flynn acquitted of charges involving minors and representing both Bugsy Siegel and Mickey Cohen. Giesler defended Lana Turner's daughter in what was ultimately ruled justifiable homicide against her mother's boyfriend, mobster Johnny Stompanato...

"So his clientele were mobsters and statutory rapists," Sheryl Ann said.

"Nice work if you can get it," Margaret responded.

"The stories you hear in this town about young girls," said Sheryl Ann. "It would curl your hair. It's sick."

"Yeah." Margaret frowned. "I've seen a bit of it firsthand." She had already told her friend about her niece and her frustration at not being able to find out more. The bartender and doorman at the Daisy had had no idea who Margaret was inquiring about; the LAPD operator told her to call back when she had something resembling actual information; Itchy Meyer at MGM wouldn't take her calls. Sheryl Ann said she would think about a way to help, but she hadn't had any ideas.

Margaret adjusted the AM dial, as if changing the station would have an impact on eradicating the evil it carried.

Former Vice President Richard Nixon, running for governor and participating in a March of Dimes parade, has been caught in the storm riding in the back of a convertible and wearing nothing but a summer suit...

The women laughed, familiar with Nixon's awkwardness and his run of bad luck.

"Poor Dick," said Sheryl Ann, switching to a music station and landing on "The Lion Sleeps Tonight" and a cascade of *a-weema-weh*s. "He has a storm cloud over his head. Like what's his name in *Li'l Abner.*"

"Joe Btfsplk."

"Yeah, him."

"Speaking of storms, the weather must have followed me and Charlie," said Margaret.

Days before, back in New York, Margaret had been overjoyed to be home with Lucy and Dwight and taking a break from the frenetic pace of their temporary California life. Even Christmas with two young children felt calm by comparison, though it was a calm interrupted far too soon. Charlie had been explaining to Lucy over breakfast that taxidermists had nothing to do with paying taxes when the phone started ringing.

"I thought you pay them and then the man gives you a stuffed bear," Lucy said, delighting her father.

"Daddy, Daddy," said Dwight, coming from the bathroom where Margaret had been brushing his hair. He ran up to his father and hugged him as Charlie tried to reach the ringing phone.

"I'll get it," Margaret said.

"Daddy, what's up?" Dwight asked, performing one of their daily routines.

"What's up is…your grandma's going to take you to the Bronx Zoo today!" Charlie said.

"Daddy, what's down?"

"Stock market's been going down for a while," Charlie said. "The Kennedy slide."

"And what's—what's right, Daddy?"

"*You're* what's right, Dwight. You and your sister are what's right with the world!"

"And Daddy, Daddy, what's left?" Dwight asked, beaming with pride.

"Only thing that's left is for me to give you a big hug," Charlie said.

They did this every morning and it was Charlie's favorite part of the day.

"Charlie." Margaret poked her head into the dining nook off the kitchen. "It's Addington White. He says it's important."

Charlie raised his eyebrows at Lucy as he got up from his chair. "Be right back, princess." Lucy returned to her cornflakes and her *Casper the Friendly Ghost* comic book. Charlie smiled, recalling the time Lucy had asked him if Casper was just Richie Rich after evil cousin Reggie finally murdered him, the natural climax of that dark rivalry for the hand of the fair Gloria. He wasn't sure if the joke was original or not, but either way, the child had a lovely, dark sense of humor, just like her mom.

He grabbed the phone.

"Charlie, we need to talk," the Justice Department investigator barked on the other end of the line.

"Merry Christmas to you too, Addison, and thank you, we did have a lovely holiday," Charlie replied, but Addison was in no mood for pleasantries.

"Meet me at Solly's at eleven. Bring Margaret."

Two hours later, with Margaret's mother, Catherine, back on babysitting duty, they arrived at the narrow, nondescript Eighth Avenue diner. Charlie supposed that White had chosen to meet in person out of an abundance of caution; it was safe to assume Hoover would be listening to their phone calls.

The bell jingled as they walked in to smells of burned toast. The cacophony of short-order cooks yelling in the back mingled with Jimmy Dean on the jukebox:

> *Kinda broad at the shoulder and narrow at the hip. And every-*
> *body knew ya didn't give no lip to Big John . . .*

In a dingy vinyl booth at the back, White raised an eyebrow in greeting while they hung up their snow-dusted coats and hats.

"Anything good?" Charlie asked.

"On this earth? I am less and less confident of that with each passing day," said White wearily. "But if you don't mean existentially, the meat loaf tends to be free of ptomaine."

"Didn't know you were such a philosopher," said Margaret, sitting down. "*Kant* say I'm particularly surprised."

"I guess he figured sooner or later we'd Sartre it out," added Charlie, waving over the waitress.

"Camus order for me, sweetie?" Margaret asked, chuckling.

"You two are a regular Nichols and May," White said, smiling despite himself.

"Eh," said Margaret. "Puns are a Nietzsche form of comedy."

The waitress came—coffee and toast for Charlie, coffee and a short stack for White, just coffee for Margaret, who often skipped meals in a constant and unnecessary attempt to diet.

"So let us move from 'to do is to be' to 'doo be doo be doo,'" Charlie said, grabbing the cream at the edge of the table and passing it to Margaret, who groaned as he attempted a pun too far. "We don't know yet what the ask was that Giancana made of Sinatra. But we have established that Sinatra is not merely friendly with mobsters, he's close to them. In just a few short weeks we met Giancana, Rosselli, and some guy named Wassy Handelman."

"Button man for Rosselli," White said.

"The publicity guy at the studio wondered if the Mob killed Chris Powell to help Frank," Charlie said. "They were romantic rivals, and Powell was some rising star. But we've seen zero evidence of that and frankly, if they were going to start killing off Sinatra rivals, Hollywood would become Stalingrad."

"The Mob killing Powell seems a real stretch," White said. "Where'd you get that from?"

"Manny Fontaine," said Margaret. "United Artists' publicist. Picture a gentile Sammy Glick."

White nodded.

"He thinks Frank does this a lot," said Charlie. "He told us the Mob muscled Tommy Dorsey to release Frank from his contract. And that Frank was supposed to costar with Powell in some new picture—"

"*Come Blow Your Horn,*" said Margaret.

"The Neil Simon play," said White.

"Right," said Charlie, "but Frank didn't want Powell to costar. And now the problem's solved."

"Hard to believe he'd have him whacked for that," said White. "He has enough juice in Hollywood to get a no-name pushed off a picture."

"True," said Margaret. "We heard some other things about Powell that might be relevant to his murder. Or not."

"Apparently he was joining some trendy new self-help religion," Charlie said.

"From the Dianetics guy," added Margaret, then clammed up as the waitress appeared to refill their coffees.

White put down his coffee cup and took out a notepad. Charlie watched him jot down *Hubbard Dianetics Powell.*

"The Scientologists," White said.

"Yeah, that's them," said Charlie.

"That's interesting," White said. "They're wired. Their first church was built on primo real estate in DC."

White offered them a quick overview. The founder of the Church of Scientology, a charismatic science fiction writer named L. Ron Hubbard, came to prominence with his bestselling book *Dianetics: The Evolution of a Science,* the latest of many self-help books for a nation-wounded by World War II and rattled by Cold War fears of a pending nuclear apocalypse.

"He writes to us a lot," White said. "To the FBI specifically. For about a decade now."

"Why?" asked Margaret.

"Hubbard's a staunch anti-Communist and, candidly, something of a loon."

"What does he write you about?" asked Margaret.

"In his first letter, he accused more than a dozen members of his Dianetics foundations—including his own wife—of being Communists," White recalled.

"Completely normal," said Charlie sarcastically.

"Yes, and like any stable person, he accuses his critics of being enemies of America," White said. "He keeps writing us, calling people who criticize the 'religion' he founded *Communist-connected personnel*. That's the term he uses, over and over."

"Are they?" asked Charlie.

"No."

"*Cuck-oo,*" chimed Margaret.

"It gets weirder," said White. "We received two sketchy pamphlets in the mail, and we immediately suspected Hubbard of sending them. One summarized Russian brainwashing techniques. The other was supposedly written by a nuclear physicist who claimed that a vitamin-supplement concoction called Dianazene could be used to combat radiation sickness. Guess what comes next?"

"Hubbard hawking Dianazene?" Margaret guessed.

"Yep," said White. "The FDA confiscated more than twenty thousand Dianazene tablets from a company with ties to Hubbard. Guy's a grifter." He lit a cigarette and took a deep drag.

"And?" Margaret finally said.

"So?" Charlie added.

White grinned mysteriously, clearly pleased with his power. "We can't ask you to go investigate a church," he said. "Constitutional issues. But needless to say, the attorney general is grateful for any information that comes his way, and he will take all assistance into consideration."

"Got it," said Margaret as Charlie fought the urge to slap the smile off Addington White's face.

"So, listen," Charlie said. "We have a couple questions for you."

"Oh?" asked White.

"We ran into my niece Violet Greeley while we were out there," Margaret explained. "She ran away from home six months ago; she's sixteen."

"Right," White said in an annoyed, almost bored tone. Margaret wondered how often he heard stories like this.

"She was with this disgusting studio exec," Charlie said.

"Itchy Meyer," said Margaret. "MGM."

"We're just wondering if you could help us track her down," Charlie said. "We've called MGM but Meyer won't talk to us. The staff of the bar where we saw her, the Daisy, say they'd never seen her before. We need to find her. She's a kid."

"I know it's low priority," Margaret said. "Young woman lost in Hollywood. But it would mean a lot to us. To me. Please."

White looked in Margaret's eyes, nodded noncommittally, then wrote down the relevant details in his notepad.

"I'll see what I can do," White said. "But to be honest, you're not really in a place to be asking anything of us. We need you to get back to work."

"We will," Margaret said. "If you agree to help, that will allow me to focus entirely on the task at hand. Charlie is one hundred percent on the Sinatra case, of course."

"Though, I have to say, we're also really worried about my dad," Charlie said, staring into White's eyes, searching for some human connection. "He's old and frail—he hasn't been the same since Mom died. We would really love to see him. Any chance I can before we head back to LA?"

White responded with a shake of his head. "Not a chance." He looked at his watch. "I gotta go. It's on me," he said and waved for the check.

Three days later, they boarded a nine a.m. flight to Los Angeles.

"Excited for my big undercover mission," Margaret said quietly to her husband. Feeling guilty about leaving the kids again, she reminded herself that she needed to help Winston and, in a different way, Charlie.

"What undercover mission?" Charlie asked.

"Scientology," she said. "Hubbard."

"You're not going on any mission in that weird church, Betsy," Charlie said. "That's crazy."

"Ah, but the Lord will be with me," she said.

"Praise the Lord and pass the ammunition," Charlie said.

They argued—quietly, politely—for most of the flight. Ultimately, they agreed that she could go if she brought along a trusted friend. Street had flown back east, so that left Charlie's former intern Sheryl Ann Gold.

Margaret kept her eyes on the snowy road. She remembered the first time she'd met Sheryl Ann Gold—well, Sheryl Ann Bernstein back then. It was January of 1954, and Margaret, three months pregnant and queasy, felt vaguely intimidated by the congressional intern's vitality and youth. Witnessing the girl's brainy, breathless charm and wholesome beauty, Margaret had worried Sheryl Ann was infatuated with Charlie, a newly minted congressman and a dashing academic with a bestseller under his belt. But she needn't have been concerned. After the adventures of that winter, Sheryl Ann moved to Los Angeles, got married, and gave birth to a baby boy named Caleb. Her husband, a struggling screenwriter, reluctantly allowed her to do part-time secretarial work at a UCLA-affiliated think tank. Her academic ambitions had fallen by the wayside.

"It's the worst of both worlds," Sheryl Ann told Margaret with a resigned shrug. "Whenever I'm with Caleb, I wish I were at work, and whenever I'm at work, I worry that I'm a bad mom."

"I sure know the lyrics to that song," said Margaret.

A radio ad caught her attention:

Norman Vincent Peale, bestselling author of The Power of Positive Thinking *and president of the American Foundation of Religion and Psychiatry, will be preaching at First Methodist on February eighteenth. His sermon—"The Tough-Minded Optimist"—is a must-listen. Come join us…*

"Another flimflam man," Sheryl Ann said, "just like our Mr. Hubbard."

"People are seeking happiness," Margaret said. "So some folks gotta sell it."

"I guess the question is," Sheryl Ann said, "were previous generations less happy or were they just more focused on the essentials, like food, shelter, and not getting the plague?"

"Post–atom bomb, there's more existential dread," Margaret said. "Hence Peale, Dale Carnegie, Dianetics…"

"You're going to want to take a right onto Hoover in a few blocks," Sheryl Ann said. "Hubbard bought the Casa de Rosas about a decade ago. You can't miss it. It looks exactly like a place that would be called the Casa de Rosas."

Margaret eased the Impala into a spot between two parked cars on Hoover. The snow had stopped as quickly as it started and was already beginning to melt; the sight of it dusting palm trees and flowering shrubs was incongruous. They climbed out of the car and shivered in the unfamiliar cold.

"Let's leave our purses in the trunk," Margaret said.

Sheryl Ann must have wondered why but she obeyed. She nervously touched her hair as they made their way to the white

Spanish mansion, climbed the steps of the concrete porch, passed a modest bronze sign on the wall that read HUBBARD DIANETICS AND SCIENTOLOGY RESEARCH FOUNDATION, and entered through its red doors. Inside, a young receptionist sat at an immaculate desk in front of a staircase, talking on the phone. Wide-eyed and no doubt an aspiring actress, she acknowledged their arrival with a slight nod of her head and waved toward two orange armchairs.

There was a bookshelf in the waiting area with dozens of books, all of them by L. Ron Hubbard, some science fiction, others religious or instructional: *Dianetics: The Modern Science of Mental Health Handbook for Preclears; Electropsychometric Auditing Operator's Manual; Self-Analysis in Scientology: A Simple Self-Help Volume of Tests and Exercises.* Above the bookshelf was an enormous movie poster for *The Secret of Treasure Island* from the 1930s.

The receptionist continued to speak softly into the phone, ignoring them. Sheryl Ann raised an eyebrow at Margaret and pushed herself out of the overstuffed armchair to examine the spines of the science fiction paperbacks: *Death's Deputy, The Kingslayer, Final Blackout, To the Stars, Buckskin Brigades.* Margaret turned her attention to the movie poster, which featured a pirate clenching a knife in his teeth, a ship on fire, a treasure chest overflowing with gold doubloons, and a shirtless captain with his arm around a busty young damsel who looked about fifteen.

"Mr. Hubbard wrote the screenplay for that film," said the receptionist, hanging up the phone and suddenly addressing her visitors. "Are you here to sign up for our new twenty-five-hour course? I can offer you a discounted rate if you both join."

Before Margaret could answer, the front door opened, and two men and three women appeared. They all looked to be in their twenties, eager, fresh-faced, attractive, the kind of young people who flocked like birds to Los Angeles every day. The receptionist greeted them warmly. "You can wait in the living room. Your auditors will be with you momentarily," she said. The group dutifully followed her instructions, none of them uttering a single word.

"I'm sorry, we're not here to sign up," Margaret said. "Our brother was a member here, and he died."

"We're trying to retrace his last few months," added Sheryl Ann.

"Who was your brother?"

"Chris Powell," Margaret said. "He was an actor."

The receptionist greeted this news with a blank expression, and just as Margaret was thinking that it was strange if not outright rude not to offer any sort of condolence, a tall man burst through the front door.

"Greetings, all!" he said. His red hair was long on the sides and back, thinning up top, and he wore a safari jacket; apparently, he was trying to look swashbuckling and avuncular simultaneously. He took off his safari jacket and handed it to the wiry, bespectacled young man in a Hawaiian shirt who trailed him, then smiled and approached the receptionist, who gasped when she recognized him. "How can we help these fine ladies?" the man said. He turned to Margaret and Sheryl Ann and greeted them with a flirty wink.

"They're inquiring about Chris Powell," she said. "They're relatives of his."

"Ah, yes," he said. "Such a loss. Can you get me his file?"

"Yes, I'll get it now," the receptionist said.

"Brilliant!" said the redheaded man with a wide smile. "Ladies, won't you please follow me?" He motioned toward the conference room to their left. "Oh, goodness me, where are my manners?" the man said. He extended a big beefy hand to Margaret. "Allow me to introduce myself—L. Ron Hubbard."

CHAPTER TEN

RANCHO MIRAGE, CALIFORNIA

January 1962

At that precise moment, one hundred miles to the east, Charlie was on the patio of Sinatra's two-and-a-half-acre Rancho Mirage estate, which was located on the seventeenth fairway of the Tamarisk Country Club and most often referred to as the Compound. Charlie, Martin, Davis, and Sinatra were wolfing down pancakes fresh from the griddle courtesy of Sinatra's valet, a fastidious young Black man named George Jacobs. It was sunny and in the mid-fifties; the cold front hitting Los Angeles remained at a comfortable distance. The day before, they had all been sunbathing by the pool.

"Son of a bitch!" said Sinatra, slamming his Bloody Mary onto the glass breakfast table with enough force to splatter tomato juice across his newspaper.

Dean Martin raised an eyebrow. "What's wrong, Il Duce?"

"These goddamn columnists. They're obsessed with me," Sinatra fumed. He grabbed the newspaper, rolled it up into a ball, and threw it onto the ground. "Assholes!" he yelled. He took a gulp of his drink and glared across his vast lawn toward the mountains in the distance. Sammy Davis leaned over to put a comforting hand on Sinatra's shoulder.

"Francis, Francis, they go after you because you're the sun, the moon, and the stars!" Davis said. "You released a dozen singles last year, and this year you'll release a dozen more! You're in the middle of shooting a picture that might win you another Oscar! People are talking about 'The Devil May Dance' winning Best Original Song! You're wooing the loveliest ladies in the world and living the life of Riley. Of course they attack you! Wouldn't you attack you if you were one of these rat-faced worms?"

Charlie marveled at the blatant sycophancy on display, but Sinatra drank it all in, then resumed his tirade.

"They're losers!" Sinatra shook his head in disgust. "Pale eunuchs. Never came up with an original thought in their lives. What would they do if I weren't here for them to write about, for them to lie about?"

"That's why they do it, Francis," Davis told him. "They feed off your life force."

"So what they do makes sense to you, Sammy?" Sinatra said with an edge to his voice.

"Hey, hey, hey," said Martin, rising from his seat. He went over to Davis and Sinatra, rubbed their backs and squeezed their shoulders. Charlie observed the trio—the king and his court—with bewilderment. All three were rich and powerful and among the most famous men on the planet, but Martin and Davis treated Sinatra as if he were royalty. It didn't seem entirely born of Sinatra's greater talent or star power or the favors he had extended to all of them. No, it felt more like what Charlie, an only child, had observed among his enlisted men in France during the war: some men naturally stood point, regardless of rank. But these soldiers, away from combat, required constant attention. These leaders—the Sinatras—needed drama.

Charlie stood and bent over to pick up the newspaper, curious about what had set Sinatra off. It was a piece by UPI's Hollywood correspondent Vernon Scott about Sinatra's return to form. It began with a low point, remembering when he'd been a "washed-up crooner" dumped by Ava Gardner. It went on from there more flatteringly, but Sinatra had focused only on that first line, ignoring the rest. Charlie shook his head. It seemed Sinatra felt tortured, somehow, by phantoms within his soul, unable to see these awful threats were the products of his own mind.

L. Ron Hubbard steered Margaret and Sheryl Ann Gold through an oak door and into a cluttered conference room.

"How about that snow!" he exclaimed, looking outside. "It shows the power of our energy, once we go clear."

The women nodded uncertainly.

"I woke up this morning and I thought it would be nice to have snow in January, even if we're in Los Angeles," Hubbard said.

Margaret shot a glance at her friend. "You mean you're the one responsible for the snow?"

"Yes!"

This strange moment was interrupted by a knock at the door: the wiry fellow in the Hawaiian shirt. Margaret wondered if the man had missed the memo on the weather pattern Hubbard was creating for the day. Hubbard motioned toward Margaret and Sheryl Ann. "These two were asking about Chris Powell."

"Julius Mercer," he said as he shook their hands. "I run our Los Angeles office. I'm very sorry for your loss." He paused. "I'm sorry, ladies, I didn't catch your names?"

"Beatrice Powell," said Margaret. "Chris was my little brother. And this is my sister Sophie." She and Sheryl Ann looked nothing alike, Margaret thought. *Cousin* would have been better. Damn it. Did she see Julius and Hubbard exchange a look?

"Let's all have a seat, shall we?" Hubbard motioned toward the conference table. This was followed by an uneasy silence as they all sat down. Hubbard slid into his seat at the head of the table so close to Sheryl Ann, on his left, that their knees were touching, and Margaret began to wonder if they'd made a mistake in coming. Sitting in the diner with Addington White, she'd thought the sleuthing seemed like a harmless task to help Winston. Now she was in the presence of the actual L. Ron Hubbard in a building full of his acolytes, and given the grim history of religious zealotry around the world, the whole assignment seemed foolhardy. Worried that Hubbard might detect her concern, Margaret smiled at him, and he returned it with a flirtatious grin.

"*The Secret of Treasure Island* isn't the only picture I worked on, you know," he told her. "You ever see *Dive Bomber* or *The Plainsman* or *Stagecoach*?" He didn't wait for an answer. "I wrote them too, but the dumb Jew producers denied me the credits."

Margaret heard Sheryl Ann draw a sharp breath beside her. "So," Margaret said firmly. "Our brother Chris."

"Chris came to us last year with a serious gambling problem," said Julius, handing a green file to Hubbard.

"What do you ladies know about our church?" Hubbard asked, looking through the papers in the file.

"Just that Chris thought it would help him," Margaret said.

Hubbard looked up. "He was right to come to us." His tone had shifted from genial host to stern instructor. "Scientology achieves things for people where nothing has worked before. It cures us of illnesses once considered hopeless. It increases our intelligence and competence, improves our behavior, brings us to a better understanding of life."

Lecture concluded, he flashed them an enormous smile.

"But it didn't help Chris," said Sheryl Ann with a tight smile.

"It sounds to me," snapped Margaret, "like you took advantage of a vulnerable man with a gambling problem."

"Beatrice," scolded Sheryl Ann, catching on. She put a warning hand on Margaret's arm.

"Oh, Sophie!" Margaret said, suddenly near tears. She pulled out a tissue and dabbed her eyes. "I'm sorry." She found herself actually weeping for this actor she'd never met. Maybe it was the strangeness of this church or these weird people, or perhaps she'd missed her calling—she should've been an actress. She blew her nose. "We need to know what he went through here, what these...doctors...subjected him to." Margaret glared at Hubbard and Julius. "Because it obviously didn't help!"

"Beatrice, it wasn't their fault," Sheryl Ann said. "Chris struggled so!"

Hubbard put a hand on Sheryl Ann's knee. "Now, now, this is all a very normal human reaction to grief," he said. "Chris was indeed a member of our church, and we worked closely with him in hopes he'd become clear, but he was not committed. In fact, though I'm sorry to bring up something uncomfortable, he still owes us quite a bit of money. Some eight hundred forty-three dollars and change. Let's call it eight hundred forty."

"Sadly, that's true," said Julius with regret in his voice. "We really tried with him." He rose from his chair. "Will you excuse me? I'll just be a minute."

As the door closed behind him, Margaret turned to Hubbard. "What does *becoming clear* mean?"

Hubbard looked at her for a few seconds as if he were deciding whether to let her in on a great secret. Then a smile—a wide, gleaming grin—erupted on his face. "I will show you, Beatrice."

Hubbard stood, ambled to a file cabinet in the corner, and withdrew from its top drawer a device that looked like a small television wired to two soup cans.

"Being clear is what we call the state achieved through auditing, which is done with this meter." Hubbard took his seat again and began fiddling with the knobs on the device. "It's difficult to pick up these concepts in just one meeting—we have classes that I highly recommend—but just to help you understand how hard we tried with Chris..." He leaned forward and placed the tin cans in front of Margaret.

"What is this thing?" asked Margaret.

"A Hubbard E-Meter," he said proudly. "Most people have reactive minds. That's the source of all of the ill behavior we see—insecurities, irrationality, unreasonable fear. The E-Meter helps us detect those problem spots. Once we get rid of the reactive mind—that's what we call going 'clear'—only then can we become our true selves. This E-Meter allows us to audit you, to figure out where you need help. It's what we used to try to help your brother." He sighed deeply and arranged his face into an expression of sympathetic sorrow. "But Chris didn't give himself over."

Margaret pointed at the metal objects in front of her. "Other than these soup cans, how is this any different from, say, Norman Vincent Peale's ideas?"

"Can Dr. Peale cure seventy percent of man's illnesses?" Hubbard demanded. "We can raise your IQ one point for every hour of auditing," he continued as if he were on a stage. "Our most spectacular feat was raising a boy's IQ from eighty-three to two hundred and twelve!"

Margaret picked up the cans gingerly and felt a slight electric current, a not unpleasant tingle. She put the cans back on the table. "Didn't Dale Carnegie make that same claim?" she asked.

Hubbard smiled. "No, no. There's no comparison."

His words alone were utterly unconvincing, but Hubbard's avuncular charm and matter-of-fact presentation carried them into the neighborhood of believability. It wasn't hard to see how someone vulnerable or eager to change or just plain hungry for human contact might be taken in.

Julius returned, looking irritated, perhaps even alarmed. He leaned toward Hubbard and whispered briefly in his ear. Hubbard rose from his seat. "Will you ladies excuse me for a moment?" The two men hurried out of the room, Julius speaking in low, urgent tones to a newly serious Hubbard. They left the door open behind them.

Margaret tilted her head toward the tin cans in front of her. "This is so weird. Can you adjust the current on the whatchama-callit there?"

"E-Meter," Sheryl Ann said.

"Yes, yes," said Margaret. "That."

As Sheryl Ann fiddled with the contraption, Margaret leaned back in her seat to peer out the open door, where she saw Hubbard and Julius in a heated conversation near the front desk. "Quick," she said, "gimme the file."

Sheryl Ann slid the folder across the table. "I'll keep an eye on the door," she whispered.

Margaret opened the folder to see a head shot of Chris Powell gazing up at her. Beneath that was a list of his credits, which tracked his career trajectory like a chart tracking population growth: bigger roles in smaller films, smaller roles in bigger films. The next page listed everyone in Powell's life who was more famous than him, from the stars of *Kid Galahad* to his romantic attachments, including Lola Bridgewater, to others more peripherally in his orbit, such as Sinatra, Martin, and Davis.

"This is strange," said Margaret. She turned the page to a memo titled "Project Celebrity."

> If we are to heal society at large, we must do something about its communication lines. A key part of this plan is Project Celebrity. There are many to whom America and the world listens. It is vital to put such persons into wonderful condition. It is obvious what would happen to Scientology if prime communicators benefiting from it would mention it now and then.

The memo contained a list of potential enlistees, including Sinatra, Edward R. Murrow, Marlene Dietrich, Orson Welles, Danny Kaye, Liberace, Walt Kelly, Sid Caesar, Pablo Picasso, Greta Garbo, and more. *These celebrities are well guarded, well barricaded, over-worked, aloof,* the memo said. *If you want one of these celebrities as your game, write us at once so the notable will be yours to hunt without interference.*

"What does it say?" Sheryl Ann asked.

"The church desperately wants celebrities to join," Margaret whispered. "There's a section here on the wooing of Gloria Swanson, and how it's helped them—"

"They're coming!" Sheryl Ann cautioned under her breath as Julius walked toward the door; Margaret stuffed the documents down the back of her dress. But instead of coming into the room, Julius closed the door—and they heard a key turning in the lock.

CHAPTER ELEVEN

RANCHO MIRAGE, CALIFORNIA

January 1962

"And here's the pièce de résistance," Sinatra proclaimed, half-hearted French accent easily defeated by Hobokenese.

He was finishing up a tour of the Compound. Outside the ranch-style mansion, on the front lawn, a sign: FORGET THE DOG, BEWARE OF THE OWNER. Throughout the property: ocotillo and saguaro cacti and citrus trees. Sinatra led Charlie, Lola Bridgewater, and Judy past the pool house, which had been converted into a briefing room in preparation for JFK's visit, then flung out his arm—"Ta-da!"—toward a sleek arrangement of concrete and granite occupying most of what used to be manicured lawn. Half a dozen masons were building a patio of sorts.

Lola looked confused. "What is it?" She had a high, chirpy voice, like a nightingale. With her bleached-blond hair, she was a near-perfect composite of Jayne Mansfield and Kim Novak. Both she and Judy were still in clingy pajamas that left little to the imagination.

"It's a helipad!" said Sinatra.

"For *Marine One*," said Judy.

Lola wrinkled her nose. *Marine One?*

"That's the name for whatever Marine Corps helicopter is transporting the president," explained Charlie, ever the historian. "Ike used a Sikorsky Seahorse. I think Kennedy uses a Sea King."

Sinatra lit a cigarette and looked at Charlie. "I loved that license-to-kill riff I hear you laid down to Wayne," he said. "Where'd you serve, Congressman?"

"France," said Charlie, "right after D-Day."

"I was four-F—busted eardrum," said Sinatra. "*Begged* them to let me join."

Charlie didn't know how to respond to men who rushed to explain why they didn't serve. He had no absolution to offer. "Well, you did as much to lift up the spirits of the troops as anyone alive," he said. "You did your part."

"There's a military picture I'm trying to get made that I'd love to talk to you about sometime, Charlie," Sinatra said. "The air force accidentally drops an A-bomb on North Carolina. B-fifty-two breaks up midair, crew has to ditch the two nukes they're carrying. One almost detonates nears Goldsboro. Two guys killed in the crash. Big cover-up." Sinatra looked right at Charlie. "You don't think it sounds far-fetched, do you, Congressman? I can see it in your eyes. Doesn't it feel like there's a part of this government that's gone off the rails? Like there are people who have no accountability and just do whatever they want? Wiretaps, thuggery, assassinations…"

"Like in *Manchurian*?" Charlie asked.

"Except real," said Sinatra.

"And you don't know the half of it," Charlie said, thinking about his work on the House Oversight subcommittee. "I'm not even sure what the foreign policy principles are anymore. Bay of Pigs was such a fiasco, it's hard to understand how the president got talked into it."

"Yeah," agreed Sinatra. "I mean, don't get me wrong—Fidel is a real Commie, not the fake kind you see in Hollywood. Rough stuff. I wouldn't cry if he slipped in the shower."

"Of course," said Charlie. "He's a monster and he's in Khrushchev's pocket. But that's not the point. It's what do we do in response."

"Exactly," said Sinatra. "It's who *we* are, not who *they* are. You're like the first sane person I've talked to about this. Everyone else is just pro-Jack or pro-Ike, pro-Commie or anti-Commie. No nuance. No conversation."

"Putting on the team jerseys," said Charlie.

"Exactly," Sinatra said again, smiling. He reached out and squeezed Charlie's shoulder, then gave him a brotherly slap on the back. Charlie felt a little foolish for speaking so candidly with the express purpose of bonding with a celebrity. But what choice did he have? It was either that or let his dying father rot in jail. Either way, Sinatra was right on the issue, and Charlie was pleased to hear a more sophisticated Hollywood take on Cuba than he'd expected.

Charlie looked at Lola. She smiled back patiently. Judy examined her nails.

"Anyway, Charlie," Sinatra said, "maybe you could read this script I got. It's similar to the point I was trying to make with the Eddie Slovik script I was working on till Wayne stuck his fat face in."

"Not the first or the last favor you did for the Kennedys," Charlie said.

"Ha," Sinatra said. "Don't bring that up in front of Sammy! But I have all the rights to this script, and contractually the studio has to make it. After my Oscar, they offered me carte blanche but then they got all hinky a few months ago when I told them I wanted to make the picture. We may end up in court. I don't get why they're so against it."

"I'd be happy to take a look," Charlie said.

"Good man," Sinatra said, squeezing Charlie's shoulder again, and Charlie was relieved that the ruse was working so well. He also had to admit it was almost impossible to resist the urge to please this man, whose moods were infectious and whose excitement about his script had a nervous edge to it, like a boy in love and afraid of how his affections were being received. "Charlie, I know you're Republican, but you know the Kennedys maybe better than any of us."

Charlie shrugged. Sinatra probably didn't want to hear that at that moment, he thought of them as cutthroat, calculating bastards.

"I think the kid brother is getting cold feet about TP staying here. Maybe you could put in a good word, let them know how fine the accommodations are," Sinatra said, and Charlie suddenly understood why he'd been invited to Rancho Mirage. "You know, Juliet and I recently got engaged; this will look like a Norman Rockwell painting by the time they get here."

Sinatra had earlier that month surprised the world by announcing he would wed South African dancer Juliet Prowse, whom he'd met on the set of *Can-Can*, though no date had been set and no one in Sinatra's circle, including the man himself, talked about it much.

"When Ike was president I had to deal with this bullshit. I wanted to go to Korea with the USO, but the army denied me clearance," Sinatra said. "I had to meet with generals, then the State Department. I told these fuck-sticks what was what. Witch-hunting! I said, 'Have any of you run a check on me?' They said there were items in the press that raised questions about my sympathies. I said, 'Gentlemen, if you feel I'm a risk, you can stick the Korean War in your ass.' Fuck them, they think I'm a risk."

Charlie was kept from inquiring further about this by the appearance of Sinatra's valet, neatly dressed in a bright white polo shirt under a dark blue cardigan and holding a bourbon (also neat) in each hand. "You have a phone call, Mr. S.," Jacobs said, placing a tumbler in his boss's outstretched hand. Sinatra nodded and turned toward the house. Jacobs gave the other bourbon to Charlie, who looked at his watch. Ten a.m.

"George, do you happen to have a smoke?" Charlie asked.

"Of course, Congressman," Jacobs said, reaching into the pocket of his cardigan. He took out a pack of Marlboros and a shiny metal lighter etched with the image of a battleship.

"Navy?" Charlie asked.

"Yes, indeed," Jacobs said. "Aide to Admiral Beatty in the Mediterranean. Then on an aircraft carrier in Korea. But nothing like you in the thick of it."

"Service is service," said Charlie.

And he knew that service of a different sort was still part of Jacobs's life.

Earlier that morning, the pneumatic drill had started rat-a-tat-tatting. Charlie had assumed that fellow hangover victim Sinatra would soon put a stop to it. But he didn't, such was the urgency to upgrade the estate for the president's arrival. So Charlie had dragged himself out of bed and headed to the empty kitchen, where coffee was already brewing. He poured himself a cup, walked outside to enjoy the fresh air, sat down on a chair next to the pool, and lit a cigarette. He took in the cloudless blue sky as a hawk passed overhead, his gaze following the creature over Mount San Jacinto. When the bird of prey was no more than a black speck in the distance, he stared blankly off into the sky. He thought about his father waking up in the prison infirmary at the Tombs, alone and afraid. Lost in those thoughts, Charlie sat in a daze, then slowly began to take notice of the shapes in front of him, the figures visible through the sliding glass door that led to Sinatra's bedroom inside the house. Sinatra was sitting on a chair wearing only a towel wrapped loosely around his potbelly. Jacobs stood behind him carefully spraying what seemed to be paint on the bald spot at the back of his boss's scalp. Jacobs then retrieved two different hairpieces from the closet, showed them to Sinatra, and placed one on his head. Seeing the great man half naked and half bald was unsettling; Charlie realized he'd been more dazzled by Sinatra than he'd wanted to admit. And in the casual intimacy of the scene, presumably one repeated every morning, he began to understand the deep bond between the two men.

They walked away from the helipad site past several one-story bungalows curving around the main house to the pool area. Judy had her arm hooked through Sinatra's in the front of the group; Lola lagged at the end, behind Charlie. She seemed bored.

"Should we go back inside?" Lola asked.

"No, the sun is so nice," said Judy. "Let's get towels and sit by the pool." Even though there was snow a hundred twenty miles away in Los Angeles, the temperature in Rancho Mirage was in the sixties. Clear skies and a cozy desert heat.

Jacobs supplied plush towels from the briefing-room closet and brought Charlie a book he'd left in the kitchen—an early review copy of *Cuba Betrayed* by Fulgencio Batista, the deposed former dictator. Batista hadn't seen Castro coming, and Charlie was unconvinced by his attempts to explain himself, though he found insightful the descriptions of fumbling and duplicitous U.S. policy. The two women positioned themselves to face the sun; Charlie took a seat at a glass table a short distance away and motioned for Jacobs to join him.

"Say, George," Charlie said quietly, putting his book to the side. "I hear Mr. S. is unhappy about a favor Mr. Giancana had asked of him. Do you know what it is? Anything I can help with?"

Jacobs looked earnestly at Charlie, seemingly taking him at his word. "I don't know, Congressman," he said. "I'll see what I can find out and get back to you. Discreetly." Perhaps Jacobs could actually help him. Charlie felt a moment of relief.

Lola propped herself up on an elbow and tilted her chin in Charlie's and Jacobs's direction. "What was eating Frank this morning?"

"Oh, the papers," said Jacobs. "Some garbage in there about the Mob."

"What specifically?" asked Judy.

"A wedding performance Sinatra supposedly gave for Angelo Bruno of the Philly Mob. Carousing with the Giacalones of Detroit," Jacobs said. "But it's nonsense," he added staunchly. "Mr. S. doesn't know them."

Lola rolled her eyes. "Why do they constantly go after him?" She affected a mock pout.

"Go after who, chickadee?" asked Dean Martin, emerging from the kitchen looking sleepy, satin dressing gown loosely tied over pajama pants and a deeply tanned torso, Bloody Mary in hand.

"Frank, Dino," said Lola. "Why does the press attack him so much?"

"Some of it's those crazy John Birchers," Martin said, collapsing dramatically onto a chaise beside Lola's. "They're convinced Frank's a Commie because he made *The House I Live In* a hundred years ago, he supported the Hollywood Ten…"

The confused expression on Lola's face spoke volumes. "Oh, Lola," Judy said, exasperated, "*The House I Live In* was this short film Frank made against bigotry, about these kids beating up a little Jewish boy. And the Hollywood Ten—"

"I know who the Hollywood Ten are," Lola said. "But honestly, it can't help that he spends time with some pretty rough guys." She unwrapped a piece of bubble gum.

"Guys like Sam?" asked Charlie.

"Oh, Sam's a teddy bear," said Judy. "He's not mixed up with any of that. He can be tough, but show me a successful businessman who isn't."

Martin looked at Charlie and rolled his eyes.

"Frank can be tough," Lola said to Judy.

"Not like hitting-you tough," clarified Judy, making Charlie wonder once again just what their relationship was. She signaled that she was dating Giancana, but the quiet looks and moments of affection between Sinatra and her were unmistakable.

"No, no," Lola said. "Like *mean* tough." She seemed to have an incident or incidents in mind. Lola was a curious sort, Charlie thought. Beneath the stereotypical bimbo veneer, she'd clearly formed some critical views of her host.

"A few years ago the papers reported Sammy said something sideways about Frank and Frank gave him the silent treatment for months," Martin recalled as he stood and walked toward Charlie's table, where Jacobs had placed a pitcher of orange juice, vodka, and ice after cleaning up the empty glasses and full ashtrays from the night before.

"What had Sammy said?" Charlie asked, lifting his drink so Jacobs could wipe the glass table with a wet cloth.

"I don't remember," Martin said. "Something true, no doubt." He sat down and poured himself a screwdriver. "Let me ask you a question." He leaned toward Charlie and said conspiratorially, "I heard from a reporter that Bobby's got a bug up his ass about Frank having Mob ties. It's all bullshit—Frank's no closer with the Mob than anyone else in showbiz." He emptied his drink in one gulp then returned to leering at the ladies.

"I don't know one singer who doesn't know at least a few connected guys," Jacobs said, lighting Martin's cigarette. "I mean, they own the clubs."

"The clubs! The studios! The unions!" Martin said. "Also, I mean, a whole lot of these cats were bootleggers back in the day, back in Jersey. Well, that's not even a crime anymore."

Charlie looked over at Judy, who was writing in a small pink journal. Weird. What could she be writing? As she scribbled away, she and Lola continued chitchatting, unconcerned or unaware that the men could hear them.

"Why did you break up with Frank anyway?" Lola asked Judy.

The two women apparently didn't know each other that well, Charlie realized. He had assumed they were friends. Blonde and brunette, Betty and Veronica, Marilyn Monroe and Jane Russell; kind of a stupid assumption, he saw now.

"Well," Judy said, seemingly taking a moment to reflect on it, "I suppose the final straw was when Frank brought this colored girl into our bedroom one night. That's just not me." Realizing Jacobs was nearby, she quickly added: "Her being colored was not the issue. A third party being in the room—that was my problem."

Jacobs nodded noncommittally, acknowledging that he'd heard it all. Charlie wondered how often he had to shrug off comments like that.

"He's a regular civil rights visionary, our Saint Francis," said Martin.

A scratchy voice suddenly blared from a speaker under one of the small tables around the pool. "All right, you halfwits, apparently you weren't aware I had this place wired for sound for TP's visit," Sinatra said. "Cut the gossip, schoolgirls." He sounded halfway on the road to fury.

Lola and Judy glanced at each other and grimaced while Jacobs walked briskly back to the house. Charlie tried to remember what exactly he'd said. Had Sinatra heard his attempts to play detective?

When Hubbard returned to the room ten minutes later with Julius, his ebullient smile had disappeared, replaced by an unnerving, stony calm. He stared silently at the women sitting at the conference table.

"Christopher didn't have any sisters," he said to Margaret. "Who are you?"

"Your IDs, please!" Julius barked, hand outstretched.

Margaret took a deep breath and tried to slow her racing heart as she pictured their purses stowed in the trunk of the rental car and wondered about their chances of escape. "We left our purses at home," she said.

Hubbard towered over Margaret. He had clearly figured out that she was the leader. "You are a *nasty* woman!" He stood close enough that a faint shower of spittle landed on Margaret, and she could see the yellow plaque that coated his teeth.

"You cannot just come into a house of worship and deceive parishioners and the church leader!" shouted Julius.

Hubbard's face was turning pink and he was breathing heavily. Margaret saw his fists clenching and wondered if he was preparing to use them.

"*Why are you here?*" he shouted. "*What do you want? Who sent you? Sara? The government? Are you even from this planet?*"

Margaret had no idea what Hubbard might be capable of. Charlie might as well have been on the other side of the earth; Hubbard and Julius could make her and Sheryl Ann disappear without a trace.

Hubbard's eyes were closed and his head was tilted toward the ceiling; he seemed to be trying to calm himself down. He cracked his knuckles. Julius had begun pacing back and forth, muttering quietly to himself. They both looked raving mad. Margaret glanced sideways at Sheryl Ann—her eyes were wide, her face white with fear.

Margaret made a decision.

As the men glowered and stormed, Margaret suddenly burst into tears. Shoulders heaving, tears flowing, she felt an odd relief in letting go like this. And her distress seemed to soothe Hubbard—his face softened and she saw him look toward Julius with an expression that seemed something like...victory? She reached blindly for Sheryl Ann's hand and squeezed gently in what she hoped would be a comforting signal. Hubbard put a beefy paw on Margaret's shoulder. His bluster was suddenly gone, replaced by an oily concern.

"I could sense your trauma when you walked in the door." He put a finger under Margaret's chin and tilted her face up to his, as if he were a grandfather trying to comfort an upset child. She tried to hide her revulsion. "We can help rid you of it."

He pulled her to her feet and embraced her. Margaret leaned into him, her arms at her side, her head bowed against his chest. She had to suppress every impulse to recoil.

"There, there," he said. He squeezed her harder.

And then Hubbard suddenly convulsed, his shoulders spasming and his head thrust back.

Julius raced to him, crying out, "Are you all right? What's wrong?"

Hubbard fell, and his body seized up; his legs kicked spastically, as if he were swimming.

Margaret grabbed Sheryl Ann's hand and ran; the two women were out the door and onto the street by the time Julius realized Margaret had grabbed the tin cans from the E-Meter and shoved them under Hubbard's arms after cranking up the electronic dial to jolt his body with a temporarily debilitating current.

Margaret and Sheryl Ann raced through the empty foyer, skidded down the snowy stairs, and almost tripped several times as they ran to their locked car. Two young men with crew cuts emerged from the house, shouting and coming at them like Olympic sprinters, followed by Julius, barking orders. Julius tripped in the slush and fell but the other two were fast; Margaret wasn't sure they were going to be able to get away.

She looked to her left when she heard another car approaching. Amazed, she saw Charlotte Goode screech up in her blue Chevy Bel Air and open the passenger door. "Get in, get in!"

Margaret was stunned, but there was no time for questions. She scrambled into the Bel Air with Sheryl Ann right behind her, and Charlotte hit the gas.

CHAPTER TWELVE

LOS ANGELES, CALIFORNIA

January 1962

They raced down the street.

Charlotte attempted to speed her junky car through the snow but it was like her tires were inner tubes. The car kept skidding, dinging parked car after parked car, nearly mowing down pedestrians.

Margaret sat shotgun. In the back, Sheryl Ann looked through the rear window. The church thugs—Julius in his Hawaiian shirt and the two crew-cut young men—trailed a block behind them, also skidding all over the road, in a blue Ford Galaxie. An actual car chase. They had become a Hollywood cliché.

Margaret looked out the side window and saw pump jacks in the distance. An oil field. Could this be Inglewood? She had lost all sense of space and time.

Goode's car hit an icy patch and they spun out, slid through an intersection, and careened into a telephone pole. The three women were jerked violently toward the pole, then back toward the front of the car.

"Jesus fucking Christ!" Goode yelled.

The car was now aimed in the wrong direction, toward where they had come from. The Galaxie slowly drove toward them.

"You okay, Sheryl Ann?" Margaret asked.

"I think so," Sheryl Ann said, patting her chin, which was bleeding.

"That's a nasty gash," Margaret said. She removed a handkerchief from her purse and dabbed her friend's cut.

Goode struggled to kick her car back to life.

"Fuck!" she yelled.

The Galaxie began speeding up.

"Why are they even—" Sheryl Ann said. Her unfinished question made perfect sense to Margaret: Why were these thugs chasing them? Because they'd tried to get information about Powell? Because they'd lied about who they were? Because Margaret had stolen that document?

"The goddamn shifter's jammed," Goode said.

The Galaxie was now close enough that Margaret could see the furious faces of the young men.

Finally, Goode got the car in gear. She slowly moved forward, then began U-turning. The Galaxie hit the same ice patch Goode had and slid across the intersection, only to be suddenly T-boned by a Chevy. There was a horrific metal crunch. The two cars skidded to a stop as Goode's car chugged away.

Dean Martin left the Compound for Los Angeles shortly after lunch; he had to catch a flight to Pebble Beach for the Bing Crosby pro-am golf tournament. About an hour after that, Charlie was downing yet another screwdriver and enjoying a cigarette on the front porch when Lawford's red Ghia L6.4 screeched around the circular driveway and came to an abrupt stop at the front door. Lawford and several attractive young women spilled out of the Italian coupe like it was the world's most glamorous clown car.

Lawford and his entourage swarmed past Charlie on a cloud of cigarette smoke and Arpège. "What are you doing out here by yourself, old sport?" Lawford said with a wink. "Join the party!"

He did. Within minutes, the young women, seemingly impervious to the brisk air, had stripped down to bathing suits, slinky one-pieces in a dizzying array of colors. Jacobs materialized with more cocktails. Sometime later they escaped the chill by migrating to the small gunite spa containing a Jacuzzi whirlpool, a new trend sweeping the estates of Southern California millionaires.

Sinatra, Judy, and two of the new arrivals—one had an impressive and loud Texas twang, the other had a delightful explosion of freckles that reminded Charlie of a Jackson Pollock—took their drinks to lounge chairs. On her way to the chairs, Lola stopped at Sinatra's impressive outdoor hi-fi and turned on the radio; "Runaround Sue" began blasting, and some of the young women started dancing. Charlie looked at their host; he seemed okay with Dion, but soon enough the song ended and another one began, and before Elvis Presley could even utter the words *When we kiss, my heart's on fire* from his hot single "Surrender," Sinatra's placid smile melted into a look of disgust and he threw his drink at the nearest speaker.

"Turn off that goddamn mumble monkey!" he yelled, and Jacobs quickly restored order to the universe by putting his boss's *Swing Along with Me* on the turntable. "Don't Cry, Joe (Let Her Go, Let Her Go, Let Her Go)" began playing.

But Texas Twang and Freckles couldn't figure out how to dance to it after the much faster song that had preceded it. Even this new "swingier" version of Sinatra's 1949 recording felt old. Charlie caught one of the young women rolling her eyes at her friend.

"Put on the covers, George," Sinatra ordered.

Jacobs brought out an LP and soon they were all listening to Sinatra singing Carl Perkins's "Blue Suede Shoes."

"Just a lark," Sinatra explained. "Made an album of rock covers for my daughters. Maybe we'll release it sometime." Everyone smiled at the privilege of being let in on the secret while dancing to Sinatra singing Richard's "Tutti Frutti," then his take on Gene Vincent's "Be-Bop-a-Lula," followed by his version of "Tequila" by the Champs.

"Fantastic," Charlie called out to Sinatra. He was half sincere, half ass-kissing, and worried for a second that he had gone too far. But Sinatra raised a glass in return and Charlie exhaled.

As the sun began to sink behind the mountains, taking its comfortable warmth along with it, Sinatra and his guests kept themselves warm with the help of Jacobs's endless supply of cocktails: screwdrivers and mai tais, then the spiciest margarita Charlie had ever had, then a surprisingly strong Pimm's cup—a purposeful nod by Jacobs to Lawford's British roots. Before long, most of the others were dancing while Charlie lingered in the hot tub, pruning like an octogenarian, and Sinatra sat at the Jacuzzi's edge, feet submerged.

"The place looks great," Charlie said to his host. "You're ready for JFK's visit."

"You know, Congressman, I don't even know for sure that TP is going to stay here," Sinatra said. "I haven't gotten a straight answer or even a call back from anyone real since the Ambassador had his stroke."

"What does Lawford say?" Charlie said.

Sinatra let out a short laugh. "Worthless. A bum." He said it loud enough for Lawford to hear, but the Kennedy in-law, well oiled by now, was focused only on the young women dancing on the pool deck. Charlie and Sinatra watched Lawford wrap a towel around the waist of the gal with the Texas twang, then pull her toward a lounge chair and onto his lap.

"Thing is," Sinatra said, "they owe me. TP owes me. Peter and I flew to Palm Beach three summers ago, in '59, to meet with the Ambassador. He had lots of asks—money, benefit concerts, a goddamn theme song. But he also wanted me to hit up Momo for help with the unions. And I did. Skinny D'Amato got the miners for the West Virginia primary, and you better believe Momo was busy in Chicago on election night. I made that happen."

Charlie took it all in. The whispers of Mob assistance had never been investigated by law enforcement, so he hadn't known what to believe. But here was the Chairman of the Board, confirming it all.

Before he could respond, Judy and Lola approached them. Judy kicked off her leopard-print mules, sat next to Sinatra, leaned close, and whispered in his ear; whatever it was, it made him smile. With one languorous move, Lola took off her shirt, revealing a bikini, and joined Charlie in the hot tub.

Lola draped her arms along the Jacuzzi edge and surveyed the scene, then leaned back and closed her eyes. Judy, meanwhile, worked double time to make sure none of the other young near-naked women were able to get Sinatra's attention.

Jacobs's next tray included much-needed solid food. Lawford reluctantly accepted a sandwich; he balanced the plate on one leg and Texas Twang on the other, as if she were a side order of chips.

"Oh, Charlie," Lawford said absentmindedly. "I saw your cousin the other day."

Charlie didn't know what he was talking about.

"That girl, the young girl," Lawford said, looking at him. "With the—" He motioned with his hands, suggesting two immense scoops of breast.

"My wife's niece?" Charlie asked.

"That's the one," Lawford said.

"Where?"

"A party," said Lawford.

"A party where? When exactly?"

Then, to Charlie's amazement, Lawford turned away and went back to the dish on his lap.

Lola's eyes were trained on Charlie. "This isn't your scene, is it?"

"I don't really ring-a-ding-ding," Charlie said.

She gave a knowing grin, rooted in the confidence of youth. Charlie had never felt that kind of assuredness. Folks might have inferred strength from his reticence or from the wounds he'd carried out of a trench in France. What trenches had Lola fought in? Charlie tried to look away but found that difficult. He felt his heart beating faster.

Lawford came over to the hot tub; he was holding hands with Texas Twang, who was in turn holding hands with Freckles.

"Loosen up, Charlie, baby," he said with a lazy grin, swaying slightly on his feet. "You're on recess."

"How long you been married, Congressman?" Lola asked.

"We've been together since '41," Charlie said. "Got married when I got back from France, in '45."

"Jeez Louise, I haven't been alive that long," said Freckles.

From the other side of the house, where construction workers had been laboring since that morning, came the sound of a power drill, temporarily drowning out everything else.

"When's the last time you did some drilling, Congressman?" asked Freckles once the noise had stopped.

They all laughed, including Lola. Charlie gave an insincere chuckle.

It had been a couple weeks. Or maybe more. More, definitely. The travel and the jet lag hadn't been very conducive to his and Margaret's love life. Charlie living in DC Monday through Friday and coming home only on weekends didn't help either. Dwight's nightmares meant that when he was back in New York, their bedroom now slept three. His drinking was also causing him to stay up later and her to turn in earlier, if he admitted it to himself.

The cold front had been making its way east. A cloud blocked the sun and now there was no denying an uncomfortable drop in temperature. The young women began to shiver theatrically. "Come inside and let's find a way to warm up, shall we?" Lawford said. Charlie marveled that this sort of line worked. His blinding smile and impressive pedigree probably helped.

Lawford and his companions headed indoors while Charlie remained in the hot tub with Lola, both sunk nearly to their chins in an effort to stay warm. He looked over at Sinatra and Judy seated at the poolside bar, wrapped in terry-cloth robes. They whispered with purpose, then they also rose to go inside. He looked back at Lola, who smiled invitingly. Nervously, Charlie looked away. Then he looked back. She was still smiling at him—brazenly, cheerfully, clear about what she was conveying.

And then she took off her bikini top.

Charlie tried to catch his breath; she was like a Botticelli. The booze was disintegrating the wall he'd constructed between righteousness and desire. No one there would care. Who would know?

He looked away, toward the large windows of the living room, through which he saw Judy take a seat on Sinatra's lap. A newly hung portrait of President Kennedy stared past Sinatra and directly at Charlie.

Kennedy. Charlie thought of the president and his brother and what they were doing to Charlie's father; he thought of the disdain he'd long had for President Kennedy's legendary extramarital duplicity. These were angry thoughts, punctuated by girlish laughter from wherever Lawford and his party had retreated.

Charlie had been with other women between Pearl Harbor and his and Margaret's post-VJ-Day nuptials. He hadn't told Margaret, and she had never asked. In France he had focused on leading his platoon and pushing aside the nihilism that threatened to overwhelm them. But there were moments of which he was not proud—a night in the Alsace when a terrified woman threw herself into his arms, in gratitude born from desperation and survival.

And there were other times, too, when Charlie felt himself on the precipice of such despair that nothing else would arrest it. No one even bothered to romanticize it. This was not *joie de vivre*. They were rats in a ship's hull. He wasn't proud of his behavior in France, but he tried to leave it behind. It was overseas, it was during war, it was before he was married.

Here in a Jacuzzi at Sinatra's compound—well, this was not war.

And with that, he permitted himself to look again at Lola, who was arching her back as she stretched—

Charlie stood up abruptly in the hot tub. "Excuse me," he said to Lola. "I just remembered I have a phone call to make."

"Doesn't look like you're thinking about a phone call," Lola observed.

He took one last look at her, swallowed, and walked inside.

Good Lord, he thought as he walked by Sinatra and Judy. She was straddling him on the sofa, though they were both still fully dressed.

"Not so easy being righteous when other dames actually want to screw you, is it?" Sinatra said loudly. Charlie suddenly wondered about the crooner's plans to marry Juliet Prowse. Maybe Frank had forgotten.

In the kitchen, Charlie found Jacobs collecting his wallet and keys and preparing for a quick shopping trip. He asked if he could join him.

"I can pick up anything you want, Congressman," Jacobs said. "No need for you to come."

"I need...I need to go with you," Charlie said. "If you don't mind."

Soon they were winding their way out of the Tamarisk Country Club.

"Not everyone can keep up the pace after hours," Jacobs said when the silence in the car became awkward.

"Lawford arriving with the party girls changed the tenor," Charlie said.

After a brief pause, Jacobs said: "Maybe it brought it all out into the open a bit more."

Charlie considered that.

"Anyway, I could all but see the angel and devil on your shoulders in that hot tub," Jacobs said. "Looked like a draw."

"That's probably being generous to the angel," Charlie said.

They drove in silence a bit longer, passing a blur of green—immense trees that served as fences, broken up only by driveways that led to mansions. The quiet seemed awkward to Charlie, although he wasn't sure why.

"I know what the favor is," Jacobs finally said, as if he'd been holding it in. "The one Mr. Giancana asked of Mr. S."

"You do?"

"Yes, sir," Jacobs said. Charlie could tell he didn't feel completely comfortable sharing it. "Or I should say, I know of *a* favor Mr. Giancana asked of him. I don't know if it's the only one or the one you were asking about."

"Okay. Sure. What is it?"

"Pretty much what you might expect," Jacobs said. "He asked Mr. S. to ask Bobby to cancel his pursuit of organized crime."

"Anything in particular?" Charlie asked.

"Momo went into quite a bit of detail," Jacobs recalled, indicating that he paid attention to matters with the diligence one would expect from an admiral's aide. "Bobby Kennedy wants the FBI to *eliminate* organized crime. Not just Giancana's guys, but all of 'em. Sending the IRS in for tax evasion, appointing a Justice Department task force to prosecute top targets—Giancana, Rosselli, Hoffa, Cohn. And on and on."

"Boy, Momo has good sources," Charlie said.

"Money gets you a lot of cooperation, especially from civil service employees," Jacobs said.

They arrived at the market. Jacobs told Charlie he'd be right back, he just needed some sweet vermouth and olives. Charlie felt better for having removed himself from the immediate temptation of Lola, although all too soon they were headed back to the Compound.

"So what did Frank do?" Charlie asked. "Did he talk to Bobby? Or the Ambassador? Or the president himself? I'm not sure what I could do, but is there any way I can help out?"

"I don't know," Jacobs admitted. "In September, Mr. S. and Mr. Lawford went to Hyannis Port, but I don't know if they talked about any of this. I stayed here. I haven't heard anyone mention it since."

They were under the carport now, the engine still running. Jacobs remained seated behind the wheel. Charlie waited to hear if he had anything else to tell him.

"I worry about Mr. S.," Jacobs finally said. "I worry about the Mob pushing him to do this, and I worry about him being rejected by the president. This time maybe he won't recover. He's still not over Ava."

"He's still upset about Ava?" Charlie said. Frank and Ava's tumultuous marriage had ended almost a decade before, when she cheated on him with a bullfighter in Spain.

"He hasn't been the same since," Jacobs said. "Might be good for the pain in the torch songs, but it's bad for him. And I cannot imagine what he will do if the president does the same thing. To be completely candid, he's head over heels in love with him too. I'm really worried, Congressman. Please do what you can to help him."

Jacobs stared off into the distance, then exhaled dramatically. He turned off the engine and got out of the car. Charlie followed. They walked into the living room, now silent, though music was coming from Sinatra's room down the hall. Charlie saw Lola outside, wrapped in a blanket like a burrito, with only her face showing.

Her face glowed in the sun; her curves were somehow even more beckoning to Charlie wrapped in the blanket.

"Ethereal," he whispered to himself.

He stood there staring at her. The pounding of bass drums from Sinatra's hi-fi shook him awake. Happy squeals from Lawford's room flew through the house like parakeets.

Sinatra bellowed to Jacobs from his room: "George, I need some champagne! Bring it in a bucket with ice!"

Charlie's visit to the Compound had borne fruit; he now knew Giancana's ask. He had escaped before doing anything truly stupid. He turned to Jacobs. "Well, I think I'm going to hit the road," Charlie said.

"Probably wise," Jacobs said.

CHAPTER THIRTEEN

BEVERLY HILLS, CALIFORNIA

January 1962

They were two bottles of Chianti into the night when Charlie felt the need to remind Charlotte Goode that the conversation the three of them were having was off the record.

"You've already said that, and I've already agreed," Goode said, "though I should be demanding the opposite. I deserve a great scoop after saving your wife from that freaky cult." She finished her glass, lifted the empty bottle for inspection, and waved down the waiter for a replacement.

"We'll give you one, I promise, when this ordeal is over," Margaret pledged. "And it should be over soon."

Puccini was packed and rowdy, with "That Old Black Magic" and other favorites blaring, so Charlie was less worried about being overheard than he normally would have been. He was surprised by what Charlotte already knew about their assignment. Much of it she had picked up from sources and shoe-leather reporting—following Margaret to the Church of Scientology, for instance—while Margaret, in a rush of adrenaline and gratitude, had filled in the rest after their dramatic car ride.

After leaving the Compound and arriving safely at the Miramar Hotel, Charlie had called Addington White and demanded a meeting. White subtly reminded him that Hoover might be eavesdropping on the line and agreed to fly to Los Angeles later that day.

Both Charlie and Margaret felt some relief. They'd been sent by Attorney General Kennedy to find out what Giancana had asked of Sinatra, and now they knew. Hopefully this would be the end of their Tinseltown mission. Charlie had enjoyed his work as a consultant to *The Manchurian Candidate*—his input had inspired some last-minute rewrites of the scene in which the American GIs were captured by the Chinese, and he liked Frankenheimer. But it was time to go back east, get his dad out of prison, and return to the life they'd built. Thinking of Lucy and Dwight and the phone conversation they'd had earlier that evening, Charlie felt an ache; he missed them *so* much.

"Honey, look," said Margaret, motioning with her chin toward the unmistakable profile of Alfred Hitchcock on his way to a prime table, diners and waitstaff forced to move aside to accommodate his considerable girth. Manny Fontaine and a top studio executive, Les Wolff, sailed in his spacious wake. Fontaine had told them Wolff's story: Tan and broad, the studio big shot was a former actor who had rocketed to the upper echelons fueled only by oily charm and the look of a CEO. Most of the other Hollywood machers were overweight or pale or chinless or all of the above.

At their table, Charlie faced the expansive mirror hanging from the wall while Margaret and Goode viewed the room. Fontaine spotted Charlie in the reflection and they waved to each other; no time to talk.

"Horrible Hitch," Goode said. "A grotesque masher. That poor girl he just plucked from obscurity to star in his latest." She tilted her head back and gulped down a shrimp from her shrimp cocktail like a ravenous seal. Charlie politely mimed to her that she had cocktail sauce on her cheek, and Goode wiped it away.

"I didn't know that about Hitchcock," Margaret said. "Charlie, that bird woman we met on set is working on that picture, his latest."

"On *The Birds*?" Goode said.

"That's the one."

"Well, she should watch out too," Goode said. "These mashers and flashers with their casting couches. MGM's Arthur Freed whipped it out to Shirley Temple when she was just twelve! There's a whole network of people making sure nobody ever hears about it and keeping hacks like me from reporting on it, but it happens every damn day." Goode pointed to an older man dining with two pretty young men. "There's Henry Wilson. An agent. He's notorious for forcing his clients into bed. Male clients. Roddy McDowall calls him the slime that oozes out from under a rock."

Margaret noticed a familiar face: Symone LeGrue. "Speak of the devil bird," said Margaret, smiling and waving as LeGrue approached their table.

"Is that a real bird?" asked Charlie.

"In Ceylonese lore," LeGrue said as she reached them. "Probably a species of nightjar or maybe a spot-bellied eagle-owl."

"We just saw Mr. Hitchcock walk in. Are you dining with him?" Margaret asked.

"I am!" LeGrue said. "Where is he?" She looked around and saw the director wedging himself into a corner booth. "Listen," she said, turning to Margaret and placing a hand on her shoulder, "I'm in LA all week. We're shooting interiors at Universal. Come by, I'll show you the birds."

"I'd love to," said Margaret.

"Call me." LeGrue took a business card out of her purse, handed it to Margaret, and waved goodbye.

"I don't know how much either of you are into stargazing," Goode said, pointing half a shrimp toward a corner booth. "But there's Natalie Wood and Rita Moreno. Have you seen *West Side Story*?"

"We did," said Margaret. She sipped her glass of wine and looked on warily as Charlie knocked back his second bourbon and waved for a third. "Bit of a sore subject."

"I hate musicals," Charlie said, slumming with a glass of wine while he waited for the bourbon.

"It's one of Charlie's seven defining characteristics, along with his freakishly keen sense of smell," Margaret said. And his drinking, which was getting higher and higher on the list, she thought.

"Lotta Oscar buzz," Goode said. "Likely nominations for both of those gals, though it's also possible Natalie gets a nod for *Splendor*." Goode, too, was drinking at a rapid clip and her mind seemed to race; she quietly started humming "Officer Krupke" from *West Side Story*, which made Charlie wince. And then, maybe reminded by the song, she brought the conversation back to their mission. "So what did the Feds say after you told them what Giancana wanted from Frank?" she asked.

"We don't talk details on the phone," Charlie said.

"Ah, right, because Bobby doesn't trust Hoover," Goode said. "Isn't that old queen more or less devoted to bringing down the Mob, just like Bobby is?"

"My guess is Kennedy doesn't want Hoover to have anything more on his brother than he already does," Charlie said.

A sudden racket of cheers and applause erupted near the door as Sinatra, Martin, Davis, Lawford, Shirley MacLaine, and several young women Charlie and Margaret didn't recognize entered the restaurant. As they were ushered toward a large table at the back, Charlie shot Margaret a look. They were caught off guard by the Rat Pack's appearance, though they felt stupid being so surprised, given that Sinatra and Lawford owned the restaurant. Spotting them sitting there, Davis broke free of the group and approached their table.

"Madame Marder, *enchanté*," Davis said, taking her hand and planting a kiss on it.

Charlie stood and shook his hand. "Good to see you again, Sammy."

Davis smiled and patted Charlie on the shoulder. "We're toasting the memory of Ernie Kovacs," Davis said. "Join us when you're done." He added pointedly: "You and Margaret." He sauntered off.

"No journalists allowed," Goode noted.

"Frank does have strong feelings about the press," said Charlie.

"As does Sam-I-am," Goode said. "Mr. Davis had my editor kill my piece excoriating him for postponing his wedding just so Frank could kiss Kennedy ass." She paused to dive into her mashed potatoes, which had arrived along with their steaks. "I wonder if the girls they have with them tonight are actresses or some of Van Heusen's hires."

"Pardon?" asked Margaret.

"Jimmy Van Heusen, Frank's songwriter," Goode said. "He supplies call girls for the singers who keep him in silk and caviar. Ships 'em in like trays of sturgeons."

"He does that? The guy who wrote 'High Hopes'?" Margaret asked, stunned.

"And lots of great romantic ballads," Goode said. "He's won three Oscars."

"Where does he get them from?" Charlie asked. "The girls."

"The lost and found?" Charlotte shrugged.

Charlie thought about Lola and the other young women at Sinatra's compound. Were they call girls? They didn't act like they had much of a say in the matter.

"Why would guys like Frank need to pay women to sleep with them?" Margaret asked.

"They don't pay them to have sex with them," Goode said. "They pay them to leave."

Margaret shook her head and excused herself to the restroom, taking in bits of conversation on her way:

Tracy, Berle, Caesar, Hackett, Jon Winters—it can't miss!
She's working on Billy Wilder's latest.
You don't remember Joe Sr. and Bobby swooping into town and stopping every issue of Hush-Hush *from hitting the stands?*
They had to cancel it because of bad weather. It's supposed to be rainy at Cape Canaveral for a few days.
Elgin Baylor had forty-two points and twenty-two rebounds!

Van Heusen's extracurriculars stuck in Charlie's craw. He recalled the time during college when he and two friends had ducked into a dark bar across the bridge, in Brooklyn, that people of negotiable standards were rumored to frequent. As they were sidling up to the bar, Charlie caught a whiff of the cologne his father wore. He turned to survey the room and saw a woman who was decidedly not Charlie's mother seated on his father's lap. Charlie had left immediately, his friends on his tail.

Goode looked over her shoulder at Margaret's retreating figure, then leaned across the table and said in a low voice, "You should know, Congressman, that *Hollywood Nightlife* recently received some compromising information about you."

Charlie felt his heartbeat quicken. "What's that?"

Goode took a bite of her steak. "We were sent," she said, sporadically pausing to chew, "photographs…of you and a topless young woman in a hot tub." She took a swig of her wine.

"Jesus," Charlie said, stunned. He reflexively reached for his glass. "Nothing happened. The girl took off her bikini top, and I got out of the Jacuzzi almost immediately." He took a big gulp. Charlie tried to think back to who might have taken the picture, and how.

"If you're wondering who the enterprising shutterbug was, some of our rivals at *Confidential* and *Hollywood Scandal Sheet* have no problem climbing trees. If you've got a Nikon telephoto, you're in business."

"You're not going to publish it, are you?"

Goode shook her head. "No," she said. "That's why I'm telling you about it. But if I have a copy, there are others. I'll see if the negatives are for sale, but let's talk later—here's Margaret."

Margaret shook her head as she took her seat. "I just can't get over it," she said. "Van Heusen writes all those lovely, romantic Oscar-winning ballads while also serving as a pimp."

"He'll probably get another Oscar this year for that song he did for Frank for *El Cid*," Goode said.

"'The Devil May Dance,'" Charlie said. It was one of those tunes that stuck with him, both for the haunting melody and the lyrics that rang too true, about compromising with evil.

Margaret's mind was packed with thoughts of such compromise as well. How did Van Heusen recruit these desperate, aspiring starlets? Who were the women who'd been with them in Vegas? Were they getting paid? How much? By whom? Was Judy as independent as she acted? It terrified Margaret that her niece might be a part of this underworld where the casting process turned into a sort of human trafficking.

Margaret grasped Charlie's hand across the table. "We can't leave Hollywood without finding Violet." Charlie nodded, slightly distracted by the thought of the photograph of him in the hot tub. How would Margaret react? Would she believe him that nothing happened?

"Well, well, well," said Goode, "look who's coming to dinner." She nodded toward two figures entering through the kitchen.

"Giancana," Margaret said.

"Was Giancana there the night Frank and John Wayne almost went at it?" Goode asked. "I don't recall seeing him."

"No," Charlie said.

"That was quite a night," said Goode.

"Yeah, two draft dodgers squaring up, then chickening out. Super-impressive," said Charlie.

"Wayne dodged the draft too?" Margaret asked.

"Three-A," Goode said.

"For dads with dependents?" asked Margaret.

"Yeah, he's got five kids," said Goode.

"Just like half the guys in my platoon," said Charlie.

"Oh, Marion Morrison," said Goode, using Wayne's given name. "He's never been 'John Wayne' in any way, and the masses will never know that, because knowing requires reading."

Charlie and Margaret exchanged a glance.

A chorus of cheers arose from Sinatra's long table—Patricia Lawford, in a rare appearance, was making her way toward the group. Her husband stood to greet her, an expression of cheerful surprise on his face. He glided over to her, kissed her on the cheek, and guided her to the chair that a waiter was wedging in next to his.

"What a sham," Goode said, rolling her eyes.

Before Charlie or Margaret could react, a dapper figure appeared by Charlie's side. "Good to see you all," Detective Ellroy Meehan said. "I trust you're enjoying our fair city?"

"We're grand, Detective," said Margaret, smiling brightly. "How are you?"

"How's your investigation into the Powell murder?" asked Goode.

"Hello, Charlotte," Meehan said, a bit warily. He looked over his shoulder, then leaned closer to the table to speak confidentially. "We've figured out which mobsters were in town that day, and we're right now winnowing down the list."

Margaret furrowed her brow. She had read that exact sentence, attributed to "a police source," in that morning's *Los Angeles Daily News*.

"You're sure it was a Mob hit?" Goode asked.

"He was in hock to the sharks," Meehan said. "The way he was killed…I don't want to be too graphic"—Goode snorted appreciatively—"but it had the signature of a specific button man."

"We know he was shot in the eyes, Detective," Margaret said coolly. "Thank you for protecting our delicate sensibilities, though."

Meehan smiled. "If it shoots people in the eyes like a duck…" he said.

She briefly considered telling Meehan about Powell's membership in the Church of Scientology and her trip to the Casa de Rosas, but then she thought better of it. For all she knew, they had filed a complaint.

Always on the hunt for someone more powerful to talk to, Meehan stole a look into the mirror on the wall behind Margaret and Goode, spotted a target, patted Charlie on the back in a moment of quick and quiet acknowledgment, and bade them adieu.

"Charlie!" bellowed a familiar voice. Sinatra, at the back table. "Congressman Charlie Marder, grab that gorgeous lady of yours and come back and join us, you little so-and-so!"

Goode winked at Charlie and Margaret and gestured for them to go ahead. They stood obediently; Margaret told Goode she would call her soon, and they made their way to the Chairman's table in back.

"Come here and revive me, you exquisite creature," Sinatra barked at Margaret, accidentally spilling valuable whiskey in her direction. "Too much death tonight. We were in the middle of toasting Ernie Kovacs when we heard Lucky Luciano croaked."

"Oh, I hadn't heard," Margaret said, as she smoothed down the back of her maroon dress and sat to Sinatra's left; Charlie squeezed in between his wife and Sammy Davis.

"Today," said Manny Fontaine, who had joined their party as well. "Crazy story. Do you know Marty Gosch? A producer. Flew to Italy to pitch a picture he wants to make about Lucky's life. Lucky had a heart attack at the airport."

"He was in his early sixties," said Giancana. The table was silent for a second as everyone waited to see how Giancana felt about Luciano's demise. "That's a hell of a ride for a guy like him," Giancana said. "We should all be taken out by God and not by a wiseguy." He raised a glass of red wine. *"Salute."* Everyone joined him.

"Cento di questi giorni!" added Martin.

"He should never have been deported," said Sinatra. "All the good he did for the U.S. during the war, he shoulda got a medal."

A young woman at the table—she had red hair and sweet pinches of baby fat that appeared when she smiled, which was often—asked Sinatra what he was talking about. The singer was only too happy to air what was clearly a long-held grievance.

"You kids! You're just babies!" Sinatra started. "Okay, so, during the war, Navy Intelligence was concerned that Italian spies were infiltrating the docks. So they reached out to Socks Lanza for help—any info to protect us from Mussolini's double agents. Project Underworld. Socks gave 'em union cards so they could be undercover."

"Socks controlled the docks," Giancana said.

"Hey, that rhymes," noted Martin. He began to croon *"Socks...controlled the docks"* to a round of titters and chuckles.

"Seussian," Margaret said to Charlie; Lucy and Dwight loved *The Cat in the Hat.* They made sad pouts at each other, missing their kids.

"You shoulda seen Socks," Martin added. "He was like a refrigerator with feet."

"And Socks worked for Lucky," Sinatra continued. "So G-men met with Lucky. In prison. Where was he, Momo?"

"Dannemanna," Giancana said, botching another name.

"Danne*mora*," Martin corrected him.

"That's the one," said Giancana. "So they moved him to Great Meadow to be closer to the city."

"Yeah," Sinatra said. "So Lucky got to work. He had nothing else to do in prison, right? He also gave 'em names of Sicilians in New York who might know things, anything to help us prepare to invade Italy. So after the war, Lucky's sentence got commuted—but he had to leave the country."

"He went to Naples," Giancana said.

"And then Havana!" said Sinatra, winking at Giancana.

Salute.

The night proceeded merrily, with a feast and copious carafes of Italian reds and the best stories the Rat Pack could tell with women present. Margaret was certain she was the soberest person at the table, except for maybe Patricia Lawford. None of the women spoke much, so Margaret entertained herself by playing zoologist and assigning hierarchical roles to the participants. Giancana was the apex predator, top of the food chain, no one around to challenge his dominance. Sinatra was the alpha, Martin the beta—his second in command. Davis and Lawford were omega wolves, assuming the court-jester roles, well liked and eager to initiate play but holding no power. She thought about the few species that practiced monogamy; there were no penguins at this table except for Charlie, Margaret, and Patricia Lawford.

Margaret then focused on Patricia, gorgeous and gracious, with the familiar Kennedy jaw and smile. She and Peter had married in 1954, and clearly the bloom was off the rose, if it had ever blossomed at all. Margaret noticed that when he reached for her hand, she flinched. When he put his arm around her, she pulled away from his touch. For his part, Lawford studiously avoided looking too long at any of the young women at the table, but Margaret thought he did so in a suspiciously unnatural way. Charlie had already told her that Lawford's fellow Rat Packers referred to his Malibu compound as "High-Anus Port," so dubbed for the wild parties Lawford threw whenever his wife was back east.

Margaret cast a benign smile in Charlie's direction. He would never engage in anything along those lines. Charlie caught her eye and smiled back at her, and for a moment she felt as if they occupied a bubble of calm floating above the beautiful, troubled occupants of the glamorous restaurant.

Soon Patricia Lawford announced that she was feeling tired; her husband escorted her outside and returned to the table without her. Her exit combined with the copious amounts of alcohol consumed by then seemed to dissolve all remaining inhibitions. The young women with them were manhandled onto laps. Bottle after bottle of wine was emptied. Stories of varying degrees of truthfulness were shared.

"Nothing could be bigger | than to play it with a ni—" Martin sang, to the tune of "Carolina in the Morning," before Davis interrupted him in the nick of time. "Tut-tut-tut!" Davis urged as Margaret and Charlie recoiled at Martin's near use of the epithet.

Davis responded by channeling Cole Porter: *"He's a wop! | Records sell like Nestle's | He's a wop! | But they don't top Presley's."*

Charlie's brain was a bubbling cauldron of concern. He felt guilty that he hadn't yet been able to rescue his dad, worried about the photos Goode had told him about, anxious about Addington White's impending arrival in town. He had a nagging suspicion they weren't going to get off the hook even though he finally had an answer for Kennedy's question. He also knew there was no way Margaret would leave without finding her niece. Despite calling Lawford several times to follow up on where he'd seen Violet, Charlie hadn't learned anything. He hadn't yet shared the news with Margaret. He didn't want to get her hopes up.

Puccini stayed open long after almost every other diner had left—Sinatra and Lawford owned it, after all—so it wasn't until roughly three in the morning that Sinatra had the idea they should all head to a cemetery to toast Death and his recent acquisitions. Forest Lawn in Glendale was thirty minutes away, barely a blink for

LA, so their nine-car motorcade proceeded like a funeral cortege through the city's empty, rain-soaked streets.

A right onto South Glendale Avenue followed by another right onto Cathedral Drive, and soon the motorcade came to its end at Forest Lawn. While Charlie parked, Margaret saw Sinatra in the distance, illuminated under a streetlamp, berating the young red-head. As she and Charlie got out of the car, they could hear more of Sinatra's tantrum.

"—the *hell* off my hair!" he yelled.

"Uh-oh," said Davis under his breath as he sidled up to the Marders, walking toward the graves.

"No touch-ay the toupee," Martin said.

Sinatra continued to berate the redhead, albeit in more hushed tones, so only the occasional word echoed in the graveyard.

"Stupid," he said, disdain dripping from his voice. "Dumb cooze."

Margaret shook her head. Sinatra was so mercurial and abusive, she no longer thought his ego was that of the mere superstar; it was something more pathological.

Instead of being disturbed by the singer's outburst, Charlie found himself experiencing an odd sense that this was familiar. He wondered why. Yes, he had now been in the scene long enough that these explosions were no longer out of the ordinary, but was that it? His mind turned to a faint memory from his childhood: He was sitting in the living room listening to "The Adventure of the Speckled Band" on NBC Radio's *The Adventures of Sherlock Holmes*. He was maybe nine? Ten? From the study he'd heard his father viciously berating his mother. Something about an ignorant statement she had made over dinner; his dad never made those mistakes in front of important company, he said. Charlie turned up the volume. His dad had scrapped his way up the ladder without any sophisticated education and never let anyone forget it. The screaming continued. Young Charlie turned up the volume again. Winston came out of the study, but before he could aim his rage at his son, Charlie ran into his room, slammed the door, and cried into his pillow.

"Do you think it's okay for us to be here?" Margaret asked Charlie as they made their way around tombstones.

"*They* seem to think it's okay," Charlie said, shrugging, coming back to the moment.

Dean Martin ran over to one of the young women and lifted up her skirt from the back. She shrieked; everyone laughed.

"'It was the wont of the immortal gods sometimes to grant prosperity and long impunity to men whose crimes they were minded to punish,'" Margaret said, quoting another great Roman. "'They did so in order that a complete reverse of fortune might make them suffer more bitterly.'"

"No one here's suffering yet, folks," Lawford said, overhearing. "But try me tomorrow around seven a.m."

They stumbled through the damp, dark grounds of the cemetery, drinking from flasks and bottles, exclaiming when someone discovered a notable burial site. It was truly a Who's Who of Hollywood's departed: Bogart, Gable, and Lombard were some of the names shouted across the headstones and tombs.

"Hey, isn't Fatty Arbuckle here somewhere?" Sinatra asked.

Dean raised a martini glass he'd somehow managed to transport from Puccini. "If so, we should pay our respects."

"Pay our respects to a fat old perv who killed a girl by shoving a Coke bottle up her yoo-hoo?" asked the redhead, disgusted.

"That's a filthy lie!" Sinatra yelled with rage. "He was smeared by that dead slut's lying friend and those yellow journalists with Hearst. Two mistrials and they kept going at him. The guy wouldn'ta ever hurt a fly! The hell he went through because of those dirty prosecutors!"

The mention of dastardly DAs made Charlie think of his father, alone in the prison infirmary. Margaret saw the expression on Charlie's face and reached for his hand.

"Fatty was cremated, anyway," MacLaine noted, taking a delicate swig from a cup of whiskey Davis offered.

Thoughts of jails and hot tubs ate at Charlie's insides like sulfuric acid; by the time Sammy fired Fat Tony's gun at the angel-adorned crypt of a long-dead racist producer, propelling stone shrapnel into Charlie's shoulder, the congressman was grateful for an off-ramp to head back to the hotel. He was relieved that Margaret was similarly inclined, a comfort that evaporated as soon as Margaret opened the trunk of their rental car looking for a first-aid kit. There lay Lola, her eyes shot out, her mouth open, her body twisted unnaturally. Margaret gasped, instinctively backing away, fleeing death. Charlie stopped breathing altogether for maybe thirty seconds. He had seen death before, had caused it before, but there was something physically painful about seeing someone who had been so full of life snuffed out callously like just another cigarette.

CHAPTER FOURTEEN

LOS ANGELES, CALIFORNIA

January 1962

"Dead bodies just happen to show up whenever you two are around," Detective Meehan observed.

Margaret—exhausted after the long night of drinking and revelry followed by the shock and horror in the cemetery parking lot—rolled her eyes. "Didn't a cop say that to Fred MacMurray in *Double Indemnity*?" she asked. "Your delivery was better, though," she added with a broad and insincere smile. She had been shaken by the sight of poor Lola, but she was not about to allow herself to be bullied by this fraud.

Meehan snorted. "Pretty glib for someone with a corpse in her trunk."

"Pretty glib for a cop who knows about the corpse only because we immediately called the police," Margaret said, cool as November.

"Chris Powell was killed shortly after you came to town, and now there's this doll," he said. "I don't want to tell my supervisors that you're not being cooperative. There was a dead girl in your trunk, Mrs. Marder."

"*Dr.* Marder," she said quietly.

"Pardon?"

"Look," she said, exhaling deeply, "we're obviously horrified.

We called and are cooperating, and we'll tell you anything you need to know. Just spare me the film noir dialogue."

It soon became clear to Meehan, though, that she didn't know much. To Margaret, Lola Bridgewater was one of dozens of young women who flitted around the edges of Rat Pack parties. "The people you should be talking to are Mr. Sinatra and his pals," she told Meehan. "Or her friend Judy. I barely knew Lola."

"Why would anyone whack her?" Meehan asked.

Like half the locals Margaret had met since she arrived, Meehan acted as if there were a camera on him; he had all the scenery-chewing subtlety of Kirk Douglas. She thought momentarily of Bugs Bunny pretending to be Edward G. Robinson: *Myah, see! It'll be coytans for you, Mugsy! Coytans!*

"I don't know why anyone would kill Lola," Margaret said. "Except perhaps to frame us, I suppose. As for who would do that, you'd have to ask my husband why we're here, but it does involve law enforcement and top officials of the Justice Department, one of whom is on his way out here as we speak."

Meehan's hard-boiled facade broke for a second around the eyes and mouth; Margaret could see the revelation not only shocked but rattled him. She often saw this in men—they were offended when a woman stood up for herself. It would rankle them as if their very manhood were on the line. Then it would come out that she had some connection to powerful men—whether her husband the congressman or, in this case, the attorney general—and the men wouldn't know what to do with their indignation.

"I need to..." Meehan said. He hesitated, then abruptly left.

When Meehan entered Charlie's interrogation room, he found the congressman at the table, his head buried in his arms, fast asleep. But he sat up as soon as Meehan walked in and delivered his "Dead bodies just happen to show up" line.

"Lola Bridgewater was her name," Charlie said soberly. "Horrible, horrible, horrible. We called you as soon as we found her."

Meehan sat down across the table from Charlie and shook a cigarette out of his pack of Marlboros. "You don't seem particularly distraught."

Charlie stared at Meehan coldly. "I don't know what that means. I didn't know her well, but it's very sad. We're very upset, Margaret and me. As for my reaction to seeing a dead body, I wish I could tell you Lola's was the first I've seen, but it isn't. I fought in France."

"Who do you think killed her?" Meehan asked after taking a long drag from his cigarette. He tilted his chair back on two legs and squinted through smoke at Charlie as if someone were filming them in black-and-white.

"I have no idea," Charlie said, which was true. "An enemy of mine? An enemy of Frank's?"

"The Mob?"

Charlie thought about it. "Maybe," he said. "But why would the Mob want Lola dead? Why would they put her in my car? Seemingly to frame me—but again, why?"

"What have you done to piss them off?" Meehan asked.

Charlie paused. "I can't really get into it in detail unless DOJ says I can, but I'm out here looking into some matters that might involve organized crime," he said. "Maybe they figured that out."

"Offing that chickie seems like pretty harsh retaliation for spying," Meehan observed. "Unless they were trying to set you up, as you say. But then what? And why her?"

There was a knock at the door and Attorney General Robert Kennedy entered, with Addington White and Margaret in tow; Meehan gasped, then tried to pass it off as a cough.

"That'll be all, Detective," Kennedy said—Boston Irish trumping LA flatfoot. Meehan scurried out the door without another word. Kennedy's suit jacket was draped over his arm; his shirt-sleeves were rolled up and his tie was loose. White, conversely, was as buttoned up as if he were walking into a baptism. Charlie rose to shake hands with them. They were the rats who'd gotten him into this fix, but he nevertheless was glad to see them.

"Let's all have a seat, shall we?" Kennedy motioned to the small table. White lit a cigarette as Margaret reached for Charlie's hand and gave it a squeeze.

"Glad you went to the police," Kennedy said.

"We suspect we weren't supposed to have found her body right then," Margaret said. "We just happened to need something from the trunk."

"I was sorry to hear about your father," Charlie said to the attorney general, an awkward bit of courtesy given his own father's status. Kennedy nodded.

"Makes more sense that whoever did this would have called in a tip and had the cops find the body," White said. "Maybe at the hotel."

"But who would do it?" Kennedy asked. "Who have you crossed out here? Giancana? Rosselli?"

"We haven't crossed any of them," Margaret said. "We've been as agreeable as a sloe gin fizz on a porch swing on a Sunday afternoon."

"Giancana has a temper," Kennedy noted. "He's into revenge."

"We were having dinner with Frank and Giancana and all the rest just hours ago," Margaret told him.

"It's possible I may have aroused their suspicions when I asked Sinatra's valet to find out what favor Giancana needed from Frank," Charlie said suddenly. "But I doubt the valet, George Jacobs, told anyone."

"And did he tell you?" Kennedy asked.

"He did: Giancana asked Frank to get you to back off," Charlie said. "Through the president, presumably. He was supposed to do it at Hyannis Port last fall, but George didn't know if he went through with it. That's it. That's the whole scoop."

Kennedy stared at him.

"Did he pass on the message?" Margaret wondered aloud.

Kennedy eyed her carefully, as if he were trying to figure out her motivation for asking. "Not to me. And the president would have told me." He paused. "That's interesting."

Margaret found it odd that Kennedy called his brother "the president."

"If I may, sir," Charlie said, "Sinatra may not be educated, and too often he's fueled entirely by impulse, but as a general rule, he's very savvy. I'm sure he knew that asking either you or your brother would be a bridge too far."

"I hate to even bring it up," Margaret said. "But what about your father? Would Frank have asked him?"

Kennedy stared at her. It wasn't clear if he was angry.

"I'm sorry for even—"

"No, no, I'm thinking," Kennedy said. "It's fine. If he did talk to Father, I never heard anything about it."

Kennedy looked down at the floor in sorrow; there hadn't been much coverage in the news about how severe the stroke was, though initial reports suggested the patriarch was partially paralyzed and could not speak.

White jumped in to change the subject. "What did you find out about the other issue, about how mobbed up Sinatra is?" he asked.

Margaret eagerly followed his lead. "He's got a lot of pals in organized crime," she said, "and while we don't know that any of their criminal acts have been done on his behalf, they're around him quite a bit. In LA, in Vegas, in New Jersey..." She turned to Charlie. "Were they with you in Rancho Mirage?"

"Rat Packers and groupies, but no mafiosi," Charlie said.

"But that said," Margaret continued, "as long as you're serious about prosecuting organized crime, Charlie and I feel strongly that the president should not stay with Sinatra at Rancho Mirage. The association is unseemly."

"We didn't see any evidence that Sinatra is part of or knows of any criminal wrongdoing," Charlie added. "But having the president stay anywhere mobsters have likely also slept…I mean, for your political rivals, it would be like manna from heaven."

Kennedy looked at White, who nodded.

"So you don't think Sinatra would have had anyone take care of Chris Powell?" White asked.

"No," Charlie said. "And not just because Powell wasn't worth it. Sinatra cares about music, movies, gossip, politics, and women. I can't imagine him ever actually asking for a hit."

"Absolutely not," Margaret agreed. "He's not a murderer. Not even close."

"Will you two step out for just a second?" Kennedy asked.

Margaret stood, but Charlie stayed in his chair. "We're allowed to leave this room?" he asked.

"Congressman, I'm the chief law enforcement officer in the country," the attorney general reminded him.

"You're not going to be charged with anything," White added.

Charlie stood and followed his wife out of the interrogation room and into the police office, which was abuzz with bookings from late-night Los Angeles life—prostitutes, thieves, fleeced tourists, all sitting at desks as weary officers tried to suss out copious claims. To Charlie's keen nose, the room smelled of coffee, cheap perfume, and sex.

They paused in front of a bulletin board covered with public service ads and departmental posters. ARE YOU INVITING BURGLARS INTO YOUR HOME? blared one flyer above a cartoon image of a house with its windows open. Another advertised the annual policeman's ball. A third listed the "Qualities of a Good Policeman," which included "the wisdom of Solomon," "the strength of Samson," and "the tolerance of the Carpenter of Nazareth." A frayed pamphlet from the previous summer reminded officers to donate to the fund for slain officer Sidney Riegel, c/o the Los Angeles Hillel Council.

Margaret sank wearily into a chair across from an empty desk. Charlie stayed on his feet.

"Think we can finally go home?" Margaret asked.

"Hope so," Charlie said, looking around. No one was close enough to hear them. "But once the Feds have their claws in you…"

"What does that mean?" Margaret asked.

"We're informants now, essentially," Charlie said. "A higher class than the average Chicago stool pigeon, but the same basic job description. We work for them. For free."

"Forever?" Margaret asked.

Charlie shrugged and turned his gaze toward the bulletin board.

Meehan abruptly appeared, grunted in their direction, and walked past Charlie to the door of the interrogation room. He knocked lightly; White opened the door and let him in.

Charlie raised an eyebrow at Margaret, then turned to look again at the bulletin board. The previous day's "Daily Police Bulletin" was tacked in the middle of the board, with mug shots and fingerprints of three arrestees: a white man picked up on four counts of forgery, a white woman in jail for four counts of petty theft, and a Black woman sporting a black eye who'd been picked up for issuing a check without sufficient funds. The charges all seemed remarkably small-bore to Charlie, especially given the dead woman in the trunk of his rental car.

He looked at Margaret; her arms were folded, and her eyes closed as her chin dipped toward her chest. He looked at his watch. Almost four a.m. Their night had started so long ago—dinner with

Goode, drinks with the Rat Pack, then their ill-fated sojourn to Forest Lawn. He thought of poor Lola Bridgewater, a captured pawn in someone's twisted game.

"Come back in, Congressman," White said, snapping Charlie back to the present. Meehan brusquely passed him again, headed in the opposite direction. Charlie leaned over and lightly touched Margaret on the knee, startling her awake. She stood and he followed her back into the room; they both sat down at the table again.

"We want to know what you learned about Hubbard," White said. Margaret told them the story.

"Do you have the papers you grabbed from them?" White asked. Margaret handed White the documents from her purse.

"What does it say, Addy?" Kennedy asked. He was facing the one-way glass, sleep deprivation noticeable in his voice.

"It's titled 'Project Celebrity,'" he said. "A list of celebrities they want to recruit. Winchell, Murrow, Dietrich."

"A bunch of gossip columnists on there too," Margaret added. "Parsons and Kilgallen. Hedda Hopper. Walter Lippmann."

Kennedy turned around and cocked his head toward White. "I suppose nowadays gossip passes for news," he said, holding out his hand for the document. Kennedy glanced at it for a few seconds, then folded it and put it in his inside jacket pocket. "What happened to the car you drove to the church?"

"We went back and got it the next night," Charlie said, impressed with the attorney general's attention to detail. "Took a cab to a spot five blocks away. No one saw us."

"The same car you drove tonight?" Kennedy asked.

"Yes," said Charlie. "It's our rental car."

Margaret didn't think anyone from the church had seen them arrive, but who knew; they were a suspicious lot and the odds of surveillance weren't negligible.

"You two can go back to the hotel and clean up," Kennedy said. "Then around lunch I need you to sit down with Addington and give a full accounting of everything you've seen."

"We've told you everything," Margaret said.

"I'll be the judge of that," White said. "We want every last detail. Projects Sinatra is working on, the behavior of various Rats in the Pack."

"Projects he's working on?" Charlie said wearily. "There's a screenplay about the U.S. accidentally dropping an A-bomb on North Carolina and covering it up."

Kennedy and White looked at each other.

"Yes, all of that," White said. "We'll go over every detail."

"And then we can go home?" Charlie said. "Back to New York."

"You can go back east when production moves back east in a few weeks," Kennedy said. "But until then, you need to figure out this Lola business."

Charlie realized what Kennedy was saying. "Wait, you want us to figure out who's framing us?"

"You're in the best position to do it," Kennedy said. "If it's the Mob that did it—and that would be my theory—stick around to see what they do next."

"Continue as a consultant to *Manchurian Candidate*," White said. "There's about five or six weeks of shooting left, Krim tells me. Soon some of it will be in New York, as you know. But you need to stay on this case until you figure out who killed the girl."

Charlie sighed wearily. Defeated, deflated. Then he sat up in his seat. "We have an ask of you too, then."

"Really?" Kennedy said, stunned. He wasn't used to folks behind the eight ball trying to rack the table.

White jumped in. "Congressman, you're really in no position—"

"No, no, Addy," Kennedy interrupted. "That's fine, I want to hear what he has to say."

"Margaret's niece is in Los Angeles," Charlie explained. "Violet. She's underage. A runaway. And we saw her briefly with a much older studio executive. We've been asking around about her, to no avail."

"And you'd like the FBI's help," Kennedy surmised.

"Actually, I have some information for you about your niece," White said, reaching into his briefcase. He opened a folder that held a typed report. "I did follow up on that note from last time we met. We found her last known address," White said, reviewing the case memo. "Violet isn't there anymore. Nor is she in the company of Itchy Meyer, or at least, she hasn't been seen with him in the past few weeks, according to our eyes and ears. Meyer says he met her for the first time that night and hasn't seen her since. The landlady where Violet briefly had a room says she fell in with a fast crowd of party girls. That's all we got." He closed the file.

"It's not much," said Margaret. She rubbed her left arm and her body tensed. She was worried about her niece and also irritated that no one other than Charlie seemed to take Violet's disappearance seriously, as if she were just a feral kitten. Did young women die in Hollywood on a regular basis the way Chicagoans died in the freezing winds off Lake Michigan? She'd begun to think it was a specifically geographical phenomenon, but here was the FBI echoing the indifference. She was grateful for Charlie pushing the attorney general on Violet's behalf. Her husband might be turning into a drunk, but he was still kind and decent.

"It's not much, but it's more than you had," Kennedy pointed out.

"We need more," Charlie said. "You need to keep looking. If we're going to stay in LA, you have to help us find her."

"She's a child," Margaret said.

"Addington will see what he can do," Kennedy said.

"Just a few other things before you go back to your hotel," White added. "Your dad has been transferred from the Tombs."

"Why?" Charlie asked. He looked at his wife, who was frowning.

"To where?" she asked.

"Sing Sing," White said. "We had to get him out of the city while this is all going on. There were threats on his life. But don't worry, he's safe."

Charlie found himself gasping, he was so stunned. "Why don't I believe you?"

White looked at Kennedy. Neither one cared. Kennedy put his suit jacket back on. "Find out who the girl was with before she showed up in the trunk of your car," Kennedy said. "Figure out who killed her."

"I don't even know who this Lola Bridgewater is," Charlie said, about ready to fall apart.

"Well, apparently she was Mary Bechmann, from Minot, North Dakota," said White.

"And Mary Bechmann from Minot, North Dakota," Kennedy added, "had only just turned sixteen."

CHAPTER FIFTEEN

FRANKLIN CANYON, CALIFORNIA

February 1962

Sinatra, in army fatigues, stood in scrubby weeds alongside a well-worn trail, shifting impatiently from one foot to the other while he waited for Frankenheimer's cue. He and a platoon of actors were gathered in Franklin Canyon, a stand-in for Korea, nestled between Beverly Hills and the San Fernando Valley. It was nearly noon, and the day was warm for February, all memories of the freak snowstorm long gone. The makeup artists scurrying among the cast dabbed away evidence of perspiration; camera crews and the production team were working to perfect every last detail. Charlie and Margaret observed it all on their Hollywood safari, accompanied by Manny Fontaine, who seemed determined to stay close to them.

"Why are they shooting this scene now?" Margaret asked Fontaine. "It's supposed to take place at night, I thought."

"It's called 'day-for-night,'" Fontaine explained unhelpfully. "He's shooting it underexposed."

"Why not just shoot at night?" Margaret asked.

"They want to do the titles over this scene," Fontaine said.

Margaret raised her eyebrows; she still didn't understand.

"It's technical," he said. Then, with a smile, he added, "I'd be lying if I claimed I really understood it myself."

"We 'bout ready, Johnny?" Sinatra called out. Charlie noted that the actor seemed in good spirits, which was notable considering that one of his recent houseguests had been found dead.

Sinatra's bad moods made him challenging to be around, but Charlie knew he was capable of great acts of decency and humanity. A key grip whose wife was suffering from cancer had suddenly learned she'd been transferred to the new Cedars-Sinai Medical Center, with a top oncologist caring for her; everyone knew how that had happened, but almost no one said anything in Sinatra's presence. An associate producer tried praising Sinatra for his kind deed, but all he received in return was a grunt.

"One second, Frank, we're almost there!" Frankenheimer shouted from the bottom of the hill where he was talking to Edmondson, his sound mixer, whose efforts to make a workable wireless microphone continued to fall short.

The scene was crucial to the plot of the film. In Korea, Captain Marco, Sergeant Shaw, and their platoon are treacherously advised by their interpreter Chunjin to walk in single file, after which they are ambushed, loaded into helicopters, and taken to the Chinese for a thorough brainwashing.

"Hey, Charlie," Sinatra shouted down the hill. "Come on up for a sec. And bring a light. If you don't have one, ask Beanie."

Brownie and Beanie, makeup and wardrobe, were never far from Sinatra's side. Charlie looked to confirm that Frankenheimer wasn't anywhere near calling "Action," then walked up the grassy slope to the actors. The sun was strong. He felt every drop of his steady diet of bourbon; his headache conjured a Buddy Rich bass drum solo. He had his own lighter and didn't need Beanie's, but he felt conflicted about now being yet another member of the retinue.

It had already been a rough morning. Outside the Miramar, as Charlie and Margaret waited for the valet to bring their rental car around, Detective Meehan had materialized like Harvey the rabbit, a cigarette in his mouth and a porkpie hat on his head. A coffee stain marred his loud red tie.

"Congressman and Mrs. Marder!" he barked in greeting.

"*Je*-sus, you scared me," Margaret said, taking a step back and putting her hand on her heart.

Meehan ignored her. He pointed a stubby finger at Charlie. "That Kennedy boy might be protecting you right now, but once you're of no more use to him, he won't care if we arrest you for Miss Bridgewater's murder."

"So I killed her and then I called you to show you her corpse in the trunk of my car?" Charlie said dryly. "Makes perfect sense. You're a regular Ellery Queen."

"Well, then, who killed her?" Meehan asked.

"Good God, I don't know," Charlie said. "But what possible motive would I have?"

"I don't know yet," Meehan said. "But I'm going to find out." And with that he threw his cigarette on the driveway, ground it into the pavement with a worn-down heel, and stormed off with his trademark panache.

"Quite the unlicked cub," Margaret said, reaching a hand up to massage Charlie's neck. "We're going to find out who did it." She tried to sound reassuring as the valet pulled up with their car. "We're going to find out who killed that poor girl."

After that uncomfortable morning confrontation, Margaret cabbed solo to a Universal Pictures soundstage where she watched a flock of ravens rip apart an ingenue.

Margaret's motivation was no mystery—she missed zoology and, more to the point, she missed accomplishing something other than tending to the needs of Charlie, Dwight, and Lucy. So she'd taken Symone LeGrue up on her invitation to visit the set of *The Birds*.

"It's going to be a hellish day," LeGrue told Margaret at the security gate after the cab dropped her off. She was holding a clipboard in one hand and had a raven sitting on her shoulder; it cawed a strange hello at Margaret.

"'Quoth the raven,'" Margaret said.

"This is Archie," said LeGrue. "He absolutely loathes Rod Taylor, so I'm keeping watch on him today. He happens to love me and does anything I say."

"What do you mean, he loathes him?" Margaret said, slowly reaching out to pet the bird. "Is he dangerous?"

"Only to Rod, and none of us can figure out why," LeGrue said. "I mean, *The Time Machine* wasn't *that* bad. Follow me."

Margaret laughed as the two walked past industrial soundstages so enormous they could have been housing cattle or hogs, though without the aroma. The Universal lot was immaculate and professional: Men and women walked briskly to various studios, carrying food or props, often dressed in costume. Policemen, soldiers from myriad armies, a barbershop quartet, gladiators, Greek goddesses, waitresses, and flappers all passed them by. A teenage boy dressed as a cowboy rode a magnificent white horse past them, *clip-clop, clip-clop.* Four young women in swimsuits walked behind the horse; they couldn't have been out of high school. They reminded Margaret of Violet, and she tried to chase that discomfort from her mind immediately.

"So why is today going to be hellish?" Margaret asked.

"We're shooting this scene where Tippi—that's the lead, she's a new girl, quite nice, Tippi Hedren—she goes up to a bedroom all alone and is ferociously attacked by a flock of ravens."

"A conspiracy," Margaret corrected her. "It's a conspiracy of ravens, not a flock."

LeGrue playfully rolled her eyes. "Oh," she said. "You're one of those." Margaret laughed. "Yes, I know, it's a conspiracy of ravens.

Or an unkindness of ravens. I confess I've dropped those fits of fancy—men out here look at me cross-eyed as it is. The Hollywood Mensa chapter is rather small, Margaret."

"Fair enough." Margaret smiled. "I know what it's like for a man to look at you like you're speaking Khoikhoi."

"But I assure you I know all of them!" LeGrue said. "A ballet of swans, a bind of sandpipers. On land or water, it's a gaggle of geese, but in the air it's a chevron. A water dance of grebes!"

"Okay, okay." Margaret laughed.

"Anyway," LeGrue continued, "Hitch had told Tippi they would all be mechanical ravens. You need to understand—this might be the most horrific part of the whole movie, like the shower scene in *Psycho*. The birds will be relentless and almost kill her."

"Sounds ugly but manageable, no?"

"No," said LeGrue. "The mechanical birds aren't working. So we have to use live ones."

"Ugh," said Margaret. She knew just how uncontrollable and vicious scavengers could get, having once seen a turkey vulture behead a baby squirrel.

"Here we are," said LeGrue, pointing to a blue building.

Inside, in the center of the long room and against the far wall, an attic bedroom had been constructed, with a hole torn in the roof and, off camera, a giant cage built around a side door, stage right. Margaret and LeGrue stood behind the cage as burly men wearing blue polyester jackets that read BERWICK ANIMAL HANDLERS gently hauled cartons of ravens, doves, and pigeons into its confines. Once the birds were freed from the cartons, they quietly grasped the metal stands and awaited their cues. They shared their cage with three prop men, all of whom wore thick rubber gloves.

"Birds have never looked less exotic to me than they do right now," Margaret said. "And I live in Manhattan, where we have fifty pigeons per person."

"Yeah, this looks like an infestation," LeGrue allowed. "That's kind of the point. This is Hitchcock, not Audubon."

The stagehands' heads turned as a pretty, lean blond woman sporting a beehive hairdo and a lime-green suit walked onto the set rubbing her arms, clearly nervous.

"That's Tippi," LeGrue whispered.

"Never heard of her," whispered Margaret.

"No one has; this is her big break. She already had one mishap on set, with phone-booth glass breaking on her face. She's going to freak out during this scene. No one wants to work with these birds. Last week we had a dozen crew members in the hospital from bites and scratches. From just one day of shooting! Birds are dangerous. Seagulls deliberately go for your eyes."

A stagehand helped Hedren up onto the set and she walked behind the faux door to the attic bedroom. Hitchcock waddled in from wherever he'd been, presumably hiding to avoid any of Hedren's complaints. "There she is," he boomed with his familiar working-class London drawl. A hush fell over the soundstage; it was quiet except for some minor stirring of the birds. "Too skinny still, but we will continue to get some curves on that road." Some of the assistant directors and crew members laughed; Hitchcock looked at them, soaking in their approval. "Blondes do make the best victims, do they not?" he asked. "They're like virgin snow showing off the bloody footprints." Guffaws erupted from the crew. A slight wrinkle in the middle of Hedren's forehead was the only indication of her discomfort, though she maintained a placid smile.

"Is everything meeting with your approval, Mr. Ridge?" the director asked a man near the cage.

"All good, sir," said a man with horn-rimmed glasses.

"That's the guy with the American Humane Association," whispered LeGrue. "He looks out for the birds."

"Who looks out for Tippi?" Margaret whispered back.

Hitchcock approached his director's chair and Margaret wondered if he was going to try to sit on it, which seemed like a risky venture. He did not. Margaret watched as the director stared at Hedren, eyeballing her as if she were a juicy steak. He licked his lips, which gave Margaret the shivers.

"Places, everyone," the director said.

A chubby male assistant stepped in front of the camera with the clapboard and slammed it down. The three prop men in the cage grabbed ravens, one in each rubber-gloved hand. An assistant director began shouting out the familiar orders as lights blazed, and through a bullhorn, someone called, "Action."

Hedren slowly opened the door to the attic and looked up at the hole in the roof as she walked in. She gasped and lifted her flashlight as the three prop men began throwing live birds at her. First a raven flew at Hedren; it turned away at the last second. It was followed by a seagull that was propelled into her hair before it could get its bearings and flap away. The stagehands pummeled Hedren with one bird after another. After each bird flew off, whether it had hit the actress or not, it continued circling around the attic in a frenzy, a tornado of feathers filling the room. Hedren was gasping, crying out; Margaret couldn't tell what was acting and what was real and she didn't know if Hedren could either. Margaret looked at LeGrue, who was as still as an oak, her eyes on what the prop men were doing, seemingly professional and focused on the task at hand because to contemplate anything beyond that would be its own sort of psychological horror.

Even later that day, on the set of *Manchurian Candidate*, watching Charlie trudge up the hill to light Sinatra's cigarette, Hedren was all Margaret could think about.

After Hitchcock yelled, "Cut," it was clear that she'd been largely uninjured, though she was hyperventilating. Cary Grant—visiting from a nearby soundstage—declared her the bravest lady he'd ever met.

"I don't know if that's the word for it," Hedren had replied. And indeed, to Margaret, Hedren's plight was all about sheer survival.

The survival of his marriage, meanwhile, was all Charlie could think about as he climbed the hill. Should he tell Margaret about the photograph of him and Lola? Surely she would believe him when he told her he'd immediately gotten out of the hot tub. He was an honorable man and had never strayed in sixteen years of marriage. He expected that she would be more likely to focus on his recklessness and stupidity. She already knew that they were in a world where he didn't belong, and now he was a murder suspect. Yes, he would have to tell her.

Reaching the top of the hill in Franklin Canyon, Charlie withdrew the lighter he'd had since the war, one he'd taken from a dead Jerry. He gently tossed it underhand to Sinatra, who caught it and lit his cigarette in one graceful motion, as if they'd rehearsed the move several times.

"Boyo, I'll tell ya, this is one of the weirdest flicks I've ever been a part of," Sinatra said.

"It's going to be great," said Charlie.

"You really think so?" Sinatra asked.

"I do," said Charlie. "I think it's going to be important. It's a compelling thriller, but it's also subversive."

"Go on," Sinatra said.

"So in the movie, the crusade against Communists is secretly led by Communists," Charlie explained. "Those who doubt the conspiracy are killed by the conspirators. Medals of Honor are awarded under the least honorable circumstances imaginable. It's all a brilliant metaphor for the Cold War."

Sinatra took a drag from his cigarette and stared thoughtfully across the canyon before he turned to Charlie with a wry smile.

"Kinda like Joe Kennedy asking me to enlist made guys to help his son win and then after he does, Bobby goes after those same guys," he said.

"Yeah," said Charlie. "Kinda like that."

Sinatra took one last drag then snuffed out the butt of his Winston under his army boot. "Do we look authentic to you, soldier?" he asked.

"Uniforms are too clean," Charlie observed.

"Yeah, no one stays clean in war, do they, Charlie?" Sinatra said with a knowing glance. He took another cigarette out of the pack. In the distance, car horns blared, then stopped as quickly as they'd begun. A soft breeze provided the waiting actors with a brief moment of balm.

"So who do you think did it, Charlie?" Sinatra asked. He was squinting and as serious as a surgeon. He put a cigarette in his mouth as if it were a lollipop and Charlie dutifully lit it for him. "Lola," he added.

"I don't know, Frank," he said. "Someone who wanted to destroy me, is all I know. I've had folks try to pull similar schemes on me in the past, but that was blackmail."

"This wasn't that, kid."

"I know. They obviously wanted me to be found with her in the car."

"When was the last time you'd opened the trunk before that?"

"No idea," Charlie said. "You don't know anyone who's mad at me, do you, Frank?"

Sinatra didn't answer right away, and Charlie wondered if he was trying to decide whether to be offended. Just then, Frankenheimer joined them, a clipboard in hand. "Everything okay?"

"Swell, Johnny," Sinatra said. "Charlie just explained to me how brilliant your picture is."

Frankenheimer paused, apparently not sure how to take Sinatra's remark. Then he must have decided, for any number of reasons, to act as if it were a sincere compliment because he smiled and spread his arms, welcoming the praise. "Well, like everyone else in this town, I'm always happy to hear about my underappreciated genius," he said. "This scene reminding you at all of your time in the service?"

"Not really," Charlie said, looking at Sinatra's fellow actors. "These guys look fresh from the beauty salon."

"We could have 'em roll around in the dirt, but it's a night scene," Frankenheimer said. "It wouldn't show up."

Sinatra took a drag and watched the smoke float to the sky as he exhaled. "You're going to be in New York with us, right?" he asked. The climax of the film would take place in Madison Square Garden during a political convention; Sinatra's character would attempt to stop a brainwashed soldier from assassinating a presidential nominee.

"You bet," said Charlie. "Can't wait to see my kids and sleep in my own bed."

"Charlie!" yelled Margaret from the bottom of the hill. "Come down here!"

"What is it?" he yelled back.

"People in New York are desperately trying to reach us!" she shouted. "The studio just sent a messenger."

"What is it?"

"Your dad!" she yelled. "He's taken a turn for the worse, and the warden says we need to get on the next plane to New York!"

CHAPTER SIXTEEN

NEW YORK CITY

February 1962

"You shoulda been here yesterday, Charlie," Sinatra said. "I fished Laurence Harvey outta the lake in Central Park."

Charlie grimaced as a gust of cold wind prompted him to tighten his coat against the morning chill.

"It was like twenty-five degrees out," Sinatra said, packing tobacco into a pipe. "Colder than today. They had to clear three inches of ice off the lake before he jumped in!"

"No business like show business," Charlie said, coughing softly as morning rush-hour traffic spewed exhaust fumes on Eighth Avenue.

They were leaning against the stone wall near the entrance to Madison Square Garden, patriotic semicircled political bunting hanging from the marquee above their heads. Hundreds of extras dressed in summer clothes streamed past them into the arena, carrying signs and umbrellas for candidates "Big" John Iselin and Benjamin K. Arthur. Sinatra, taking a smoke break, was in full army uniform as Bennett Marco, complete with his service cap, a poor substitute for the crooner's signature fedora. Standing on the dirty street, braving the cold, he looked every bit a man of the people—but the police, private bodyguards, and yellow wooden barriers keeping gawking crowds at a safe distance told the real story.

Sinatra's entourage continued its excessive doting; Brownie approached him to take his tobacco pouch so as to avoid a bulge in his pressed military jacket.

"How you holdin' up, boss?" Brownie asked. "You take any bites outta the Big Apple last night?"

"I've often gone to bed at seven a.m. here," Sinatra said. "This is the first time I've *gotten up* at seven a.m."

Brownie smiled, then jumped onto the sidewalk after a garbage truck honked at a taxicab.

The actor took a long drag from his pipe. "The acting in this one is a challenge, Charlie," Sinatra said. "What with Marco having been brainwashed. I'm not a trained actor, so it takes a lot of doing. I hope it comes out all right."

Charlie nodded. "I'm sure it will be great," he said.

"You saw that the White House announced the California trip," Sinatra said. "It was in the papers."

"I saw," said Charlie.

"Secret Service came to Rancho Mirage the other day to do an inspection," he said, then added wistfully, "but they said they were looking at several properties, including something else in the neighborhood and even High-Anus Port."

Manny Fontaine emerged from the nearby arena door with urgency, looking out of place on the gray New York street with his deep tan and bright blue sport coat. "Mr. Sinatra, I come bearing wonderful news," he said, beaming, as he approached. "The Oscar noms are out and you're up for best song!"

"That's fantastic, Frank!" Charlie said, slapping him on the back.

"Who else?" Sinatra asked.

Fontaine pulled a list from his inner pocket. "Best Picture: *West Side Story, Guns of Navarone, The Hustler*—"

"No, no, no, Manny, who am I up against for Best Song?" Sinatra asked.

"Um, um…here it is: 'Moon River,' 'Town Without Pity,' 'Pock-etful of Miracles,' and 'Bachelor in Paradise.'"

"You can beat them," said Charlie.

"'Moon River' will be tough," said Sinatra. "Let me see that list, Manny."

"*Judgment at Nuremberg* and *West Side Story* are nominated for eleven Oscars each," Fontaine said. "Nine for *Hustler*." He passed the list to Sinatra and shivered. "Jesus, you two, it's colder than a witch's tit—how does anybody live in this place?"

"Oh, good, Monty is up for Best Supporting," Sinatra said. "And so is Judy!" Charlie assumed he was referring to his *From Here to Eternity* costar Montgomery Clift and one of Sinatra's many former paramours, Judy Garland. While Sinatra perused the list, Fontaine blew warm air into his fists and crossed his arms tightly across his chest. He turned to Charlie.

"Congressman," he said in low voice, "I just want you to know, at the behest of Les Wolff, I spoke with the proper folks at the LAPD about the, uh, incident the other night at Forest Lawn. And we're on top of it. The studio is cooperating with the investigation, and we will do everything we can to keep your name out of it."

Charlie looked at Fontaine. Shit. He hadn't known word had spread. "Thank you," he finally said.

Sinatra cleared his throat and looked at Charlie. "I talked to our friend about Lola. He says he doesn't know anyone who would do such a thing." It took Charlie a second before he realized Sinatra was likely referring to Giancana. Fontaine looked pointedly up at the sky, the very picture of a man who hadn't heard what he'd just heard.

Charlie nodded and took a deep breath, inhaling the pipe smoke Sinatra blew his way. It reminded him of his father's pipe tobacco, of scotch and his dad's dimly lit study, and of how badly, despite the early hour, Charlie wanted a drink. His jitters were getting worse.

He couldn't quite see his way out. His dad was lying in a bare-bones hospital ward in federal prison, his niece was still missing, and yet with all this angst, he couldn't allow himself an ounce of self-pity for being so reckless with Lola. Such a photograph could end his political career in a second.

"I mean, that girl got around," Sinatra said. "Not saying she had it coming. Just that who knows who she upset."

"Speaking of which, Frank, I caught Beans phoning a florist in North Dakota," Fontaine said.

"Yeah?" Sinatra said, confused.

"Sending flowers to the Bechmanns?"

"Who?" Sinatra asked.

"Lola's real name was Mary Bechmann," Charlie said.

"Ah," said Sinatra.

"Did you ask Beans to send her family flowers?" Fontaine asked.

"I may have," Sinatra said, irritated, looking up from the Oscar nominees. "Is there a problem?"

"Do you think that's wise?" Fontaine asked. "No one knows you knew her. Why let the parents know?"

Sinatra frowned. "Just tryin' to be nice."

"Of course, of course," Fontaine said reassuringly. "But let the studio take care of that. Lola was working on *Kid Galahad*, she had a bit part, so UA is going to send flowers. Okay?"

"She was a fun time, Lola," Sinatra said. "But young, you know?"

"Sixteen," Charlie said.

"What?" Sinatra said, genuinely shocked.

"That's what the cops said."

"That can't be true!"

"It is, Frank," Fontaine said.

"That's horrible," Sinatra said. "Looked a lot older."

"At least eighteen," Fontaine said.

Charlie couldn't tell if he was joking.

"I met her at a party at Lawford's," Sinatra recalled. "She walked in wearing one of those short skirts." His facial expression made it clear his memory was taking him down a tawdry path. "Oh, Charlie, don't get so high and mighty," Sinatra said, noting his look of disgust. "I saw you talking to her. You weren't discussing the Bay of Pigs."

"I didn't say anything!" Charlie protested.

"Your face is a Sunday sermon," Sinatra spat.

"Who else was she with?" Charlie asked. "Who else did she date?"

"Everyone," Sinatra said. "Powell, obviously. Last time I saw her was at a party at Van Heusen's."

"Whatever happened to that?" Charlie asked. "Powell."

Fontaine shrugged. "Last I heard, it was Mob debts," he said.

"That doesn't make any sense," Sinatra said.

Though Charlie and Fontaine had been shielding Sinatra from the street and police barriers prevented fans from approaching them, Fontaine looked around nervously. "Let's change the subject," he said.

Sinatra put a concerned hand on Charlie's shoulder. "How's your pa?" he asked.

Not great but alive, was the answer. After landing at Idlewild Airport a few days before, Charlie and Margaret drove the fifty miles north to Sing Sing Correctional Facility in Ossining. In its 137-year history, the prison had housed many celebrities, from Lucky Luciano to bank robber Willie Sutton to Tammany Hall political boss Jimmy Hines. And now Winston Marder.

They were met at the gates by Wilfred Denno, the warden. Bald and ingratiating, Denno was so eager to show off the prison to a New York congressman and his wife that he seemed to have briefly forgotten they were there to visit his ailing inmate

father. It was a straight line from the entrance to the grounds to
the prison infirmary, and Denno's travelogue was unceasing: "The
train tracks that bisect the property are underneath us in a tunnel"
and "The stained-glass windows in the chapel were made by
convicts out of old pharmacy bottles" and "The prison shops make
more than a mil a year from dog licenses and shoes, brooms and
paintbrushes"—until Margaret politely reminded the warden that
although there were eighteen hundred prisoners in the five-tiered
maximum-security cell blocks, they were there for exactly one, an
ailing man in the prison hospital.

Hospital was being generous, Charlie thought. It was just a
long room in an industrial building that also housed the prison
gymnasium, which provided a constant background of banging
and clanking, shoe-squeaking and occasional shouts. Patients were
lined up in cots just feet from one another on both sides of the
room, some of them shackled to the bed. Charlie was temporarily
distracted from the dismal sight by its echoes of Lucy's favorite
bedtime book, *Madeline*; this was a darker version of that orphan-
age, with his own aged father occupying a cot at the far end. As they
approached his bed, the old man seemed to sense their presence,
and through the tangle of IV tubes suspended from the wall above
him, Winston turned his head toward them. When his eyes met
Charlie's, he smiled weakly.

His father looked older and frailer, gray and shriveled. Charlie
and Margaret could hear his heavy, labored breathing.

"Charlie," he said, his voice reedy and raspy. He extended a
trembling hand to his son and beckoned for him to come closer, so
Charlie took a nearby wooden chair and pulled it up to the bed.
Margaret stood at the foot, her face grave with concern. Denno
nodded his approval to the guard.

"I...know," Winston said, his voice strained. He tried to push
out a third word but couldn't.

Charlie looked at the warden, worried about his father's health, secondarily worried about what his father might say.

"You...need—" Winston began to cough; what started as a throat-clearing quickly turned into a deep hacking. Charlie softly patted his father on his shoulder, looking sadly to his wife. What a thing to witness, the rapid erosion of a mountain.

"We think there's a chance your father may be coming down with pneumonia," Denno said. "Doctors are watching him around the clock, of course."

"What doctors?" Margaret asked. "I don't see any here."

Denno scanned the room and shrugged. He wandered off, presumably to find one.

Something distant in Winston's eyes lit up; he leaned into his son. "Trust," Winston whispered in Charlie's ear. "Don't." He collapsed heavily onto his pillow.

Charlie thought back to when he was a child lying beside his father in bed, listening to serials on the radio Charlie had built by hand in Cub Scouts. They'd started with comedies like *Sam 'n' Henry* and *The Goldbergs* and moved on to dramas: *Aunt Jymmie and Her Tots in Tottyville*. Eventually they'd graduated to Westerns, do-gooder tales, mysteries, and true-crime: *Empire Builders*, *The Air Adventures of Jimmie Allen*, *The Adventures of Ellery Queen*, *The Bishop and the Gargoyle*. When a show ended, Charlie would turn off the radio and he and his dad would talk about the plot, the twists, the actors whose voices they'd come to recognize. They were a team, a pair of aficionados, critiquing the sound effects, raising their fingers when a common trope was leaned upon too heavily. Those were some of Charlie's happiest memories.

Occasionally, on the nights when he smelled as if he'd been pickled in gin, Winston could get a bit silly. The popularity of radio serials exploded in the 1930s, and demand apparently exceeded the supply of new ideas and good writing; Charlie had noted the frequency with which some freshly wounded victim would spit out his last utterance with the only fight left in him, economizing the words so that "The murderer's name is" would exhaust all remaining oxygen, leaving the identity of the killer a mystery unless the victim was able to point to some object that at first glance made no sense. Charlie would pretend to take one in the gut and then gasp, muttering, evoking laughter from his father. When Winston was sufficiently in his cups, the two would act it out together, collapsing on each other's chests with the ridiculous last words: *"The...murderer's...name...is..."*

Winston's current state recalled that theatrical shortness of breath; Charlie couldn't help but smile despite it all. Winston saw him smiling and reached out to touch his cheek.

"Pa," Winston exhaled.

"Pa?" Charlie asked.

"Calais," he added, then started hacking again. He held up his right index finger, then used it to reach out and touch Charlie's nose. The cough then seized him and pulled him back, his body convulsing. Charlie looked at Margaret, now in tears. Warden Denno returned alone, no doctor in sight, and stood by uselessly. As Winston coughed violently, two orderlies ran to his bed and sedated him. It reminded Charlie of a time in France when his men were choking on nerve gas left over from the previous war. He desperately needed a drink.

Escorting Charlie and Margaret from the infirmary to the front gate, the warden asked if they had any idea what Winston was talking about. If it was something that would be helpful to the doctor, Denno said, he could pass it along.

"No clue," said Charlie. "Though it's good to hear that somewhere in this complex, there's an actual physician."

Embarrassed, Denno grimaced. "He's usually here by now; he's just late today." He cleared his throat, filling the awkward silence with something, anything. "Did he say *Pa?* Did you call him Pa?"

"Thanks for your time today," Charlie said, ignoring his question. They reached the front gate, and he shook the warden's hand with all the politeness he could muster, balancing his disgust with his father's predicament against the fact that the warden could make it much worse. "Really appreciate your help, Warden."

Once they were on the highway, Margaret answered Denno's question. "Pas-de-Calais," she said.

"That's my guess too," Charlie said. He had a flask hidden somewhere. He needed to get at it. Without Margaret seeing.

"What does a northern French state have to do with anything?" she asked.

Charlie frowned and looked in the rearview mirror for police. His foot pressed harder on the gas pedal. Margaret was familiar with this particular brand of silence. This was when he felt he had information he couldn't share. To Margaret, it was an aggressive silence, almost showing off.

"We are well past keeping secrets here, Charles," she said.

He sighed; she was right.

"It was called Operation Fortitude," he said. "Most people still don't know about it. I didn't even know about it at the time—I only learned about it on House Oversight." He looked at her.

"Go on," she said. "Keep your eyes on the road and keep talking."

"So part of Fortitude took place in Pas-de-Calais, with the First Army Group," he continued. He stole a look at her, then wondered if there was a rest stop where he could sneak a drink.

"First Army Group?" she said. "Never heard of them. And I read *everything* when you were over there."

"There's a reason for that," Charlie said.

"Which was?"

"It didn't exist," Charlie said. "Deception campaign. Army even built these things they called Bigbobs. Fake landing craft. Inflatable. Dummy tanks."

"Holy smokes, I can't believe I haven't heard about this."

"It's one of the most amazing stories of the war," Charlie agreed.

"So was your dad holding up one finger to signify the First Army Group?" she asked.

"Oh, I hadn't thought that," he said. "Maybe. I thought it was something else. Huh. You may be right."

"How did your dad even know about it? You confided in him?"

"Believe it or not, *he* told *me*," Charlie said. He pointed to an exit. "I'm going to get some gas," he said.

"He did?" she asked.

"Yeah, one night, maybe ten years ago? It was late, we were in his study drinking scotch. Turns out he knew about it because he helped with the pneumatic-rubber construction. Dad made a lot of money during the war, doing these...odd jobs. For the Allies."

"And then violated some promise and spilled the beans."

"We were drinking," Charlie said.

"Yeah, well," said Margaret. "People do stupid things when they drink too much."

Charlie looked at his wife to see if she was speaking about his obvious general problem or alluding more specifically to the Lola incident. Although he still had not told her about it; had Charlotte? She didn't return the glance. He pulled into a gas station and an attendant ran out.

"Fill 'er up," Charlie said. He turned back to Margaret, who was powdering her nose. "You want to use the facilities?" he asked her.

"Sure," she said.

A few minutes later, she returned to the car and stood outside his window. "Find your flask? Feeling better?"

"I'm fine," he said sheepishly.

"Why don't I drive so you can keep drinking."

He slid over to the passenger side. Margaret got behind the wheel, handed the attendant a five-dollar bill from her purse, and started driving.

"Anyway, it was a deception campaign," Charlie said to his wife, who was staring at the road.

"What did you think it was?" Margaret finally asked.

"Huh?" Charlie asked.

"You said you thought it was something else when your dad raised his index finger—what did you think it was?"

"Oh," Charlie said. "Dad loved this essay Orwell wrote after the war about how the Krauts and Japs lost because their rulers weren't able to see the reality in front of them, facts plain to any dispassionate eye. The quote was 'To see what is in front of one's nose needs a constant struggle.'"

"He touched your nose," Margaret said.

"Right," Charlie said. "I thought he was referring to something obvious that we're missing."

"So, a deception campaign," Margaret said. "Something in front of our noses that we're missing. What are we missing? Lola? Powell? Giancana?"

"I don't know," Charlie said.

"Lot of deception, I guess," Margaret said pointedly.

He was ashamed that Margaret knew enough about his drinking to be disappointed in him but decided to make the most of the moment. He told Margaret everything then, about the photograph of him and Lola in the hot tub and about how he couldn't stop drinking. She listened, and when he finished, she kept driving in silence south toward their Manhattan home, the bare trees and milky light of the late-winter afternoon adding to his already pronounced sense of despair.

CHAPTER SEVENTEEN

NEW YORK CITY

February 1962

Midway through another night of revelry, Sinatra surprised the crowd in the restaurant by standing up at his long table in the middle of the room, raising his highball, and toasting his fiancée. Their engagement had been announced in January but few had seen him with Juliet Prowse, a statuesque, full-lipped redhead who'd costarred with her beau in *Can-Can* two years before. She stood and beamed a smile toward her future husband while the guests clapped and hooted appreciatively, then sat back at her table with Frankenheimer, Laurence Harvey, Janet Leigh, and Angela Lansbury.

Shooting of *The Manchurian Candidate* had wrapped earlier that day, and the cast and crew, along with invited guests, were gathered for a celebratory dinner Sinatra was hosting on the third floor of Toots Shor's legendary restaurant. Charlie and Margaret, like other honored-but-less-important guests, occupied a small table on the outskirts. They'd arrived late after reading bedtime stories to Lucy and Dwight, then leaving them in the care of Margaret's mother—again—and tiptoeing out of the house with renewed pangs of guilt.

Margaret's response to Charlie's admission of having been photographed in a compromising position with Lola was mixed.

Fortunately, she believed him and had no doubts of his fidelity. That was the good news. But after he told her the story on their drive back from Sing Sing, it was almost as if a barrier had been constructed between them, one built out of disappointment and embarrassment.

"Well, there's Meehan's motive," she had noted. "If he ever gets that photograph, he'll come at you like a bull." She didn't mention that he'd imperiled their entire world. Scandal, blackmail, defeat—anything was possible. She remained civil to him, but distant. He figured he was getting off easy, so he didn't fight it. He'd been overjoyed when she'd agreed to come with him to Toots Shor's tonight.

"I thought this place was on Fifty-First Street," Margaret said.

"It used to be," Charlie said. "Then some real estate guy who was trying to build a skyscraper told Toots he would rebuild his place one block over and give him one and a half million dollars if he moved."

"Quite an offer."

"Isaiah says Hoffa put up a loan from the Teamsters' pension fund to underwrite it," Charlie said. "Four million!"

New York City was full of swanky restaurants with award-winning chefs and gracious service; Toots's place offered neither. It was a saloon with a pedestrian menu and a fabulous clientele, frequented by the likes of Sinatra, Babe Ruth, Jackie Gleason, Joe DiMaggio—all of whom were forced to wait in line and suffer occasional insults from Shor himself.

The Fifty-Second Street version was almost the same as the Fifty-First Street version, with plank oak floors, pine-paneled walls, and spacious and brightly lit rooms dominated by murals of sporting triumphs. The first and second floors each had an immense circular bar, and each dining room had an enormous fireplace with a bronze hood. The third floor, where Sinatra hosted his party, was accessible by elevator and winding staircase and fit three hundred people, though fewer than a hundred were present tonight.

"It feels like what I imagine a men's club would be like," Margaret observed. "Which is saying something, given how much of regular life in America is a men's club."

"What do you mean?" Charlie asked.

"You know," Margaret said, sipping her martini. "We're dames. Usually off camera. Like the First Lady. Or Juliet Prowse. Or sidekicks like Shirley."

"You're no sidekick," Charlie protested.

"Not to you," Margaret said. "But to them." She tilted her head toward Sinatra and his crew. "And then there's that other role women can fill…" Margaret nodded toward a corner table where Lawford and Giancana chatted with Judy and another young woman, this one in the process of slowly wrapping herself around the Kennedy in-law. Giancana's face was lit by a wide, lascivious grin, clearly inspired as much by both women's attention as by Lawford's conversation. Charlie had long felt a pang of sympathy—or maybe *pity* was the better word—for Lawford, a showman who hung out with and had married into groups of more compelling performers. He existed alone in his Venn-diagram circle, a tenuous and less respected member of both the Kennedys and the Rat Pack, constantly overcompensating as he flitted among roles as a diplomat, actor, and bon vivant, failing miserably at all but the last.

"What are those women anyway?" Charlie said. "Heiresses and divorcées? Trust-fundees? Something…more commercial?"

"What was it that Lord Beaverbrook said about haggling over the price?" Margaret asked. Charlie knew the answer but didn't respond.

Several martinis later, Margaret was deep in conversation with Janet Leigh at a two-top. It was that time of the night—or, technically, the morning—when parties take on lives of their own and libations explain almost any detour.

Their conversation had started innocently enough with Margaret reintroducing herself to Leigh at the sinks in the ladies' room.

"It's probably a cliché at this point for someone to tell you she hasn't taken a shower without fear since seeing *Psycho*," Margaret said as she reapplied her lipstick in the mirror to a knowing chuckle from Leigh, "but I have to wonder if it was traumatic for you too."

"Are you kidding? I almost stopped taking showers," Leigh said, dabbing her nose with a powder puff. "And I'm always facing the door, watching, no matter where the showerhead is."

Margaret laughed. "You have no idea how much better that makes me feel."

Leigh reached over and gently caressed Margaret's cheek as a sister might. The two closed their purses, wandered to the bar, then found a table, drinks in hand. The shower scene, Leigh confided, was the most difficult shoot of her life; though it lasted just forty-five seconds in the movie, it was composed of fifty-two cuts requiring seventy-eight camera setups. It took more than seven days to film, Leigh said. The shower water was ice cold, the blood was Hershey's chocolate sauce, the sound effects came from a knife plunging into a casaba melon, and a body double was used for every shot in which the audience didn't see her face.

"Marli Renfro was her name," Leigh said. "A stripper from Dallas. One of the first *Playboy* cover girls! She's shooting some dreck right now, a soft-core comedy, the only gig she could get." She tsked knowingly and took a sip of her cosmopolitan.

"Well, at least she's safe from these octopuses," Margaret said. "Octopi," she corrected herself.

Leigh laughed. "They're a handsy bunch, aren't they," she said. "As soon as they found out Tony was leaving me for that teenager, every one of them stepped right on up for a piece."

It hadn't hit the papers yet, but Leigh's husband, actor Tony Curtis, had filed for divorce and was leaving her for Christine Kaufmann, his seventeen-year-old costar in the film *Taras Bulba*.

"Frank was first in line, of course," Leigh continued. "Tony had me served right before we shot the train scene on *Manchurian* and the attempts to 'console' me began shortly thereafter." She smiled modestly. "But I've heard far too many horror stories."

"What do you mean?"

Leigh looked around the room. Charlie and Lawford were deep in conversation, as were Giancana and Judy, but most of the remaining crowd was gathered around the main table where Sinatra, Frankenheimer, and others regaled the guests with uproarious tales.

"Don't get me wrong, Frank is a real charmer," Leigh said. "He's just also kind of, well, unstable."

"He has moods," Margaret agreed.

"Sammy even gave those dark moods a nickname—'Stormy Weather.'" Leigh chuckled. "But I'm talking about real problems. He tried to kill himself a couple times after breakups with Ava. And I don't mean like threatening to do it or taking two extra aspirin or any of that bullshit Hollywood drama. I mean gun in hand, Ava trying to wrestle it away, bullet goes through the door. Scary stuff."

Leigh reached into her purse and withdrew a pack of cigarettes and a gold lighter. She offered a smoke to Margaret, who accepted, feeling wild.

"I don't know much about…celebrities' personal lives," Margaret said not particularly truthfully, searching for a more respectful term than *gossip*.

"You don't?" Leigh asked. "Well, I wish more people were like you. It's bad enough Tony's shtupping a teenager, but soon enough the whole world's going to find out." She downed her cosmo and motioned for another. "Worst thing is, Charlotte Goode tried to warn me and I dismissed her."

"You know Charlotte?" Margaret asked.

"Everyone knows Charlotte—and she knows everything," Leigh said. "Thank God she prints only a fraction of it."

"Really?" Margaret asked. "Why does she hold back?"

"I don't know," Leigh said. "She's barely touched anything relating to Frank. She wrote about how horrible Ava was to him, though— just awful. Really cruel. But she didn't print anything about the abortions Ava got that broke Frank's heart. Or his suicide attempts."

"How do you know Charlotte even knew about them?" Margaret asked.

"Sweetie, Charlotte told me herself," Leigh said. She sighed and looked at the main table. "And now Frank is getting his revenge on our whole gender. Poor Juliet better watch out or she'll end up just like Betty."

Margaret knew "Betty" was the actress Lauren Bacall, the widow of Sinatra's idol Humphrey Bogart. But that was where her understanding ended.

Someone in the dining room turned up the volume of the background music, blasting Joey Dee and the Starliters singing "Peppermint Twist": *In a night like this, a peppermint twist. Round and round, up and down…*

"I'm afraid I don't know what Frank did to Betty," Margaret said.

Leigh looked around to make sure no one was listening. "Frank idolized Bogie, you know. Worshipped him. Him and Bogie and Bacall and Judy Garland—they were the original Rat Pack, the *real* Rat Pack. This is all just nonsense." Her expression turned sour and she waved her hand toward the main table and then around the room, as if everything at Toots Shor's that night was a joke.

"So Bogie got cancer and died in…when was it?" Leigh continued. "In '57, I think. And then Frank started dating Betty. It got serious—quick. He proposed. But he wanted it to be a secret. Bogie had died only like a year before. One day she went out to see a picture with Swifty—Lazar, you know, the agent—and a reporter was there and asked about the engagement and she told the truth. She admitted it. I mean, why not, right? So it was going to hit the papers and Betty called Frank—I think he was in Miami or something—to explain how it had happened and apologize, and Frank lost his mind. I mean, deranged. Yelling. Punching the walls. The whole nine."

She stubbed out her cigarette and lit another. Margaret sat patiently, waiting for the rest of the story.

"And then he did something that rivaled the cruelty Ava had subjected him to—he never spoke to Betty again. He didn't answer the phone. He didn't return her calls. This is a relatively recent widow, remember, so she was already something of a mess. But he just—*pfffftttt*—snuffed out their relationship as if Betty Bacall had never existed. Imagine the kind of screwy wiring you have to have to do that to your fiancée merely because she told someone that the two of you were getting married. I mean, I love Frank and all, he's a close personal friend and a marvelous performer, but let's be honest—that's psychotic."

Across the room, Peter Lawford noticed Margaret's empty seat and sidled up to Charlie.

"Congressman," he said. "May I sit?"

Charlie extended his hand, offering the chair. The music continued to blare; the lights dimmed and under the cover of the artificial dusk, several guests stood and began to dance.

Who put the bomp in the bomp bah bomp bah bomp? boomed Barry Mann. *Who put the ram in the rama lama ding dong?*

"I've been trying to reach you since Rancho Mirage, but you're impossible to track down," Charlie said.

"I've seen you since then, have I not?" Lawford asked, pouring on the British charm as he poured more martini down his gullet.

"Not anywhere we could talk," Charlie said. "I've been hoping you could tell me more about Margaret's niece Violet. You said you saw her at a party."

"Indeed I did, old chap. It was late, quite late, and I was party-hopping with a group of rich expats I'd met at the Daisy." He leaned forward. "I will be honest. I'm not unfamiliar with the experience of intoxication—none of us are, and you're a dog that runs right with the rest of us hounds, Charlie—but on this particular night, I was quite smashed, and all of a sudden I was in this party in, oh, I don't know...Malibu, maybe? Santa Monica? Venice? We were driving—"

Charlie raised his tumbler and downed more bourbon to hide his irritation. Lawford fancied himself quite the raconteur, but like most of the actors Charlie had encountered in Hollywood, he mistook the clever lines written for him by others as his own cleverness. That Americans were so easily seduced by an English accent only compounded the delusion.

"—then we were in this party, I have no idea who was throwing it, and it was full of old men and young girls. And somewhere in that blur—I kind of came to in the midst of this bacchanal, and there she was, this girl, I recognized her but didn't quite know how, and you know, to be perfectly honest, it was her chest that I recognized. I mean, certain works of art one just remembers forever." He smiled lasciviously, then seemed to recall that Violet was missing; he winced in regret and gulped a new martini that had been placed in front of him by an attentive waitress.

"You're sure it was her, though?" Charlie asked.

"As sure as I can ever be of anything after a night like that, I suppose," Lawford said. "But listen, old sport, I have a favor I'd like to ask of you."

"Ask away," Charlie said.

Lawford checked over his shoulder to make sure no one could hear him. The music was blasting and no one was within earshot.

"I got a call from Bob earlier today," he continued. "Jack is *not* going to stay with Frank next month. Bob won't let him."

Charlie nodded as if this were news to him.

"Needless to say, Frank is going to flip his lid. And I have to deliver the news."

"I'm picturing one of those Tasmanian Devil cartoons," said Charlie.

"I know," Lawford said, sighing deeply, "but as the Kennedy ambassador to Hollywood, I've been told this is my job. So you, my friend, have got to be there with me. Might help keep him under control. Please."

Charlie wasn't sure when he and Lawford had become friends. "There?" asked Charlie. "Where? And when? Not tonight. I'm not going anywhere near a blotto Frank bearing bad news."

"No, no, no," Lawford said, leaning back in his chair and lighting a cigarette. "Not tonight. When we're all back in Los Angeles. I'll pick you up and we can drive there together—strength in numbers. Frank respects you, and it will be over quick, then we can go have a good time."

Charlie thought about it. He didn't really have to do this. Since December, he'd been on a mission he had no desire to carry out, one a different Kennedy was forcing him to undertake. And now this? There was nothing appealing about the proposition.

"I'm sorry, Peter," he said, "I'm afraid I have some business I need to attend to that day."

"What day?" Lawford asked, shocked.

"Any," Charlie said. "Any day."

Clearly not unfamiliar with hitting the limits of his charm, Lawford looked sideways at Charlie. "Okay, friend, tell me what you'd like in exchange."

Charlie scratched his head. "There is literally nothing you have that I want," he said. He looked around the room for his wife, finally spotted her absorbed in conversation with Janet Leigh. And then he had an idea.

"Well, actually, there is something I'd like from you," Charlie said. "But you cannot tell anyone—not even Frank."

CHAPTER EIGHTEEN

LOS ANGELES, CALIFORNIA

March 1962

"We have three young daughters ourselves, so I feel strongly about protecting children from material intended only for mature audiences," Stanley Kubrick told Charlotte Goode, who raised a skeptical eyebrow. "That said, when Nabokov's novel came out, I knew I had to bring it to the screen."

After days of having her calls go unreturned, Margaret had found Goode at Grauman's Chinese Theatre at a film premiere, on the wrong side of the rope blocking off the red carpet. She didn't want to interrupt her work, so she stood next to her quietly as she talked with Kubrick.

"But didn't you shoot the film in England to escape American censors?" Goode asked.

Kubrick looked to his right, hoping someone would rescue him, but alas, the MGM public relations escorts were tending to the needs of Peter Sellers, James Mason, and Sue Lyon, the teenager who played the eponymous nymphet. The paparazzi and fans called out to her by the name of her character. "Lolita!" they cried. "Lolita! Over here!" The actress swiveled seductively and it broke Margaret's heart. A teenage girl given so much immediate short-term fame in exchange for unnamed sacrifices was just plain wrong. It made Margaret wonder where Violet was and whether

Goode would ever be of any help. She kept asking, and Goode kept saying she hadn't found anything yet.

"No," Kubrick said. "Shooting it over there was more about control. It's nice to have the studio an ocean away."

"What were you worried about them controlling?" Goode asked. "The degree to which you put a twelve-year-old girl in perverted situations?"

Kubrick turned his head toward the theater as if someone had called his name. He took a subtle step in that direction, signaling that the interview was coming to an end. "Sue is fifteen," he said uncomfortably. "And we made some adjustments to the book so it would be less shocking. Look, if you see the film, I mean, *Lolita* is one of the great love stories, isn't it? If you consider *Romeo and Juliet, Anna Karenina, Madame Bovary*, they all have this in common, this element of the illicit! And in each case, it causes the couple's complete alienation from society."

"I saw the film, Stanley," Goode said. "And it doesn't matter whether she's twelve or fourteen—how do you think the National Legion of Decency is going to respond to the reference to Camp Climax for the girls or that line about 'Your uncle is going to fill my daughter's cavity on Thursday afternoon'?"

Kubrick coughed and took another step away from Goode. "The general public is a good deal more sophisticated than most censors imagine and certainly more than these groups who get up petitions believe," he said. "I have to move on now, thank you for your questions!"

Goode tried to squeeze in another but Kubrick had escaped. She turned to Margaret.

"When you were twelve, were you interested in getting your jollies with grown men?" she asked. "Men in their fifties?"

"When I was twelve I had a slight crush on a boy in the eighth grade, but even he seemed too old for me," recalled Margaret. "I was busy with school and a job at the local grocer's."

"The men in this town," Goode said. "They should be put in a hospital for the criminally insane, not given Oscars. Look at the poster! The little girl barely has breasts and she's all sultry in a bikini, the lollipop in her mouth." She exhaled like she was blowing her anger out of her body. "What are you doing here?"

"You haven't been returning my calls."

"I haven't gotten any messages."

"I left several with that creepy guy, what's his name, Tarantula."

Goode laughed. "Tah-ran-*too*-la," she corrected her. "Ick. A toad. And a horrible colleague."

A small ruckus sounded as costar Shelley Winters emerged from her limo and eagerly posed for pictures and waved to fans. Red Buttons, Joan Fontaine, Hugh O'Brian, and other stars slow-walked into the theater, stopping to grin for cameras, sign autographs, and offer up quotes to the press.

"Can we talk somewhere?" Margaret asked as an usher with a brass gong and a rubber mallet alerted any celebrities still on the red carpet that the film was about to begin.

Goode nodded. "Come with me," she said. She led Margaret out of the crowd, down Hollywood Boulevard, and onto North Orange. The neighborhood immediately turned seedier, with vagrants, hucksters, and star-maps salesmen. Storefronts advertised ALCOHOL and SOUVENIRS.

"Everything in New York is jake?" Goode asked. "Kids good?"

"All well," Margaret said. "Growing like weeds. It was wonderful to be home. And it looks as though Charlie will have the challenger of his dreams this November, a city councilman who's been indicted like three times."

Goode grunted supportively, turned down an alley, and walked up to a sturdy green metal door sealed by three different locks she needed three separate keys to open.

"Welcome to *Hollywood Nightlife*," Goode announced as she hit the light switch and led Margaret in. Much to Margaret's surprise, the square, windowless newsroom was relatively immaculate. The walls were covered in calendars, posters, and schedules pinned on floor-to-ceiling corkboard. At the far wall stood ten filing cabinets, different colors, each secured with a thick padlock. Goode walked to her desk in a nook in the far left of the room, Margaret following closely behind.

"It's shockingly organized," she said.

"You mean for a crappy scandal sheet?" Goode asked, reaching into one of her desk drawers.

"For any press outlet," Margaret said, though Goode had read her correctly. Charlotte took a long swig from a silver flask sitting on her desk, then began perusing her reporter's notebook, occasionally marking passages with a felt-tip marker.

"It's not usually this empty," Goode said, distracted.

Margaret walked to the file cabinets, which were thick metal, almost safety-deposit-box quality. The drawers were marked with anodyne labels—years, the names of film studios, awards, and some that didn't make sense to Margaret, like TOYS and TOTS and TULIPS and DAISIES.

"So where's Charlie this evening?" Goode asked, not looking up from her task. "Rancho Mirage?"

He was, in fact; he'd been picked up by Lawford in the late afternoon. "How did you know that?"

Goode shrugged. "We know everything." She leaned back in her chair and stretched like a cat in the sun. "We have this whole town wired. Cops. Nurses. Bartenders. Doormen."

"I'm impressed."

"The proletariat work for scraps, but the tsars have other motivations," Goode said, "ones contained in those file cabinets." She pointed vaguely in their direction. "Feel free to take a look around the office," she said, clearly distracted. "I'll be done in a sec."

"Please," Margaret said. "I'll just freshen up."

"Oh, sure, right over there," Goode replied, pointing toward a door in a corner.

Margaret walked into the cramped bathroom, painted yellow and barely more spacious than a restroom on an airplane. The most recent edition of the tabloid sat on the floor under the toilet paper roll. "Sinatra and Prowse Splitsville" blared the headline next to an illustration of a torn photo of the couple. "Dancer's Refusal to Embrace Motherhood Leaves Blue-Eyed Crooner Blue."

Was that what had happened? Margaret wondered. Sinatra was mercurial and the sudden engagement had seemed to surprise even his friends. After what she'd seen and heard, Margaret doubted *Hollywood Nightlife*'s version of events, though she knew, given the power of the tabloid, that it would be accepted as gospel. She supposed it wasn't surprising that the breakup would be blamed on the less famous partner.

Smaller type highlighted the travails of lesser stars: "Did Bobby Darin Only Marry Sandra Dee to Get More Famous?" "Is Natalie Wood Ignoring the Woman Who Did Her Singing in *West Side Story?*" "Brigitte Bardot's Latest to Be Directed by Her Ex!"

Where am I? Margaret wondered. Not long ago she was raising her kids, reading zoological journals, and helping Charlie steer his political career. She'd had a weird hankering to learn how certain cloven-hoofed animals of the Paleozoic were related to the modern equine and a few thoughts on how to restart her research, but she'd wait until her kids were in grade school to find out. But now, she was trying to figure out who might blackmail her husband with the body of a dead teenage girl, how she could get her father-in-law out of prison before he died there, and where she might track down her runaway niece. And she was contemplating it all from the shoddy restroom in the offices of a tawdry Hollywood scandal sheet.

And then she heard someone talking.

"What the hell, Charlotte!" blared a man's voice.

Margaret carefully turned the handle to crack open the door and better observe. Tarantula had shown up in all his slime and hideousness, a camera hanging from a weathered strap around his doughy neck.

"We don't pay you to lecture directors on red carpets," he hissed. "I'm fucking serious here. If this happens again, there will be consequences!" Margaret couldn't see his face, but Goode appeared chastened and perhaps even frightened. He began turning his ample frame toward the bathroom. Margaret ducked behind the door. Her heart skipped a beat. Was she even allowed to be in these offices?

"The toilet's broken," Goode said, answering the question. "I called the plumber."

"Good fucking Christ," Tarantula said, cursing at the floor. "I'll be at McGill's." A few seconds later Margaret heard the metal door slam.

Margaret peeked her head out again. "Yikes," she said.

"I'm so glad he bought the toilet excuse," Goode said, exhaling. "Not sure what he'd have done if he found you in there." She lit a cigarette, her hands shaking. "Jesus, I'm fifty today."

"Happy birthday," said Margaret. "Let's celebrate. Unless you have plans?"

"I had plans," Goode said, and she took another swig from her flask. "I was going to write the next *His Girl Friday* or *Bringing Up Baby*. I thought by age fifty I'd have won a screenwriting Oscar or two. Not…this. Maybe Peg Entwistle had the right idea."

Margaret racked her brain and then recalled the story of the ruined actress who'd dived off the *H* of the Hollywood sign. Silence filled the room.

"Charlotte, I need your help," Margaret finally said.

* * *

And Lawford needed Charlie's help. Earlier that day, he'd picked up Charlie in his Ghia, and now they were heading to Rancho Mirage.

"He's going to blow his stack," Charlie said. "I'll be there for moral support, but you have to light the fuse."

"Thanks," Lawford said. "That won't be hard to do."

Charlie had little confidence in Lawford's pledge, and the distrust hung in the air awkwardly until Lawford turned on the radio.

…the youngest brother of the president, who is seeking his older brother's former Senate seat, admitted today that in his freshman year at Harvard he was asked to leave the college after he was caught cheating on an exam—

"Oh, Teddy." Lawford sighed.

"Lot to live up to in that family," Charlie said.

"You don't know the half of it," Lawford said, a rueful smile on his face. He changed the station.

…twelve hundred defendants, sitting in a basketball court in the Principe Prison, facing Castro government charges that remain secret but clearly relating to the Bay of Pigs fiasco. Cuban defense lawyers say they believe prosecutors will seek various punishments including the death penalty—

Lawford sighed again and punched in another station, this time one that played music, producing a familiar crooning from the man they were about to confront.

> *…like the love of Ant'ny for Cleo,*
> *When I left my heart down in Rio*
> *What is more sad than a good love gone bad*
> *I was an Aries devoured by a Leo!*

Sinatra's light baritone prompted Lawford to grimace. He changed the station.

In '43 they put to sea thirteen men and Kennedy
Aboard the PT-109 to fight the brazen enemy...

"PT-109" by Jimmy Dean was climbing to the top of the country chart, but Lawford was clearly not in the mood for the hagiography, and he shut the radio off completely.

The report from Cuba, meanwhile, had prompted Charlie to ruminate about the classified Oversight Committee hearing a week before where a terrified lieutenant had told him and two other House Republicans about Operation Northwoods.

Charlie couldn't believe his ears as the officer explained the false-flag scheme he claimed the Joint Chiefs chairman, General L. L. Lemnitzer, had presented to Defense Secretary Bob McNamara days before: the U.S. would stage a "series of well-coordinated incidents" at or near the U.S. base at Guantanamo "to give genuine appearance of being done by hostile Cuban forces." Fake saboteurs, fake riots, burning our own aircraft, even staging funerals for mock victims. The document the lieutenant presented was hideous: "We could blow up a U.S. ship in Guantanamo Bay and blame Cuba," it stated. The general proposed staging terrorist operations against Cubans in Miami and Washington, DC, sinking a boatload of Cubans, real or imagined, an "incident" where a Cuban aircraft shot down a chartered civilian airliner on its way from the U.S. to Central America, or an "incident" where Cuban MiGs destroyed a USAF aircraft over international waters in an unprovoked attack. This, of course, would prompt a massive U.S. invasion of Cuba. *Adiós*, Fidel.

Charlie and his fellow congressmen promised the lieutenant they would protect his name. Who knew what a Pentagon willing to hatch and carry out such deranged orders might do to a leaker? And what the lieutenant didn't know was that he was not the first officer to tread outside his chain of command. Charlie had previously received an anonymous letter detailing the CIA's Operation Dirty Trick, a plan to blame the Cubans if anything had gone wrong with the Mercury orbit the month before. A different source told them about Operation Good Times, which would spread throughout Cuba a fake photo of "an obese Castro with two beauties in any situation desired" next to a "table brimming over with the most delectable Cuban food with an underlying caption (appropriately Cuban) such as 'My ration is different.'"

After several years on the Oversight Committee, through the Eisenhower and now Kennedy administrations, Charlie had reached many disappointing conclusions about the wisdom and even the emotional stability of those tasked with keeping the United States safe, mostly those at the CIA, run by men to the manor born, *boola-boola* Brahmins with no sense of humility. The worst of these unaccountable operatives was the one known as "the most brilliant man in Washington," Richard Bissell—he of Groton, Yale, the Skull and Bones, the Marshall Plan, and the Ford Foundation—the agency's deputy director for plans ever since the man who'd recruited him for the job, Frank Wisner, had had a mental breakdown in '58.

Charlie first met Bissell in a closed-door hearing after his much-heralded high-altitude U-2 spy-plane program, which had been collecting reams of data through its illegal flights over the USSR, was ignominiously exposed after one of its planes was shot down over Sverdlovsk and its pilot captured. This happened literally days before President Eisenhower and Premier Khrushchev had been set to meet in Paris to discuss possible nuclear disarmament and a test ban. Eisenhower ultimately was forced to admit the United States had been spying on the USSR. Behind closed doors to the House Oversight subcommittee, Bissell demonstrated no contrition, no repentance, nothing indicating that he accepted responsibility for actions that had put the nation at greater risk.

Bissell next appeared before Charlie after the April 1961 Bay of Pigs disaster. The attitude, again, was pure hubris. Under questioning by Charlie, Bissell revealed that he'd feared that sharing a candid assessment of everything that might go wrong could frighten President Kennedy and keep him from taking any action, which he could not allow to happen. Again, he took no responsibility for the fiasco, the loss of life, or the embarrassment the president felt.

Charlie had spent a great deal of his time in Washington, DC, feeling staggeringly dismayed at the sad state of intellect in the nation's capital. It wasn't that they weren't smart, the Eisenhower and Kennedy administration officials, congressional leaders, and members of the military-industrial complex Ike had warned everyone about in his farewell address. It was that they thought they were smarter than they were. They came up with plans that were so convoluted that if they backfired, they caused repercussions that lasted for years and only grew in their destructiveness. And here we had CIA officers and generals—the goddamn chairman of the Joint Chiefs of Staff—

"Charlie." Lawford interrupted Charlie's furious train of thought. "Do you watch *The Twilight Zone*?"

"Sure," said Charlie. "Rod Serling's a genius."

"A few months ago they had this episode where this kid, I think his name was Anthony, had terrifying powers and could just wish people into the cornfields or transform them into horrific creatures. Did you see it?"

Charlie had. "Yeah. Creepy. Everyone's afraid of the kid so the family turns into a bunch of sycophants. 'It's good you're making it snow. A real good thing!'"

"Yeah," said Lawford. "Exactly." He shifted uncomfortably in his seat. Charlie was about to ask why he'd brought up the episode, but then he understood. They pulled into Sinatra's Rancho Mirage estate.

They knocked on the door, and George Jacobs opened it while pouring from a shaker into two martini glasses. Despite the festive greeting he was offering, his tone was grim: "The boss has a cold," he warned them.

"Oh, that's too bad," Charlie said, wondering what that might mean in terms of Sinatra's mood.

"How bad?" Lawford asked. "His pipes clogged?"

"He's worried about his ability to perform," Jacobs said. "At the Oscars."

"Hoo-boy," said Lawford as they walked into the house.

Sinatra was sitting on the sofa in pajamas and a bathrobe, drinking a bourbon on the rocks. "Gentlemen, to what do I owe this honor?"

Charlie looked at Lawford awkwardly but Sinatra changed the subject before they had to confront their task.

"You went to the Globes, right?" Sinatra asked Lawford. "I heard Marilyn could barely walk." The Hollywood Foreign Press Association had given Monroe and Charlton Heston their top awards a few weeks before.

"She was not in good shape," Lawford agreed as he sat in a plush armchair across from Sinatra.

"'Town Without Pity' won," Sinatra said, referring to the Best Original Song winner. "That and 'Moon River' are going to be tough to beat."

"I've got my eye on some of the Globes' 'New Star of the Year' girlies," Lawford said. "Jane Fonda. And that Ann-Margret!"

"You and me both, pally," Sinatra said, toasting his friend.

"Warren Beatty got one of those awards too," Lawford said. "The kid is quite a swordsman."

"That whole evening is ridiculous," Sinatra said. "Foreign Press Association. It's like five guys wearing fezzes—no one even knows if they write for actual papers."

"Nothing like an Oscar, I'd imagine," said Charlie, positioning himself on the other side of the room.

"That was something special," Sinatra said. "Hey, Charlie, I got Joey tickets to the Oscars this year but per usual, he'll be a no-show. You want 'em?"

Rat Pack member Joey Bishop was almost never around, working steadily on his new sitcom and preferring a comparatively normal life with his beloved family. Bishop's membership in the Rat Pack was pretty much confined to movie sets.

"Yes, of course," Charlie said.

"You'll need to stand up and applaud like hell when I sing!" Sinatra said playfully.

"A given," Charlie said.

"George!" Sinatra called. His valet walked into the room. "Go get Joey's Oscar tickets that he's never gonna use and bring them to Charlie. Put them in the car so he doesn't forget them."

"At once, Mr. Sinatra," Jacobs said. "Do you want me to give him the screenplay you asked him to look at?"

"What's this?" asked Lawford.

"Oh," Sinatra said. "A picture about the U.S. accidentally dropping an A-bomb on North Carolina. Charlie's going to give it a scrub to see how realistic it is."

"Peachy," said Lawford.

"Oh, and I got something else for you, Charlie," Sinatra said. "An LP. Listen to it when you get back to your suite."

"Will do," Charlie said.

"What is it, Pope?" Lawford asked. "No parting gifts for me?'"

"Oh, it's nothing, Pete," Sinatra said. "I was fiddling around the other night in the recording studio out back, and we recorded a jazzier version of 'The Devil May Dance.' We cut a few thirty-threes. I have one extra. I can get you one next time."

Small talk continued for another hour, with Sinatra minorly

obsessed with Jack Paar's departure from *The Tonight Show* that week, his last live show airing the night before. Paar had said he was leaving because the daily grind had grown too tough, which Sinatra found silly: "Some of this showbiz stuff is long days and hard work, but c'mon, we aren't coolies building the railroads!"

What most animated Sinatra, however, was that Paar, who would be replaced by Johnny Carson in the fall, had devoted way too much time in his last show to settling scores with his enemies in the press.

"I mean," Sinatra said, "it's all pussy and jelly beans. What is he bellyaching about?"

Paar had taken some hits a year before for comments he'd made defending Castro—credulous and naive homages to the Cuban leader about how beloved he was and how he wasn't a Communist. And although Castro's declaration that he was a Marxist-Leninist the previous December had prompted Paar to admit he'd made a mistake, on his last night as host of the show, he was unabashed and untethered and determined to exact revenge. "Phony patriotism," Paar had said of columnist Walter Winchell. "He wrapped himself in the American flag whenever you criticized him, and he wore the American flag like a bathrobe."

"Why even bring that shit up?" Sinatra asked. "No one watching was thinking about Castro. People don't put on Jack Paar because he's talking about Cuba. They put him on because he doesn't."

Charlie glared at Lawford. There was never going to be a better moment for Lawford to drop the bad news on him like an A-bomb on Goldsboro. But Lawford was looking down, still clearly afraid.

"Speaking of current events," Charlie said. "Peter has some news on the JFK visit."

"Yeah?" asked Sinatra, crossing his arms. "I wondered when I was going to get the final word—he's supposed to be here in a week and a half!" He looked at Charlie, who nodded toward Lawford. "Yeah?" he said directly to Lawford.

"I'm afraid it isn't good news, Frank," Lawford began.

"It was fucking Bobby, wasn't it?" Sinatra asked, his face turning pink. "Fucking choirboy. Fucking Puritan."

"I pleaded with him to reconsider," Lawford said. "They say it was a Secret Service decision. Security. They don't think this compound is safe enough for a visit. It's nothing personal, Frank!"

Sinatra stood, enraged. "George! Get the president on the phone! This is fucking bullshit!" He grabbed a decanter of bourbon in one hand and a tumbler in the other, poured some bourbon, took a swig, then replenished the glass. "George!" he bellowed. He started pacing around the room maniacally.

Jacobs yelled from the kitchen: "Just got through to the White House! I'm on hold!"

"Let me know when you get that son of a bitch on the phone," Sinatra snarled. He turned to Charlie. "The president's been dodging my calls for months."

"Look, Jack called Patricia," Lawford continued, an emotional dam having been broken. "He said that as president, he just couldn't sleep in the same bed as Giancana had. She protested, but—"

"That hypocritical fucking mick," Sinatra said, shaking with rage, spittle forming at the corners of his mouth. He stared at Lawford, then threw his tumbler across the room; it shattered against the wall, leaving a stain.

"I cannot fucking believe the nerve of this guy, his brother, his whole fucking family," Sinatra said. "Your fucking family, Lawford!"

Jacobs came into the room. "Mr. S., I'm sorry, but President Kennedy can't come to the phone."

"Call fucking Bobby, call that goddamn rat-fink choirboy motherfucker and get that fucking piece of shit on the phone right now!"

Sinatra yelled. Jacobs nodded and retreated to the kitchen. His boss stared out the window toward the pool. No one said a word.

"So where is he fucking staying?" Sinatra finally asked. "He's coming to California, right? That's been announced. Where is he fucking staying?"

Lawford swallowed. Charlie took it all in, half horrified and half thrilled to witness it.

"He's...he's staying with the Crosbys," Lawford said softly.

Sinatra's blue eyes seemed to turn ice white. "Bing?" he yelled. "He's staying with fucking Bing Crosby? *Fucking Republican Bing Crosby?* Right here in *goddamn fucking Rancho Mirage?*"

Shaking, he picked up a vase containing daisies and tulips and threw it at Lawford, who ducked. The vase smashed against the door to the kitchen.

"Fucking Bobby, if the old man hadn't stroked out, he would have taken care of this!" Sinatra spat. "Fucking Bobby is a rat-fink motherfucker and you, Lawford, are a worthless piece of shit. You will never be in another picture with us, you will never be in another show with us, you are dead to me. Dead. Do you hear me? Fucking dead!"

Charlie kept waiting for Jacobs to pop in again to calm his boss; when he didn't, Charlie realized the valet was likely hiding.

"I did everything I could, Frank!" Lawford protested. "I told the president all the work you'd done to the place, that you'd had a switchboard put in for his calls, that you'd built him a heliport. I said that you'd even erected a flagpole just for the presidential flag after you saw the one flying in Hyannis Port!"

Sinatra started rubbing his cheeks with his right hand, up and down, as if feeling his beard, up and down, as if he were trying to wring an answer from his own head. He stopped, raised a finger, and shook it as if he'd come up with the one solution to all of this. He strode to the door to the pool, swung it open, and marched off.

Charlie and Lawford looked at each other, then began scrambling after their friend. In his present state, who knew what he was capable of?

It was late afternoon and the sun was beginning to disappear behind Mount San Jacinto. Charlie followed Lawford around a corner of the mansion. Sinatra had grabbed a sledgehammer from the construction equipment scattered around and was walking toward the helipad.

"What are you doing, Frank?" Charlie asked.

"Don't, don't do that, Frank!" Lawford pleaded.

The singer was not exactly in top physical shape, his diet and exercise regimen consisting of whiskey, cigarettes, and poker. He focused the giant hammer on the paved circle of the helipad, hoisted the sledgehammer above his head, then brought it down with every ounce of strength he had. It made a thick sound, an ugly *clunk*!

He was already sweating as he brought the hammer down again. And again. A hole appeared in the asphalt; cracks spidered out from there, destroying the pristine construction. He looked up at Lawford and Charlie, wiped his forehead with the sleeve of his bathrobe, and lifted the tool high above his head once more.

"You having fun watching this, you pieces of fucking shit?" Sinatra snarled at them. "You fucking traitors? Get the fuck out of here!"

The two men backed away from the helipad and returned to the house. After bidding Jacobs a quick adieu, they rushed into Lawford's sports car, and he stepped on the gas.

A few blocks away they both exhaled.

"Jesus Christ," said Charlie.

"That went about as well as we expected," said Lawford.

"And now it's your turn to do me a favor," Charlie said.

"Oh, goody," said Lawford.

CHAPTER NINETEEN

ANAHEIM, CALIFORNIA

April 1962

The phone rang. Charlie looked at the hotel clock: just after midnight. He was reminded of when the phone had rung early that December morning and he found out his dad was at the Tombs, changing his life forever. He looked at Margaret, beside him in bed. She had been sound asleep when he got back to the room from the hotel bar. The cold front between them that had rolled in on the way home from Sing Sing when Charlie told her about the photo with Lola felt like the beginning of the end. He'd stopped any pretense of hiding his drinking, and Margaret had ceased concealing her disdain.

"Another one?" she would ask when he poured a drink for himself in the kitchen or entered the living room holding a half-empty glass. This soon became an assertion rather than a question: "Another one," as if she were stating it for the record. And that became part of their new routine, her disapproving glance implying some new level of disgust. Somehow the subterfuge, pouring the drink out of Margaret's line of sight, had provided a degree of respect that openly pouring bourbon into his morning coffee did not.

"Hello?" he mumbled into the phone. It was Addington White. With a lead on his niece's location.

"Wait, she's where?" Charlie asked, taking a second to absorb it all.

"Tip came in," White said. "I told you we'd help!"

Charlie hung up the phone, made a note on a scrap of paper, and called Lawford. Thirty minutes later, they were speeding east on the Santa Ana Freeway to Anaheim. Lawford was behind the wheel of the Italian coupe, Sammy Davis Jr.—who'd been drinking with Lawford—was in the passenger seat, and Charlie was crammed in the back.

"I can't believe we're going to fucking Disneyland," Lawford said. He wasn't the only one.

Sinatra had attempted to ignore President Kennedy's visit to California, but photographers and local TV news had followed the president to every stop on the way, from Naval Air Station Alameda, where he landed, to the campus of the University of California, Berkeley, where he was given an honorary degree. Then it was back to Alameda to fly to Vandenberg Air Force Base for an inspection and the launch of the Atlas 134D intercontinental ballistic missile, which theoretically could deliver a nuclear weapon. It was intended as a clear signal to Khrushchev and any of his friends in the neighborhood—primarily Castro. Next a hop to Palm Springs Airport to the home of Bing Crosby and a quick visit with Palm Springs' newest resident, President Eisenhower. Charlie and Margaret had watched much of this unfold live on their suite's television at the Miramar.

"Charlotte says the president met Marilyn Monroe at Bing's," Margaret said in an attempt to fill the void between them and fight off her loneliness. "Says the whole scene was wild—amyl nitrite, interns. Bing wasn't there."

Charlie leaped at the chance to have a conversation with her, but it took just seconds for the topic to remind Margaret of Lola, and her terse responses resumed.

That evening, Charlie had just grunted on his way out the door.

He had begun taking his dinner in the lobby. His meals were mostly liquid at this point, anyway. He had convinced himself he was the aggrieved party here, that he was unappreciated, that she was being too tough on him. But now, with this new lead on where he might find Violet, he felt something he hadn't experienced in some time: hope.

Charlie updated his friends in the car: An FBI tipster had heard about a party being thrown at Disneyland, the theme park that had opened seven years earlier and was now a full-on international tourist attraction. White had said there were a number of underage girls being brought in for the party. The tipster had previously been shown a photo of Violet at the FBI Los Angeles field office and believed she was one of the girls who would be there.

"You ever make a Disney picture, Peter?" Davis asked, clearly trying to lighten the load of the conversation.

"Nope. You?"

"Nope," Davis said.

"I assume Walt wouldn't, like, officially permit this kind of party at his Magic Kingdom," Charlie said. "How would these creeps get the keys to the castle?"

"I'm sure Uncle Walt doesn't know," Lawford said. "Do you have any idea how many layers of bureaucracy exist between him and the guys who watch the park at night?"

Lawford made a right on Harbor Boulevard, and soon enough he was pulling his sports car into a parking lot with plenty of other shiny, exotic vehicles: Jags, Aston Martins, Caddys, and a Rolls or two.

"Someone's going to make some bank off this shindig," Charlie said.

"This is Hollywood, mate," Lawford said. "Everything is for sale." Davis mimicked the sound of a cash register as Lawford put the car in park.

The three men got out and began walking toward the empty ticket booths; the American flag fluttered in a light wind, and music emanated from somewhere in the darkened theme park.

Charlie's drunken clattering around in the bathroom on his way out the door had, in fact, woken up Margaret. After he left, she checked the time, then rolled over in a huff. She was surprised when, not thirty seconds later, the phone rang again.

"It's Charlotte," said the shaky voice on the other end of the line.

"Are you okay?" asked Margaret, sitting up.

"Listen," she said. "I pinched the keys and opened the files."

"Holy crap," Margaret said as her pulse quickened. As a favor to Margaret, Goode had been trying to track down anyone who might have any details of Lola's life. They needed to find out what enemies she had, who might have preyed on her.

"I found some stuff on your girl," Goode reported. "Most of it in Tarantula's chicken-scratch handwriting, which is almost as repulsive as he is."

"Are you at the paper right now?"

"No," Goode said. "I'm home. I can't risk being caught with these documents. I snuck them out and hid them someplace nobody will ever find them."

"I don't understand," Margaret said. "You're a journalist. You have files of information, of research. Of dirt. What's all that research good for if you and your paper don't use it?"

There was silence on the line. Finally, Goode said: "Leverage."

"For what?"

"For anything they want," Goode said. "Money. Sex. Real estate. Power. Favors. Whatever they want."

"Who's *they*?" Margaret asked.

"We can talk about that later," Goode said. "Let me tell you what I have about your girl."

"Tell me," Margaret said. She'd agreed to come back to Los Angeles to help Charlie, to figure out who this Lola was and maybe save her husband's hide. She'd reached out to Manny Fontaine, to John Frankenheimer, to George Jacobs, but everyone pleaded ignorance about where Lola had come from or who her friends were. Fontaine said he'd seen her at the Daisy and at Puccini, but the maître d' only faintly recalled her. Her demise seemed to have caused everyone in LA to forget she had existed.

"These girls, they come to town like moths to a flame," Goode said, "all of them told since they could walk that they oughta be in pictures, they're as pretty as any movie star." Margaret heard Goode light a cigarette and take a drag. "They spot 'em at the Greyhound station or at a casting call or walking down Santa Monica Boulevard. Some end up at those parties and become known for providing a good time. Your girl might have a dope habit too, sad to say."

"She might have—" Margaret was confused. What was with the present tense?

"Yeah, I think I may have an idea of where she's currently crashing," Goode said. "You can't go alone, though, if you try to go. Bring a friend."

"Wait," Margaret said. "I thought you were telling me about Lola Bridgewater."

"No, this is your niece I'm talking about," Goode said. "Violet."

Charlie jumped when he noticed that in the shadow of the ticket booth was a tall, broad man in a dark suit. The man waved Charlie and Lawford through the turnstile. Charlie didn't know what he was walking into, nor did he know how much he could rely on his Rat Pack pals. The constant boozing and the estrangement from Margaret had destabilized him; it was like removing ballast from a ship.

Charlie, Lawford, and Davis proceeded under the Santa Fe and

Disneyland Railroad locomotive, which circled the perimeter of the park, and onto Main Street. Even in the dim streetlamps around the town square, the shiny red of the horse-drawn Disneyland Fire Department wagon popped out from the grays and blacks of the night. Down the faux avenue they strolled, passing the Wurlitzer Music Shop and the Main Street Cinema.

"Why *here*?" Charlie asked. "Why not at some Xanadu at the Hearst Castle? Behind locked and guarded gates, far from the street, away from any chance of discovery."

"Getting away with it is part of the rush," Lawford said.

Davis pointed to a giant cartoon image of Mickey Mouse hanging in a storefront, illuminated by an old-time streetlamp. "Always amazes me how minstrel Mickey is," Davis said.

"What?" asked Charlie.

"Look at that mouse, man!" Davis said. "The elastic black arms and legs, the white mouth, the gloves—the whole thing is a classic coon character. Oh, man, this gets me crazy."

"Don't get him started on that fucking mouse, Charlie," Lawford said, chuckling. "He'll take it back to *Steamboat Willie* and 'Turkey in the Straw.'"

They crossed the street, went past the Crystal Arcade and the Carnation Ice Cream Parlor.

"Who are the girls at these parties?" Davis said. "I assume if this is *verboten*, the *fräuleins* are of ill repute."

"The question is whether they're of ill repute willingly," Charlie said.

They came to a large wooden map and Lawford took out his lighter and flicked its spark wheel to see better.

"Tomorrowland, man," Davis said, pointing to the top right corner of the map. "That's where Frank and I rode on that little motorway in 1955 in that TV special when they opened the park."

"Neat," Lawford said.

"Disaster," Davis corrected him. "Traffic jam on the Santa Ana—I mean a horror show, even for SoCal. Hundred-degree heat meant gummy tar on Main Street, snagging the moms' high heels. Counterfeit tickets, so sardine-can crowds, which meant the vendors ran out of food and drink. Plumbers' strike, so no water fountains. The company rushed the open, so the best rides weren't even running yet. Only thing really open was Autopia, which was just regular cars. Tomorrowland was pretty much Todayland."

"We're going here, to Frontierland," Charlie said, pointing to the top left corner of the map.

"Lead on, Macduff," said Lawford.

"I came in early this morning and Tarantula was dead drunk at his desk," Charlotte continued on the phone. "He'd dropped the keys in the bathroom. I unlocked the file cabinet. After about twenty minutes I figured out the filing codes and found a bunch of stuff about young girls. And boys. And that's where Violet was. She's one of a number of young women who live with this investment manager, John Boyle. It's sick, Margaret, sick. They pass these girls around like canapés."

"Where can I find Violet?" Margaret asked.

"I've seen a lot of horrors in my day and on this beat," Goode said. "I covered Black Dahlia and Lupe Velez. I covered Jeanne French, her face beaten into pulp, 'Fuck You, BD,' written on her torso in her own lipstick."

Margaret could hear Goode puffing on her cigarette at a rapid clip. Something was off. Her friend's mind seemed to be unspooling.

"There's no way I would ever be able to get any of this into print. You have no idea the stories they've killed. Amazing stories, multiple sources! Studio bosses forcing Bette Davis to have an abortion! Joan Crawford's skin flick! Why Hearst killed Thomas Ince! A three-part series on Uncle Walt rolling out the red carpet for Leni Riefenstahl! Clark Gable's secret love child with Loretta Young! On and on. All of them buried."

"Charlotte, what did you find out about Violet?" Margaret said. "What's wrong?"

"I have never seen anything like this, and I covered Chaplin marrying two sixteen-year-olds! Not at the same time, of course. And Errol Flynn's statutory-rape trial. Benny Benson! Ed Tierney! Natalie Wood! Vicious! Everyone knows that these men like girls—literal *girls*! But this takes it to a new level of sickening! The question is what can I do about it. *Nightlife* will never print it—"

Her rant continued unabated. This wasn't Charlotte's normal almost-manic state; this was something more extreme, her words almost indecipherable, her breathing frenzied.

"Charlotte, honey, calm down," Margaret said. She might need to go to her friend, see for herself what had triggered Charlotte. "I have your home address. I'm coming. Stay put, okay?"

The line went dead.

Charlie led the way across the park, Lawford and Davis following him, past the Frontierland Shootin' Gallery, where two armed guards stood, guns in their chest holsters, jackets off. They looked somewhere between Mafia thugs and FBI agents, Charlie thought, in that twilight space where private security guards dwell, tough and not to be trifled with, but badgeless.

They entered the Mexican town square, El Zocolo, where a mariachi band performed "La Bamba" on the Mexican bandstand, and a crowd of men salivated while watching two dark-haired teenage girls dancing some kind of courtship dance. One of the girls was dressed in a formfitting blouse and high-waisted skirt approximating the traditional china poblano; the other was clad as a charro, with an enormous black sombrero. Charlie paused and looked at their cherubic faces, which made him think of a child, of his own daughter, Lucy, though these girls' outfits were made to convey a sexuality they wouldn't grow into for years.

"Come on, amigo," Lawford said, pulling him along, "vámanos."

A song began blaring from behind them; Charlie turned to see the Golden Horseshoe, an ersatz saloon that was currently serving as a very real one. They walked up the porch and looked inside, where a burlesque singer dressed as a cowgirl regaled the audience with a song.

"*A miner from the Klondike came a-strollin' in the place,*" she sang. "*With nuggets in his knapsack and whiskers on his face. He said, 'A kiss I crave,' and I said, 'Sir! Not until you shave!' A lady has to mind her P's and Q's!*"

The saloon was packed with drunken men and girls who could be their daughters or granddaughters.

"Do you see her?" Lawford asked.

"No," said Charlie. "Not here."

They stepped back from the saloon doors.

"We probably shouldn't act as if we're looking for someone," Davis said. "We should blend."

"If we really want to blend, we need to grab girls," Lawford said. Seeing Charlie's and Davis's alarmed faces, he quickly added: "I don't mean that literally. I'm just saying, we're sore thumbs here. Especially Sammy."

"Hey!" said Davis.

"What's over there?" Charlie asked, nodding to the river, beyond which sat Tom Sawyer Island, festooned with tiki torches, bubbling with human activity. He walked over and onto the dock, where an immense steamboat sat still in the man-made river, bathed in moonlight. Lawford and Davis joined him. In the distance came the faint deep beating of shamanic drums.

"It sounds like the climax of *Sergeants Three* over there," Lawford said.

"The pornographic version, maybe," Davis said. "Our version doesn't have full-frontal."

"The version in my trailer did," said Lawford. "Firewater, squaw, smoke-um big peace pipe."

"Different kind of climax, Peter," Davis said.

Charlie looked back at Tom Sawyer's Island. He heard a woman's laugh echoing across the water. He knew exactly why he was there: If he could save Violet, he could redeem himself with Margaret. And then he could quit drinking and get his dad out of jail and be the man Margaret believed he could be. Not this other man, the one he was on his way to becoming.

"We need to get over there," he said.

CHAPTER TWENTY

LOS ANGELES, CALIFORNIA

April 1962

Margaret drove slowly on Sunset trying to spot where Charlotte Goode lived. It was two thirty in the morning.

"I think this is it," Margaret said, pulling the car to the curb and hopping out. Sheryl Ann Gold sleepily followed her, probably trying to will herself into the right state of mind for the potentially dangerous situation before them. As soon as Charlotte's phone had gone dead, Margaret called Sheryl Ann and pleaded for her company.

Goode's house sat behind a row of palm trees. The front door, beneath a brick porch, was bracketed by lanterns, now dark.

"I can't see anything," said Sheryl Ann.

Margaret took out her cigarette lighter and held it in front of her; she could make out a stairwell leading to a cellar door.

"This must be it," she whispered.

She walked slowly down the steps, at the bottom of which the door was ajar. Margaret looked back at Sheryl Ann, then slowly pushed it open and felt around on the wall for the light switch.

The room inside had been turned upside down: pillows gutted, cushions torn apart, papers strewn, drawers open. Margaret and Sheryl Ann cautiously stepped through the small living room. The kitchen was just as torn up—cabinets emptied onto the floor and the oven and refrigerator left open, casting light onto the disarray. Margaret kept walking, quietly, to the bedroom; she steeled herself before turning on the light, glancing over her shoulder and feeling a reassuring pat from Sheryl Ann.

Margaret turned on the light.

Charlotte Goode lay on her bed, her eyes and mouth open. Her shirt and the sheets were smeared with blood.

"*Je*-sus," exclaimed Sheryl Ann, jumping back.

Oh no, Margaret thought. *Oh God, no.* Her heart began to race. She ran to the bed and felt Charlotte's neck for a pulse.

There was none.

Margaret felt as if her insides were being torn out. She started to cry. Sheryl Ann put her arms around her, attempting to comfort her. After a minute had passed, Sheryl Ann patted Margaret on the shoulder to bring her back to the urgency of the moment, not just its tragedy.

"We should call the police," Sheryl Ann said. "Where's the phone?"

Margaret looked around the room, then back at Goode. "It's around her neck," Margaret said, pointing to the cord that circled Goode's throat and trailed onto the floor on the other side of the bed.

Sheryl Ann walked around the bed, picked up the receiver that dangled at the end of the cord, and lifted it to her ear. "No dial tone," she said.

Margaret looked down at Charlotte. She noticed weird blood smears on the sheet near her right hand. Circles and lines. She ran around to the far side of the bed to take a closer look.

The Mark Twain Steamboat was anchored for the night, but Davis noted that a Tom Sawyer Island motorized raft appeared to be bringing some guests from the island. The raft could fit thirty

visitors, but the captain was depositing only four back on the main-
land, two men and two girls. The men were in their sixties, tripping
and stumbling, wearing coonskin caps, guffawing and grasping at
their dates. The two girls were done up in raunchy Disney-squaw
garb—fringed leather bikinis and skirts, eagle feathers, braids.

"All aboard!" said the raft operator, a young man in an unkempt
country-boy Huck Finn costume.

"I'm way too sober," Lawford said as they all climbed on.

"We have heap big firewater on the island," the raft operator said
robotically, cranking up the motor and steering the craft to Tom
Sawyer Island.

"It's weird how no one seems to notice you two," Charlie said.
"I mean, not only no autograph requests, but it's as if they don't
recognize you!"

"No one notices anyone because this event isn't happening,
man," Davis observed. "You're not here, I'm not here, no one is
here." The raft operator nodded approvingly.

As they chugged forward, Charlie could see more of the island,
some of which was illuminated by tiki torches and lanterns. A
fishing pier sat by the docks, adjacent to an old mill, and off in the
distance at the northern tip sat what appeared to be a cabin on fire.
Beyond the party sounds of music, murmurs, and revelry came the
rhythmic warpath drumbeats of the Ugga-Wugga Wigwam tribe
from *Peter Pan*.

The operator tied the raft to a post in the Tom's Landing dock
and as Charlie disembarked, he noticed shapes on the muddy shore
illuminated in the moonlight. It was a young woman on her back,
naked from the waist up, gazing patiently if dead-eyed into the
sky, and a big, broad, heavy, hairy man on top of her.

The sight transported Charlie back to a night in France during the
war. Along with the rest of First Battalion, 175th Infantry, Charlie

landed at Omaha Beach on June 17, 1944. He and Company K seized Isigny-sur-Mer, secured the bridge over the Vire River, recaptured Saint-Lô, and proceeded northeast. By late August, Charlie and his weathered platoon had reached a bank on the eastern estuary of the Seine River southwest of the Pays de Caux. The nearby city, German-occupied Le Havre, was France's biggest channel port, and beginning in the early evening of September 5, the Royal Air Force dropped almost ten thousand tons of bombs on the town, destroying more than 80 percent of the buildings and killing two thousand French civilians. Soon, from the ocean, the monitor HMS *Erebus* and battleship HMS *Warspite* began pummeling the port town with more than four thousand long tons of shells.

Charlie and Company K had watched it all in horror, hiding in the woods a kilometer away. On September 12, the British and Canadian forces entered Le Havre, and the Germans surrendered. Six days later, Charlie was with the American forces entering the town, a trek through rubble and concrete, over glass and viscera. The troops had to cover their noses with scarves and rags to avoid the stench of rotting carrion. Most of the townspeople were homeless, and food was scarce. The citizens of Le Havre had been pulled quickly into degraded states. They were focused solely on survival, with only the occupying forces to try to keep order.

Charlie had spent only five days at Le Havre, but he spent much of the next decade trying to forget what he saw. Starting with what he found when he followed the sound of a mournful wail into what had once been a storage facility for the hospital. He had assumed someone was dying and needed help. He ducked into the rubble and entered a dark room barely illuminated by a flickering lantern. Squinting, he approached two shapes that turned out to be a large man in fatigues—he couldn't tell which army—humping a young girl, barely pubescent. Charlie recoiled, then stepped closer. The girl wasn't actually moving. He kicked the soldier off her, and the man grunted, stunned, having not even known Charlie was in the room. Charlie knelt next to the girl.

She wasn't breathing.

What's more, she was cold to the touch. She had been dead for some time.

Charlie backed away, horrified at his realization, as the soldier quickly ran out of the rubble.

What have we become? Charlie wondered.

Or maybe the question was even more disturbing than that: *Is the war only now revealing what we have always truly been?*

Now, without thinking, Charlie jumped down into the mud, took the man by his throat, pulled him off the girl, and threw him onto his back. His eyes met the man's, and Charlie thought, for a moment, about crushing his skull. The frustration of these past months surged in him, this disoriented feeling he couldn't shake and his anger at himself for his own stupidity and laziness. He caught his breath, then said to the man through clenched teeth, "Get out of my sight before I fucking kill you."

The man stood up, shirtless, shocked, and terrified. He grabbed the waist of his pants and, without looking back at the girl, sprinted for his life. Charlie watched him for a moment, then knelt to help the girl. She skittered away from him, eyes wide, then stood, hauled the skirt of her dress over one shoulder, and took off.

Charlie sank to his knees in the mud.

"Charlie, boyo, you okay?" Lawford asked, gently shaking his shoulder.

He didn't know what had just happened.

Charlie looked to the docks of Tom Sawyer Island. "Sorry," he said. "It reminded me of the war."

It took him another second before he fully rejoined his friends.

"Bad memories, man," Davis said. "They can pop up and block everything else out. Like Nosferatu, man."

"Let's just focus on your niece for tonight," Lawford suggested. "And not try to save every woman in Disneyland."

They walked from the docks, passed a giant faux Old Mill to their left, and proceeded straight down a row of tiki torches as if headed to a Hawaiian wedding, signs beckoning them to stray and explore other sights: Injun Joe's Cave, Smuggler's Cove, Tom and Huck's Treehouse.

Three lanky, skinny teenage girls walked toward them, dressed as stereotypical squaws.

"...said he had the opportunity of a lifetime for me," one of them was saying. "He said he would introduce me to the most important man I could meet."

They were young and blond and gawky. It was difficult to see their faces in the dark, but they resembled so many Hollywood teens, girls with big Keane-painting eyes. They noticed Lawford and Davis, did double takes, and approached them.

"You boys going to Fort Wilderness?" one of them asked.

"What's that, doll?" Davis said. The words were characteristic Sammy Davis charm, but to Charlie they rang hollow, suggesting the singer was maybe as nervous as he was.

Davis put a cigarette in his mouth and was about to light it when the girl closest to him reached over and took it. He lit it for her, then held out the pack for the other two to partake. As they leaned toward the lighter, Charlie got a better look at their faces. *Kids*, he thought. They were just kids.

The first one took a drag of the cigarette, exhaled, then said: "Fort Wilderness is where all the fun is happening. Keep going down the lane."

"Do you know a girl named Violet?" Charlie asked. "About your age, from Ohio?"

The three girls looked at each other, rolled their eyes, and laughed.

"There are a lot of girls there," said the first. "Dunno names. We're heading to the treehouse, there's reefer there." They tee-heed and ran off.

"Jesus, it's past their bedtime," Davis said.

"Weird that no one has asked if we belong here," Charlie noted.

"When you're famous, no one stops you to ask questions," said Lawford.

The three men continued down the dark path, the sounds of music, drums, and revelry growing louder.

Sheryl Ann cautioned Margaret to slow down as they proceeded east on Sunset.

"We can't get pulled over," she said, looking at the dashboard clock: 3:04.

They had rushed out of Charlotte Goode's basement apartment, walked briskly to the car, and tore down the street.

"Should we call the police?" Sheryl Ann asked.

"Why? To bring her back to life?" Margaret said. She'd retreated into pure survival mode. "I'm worried about them placing us at the scene. LAPD is already trying to frame us." She took her foot off the gas pedal.

"The sooner LAPD gets there, the better the chance they have of finding her killer," Sheryl Ann said.

Margaret considered that. She spotted a phone booth near an empty corner, pulled over, and called the cops. After giving them the address and saying she suspected wrongdoing, she hung up. Next she called Addington White, reversing the charges. When he answered, she offered a quick description of what she'd seen, save for the clue Charlotte had apparently written on the sheet with her own blood. White thanked her for the call and assured her he'd have field agents from the FBI's Los Angeles office head there at once.

Back in the car, Sheryl Ann directed Margaret to their destination as best she could figure it out: Sunset to Highland to Hollywood Boulevard to Beachwood Drive. The fancy homes they whizzed by came in four styles: Spanish, Mediterranean, French Normandy, English Tudor. One after the other, like the repetitive backgrounds of Bugs Bunny cartoons to which Frankenheimer had once referred.

"Why are you so convinced we need to do this?" Sheryl Ann asked.

"Charlotte told me she had documents that were shocking that she'd taken from the locked file cabinets at work," Margaret said. "She must not have brought them to her home, though. I'm certain that's what they were looking for when they killed her."

"But why are we going to the Hollywood sign?"

"The *H* she drew in blood on the sheet," Margaret said. "And her obsession with Peg Entwistle, who jumped from it."

"Take a left here on Ledgewood," Sheryl Ann said. "And we're going to take a quick right to get to Mulholland. How good a hiker are you?"

"I wouldn't call the incline from the Lower East Side to the Upper East Side particularly steep," Margaret said. "Except socially."

They hit the end of the road, parked, and hopped out of the car. The sign was lit above them, but beyond that the mountain was dark. So as to not trip on rocks and brambles, Margaret illuminated the ground in front her of her with her cigarette lighter while Sheryl Ann followed. Behind them, the lights of downtown Los Angeles shimmered as the two women began to scramble up the canyon to the Hollywood sign. They felt as distant and remote as the stars above them.

CHAPTER TWENTY-ONE

ANAHEIM, CALIFORNIA

April 1962

Charlie felt nauseated. On their way to Fort Wilderness, he and the Rat Packers kept coming across middle-aged lechers and their victims rolling in the fake flora. It was impossible to tell the women who might be willing participants from the girls—children, really. And it was difficult to reconcile the debauched criminality with the Disneyness of the setting: the wholesome plastic artifice, the aggressive Americana, and the bland mainstream music, including the song emanating from the fort right now— "Wringle Wrangle," from the Disney Western *Westward Ho the Wagons!*

With a dollar's worth of beans, a new pair of jeans, got a woman to cook and wash and things, blared the recording of Fess Parker, who'd acted in the film as well as played the lead in Disney's erstwhile Davy Crockett show.

"Remember this song?" Davis asked Lawford.

"'Course," Lawford said.

"Whatever happened to ol' Fess?" Davis asked.

"He wanted to play more than cowboys, but Uncle Walt only saw him with chaps," Lawford said. "He refused to do some picture with a bit part, and that was that. Haven't seen him since."

"Can't be a starter if you won't play ball," Davis observed.

Their trail veered right and suddenly Fort Wilderness was before them. Constructed out of ponderosa pine logs as if it were an actual U.S. outpost in Texas, the fort sat atop a bluff on the western bank of the island, adjacent to an ersatz Missouri River. Four men stood at the gate dressed as U.S. Army soldiers from the early 1800s, around the time of the campaign against the Creek Indians. Seemingly working for whoever was throwing the party, they nodded to Charlie as he led the group in.

Charlie, Lawford, and Davis stood and surveyed the decadence. Across the fort grounds were girls who looked like they should have been preparing for JV cheerleading tryouts paired off with men who looked like their fathers or grandfathers. Bonfires flickered, illuminating the parade ground as Charlie searched for Violet. A staircase led to a porch; beyond the parade ground stood a graveyard, some teepees, and, in the distance, the burning cabin they'd seen from the river, the controlled flames on its roof purposely fed by propane.

Some laughed or sang, the men in cowboy gear, the girls in Indian leather playing their parts as dutiful conquests. Waiters in army uniforms brought them drinks in copper tankards.

"Do you see her, old boy?" Lawford said as he scanned the scene.

"I don't," Charlie said. He stared at the faces. Couples sat at tables or around the bonfires, drinking. Some danced. An older man, white-haired with a belly, struggled to his feet. He laughed and extended his hand to the girl by his side; she was dressed like a squaw in a B Western with feathers in her headband and a short, fringed, clingy faux buckskin dress and beaded moccasins.

It was Violet.

Charlie gasped.

She followed the older man into the fort through a doorway marked APOTHECARY. Charlie saw a different couple exiting the same room through a side door as a soldier waved the new couple in.

Charlie gestured at the couple going in. "That's her."

"Where?" asked Lawford.

Before he could answer, a young soldier approached them. "We have two girls available," he said. "One of them is a mulatto if you're interested, Mr. Davis. Would you like to come with me?"

He motioned toward the wooden stairway.

Sweaty and panting from the steep ascent, Margaret and Sheryl Ann finally reached the Hollywood sign. Each letter was huge, fifty feet high and thirty feet across, made up of three-by-nine panels of sheet metal painted white on one side and held up by utility poles and wooden beams. Margaret walked along the front of the sign while Sheryl Ann walked on the opposite side.

"Nothing here," Sheryl Ann said. "Do you know where Entwistle died?"

"She climbed to the top of the *H*," said Margaret. "And then she jumped."

Sheryl Ann slowly walked along, surveying the rocks and bramble in the predawn light. She lifted her head and gazed at the top of the *H*.

"That's the lore, anyway," Margaret said. "Couldn't have been any more of a metaphor if she'd been nailed to the *H*."

"How did she get up there?"

Margaret noticed just above her head a white ladder fastened to the back of the letter. At the top, there appeared to be something wedged between the sheet metal and a utility pole.

"Come here," Margaret said, beckoning to her friend.

Sheryl Ann joined Margaret behind the *H*.

"I need a boost," Margaret said. "Clasp your hands."

She hauled herself up to the ladder and climbed. Each rung made a loud creak. She tried to focus on the inches in front of her and not the broad-view insanity of what she was doing.

* * *

Charlie hatched the plan in a panic. "I want to stop him," he told Lawford and Davis as they approached the wooden steps. He told them what to do and they nodded their assent. The two walked to the front of the fort and whispered to a couple of the guards. Then they strode to the center of the parade ground.

"Hey there, kids!" Lawford said as the loudspeakers blared the *zzzzzip* of a needle being clumsily removed from the record. Charlie—slowly walking toward the apothecary—was surprised at how his friend's voice boomed throughout the fort without the aid of a microphone.

"Since this is all *entre nous*," Davis said, "we thought you cool cats and chicks might appreciate a song or two."

"So unless you're otherwise indisposed, my friends, let's celebrate!"

The old man with Violet poked his head out of the room and smiled to see the special mini–Rat Pack concert. Violet followed him out, seizing the respite to lean against the wall.

Davis had grabbed a recorder from a girl dressed as a squaw while Lawford beat on tom-toms.

"*¡Revolución cubana!*" the two men shouted from the center of the parade ground, commencing with a popular one-hit wonder from the mid-1950s, before the Castros and Che landed at Playas de las Coloradas from Mexico.

> *¡Revolución cubana!*
> *I just fell in love in Havana*
> *She ran for the Puerto*
> *And wished on me muerta*
> *And left me with just my banana!*

"*¡Olé!*" the singers shouted, prompting clueless cries of "*¡Olé!*" from the crowd. Some of the teenage girls started to dance. Charlie wondered if they were drunk or trying to avoid their "dates" or just having a little harmless fun, the kind kids their age should be having in purer settings.

He looked at Violet; her "date" stood a few feet in front of her. Charlie stared at her; he didn't want the old man aware of his presence. Finally, sensing the eyes on her, Violet glanced to her left and saw Charlie, who motioned with his head that he wanted her to follow. Violet's face registered no reaction. Charlie realized that she probably figured he was just another pervert. Then, as if something had snapped in her brain, she looked at him again and her eyes opened in recognition. *Uncle Charlie?* she mouthed, and he nodded.

> *¡Cubana revolución!*
> *Batista retribution!*
> *He calls CIA.*
> *And they say come-what-may*
> *No, no, no to wealth redistribution!*

> *Señorita—*
> *Your skin—leche con café*
> *On your Sierra Maestra I want to play*
> *While I attack in the valley beneath Escambray*

Charlie put a finger to his lips, then pointed upstairs. Violet understood.

> *¡Revolución cubana!*
> *Now I'm back in ol' Indiana*
> *I loved to do pillage*
> *In each sexy village*
> *Every lady like heaven-sent manna!*

Charlie casually strode to the stairs, followed by Violet, who seemed nervous and eager to flee. The porch wound around the back of the fort and they ducked into a room, at the far end of which was, luckily, another door to another set of stairs. Beyond the fort lay the banks of the faux Missouri River, on which they were relieved to see a canoe.

Borrowing some of the light cast on the immense *H*, Margaret held the first document close to her face. It was a bill from a costume designer for seventy-five squaw costumes. The next was a bill from the same costume designer for fifty flapper outfits. That was followed by dozens of other bills for dozens of costumes—leprechauns, witches, plantation, Kentucky Derby, and the like—dating back to 1953.

Margaret looked back at the most recent bill. It was dated two weeks ago.

Sheryl Ann studied a different stack of papers in the light projected onto the giant *O*. "Here's a photo of Chris Powell at some film premiere," she said. She held it up. Powell and his date were smiling.

"That's Lola," Margaret said. "The dead girl."

Sheryl Ann sifted through the stack. "What's this?" she asked, holding up bookkeeper vouchers, records of debts paid. "Payments from Paramount and Warner Brothers Studios to someone named Marie Antoinette."

Margaret dug through the file folder she'd found wedged behind the *H*. "There's a film reel here too," she noted, digging into the bottom of the container.

"Does it make any sense that Charlotte died for...this?" Sheryl Ann asked. "What is this? Some bills, bookkeeper vouchers, some photos, and a film reel?"

From above them, at the top of the mountain behind the sign, they heard a car slowly driving over gravel.

"We should get going," Margaret whispered. The steep canyon wall blocked her view of the car. They heard footsteps and Margaret stuffed everything back in the folder, and the two women began cautiously walking down the mountain.

Some rocks dislodged above them and rolled by. Margaret looked over her shoulder to see the silhouette of a large man determinedly moving down the hill.

"Sheryl Ann!" she cried.

"I see!"

It was difficult to go much faster, given the steep precipice and the dim light; Margaret stumbled on a bush. She recovered, reclaimed the folder, and continued her controlled rush down the mountain. When she found the semblance of a trail they'd used on their way up, she paused and looked back and saw Sheryl Ann fighting off the man. With his free hand, he pulled out a gun, aimed it at Margaret, and fired.

CHAPTER TWENTY-TWO

ANAHEIM, CALIFORNIA

April 1962

"Hop in front," Charlie said as he and Violet scurried to the canoe. He had originally planned for them to swim and couldn't believe their luck.

He looked back at Fort Wilderness. Lawford and Davis continued to sing, the crowd was still cheering, no one seemed to have any idea they had left.

"Okay," Violet said as she stepped into the boat. "Thank you."

He looked at her, hoping she was still the same good-natured kid he'd met some Christmases ago given that she'd been through God only knew what since running away from home. Margaret was going to be so happy, so relieved, so grateful, he thought. He slid the vessel off the banks and into the water, stepped in, knelt, found an oar, and began paddling.

"How do we get out?" she asked. They were cloaked in the night as Charlie guided them through the imitation Missouri, but he gently whispered, "Shh," as he clutched the oar. She nodded. She got it.

With Tom Sawyer Island on their left, he paddled past a dock, a small forest, and keelboats on their right. A sign announced FOWLER'S HARBOR and beyond that stood a structure that advertised NEW ORLEANS SQUARE. If they kept paddling to the left on the circular river, they would soon be back at the Mark Twain Steamboat area, which teemed with activity, so Charlie figured New Orleans was a better route. He put some muscle into his stroke to land on the banks in front of him.

"We're getting off here?" Violet asked.

"Think so," he said. The canoe skidded onto the muddy shore and Charlie began pulling the boat all the way onto land so Violet could climb out. But suddenly he felt a sharp whack on the back of his head, and everything went black.

The bullet ricocheted off a large rock maybe a foot from Margaret. She ducked, gasped, then turned and ran down the mountain. Her pursuer fired another shot. Margaret heard it whiz by her head; she felt the wind of it. She ducked again and started zigzagging down the hill.

A minute passed. She skidded behind a bush then stole a look uphill. No one was there. It was quiet and still. The Hollywood sign stood indifferent to the drama.

She stood and once again heard the crack of the gun. She turned and ran, straining her eyes to see the path in front of her. Her run down the mountain took on a pattern: hop-jump-skid, hop-jump-skid. Her thoughts drifted to Charlie, wherever he was, then Violet, then she remembered Charlotte. *God. Charlotte.* She'd put the dead woman out of her mind as she raced to find the hidden trove of evidence, but Margaret couldn't believe she'd been murdered. What secrets would be worth killing someone to preserve?

Hop-jump-skid...

Lord Almighty, she wanted to see Charlie. She needed his help in rescuing her friend, of course, but it was much more than that, she realized.

She loved Charlie at his best, and when he was at his worst she was mad at him for not being who she knew he could be. She'd been too hard on him, she decided, confronted as she was now with finality, with mortality. Perhaps she too readily compared him to the dashing, brilliant Columbia senior she'd met in the stacks that romantic winter night in 1941. Maybe she'd had a vision of the man he would become and was struggling with the chasm between that man and the reality of Charlie at forty-one, shell-shocked, booze on his breath, still unsure of how to negotiate his finely tuned sense of black and white on a planet of grays.

Yes, he was, of course, making stupid mistakes, ones that maybe seemed small in the context of the Rat Pack bacchanalia but were nonetheless out of character. There remained so much in Charlie that was good—not just his virtue, but his tenderness with Lucy and Dwight, his kindness to her mother, his devotion to her. Margaret would help him. The fundamental issue she had, she knew, was not with her partner; it was with their enemies, those who sought the erosion of standards and fundamental decency. The American way of life was built on the honor system, but that depended on all the players having a sense of honor. Others might not, but Charlie did, and that was all that mattered, truly. Yet both of them had become so focused on the minutiae of day-to-day decisions and slights, they were blind to the overall wonder of their lives.

Hop-jump-skid...

She stopped to catch her breath and turned to look up the mountain. There was nothing but the letters, illuminated by both the floodlights and the pinkish-orange light preceding the rising sun to the east, past the reservoir. The shooter and Sheryl Ann were both gone. Before her, the glittering grid of Hollywood and the sprawl of Los Angeles, Inglewood, Compton, Lakewood, Torrance. And beyond that, the inky black where the Pacific rumbled. She would run to the bottom of the hill, get into her car, and go find Charlie. He would help her, she would help him, and they would defeat the nefarious forces that once again had found them and were trying to

234 • JAKE TAPPER

destroy them. She would do whatever she needed to get him back to full strength. They had no choice; she had no choice.

As Charlie rolled over, he caught a glimpse of the imprint his face had made in the muddy bank of the fake river; it looked like the death mask of Napoleon Bonaparte. He tried to sit up, but a foot suddenly came at his chin. Charlie jerked away and the kick bruised his shoulder.

When Charlie had told John Wayne about his hand-to-hand training at Fort Benning, he meant every word of it. He'd learned to fight dirty, to kill or be killed. His instructor, Master Sergeant Tom Ladzinski, would repeatedly say, "Fuck the Marquess of Queensberry" while demonstrating how to rip out a man's throat. Ladzinski destroyed the idea that men should put up their dukes and instead showed them how to tap into the viciousness within themselves.

Charlie was older and slower on the banks of Disneyland's sham Missouri than he'd been at Fort Benning or in France. As he stood, he saw that his opponent was a good deal smaller, sinewy, with a floral-print shirt and horn-rimmed glasses, currently focused on trying to pull Violet, who had collapsed in the mud, to her feet. Charlie didn't recognize him, but he realized that Violet's flop onto the banks, purposeful or not, gave him an opportunity. Charlie charged.

The man sidestepped Charlie's lunge and tripped him. Charlie staggered and turned just in time to take a judo kick to his abdomen, which knocked the wind out of him, bringing him to his knees. The man attempted to kick Charlie in the chin, but Charlie grabbed the man's leg, lifted him, and tossed him onto his back.

He suddenly wondered if this man truly sought to kill him and whether lethal force was necessary. It was in that moment of hesitation—the precise second-guessing that he'd been warned about at Fort Benning—that Charlie heard the click of a switchblade, then saw its metal gleaming in the moonlight, the foil grip held in the right hand of his opponent.

The knife came for Charlie, the assailant lunging for his abdomen; Charlie jumped to his right, splashing into the shallows. He snapped to it, chasing away any questions about whether both men would be able to walk off this beach. He ran and dived into the man and felt the tip of the blade enter the back of his left shoulder. He felt it again and again, going into the muscle in his back. Then the man tried to bring the knife to Charlie's throat. Charlie grabbed the man's head, ripped off his glasses, and plunged his thumbs into his eyes.

He locked his elbows, sat forward, pushed his thumbs deeper, and dragged him headfirst into the water. The man writhed and splashed, swinging to bring the blade back to Charlie's throat. Charlie looked away as the man's spasms weakened. A sign at a nearby wooden building advertised AUNT JEMIMA'S PANCAKE HOUSE.

The man stopped resisting.

The knife fell into the water.

Charlie felt light-headed. He vomited, violently, into the faux river until everything inside him, every drop of liquor that wasn't in his bloodstream, dissolved in the water. He felt utterly sick. In his body, in his heart. The bile and alcohol, like poison in his throat, on his lips.

He crawled out of the water and collapsed from exhaustion. Minutes passed; Charlie didn't know how many. Then his mind reentered the full context of his situation. Music echoed from down the river.

A whispered voice: "Charlie, that you?"

It was Sammy Davis Jr., standing at the edge of New Orleans Square. Violet was with him. In the dark of night, neither of them seemed to see the corpse in the water. Or if they did, they didn't acknowledge it.

"We gotta get out of here," Davis said. "Now!"

CHAPTER TWENTY-THREE

SANTA MONICA, CALIFORNIA

April 1962

The morning sun had already begun to beat down on the beach town when, half a block from the Miramar Hotel on Ocean Avenue, a blue Rambler American swerved up to Lawford's Ghia and honked. Charlie sat, spent, in Lawford's back seat, Violet asleep with her head on his shoulder. Neither of them paid attention to the horn. Lawford followed the Rambler into a Howard Johnson's parking lot a mile away.

Few words had been spoken during the drive from Anaheim. In the front, Lawford and Davis spun the radio dial between music and news. Violet had nodded off immediately, almost as if she were trying to catch up on years' worth of sleep. She was only sixteen but she looked ten years older, Charlie thought, and not just because of her dress and makeup. He wasn't sure if the trauma she'd experienced was as bad as what he'd gone through during the war, and there wasn't much sense in trying to compare the two; he just knew she'd be fighting to get back to who she'd been forever. She'd learn to numb herself, forget her pain for a few minutes here and there.

Despite the events of the past few hours and the stab wounds that throbbed and continued to bleed beneath his makeshift bandages, Charlie felt more like himself than he had in years.

He knew intellectually that in the weeks to come, he would start second-guessing his actions on the riverbank, but had he not killed the man in the floral shirt, Lucy and Dwight would be without a father and Margaret would be a widow, to say nothing of Violet being left in hell. Saving his niece, bringing her back to his wife, filled him with pride, an emotion he hadn't felt in a long time.

"Heads up, Charlie," Sammy said from the front passenger seat. He pointed to the Rambler as Lawford pulled up alongside it.

Charlie looked up to see Margaret running to him. His heart jumped as she opened the Ghia's door and gave him a tight hug.

"Guess who I found," Charlie said. Margaret reached over to touch her niece, caress her cheek. Violet woke up and they all got out of Lawford's car; Violet buried her face in Margaret's shoulder and began heaving with tears.

Charlie turned and was stunned to see Isaiah. They shook hands, Charlie so overwhelmed he was tempted to hug him, though he could muster only enough energy to add his left hand to the shake.

Feeling no such inhibitions, Davis stepped in and gave Street the strongest embrace a person of his diminutive stature could manage.

"Sorry about the detour; I saw some shady characters staking out the Miramar lobby," Street said. "I called up to your room and told Margaret to sneak out the back, then we drove up the block and waited for your car to arrive so as to warn you."

"Who are they?" Charlie asked.

"Dunno," said Street. "Some fishy-looking white people. Undercover cops?"

"Maybe the same people who have Sheryl Ann," Margaret said.

"What?" Charlie asked.

"She's been snatched," Margaret said. "We need to find her. Now." Charlie nodded.

"Where were *you?*" Street asked.

"Disneyland," Charlie said. "Long story. One best not shared in a HoJo's parking lot."

Davis wagged his finger. "You can tell Congressman Street, but beyond that, it's imperative that this remain *entre nous, mon ami.*"

"*Absolument,*" Charlie said.

"I still cannot believe we got in and out with no real fuss other than Sammy and me serenading that crowd," Lawford said sunnily. Charlie frowned to himself at what his coconspirators did not know. All he could hope for now was that whoever was throwing the illicit party would consider the corpse just one more unfortunate item to clean up and make disappear.

Lawford reminded them all that the Academy Awards were that night, and they'd better go home and clean up.

CHAPTER TWENTY-FOUR

SANTA MONICA, CALIFORNIA

April 1962

Street didn't think it was safe to go back to the Miramar, so they drove to the nearby Georgian Hotel. They took Violet to Street's suite, where she collapsed onto the couch. Margaret phoned her sister in Ohio to give her the news and tell her to book the next flight to LA. When they hung up, Margaret spoke in hushed tones with her niece. She gave her another warm embrace, after which Violet turned onto her side and fell asleep again. Margaret grabbed a blanket from the closet and laid it gently atop her.

Margaret, Charlie, and Street proceeded to the veranda restaurant, with its glorious view of the Palisades bluff and the Pacific. Over coffee, bacon, and eggs, they recounted the events of their nights. Margaret led with the news that Sheryl Ann had been abducted.

"We started with one damsel in distress," Charlie said, "and we've still got one. We've only succeeded in swapping her out."

"And we don't know if it's the same kidnappers," Margaret added.

"How could it not be?" asked Street. "A group of guys running a sick sex party with underage girls at Disneyland and another group of guys pursuing the documents proving these parties have been going on for years. Have to be one and the same, no?"

Street motioned to the documents, photographs, and film

Margaret had uncovered at the Hollywood sign and brought with her. After ensuring no one in the restaurant had any interest in who they were or what they were doing, Charlie and Margaret lined up the bills from costume designers beside checks from studios made out to Marie Antoinette. The amounts being charged matched. Street noted that the Disneyland costume department sent an internal invoice for $87.54 for squaw costumes, presumably the ones Charlie had seen the night before. The same amount, $87.54, was on a Disney Studios invoice to Marie Antoinette.

"So it's a shell corporation that funds it all?" Street said.

"Not the most sophisticated way of hiding it," observed Margaret.

"No, but you wouldn't give it a second thought, would you?" said Street. "It only makes sense as a conspiracy when you see all of these bills at once showing all the studios doing the same thing. Otherwise, who would even notice?"

"I gotta believe there are other charges hidden in the books of the studios for much more than just costumes," Charlie said. "This is just the one that someone leaked to the tabloid."

They grabbed the stack of photographs and tried to make sense of them.

The red-carpet paparazzi snapshot suggested Powell and Lola Bridgewater had dated, as did other photos: Powell and Lola out for lunch at Taylor's Steakhouse, frolicking in the surf, laughing and drinking at the Daisy.

"This one is a much younger Lola," Charlie said, turning the photo to show the other two. In the picture Lola was attempting to imitate a grown woman's flirty glance. She was in bed, likely naked under the covers, her breasts partly exposed.

"Jeez, she can't be more than fourteen," Margaret said.

"You think this means she was caught up with the same folks from last night?" Street asked Charlie.

"Could be," Charlie said. "I don't know. I mean, it seems likely, but..."

Margaret frowned. "I appreciate my husband's healthy skepticism," she said, "truly I do, and let me add it's about time. But that said, let's at least concede that these groups are so secretive, it's highly unlikely the two of us would independently and separately stumble on two different grand conspiracies, right?"

"I so concede," Charlie said.

"So it's the same gang, the same bad guys from Disneyland," Street said, grabbing the invoices in the pile in front of them. "These receipts are for the costumes for these poor young girls, for these sick parties."

"And people at the studios are footing the bills," Charlie said. "And hiding the costs."

"And that would mean the guy who killed Charlotte and tried to kill me and who snatched Sheryl Ann is also part of this," Margaret said.

"And theoretically," added Street, lifting up the red-carpet photograph, "so is whoever killed Lola and Powell."

"Remember, Fontaine and Meehan both told us that Powell was a Mob hit, shot through the eyes," Charlie said.

"The Mob certainly has its hands in human trafficking, prostitution," Street said. "But the timing doesn't make sense."

"What do you mean?" Charlie asked.

"He means that whoever is hunting us was onto us even before we began poking our noses into these files and the parties," Margaret said.

"Exactly," said Street.

"So they began targeting us when?" Margaret asked. "With Lola in the trunk?"

"What about before that," Street said, "when you were fleeing those Scientology creeps?"

"How did you know about that?" Margaret asked.

"Who do you think T-boned their Galaxie?" Street asked.

Margaret smiled.

"I told you, Ike asked me to keep an eye on you two," Street said.

"Would the church thugs do this?" Margaret asked. "Just because we came to them and asked about Chris Powell? That makes no sense."

"Not if that's the reason," agreed Charlie, "but what if there's something we don't know about?"

Street was staring into his coffee.

"What, Isaiah?" Margaret asked.

"Is it hard to imagine that wholesome church crew involved in murder and prostitution?" Street asked.

"I don't have any problem imagining any group of men, clerical or not, involved in the unimaginable," she said.

"I'm just trying to picture what those clean-cut missionary-looking freaks and the skinny guy in the Hawaiian shirt would be capable of," Street said.

"Skinny guy in a Hawaiian shirt?" Charlie repeated.

"What is it, Charlie?" Margaret asked.

"What are you thinking?" asked Street.

Charlie took a sip of coffee. "I ran into a guy at Disneyland who matched that description."

"Horn-rimmed glasses?" asked Margaret.

Charlie nodded.

"That's Julius from the church," Margaret said.

"He was...not pleasant," Street noted, lighting a cigarette. "To be fair, I'd just plowed my car into his."

"So the church, or at least Julius—assuming it's the same man—is part of this too," Margaret said. "But how and why? This simply can't be just because Sheryl Ann and I pretended to be Chris Powell's sisters. There must be more to it than that. And either way, we need to figure out where Sheryl Ann is and find her before…"

Her voice trailed off; she was unwilling to speak the unthinkable.

Charlie picked up the 8-millimeter film canister and stared at it.

"I think," Charlie said, "we need to see what's on this film."

Street had a list of names, numbers, and addresses—all the information he needed for this mission. Charlie perused the names: Frankenheimer, Sinatra, Martin, Davis, Giancana, Janet Leigh, Les Wolff, Manny Fontaine, and more.

He pointed to the paper. "Why is L. Ron Hubbard's name crossed off?" he asked.

"He flew back to London the day after Margaret and Sheryl Ann paid him that visit," Street said.

Charlie handed the list back to Street and signaled for the check. They needed to make a phone call.

Thirty minutes later they were knocking on Frankenheimer's door. The director opened it, squinting as if he hadn't seen the sun in weeks. He welcomed them into his abode.

Frankenheimer was being sued for divorce by Carolyn, his second wife and mother of their two daughters. While rumors had swirled that he would end up with actress Piper Laurie, whom he had directed on *Playhouse 90*, he was currently living with the actress Evans Evans, who greeted the group.

"Sorry for how the place looks—John has been editing," Evans said. "I must look a fright!"

Both she and the house looked lovely, of course, which Charlie and Margaret made clear after they introduced them to Street.

"So what brings you here?" Frankenheimer asked as Evans guided them all into the living room.

"Do you have an eight-millimeter film projector?" asked Margaret, holding up the canister. She was struggling to contain her sense of urgency, knowing that soliciting help would be more easily accomplished if she operated according to LA's laid-back ways.

"Of course," he said. "Why?"

Margaret and Street looked at Charlie.

"Uh," said Charlie, "this is a long and complicated story. There's probably salacious, maybe even criminal, material in here. I wouldn't impose if this weren't incredibly important."

Frankenheimer mulled that over for a second, then led them to the edit room, a small converted bedroom, its windows covered by black sheets tacked to the wall. A giant framed poster for *Birdman of Alcatraz* leaned against the back wall next to a couch covered with notebooks and papers. To the side of the edit desk stood a folded-up portable movie screen.

"Now, this is an actual fright," Margaret said. She was trying to lighten everyone's mood, but she remained terrified about Sheryl Ann. They needed to figure out who was behind this, then maybe they could save her.

"It's a Bell and Howell," Frankenheimer said of the projector, sitting in a rickety chair in front of it. "Wish I could give you your privacy, but I don't let anyone else operate it. They break easy." He held out his hand and Charlie gave him the film. The director unspooled an inch or so, then loaded it in the machine. He looked at Evans, standing by the door, and she turned off the lights.

The film flickered on a small screen, roughly eight by ten inches. Charlie and Margaret pulled folding chairs closer, while Street and Evans stood behind them all. Outside the window beyond the black cloth, finches chirped at each other.

The first image was too bright to make out, but soon things came into focus: an industrial area, concrete and palm trees, a sunny day, a man in sunglasses and a light-colored suit walking purposefully.

"Is that Chris Powell?" Charlie asked.

Frankenheimer squinted. "Could be," he said.

The man walked upstairs into an office building.

"Is that United Artists?" Evans asked, leaning forward.

"Yes, it is," Frankenheimer said.

The film abruptly cut to another location, shot from inside a car: Chris Powell walking out of a different building and making his way down the sidewalk.

"That's the Church of Scientology," Margaret said.

Powell stopped in his tracks; someone had called his name from back at the house. He turned to see a thin man in a floral shirt and horn-rimmed glasses.

"That's Julius," Margaret said.

Charlie recognized him from Disneyland. He absorbed the news and was able to keep it clinical, intellectual. Julius had wanted to kill him; Charlie had done what he'd had to do. He had taken life before and knew that the guilt would come for him eventually, but in the thick of their continued battle—now to save Sheryl Ann Gold—he didn't have time to indulge the anxiety he felt. And oddly, perhaps because he'd been so drunk when he killed Julius, he didn't want a drink. He would have to soldier through.

The film cut to evening, an outdoor café, maybe at a hotel. Bathers in swim trunks walked by tables and palm trees. The light and the more formal dress of the diners suggested dusk.

"Where is that?" Evans asked.

"It looks kind of like the Miramar," Charlie said. "What other hotels have a view of the ocean?"

"Too many to name," said Frankenheimer.

The camera panned to the ocean, then followed a man in a short-sleeved shirt, untucked, as he walked from the direction of the beach into the restaurant.

"That's that guy, what's his name...um...Maheu. Remember him, Margaret? From Vegas? He showed up with Rosselli," Charlie recalled. "Didn't say much."

"And speak of the devil," said Street, pointing to the right corner of the small screen. "Isn't that Handsome Johnny?"

Everyone squinted at the figure as Rosselli's profile came into view. Rosselli turned to his left. Another familiar face popped up.

"Giancana," said Street. The Chicago mobster sported his usual thick glasses and deadpan expression as he followed Rosselli into the hotel.

"So Maheu met up with Rosselli and Momo," said Margaret. "So what?"

"I agree," said Charlie. "We know Maheu knows Rosselli, and Rosselli knows Giancana."

"So what are we missing?" Street asked as the film ran out and the tail end of the strip began clanging about. Frankenheimer turned the machine off.

"Wait, John," Evans said. "Can you roll that last scene again?"

"Of course, darling," he replied. He respooled the film and everyone watched Rosselli and Giancana walking backward out of the hotel, followed by Maheu traipsing backward in the opposite direction, toward the ocean. In the background the waves began in the sand and rolled toward the sea; birds flew in reverse.

"Look," Evans said, pointing at the ocean. "No sunset."

"I don't follow," said Frankenheimer.

"It's dusk but the sun isn't setting over the ocean," said Margaret. "This isn't Los Angeles. This isn't even the West Coast."

"But the palm trees," said Charlie.

"It's Florida, Charlie," said Evans.

"Miami!" exclaimed Frankenheimer.

"Darn it!" said Street. "I should have recognized it. That's the Fontainebleau."

"Which means what, though?" asked Evans.

"Which means the mobsters were meeting with other people too, and it had nothing to do with Hollywood," said Margaret.

Downstairs, the doorbell rang.

"I'll be right back," Evans said, leaving the room.

"Cuba," said Charlie. He looked at Margaret, who was staring back at him. Each reached over to touch the other's nose.

"What's that?" Street asked.

"'To see what is in front of one's nose needs a constant struggle,'" Margaret said.

"Orwell," said Frankenheimer. "This is going to be one hell of a story when you finally tell me."

"We're still figuring it out," Charlie said.

"Mobsters," Margaret said. "Miami."

"It's only slightly less plausible than the Chinese brainwashing an American war hero," Charlie said.

"Charlotte wanted us to see *all* of this," Margaret said. "Not just Chris Powell at United and at the church, but Miami too."

Frankenheimer smiled and stood. "I'm going to see who's at the door," he said just as Evans reappeared with Manny Fontaine.

"Manny, to what do I owe the pleasure?" Frankenheimer asked, shaking the publicist's hand. Fontaine was impeccably dressed in a casual Sunday-brunch outfit—blazer and pocket square, open blue oxford shirt, dark sunglasses, and loafers—but he seemed nervous.

"I need to talk to Charlie and Margaret," he said.

"How did you know we were here?" Charlie asked. He and Margaret were sitting on the back porch with Manny, the finches chirping and the salty sea air potent.

"You got a call through the studio switchboard; you weren't at your hotel," Fontaine said. "The guy on the other end of the line insisted that the operator patch him through to someone who would convey the message." Fontaine patted his forehead with a white handkerchief he withdrew from his pocket. "That job fell to me."

Charlie looked at Margaret. "That doesn't really explain how you knew we—"

"Right," Fontaine interrupted. "I was calling around to see if anyone knew where you were, and I called here."

The explanation seemed unlikely, but Margaret put her hand on Charlie's, a way to urge Manny to move on to *why* he was here. Surely, she thought, this had to do with the previous night's events and Sheryl Ann. Fontaine reached into his left jacket pocket and took out a pack of Marlboros.

"So what was his message?" Margaret asked.

Fontaine lit the cigarette, took a deep drag, and exhaled. "The man said: 'If you want your friend, bring the file tonight, including the film.'" He looked at Charlie. "What friend?" he asked. "What file? What film?"

Charlie glanced at Margaret, who asked: "Where are we supposed to bring it?"

"To the Santa Monica Civic Auditorium," Fontaine said. "To the Academy Awards."

CHAPTER TWENTY-FIVE

SANTA MONICA, CALIFORNIA

April 1962

"Good evening," Bob Hope said, "and welcome to Judgment at Santa Monica." He wore a white tie and tails and received a steady stream of polite laughter.

Sitting on the aisle in the Santa Monica Civic Auditorium in a rented tux, Charlie wondered whether the laughs were real or just a sign of relief that the interminable opening—national anthem, orchestral overtures, and a stem-winder by the chairman of the Academy—had ended. Charlie fidgeted.

"Yes," Hope said, "here we are at Santa Monica for the real *West Side Story*." More rote ha-has.

Margaret, in an aqua dress she'd borrowed from Evans, allowed herself a moment to stargaze. Having already said hello to Sinatra, Martin, Davis, and Lawford, who had seats in the first few rows, she spotted Paul Newman and Joanne Woodward, Warren Beatty and his girlfriend, Natalie Wood, Audrey Hepburn...

"In the lobby before the show everyone was shaking hands and smiling," Hope continued. "And in a few minutes the suspense will be over, we'll all know who to hate."

Ha-ha-ha-ha. Margaret pushed out an obviously fake laugh, amusing Charlie, who adored her occasional displays of discreet subversiveness. He knew that in a different situation, one less anxious, Margaret might commit to this fake laugh for the entire Hope routine just to please Charlie (and fend off her own boredom). Hope had quickly descended into tiresome inside jokes about studio bosses and pictures in perpetual turnaround and complaints about not being nominated for an award for his first feature film, *The Big Broadcast of 1938.*

"There's Fontaine," Margaret noted, back to business, pointing to the nattily dressed flack as he strode purposefully from the front of the auditorium toward them.

Apparently the man who had reached out to Fontaine that morning had also told him to be by his office phone at five p.m. to be notified on how the quid pro quo would go down. Presumably, Fontaine was about to share that information.

When Fontaine had told them that the handoff of the secret file in exchange for Sheryl Ann would take place at the Oscars, Charlie and Margaret were stunned. But Fontaine—who seemed to have a vague idea of what was going on—argued it made a certain kind of sense. Crowds and cameras could guarantee a layer of security.

Fontaine smiled as he approached now, holding out his arms approvingly as if to say, *Look at this wonderful display, look at these two handsome creatures.* He took a knee and whispered into Charlie's ear. "We're gonna go to the East Wing Meeting Room, which United Artists rented for a reception. Your name's on the list, so you should be able to get in. I'll come with you just to make sure it's okay. I don't know if anyone will be there. There's an ice sculpture of a rumble on a table with a long tablecloth. You're to leave the packet under there."

"A rumble?" Charlie asked.

"Like Jets versus Sharks," Fontaine said. "To honor *West Side Story.* It's a carving of two teenage hoods with switchblades. I don't know, it wasn't my idea. It looks pretty good, though." He realized he was talking nonsense. "We need to go."

Charlie turned to Margaret. "I need the file."

She reached into her purse and grabbed a folder she'd rolled into something resembling a tube so she could wedge it into her stylish barrel-pouch bag. Charlie received the baton and headed off with Fontaine. Margaret second-guessed their decision to leave the film canister back at Street's hotel suite; there was no room for it in her purse and it would have been too odd to carry it around at the Oscars. But now she worried that these thugs knew of its existence.

The auditorium was packed with ushers and publicists and members of various entourages who had somehow managed to access the event without tickets. There were also agents, managers, valets, and wardrobe and makeup artists. Fontaine steered them through the chaos to the meeting room. An usher checked their names and stepped aside.

"Charlie!" a woman cried from behind them.

Before they could enter the room, the congressman turned to see Janet Leigh, lovely in an emerald gown, drinking a Coca-Cola from a plastic cup and smiling as if she'd just won a gold statue.

"Already bored?" the actress asked.

Fontaine wiped an expression of irritation off his face and replaced it with a battalion of shining white teeth. "Hey, Janet!" he said. "Where's Tony? Oh, wait, never mind. Sorry!"

Charlie knew that a smart, calculating publicist like Fontaine would never let something so mean slip out by accident. His intent was to wound her; God only knew why. These people were vicious, as casually cruel as their counterparts in the snake-infested swamp of DC politics.

"Where are you guys headed?" Leigh asked, ignoring the question. "The event's in there." She thumbed toward the auditorium. Charlie looked at Fontaine.

"Just grabbing a drink," the publicist said.

Leigh hooked her arm through Charlie's as naturally as putting a hand into a mitten. "Well, say no more," she said. "Lead on."

Charlie looked at Fontaine, who shrugged, and they entered the East Wing Meeting Room. Fontaine walked ahead while Charlie whispered to Leigh.

Beyond the bartenders and cocktail waitresses, three stocked bars lined the walls, their shiny bottles arranged in neat rows. Charlie felt a twinge of—what? Love? Nostalgia? Regret? He wasn't sure. He changed his focus, examining the ice sculpture looming over a buffet of delicacies. It was even more impressive than advertised, a detailed rendering of Richard Beymer as Tony lurching and stabbing George Chakiris as Bernardo. A knife fight. Charlie recalled another knife fight on the banks of the faux Missouri river and that bilious taste in his mouth when it ended.

"Well, that's sure weird," said Leigh of the sculpture. She turned to Charlie. "Champagne?"

Charlie smiled, unsure. Fontaine grabbed her shoulder. "Why don't I escort Miss Leigh to the champagne while you admire the melting artwork?" Fontaine said. He steered Leigh away.

Charlie stepped closer to the ice sculpture, bent down to tie his shoe, placed the papers on the ground, and pushed them under the folds of the tablecloth. He stood and watched Leigh accepting a flute of bubbly from the bartender. Fontaine winked at him as they walked back to Charlie.

After a few minutes of conversation, Fontaine observed it was probably time to head back to their seats, so they did. Leigh lagged behind, chatting with a cocktail waitress, sipping her champagne.

A young woman in a caramel gown with a pink rose corsage on her wrist was sitting in Charlie's seat on the aisle. Upon seeing Charlie, she stood immediately. He was surprised but he eased back into his seat.

"She's a seat-filler," Margaret whispered to him. "That's

apparently a profession in this town. She and a whole bunch of other young people—all of them with pink roses as corsages or boutonnières—run around and make sure no chairs are empty should the cameras pan this way."

Onstage, Hope began mocking George C. Scott, a Best Supporting Actor nominee for *The Hustler*, for not showing up to the awards ceremony, which Scott had called "a weird beauty or personality contest" that corrupted the craft of acting. "He's sitting at home with his back to the set," Hope said. "He's the one person in our audience who will come back into the room for the commercials."

"Manny came back a minute later." Janet Leigh had suddenly appeared at Charlie's side and was whispering in his ear. "He grabbed the file. I followed him down the hall. He was with a man I didn't recognize. Also in a tux."

Charlie looked up at her. "Thanks," he said. Leigh smiled, waved at Margaret, and returned to her seat.

"Great idea to enlist her help," Charlie said. Margaret had called Leigh that afternoon and explained that they desperately needed someone to keep an eye on a folder Charlie was going to drop off. It was seriously a matter of life and death, one Margaret would tell her all about later over drinks, but for now she needed her help. Leigh was tickled to be recruited for actual cloak-and-dagger work, not just playacting, and immediately agreed.

"So what now?" Margaret whispered.

Charlie scanned the audience. "Keep our eyes open," he said.

"For?"

"I'm not exactly sure," he said. "An anomaly. Maybe someone returning to his seat after meeting with Manny. Or maybe Manny coming back to talk to someone here."

They surveyed the scene before them. Hope continued with his jokes. The audience sat there, responding obediently. The aisles were empty. In the corners and along the back of the auditorium, seat-fillers loitered. Up front, the orchestra began their next number.

Margaret pointed out a skinny young man wearing a pink rose boutonnière. He quickly stood to make room for a man returning to his seat.

"Who is that?" Charlie asked.

"Can't tell," Margaret said. "Should I check?" Charlie nodded.

She edged past him and exited the auditorium.

Outside in the hall, Margaret stood nervously for a second.

It was entirely possible that their foes intended to take the file and kill her friend Sheryl Ann Gold. But despite their precautions and plans for the night, it was clear that their enemies' response would depend on their own—and their friends'—ability to ad lib.

Margaret walked down the hall and up a few steps into a control room in the back of the theater. She opened up a heavy door to see a producer with a headset and a map looking out to the audience.

"Richard Widmark leaving his seat, copy," he said, glancing down at the map. "Row fourteen, seat H, gamma sector. Row one-four, seat H, as in *hotel*."

"Copy," said a voice from the radio.

Margaret took a step closer to the man. "You're sending out the seat-fillers."

The man jumped, startled. He looked at Margaret, quickly assessed that she was a harmless rich lady, and returned his attention to the audience.

"Yes, ma'am, our scouts sit up front and watch who's getting up, and we have four teams scattered throughout so the odds of a pan to the audience showing an empty seat are close to nil—"

He was interrupted by a call on his walkie-talkie. Margaret noted he had several devices for communication—a headset, two walkie-talkies, and probably more.

"Shirley Jones is on the move," the voice crackled.

"Copy that," said the man, scanning his seating chart. "That's row twenty, two-zero, seat B, as in *bravo*, also gamma sector, Carlos."

"Copy," said Carlos.

"This is so cool!" Margaret said.

The man smiled, happy to be appreciated and gushed over.

"You're single-handedly making sure that there aren't any empty seats!" she said, really selling the notion that this constituted an achievement. "Are a lot of people out of their seats?"

"Nah," he said with false modesty, motioning toward a hand-written list on a legal pad. "A couple dozen so far."

Margaret walked over and looked down at the list. She scanned the names, then tapped the pad twice with her finger, seeing one that she recognized, one that made sense.

"First time at the Oscars?" he asked, but she was already gone, the door slowly closing behind her.

CHAPTER TWENTY-SIX

SANTA MONICA, CALIFORNIA

April 1962

"Let's split up," Margaret whispered.

She and Charlie stood in the hall out of earshot of the ushers.

"You don't think we should wait for them to come to us," Charlie clarified.

"We need to get the drop on them," she said. "They have Sheryl Ann, and they think they have the file—the only advantage we have right now is the element of surprise. They think we're meekly waiting for them."

"We don't know where they are," Charlie said. "We don't even know who is a part of this, other than your speculation based on a name you saw on the seat-filler list."

"That's my point," Margaret said. "We need to figure it out. Back here in ten?"

Charlie nodded and they began walking in opposite directions.

The loudspeakers in the hall continued to broadcast the events onstage. Shelley Winters, who'd won a Best Supporting Actress award two years before for her performance in *The Diary of Anne Frank*, presented the award for Best Cinematography together with Vince Edwards—television's Ben Casey. It struck Margaret as crass to have Winters—who'd donated her Oscar to the Anne Frank House—alongside some cheesy TV doctor, but then again, Hollywood was crass. Ben Casey made as much sense on that stage as Howdy Doody or Mr. Ed. These people were acting. They were paid to pretend. None of it was real.

Margaret continued down the hall.

There—in the distance, near a scrum of photographers waiting to enter the auditorium—was Manny Fontaine walking solo. She followed him back into the auditorium as the audience seemed to suddenly tense up. A young man had jumped onto the stage and grabbed the microphone, interrupting Edwards and Winters.

"I'm the world's most famous gate-crasher," he said, "and I just came here to present Bob Hope with his 1938 trophy." He plunked down on the podium a miniature faux Oscar, the kind a tourist might purchase at a souvenir shop. Except for some gasps, the audience was silent.

"We'll give it to him," said Winters, trying to end the awkward moment, which was compounded by the gate-crasher's unfounded confidence that anyone found this remotely amusing or charming.

Margaret hadn't noticed much security around that night. There were a couple of boys in blue out front, and a private auditorium guard had surveyed the stars as they walked in. But now, with the gate-crasher on the stage, a dozen men—some in uniform, most not—appeared and rushed out to remove him. Margaret was pushed forward and collided with several seat-fillers and Fontaine himself. He turned to see who had rammed into him, then did a double take. To avoid being crushed as the crowd continued to bunch up at the corner of stage right, Fontaine walked up the stairs onto the stage and then behind the curtain, out of view.

"Crazy, huh?" Margaret said, right behind him.

Fontaine shot her a look. "Where's the real file?" he asked, dropping all pretense and barely concealing his rage.

Charlie made his way to the opposite end of the hall. No sign of Fontaine or anyone who might be involved. He opened a door marked NO ENTRY, revealing an industrial stairwell with worn steel railings and a buzzing fluorescent light. He entered, and the door closed behind him, but before it could snap shut a Santa Monica Police cadet burst in. He moved his right hand to his holster and unsnapped it. "Sir, what are you doing here, sir?"

"I'm, um," Charlie said, "just looking for someone."

"Sir, we need you out of here, sir," the cadet said. He put his right hand on his gun. Charlie studied him. He looked barely old enough to vote.

"Son, I'm a U.S. congressman," Charlie said.

The cadet panicked, drew his gun, flipped off the safety, and yelled, scared, "Sir, I need you to put your hands in the air, sir!"

The cadet was too hyped up to reason with. Charlie complied; who knew what could happen in such a situation? The cadet marched him out of the stairwell, down the hallway, and out the doors of the auditorium. He continued trying to explain that the kid had it all wrong, but fear had taken over the cadet and Charlie knew the best he could hope for was that an older, wiser officer would realize the insanity of the situation and release him.

But bedlam—not a wise police supervisor—was all that awaited Charlie outside the auditorium. Three police cars, lights flashing, pulled up onto the red carpet. Their occupants got out and ran into the arena, keys, cuffs, and weaponry jingling. More police stood in front of the doors, and sirens in the distance suggested yet more were on the way. Charlie was relieved when the cadet, perhaps desiring to be in on the real action, pushed him forward and released him like a fish before heading back into the building. Charlie stood for a moment.

"I need to get back in there," Charlie told the officers, holding up his ticket, but the men ignored him, stone-faced, forming a wall of blue. His heart sank as it dawned on him that he was now trapped outside with no idea what to do next.

"Where's Sheryl Ann?" Margaret asked.

They were tucked in the far corner backstage, away from the stagehands and dancers preparing for the next number.

"Safe," he said. She wondered if he was still attempting to convince her that he was a mere go-between in this evil trade.

"We're not giving you anything until she's back with us," she said, staring into his beady brown eyes.

"I'm not *running* this," Fontaine insisted. "I'm just trying to help."

Margaret raised an eyebrow skeptically. She heard a familiar voice and turned to see Sinatra in the wings, receiving last-minute hair and makeup assistance. A flock of two dozen dancers appeared, all wearing black tights, long red devil tails, and headbands festooned with pointed red horns. The ladies flooded past Margaret and Fontaine, their high heels clacking, and made their way through the scaffolding and sets and ropes attached to sandbags to their places around Sinatra.

Margaret was about to call Sinatra's name, but before she could, Fontaine grabbed her arm. At that moment, the curtains parted. "Ladies and gentlemen, here to sing Academy Award–nominated 'The Devil May Dance' from the motion picture *El Cid*, Mr. Frank Sinatra!"

As the audience erupted in applause, Margaret broke from Fontaine's clutches and ran, instinctively grabbing a rope tied to a sandbag as the curtains opened. Holding tight, she was whisked up into the rafters as Sinatra and his dancers made their entrance and an elaborate backdrop was lowered to the stage. Fontaine, stunned, watched her fly up like a superhero and then coolly step onto a narrow wooden plank, part of an intricate network of scaffolding out of the audience's view.

Okay, she thought, slightly amazed at what she had just pulled off, *I'm safe for the moment. But where the hell is Charlie? And what do I do now?*

CHAPTER TWENTY-SEVEN

SANTA MONICA, CALIFORNIA

April 1962

"*The first time the devil comes calling,*" Sinatra sang, "*he's wearing the face of someone you love / He tells you your hopes are just silly / With no mettle, you settle, what dreams were made of.*"

The audience fell under the spell of "the voice." His ice-blue eyes at once romantic and predatory, Sinatra held the stand tenderly and embraced the microphone. The set behind him, depicting hell—molten lava erupting from small eddies, dark clouds, demons torturing damned souls—had landed onstage beneath Margaret as she'd flown upward. Now, two stories above and out of view of the audience, she stood on wobbly scaffolding, her familiar urge to swoon over the crooner now shoved to the margins of her mind. She watched Frank below as he closed his eyes and sang:

> *Next time the devil rings your doorbell*
> *He's your closest of friends and he says look away*
> *The devil comes not bearing sharp horns*
> *Or with hooves now*
> *But with friendship, with memories*
> *A fragrant bouquet*

Wahhh-waaahhhh-wahh! From the orchestra pit, horns wailed and drums boomed, echoing throughout the building and causing the scaffolding to tremble slightly beneath Margaret's feet.

She looked around to get a better sense of the space she was in. Above and behind her were steel-framed platforms, sets for musical numbers that had already happened or would follow Sinatra, that could be lowered onto the stage. Above that, lighting, props, whatever, hung from the rafters. The hellscape backdrop that had landed behind Frank would soon be hauled up behind a thick black curtain that kept everything out of view. On the brick wall behind Margaret was a steel door from an exterior hallway on what must've been the top floor of the auditorium; anyone who opened it and stepped through would plunge to the stage. And between her and the crowd, Sinatra sang with every fiber of his soul:

> *You will not know the circumstance*
> *He hugs you, he loves you, and he enchants*
> *And the devil may dance*
> *The devil may dance*

Margaret negotiated the scaffolding, quickly realizing that at this height and with the musical performance so loud, no one could hear her. With each step she took, the scaffolding wobbled; it was secured only from above. Her safest path seemed to be to follow the beam she was on to another piece of scaffold, jump onto it, then onto another, which led to a sturdy-looking ladder leaning against the wall.

> *Third time the devil's at work now*
> *Success is yours if a corner you cut*
> *No one will be wise to this sad compromise*
> *No one but you and the ache in your gut*

A quickly pulsing bass-drum roll led into an extensive instrumental section—crying trumpets, sympathetic violins, disorienting cymbals. Beneath Margaret, the devil dancers sashayed around the stage and subtly gyrated. Slowly, cautiously, she walked to the end of the scaffolding, grabbed the thick black chain for balance, and began shifting her weight onto the next beam.

Above her, the random top-floor door opened, revealing the silhouette of a man. The figure was too stocky to be Charlie, but Margaret had allowed herself a moment of fantasy to imagine that it was. Where was Charlie now? The man retreated, then a different silhouette appeared, this one clearly Manny Fontaine, tux jacket gone, sleeves rolled up. He watched her for a moment, then, unbelievably, he leaped through the air and grabbed hold of a chain. It swung, and he shimmied down to the scaffolding she had just left with an athleticism that surprised her.

"The folder," he said.

The deep chords of a pipe organ filled the arena, conveying menace. The sound almost drowned out Fontaine's words. She stepped carefully along the narrow metal plank. *Goddamn high heels.*

"I don't have it," she said.

He jumped to the end of her plank, causing it to wobble and wheel. They both braced themselves as if they were surfing.

"You do," he said. "And we have your friend."

She suddenly realized he was right; she did have the real papers—not the forgeries Charlie had delivered earlier that evening. They were rolled up into a tube and crammed at the bottom of the purse she still had over her shoulder, though she wished she had remembered to ditch it along the way. She could just give him the papers, she thought, but then she'd have no leverage.

"Is this all worth it?" she asked, jumping to a lighting rig that swung back and forth like a carnival ride. "To cover up your sleazy sex club with little girls?"

"You're an idiot," he said, shaking his head in disbelief, continuing toward her like a cat.

The door above them opened again. From her new vantage point she could see the same man whose name had been recorded earlier as requiring a seat-filler, the United Artists executive Les Wolff.

"Cut the shit," Wolff hissed.

One slip and she or Fontaine or both of them could crash to the stage while tens of millions watched on television.

"You can chalk it up to hap-pen-stance!" Sinatra sang, the choreographed section over. Even in this state of hyper-attention to her balance and her goddamn high heels and the movement of the lighting rig, Margaret couldn't help listening, and she glanced down at the stage. He was really cooking now, impassioned and selling it with his whole heart.

> *You convince yourself and you're entranced*
> *And the devil may dance*
> *The devil may dance*
>
> *What does Satan have on you now?*
> *What have you done that fills with remorse?*
> *A corruption, an evil, you cannot disavow*
> *And you're fearing no clearing, so it's jail or divorce*

The realization hit her like a punch. "You're not just running a kiddie-sex ring, you're running a blackmail ring," she said to Wolff.

He didn't respond.

"You film everything!" she said. "And Chris Powell found out. Maybe through the church." She was deducing it all on the spot, but for the first time the randomness made sense.

"What a diabolical scenario," Wolff said. It was dark, but Margaret could discern a smirk.

"It's brilliant," Margaret said. "A bunch of predators—why not victimize them? They deserve it. And they won't complain about it!"

Wolff chuckled. "You've seen too many movies where the bad guy confesses everything before he kills the pretty girl," he said. "You're not Ingrid Bergman, and I'm not Charles Boyer. We just want the papers."

"The thing I can't figure out," Margaret continued as if he hadn't said a word, "was why you didn't just blackmail Powell."

Wolff didn't say anything.

"I'm a very bright woman, Mr. Wolff, I have a PhD in zoology. But I confess I don't have your genius when it comes to evil. Educate me."

Wolff laughed, amused by her effrontery.

"I'm serious—you've clearly outwitted not just me but this whole city. I don't know where you went to school or if you have much of an intellect, to be perfectly candid. I mean, I get that out here a deep tan, charisma, and a certain look—not to mention your ability to act the part—can go a long way. But I gotta admit, you're pretty brilliant with this stuff."

"You have to remember," Wolff said, "not everyone can be blackmailed. Some people care more about other things than about their careers or reputations, so blackmail doesn't work."

"And Powell loved Lola more than his career or reputation?" Margaret asked. "Or maybe he was just disgusted that you used her as a whore when she was a child."

"Who knows what motivated him," Wolff said with all the nonchalance of someone wondering if it might rain. "Just an actor. A speck of dust."

Margaret reached the end of the lighting rig, grabbed one of the chains, and jumped to the last remaining piece of scaffolding, causing the beam to sway wildly away from her. She clung to the chain as Fontaine, below, tried to grab her. He almost fell after attempting to lunge but caught himself and swung back onto the metal ledge, deploying his Special Forces training and Eighth Army Ranger expertise to help neutralize a mom trying to stop a child-sex-slave ring.

"I don't know where you think you're going," Fontaine said.

The water grew warmer o'er the span of a lifetime
Now it's boiling, you're roiling, you look to your friend
But that pal you saw dancing, advancing, romancing
Wants your soul, that's his goal, and this is the end

Margaret steadied herself, then inched along the swinging beam to the ladder. She was almost there when Fontaine jumped onto her scaffold. Margaret lost her balance; her flailing right arm hit the ladder, and she grasped a rung. Fontaine slid forward on his stomach, grabbed her by her hair, and yanked her toward him. She was still holding on to the ladder, which pulled away from the wall.

Margaret tried to hit him, claw him, scratch him, anything, with her free hand. She was holding on to the ladder with all of her strength, but she knew she couldn't do it for much longer. Part of her just wanted to give up.

She instinctively let go of the ladder and grabbed Fontaine's right arm, half dragging him off the swinging metal beam. He clutched Margaret by her hair but she tightened her grip on him and pulled herself up on his arm, relieving the pressure on her scalp. They hung there at this impasse for seconds, though it felt longer, neither sure of what to do.

Margaret looked up at the rafters of the building, then down at the floor, then at Fontaine. He appeared furious and terrified in equal measure.

She lunged for the chain holding up one corner of the beam on which Fontaine was lying. After grappling with it blindly for several seconds, she managed to release the clasp—it was the same kind she'd used on the bridle of her pony as a kid. The beam jerked and Fontaine let go of Margaret and grabbed at the air around him.

The next few moments for Margaret seemed to pass in slow motion; released from Fontaine's grip, she pushed herself away from the scaffold and lunged for the ladder.

Onstage, Sinatra was bringing the song to its boisterous, soulful climax, the deep menacing notes from the pipe organ serving as a musical rumbling of the beast, Satan, as Sinatra cautioned the crowd with his closing refrain:

> *Don't say you weren't warned in advance*
> *You can't hide safe ensconced in your manse*

Fontaine seesawed left and right.

> *You felt safe in his eyes at first glance*
> *And now inside you's a hate you can't lance*

The chain she'd released flew upward and the sandbag fastened to its other end shot down and hit Fontaine's head with the force of a speeding Mack truck.

> *And the devil may dance*
> *The devil may dance*
> *The devil may dance*

The song crescendoed under Sinatra's desperate pleas; cymbals crashed and bass drums erupted. A wild standing ovation from the audience drowned out the noise of Manny Fontaine and the sandbag hitting the floor.

Margaret grasped a rung of the ladder and clung to it as it thunked back against the wall. She settled herself, then carefully descended to the stage.

CHAPTER TWENTY-EIGHT

SANTA MONICA, CALIFORNIA

April 1962

Margaret reached the final rung as several dozen she-devil dancers exited the stage, grinning exuberantly as they poured into the wings. Les Wolff emerged from the dark, grabbed Margaret, and yanked her back into the shadows. She reached for the dancers around her and desperately shouted for help, but it played as a lark.

"I'm serious! Help me!" she called out, but Wolff laughed and held her tighter.

"Oh, Margaret, you're too much," he said, smiling, pulling her arm behind her back and jamming it up. He steered her toward the stage and down a separate hallway.

"Help!" Margaret cried. "He's kidnapping me!" Heads turned. Wolff slapped a hand over her mouth. She shook her head from side to side. Wolff employed his acting chops and Hollywood charisma. "It's true!" He laughed. "I'm kidnapping her!"

Margaret looked around wild-eyed, hoping to find a friendly face. But the actors, dancers, stagehands, and producers backstage were unsure about the sincerity of her panic and happily smiled back at Wolff, who was well-known and who, they knew, could make or break their careers. He pushed her past a cluster of official-looking men and women at a table full of gold statuettes.

"Help me!" she said, turning away from his big, hot paw. He

kept his hand over her mouth, smiling at the people glancing over at them. "She forgot to take her pill this morning," he said and shoved her through an exit door. It shut behind them and they entered a silent corridor beside a dark stairwell with an open door at the end of the hall.

Margaret bit his hand. "Fuck!" he exclaimed. He slapped her face, stunning her silent. "If you want to survive this," he said, "you need to behave." He grabbed her arm again, pulled it back behind her, twisted it harder.

The open door down the staircase led to organized chaos—theater ropes and bright lights and women with clipboards; some kind of press area for Oscar winners?

With her free hand, Margaret rubbed her reddened cheek. "Big studio boss going to kill me yards away from paparazzi?" she asked. "Seems unwise."

"You'd be amazed at what journalists don't cover," he said.

A tall young man in a black suit entered the stairwell from backstage. He had dirty blond hair and was clean-cut and chiseled, a Tab Hunter knockoff.

"Oh, good," Wolff said. "We need to figure out a way to get her out of here."

"Who are you?" Margaret asked. He ignored her.

"You need to move. Whoever wins Best Supporting Actor will come right through here in about ninety seconds," the young man said. He hopped down the stairs, then peered out the open exit door. "Easy path for us as long as she keeps her mouth shut."

"Which she'll do if she wants this to end well," Wolff said. "She'll give us the file too." With his free right arm, he suddenly grabbed her purse and violently yanked it from her, breaking its strap. He tossed the purse to the young man, who began rummaging through its contents. He plucked out a roll of papers as if he'd found the Dead Sea Scrolls, unspooled it, skimmed through, and gave Wolff a thumbs-up.

"So you did bring the real ones," Wolff said.

"Where is Sheryl Ann?" Margaret asked.

"We can tell you that as soon as we get out of here," Wolff said. "You and the congressman can go back to Washington, and everything'll be hunky-dory."

The poor man's Tab Hunter walked outside the exit door for a few seconds and quickly returned. "I see some friendly faces out there. They can help us escort her out."

"You think I'm going to let you drag me out that door?" Margaret asked.

"Yes, unless you trip and knock yourself unconscious and we have to carry you to safety," the young man said with a malevolent glare.

"Where are we anyway?" Margaret asked, though she seemed to be talking more to herself. Adjacent to the stage, on the side of the building—she was trying to get her bearings.

The wannabe Tab Hunter went down the hall to gather those friends.

"So Lola told Chris Powell, and he confronted you," Margaret said to Wolff. "And you killed him."

Wolff smirked. "No, I would never do anything like that," he said. "That's crazy."

"Well, of course *you* would never do it," Margaret said. "You're too important, too powerful. You probably haven't even clipped your own nails since Truman."

Wolff laughed. "That's probably true."

"No, you wouldn't do it," Margaret continued. "So someone else would do it. For you. Someone who has a lot of zealots at his disposal, people who will do whatever he tells them to do. Someone who heads an organization trying to curry favor with powerful people and recruit new members. Maybe a religious organization. Kind of."

272 • JAKE TAPPER

Wolff continued to smile at her. He was impressed, and Margaret saw she was right.

"So the church is wrapped up in this too," she said. "They're your henchmen."

He was staring at her, almost amused. "I'll tell you, you can say what you want, but those folks are smart. And efficient."

"You have"—she chose her words carefully—"a lot of friends. Cops, mobsters, church elders."

Wolff thought about that. "It's good to have friends," he finally said. "And that's why you and your husband can't win. Powerful men need a safe place to unwind, away from the prying eyes of the public and the press. Pursuit of happiness is in the Constitution, lady."

"Actually, it's in the Declaration of Independence," Margaret said.

"So you went to the better school," Wolff said.

"I don't think the Founders were condoning statutory rape," she said.

"Those girls are old enough to know what they're doing," Wolff said.

"And yet young enough to be blackmailed over."

Wolff sighed. "Your husband is a congressman. I'm amazed you're this naive," he said. "Leverage is the key to any negotiation, whether it's a three-picture deal or tax breaks. Everyone is always pursuing leverage."

"So that's why you stuffed Lola's corpse in our car—leverage. To get us out of town."

"I didn't stuff anyone anywhere," he said.

"My mistake." Margaret smiled. "But that's why you had it done, right? I mean, it's pretty brilliant. Appeared to be a Mob hit, and we're out here looking into Sinatra and the Mob…"

"Thanks, I thought it was pretty inspired myself," he said.

"You're remarkably smart for a former actor," Margaret said.

He laughed. "You interviewing me? You doing a feature for the *Times*?"

"Sort of," Margaret said. "You know how Charlie and I were working on *The Manchurian Candidate*?"

"Yeah, whatever, sure."

"You know John Frankenheimer, the director, and Joe Edmondson, his soundman?"

"I know John," Wolff said. "I don't much focus on the best boys and key grips."

"John and Edmondson have been trying to figure out a way to mike a scene from a distance. Keep the booms out of the shots. Wireless-microphone technology. Heard about it?"

She watched Wolff's face. His expression at first was confused; why was she talking about this? Then it clicked. A fire ignited in his eyes.

"No," he snarled.

With her free hand, Margaret reached into her décolletage. "Edmondson's been with us the whole time, listening on this microphone," Margaret said as she struggled to retrieve the device from underneath her dress. "He's been in a van outside the auditorium, recording this all."

"You fucking bitch," he said.

Margaret screamed, *"Charlie Marder!"* as loud as she could as Wolff grabbed her by the throat.

Down the stairwell and outside the exit door she saw the commotion as cops were shoved aside and paparazzi approached, waving cameras. Charlie barreled through the rapidly forming crowd. Wolff sensed the congressman rushing up the stairs and turned in time to see Charlie ram him against the wall. The studio executive, stocky and strong, was temporarily winded. But he quickly shook it off and tackled Charlie, and together they plummeted down the stairs.

CHAPTER TWENTY-NINE

SANTA MONICA, CALIFORNIA

April 1962

Charlie hit Wolff's sturdy mass so hard that he knocked the wind out of himself. For a few seconds he couldn't breathe and was worried a rib might have punctured his lung.

Wolff had no such problem. He sat up on the congressman's torso and began punching him in the face—once, twice. At first, Charlie wasn't able to respond, and then only defensively, holding up his arms to block the pummeling. The stab wounds from last night didn't make things any easier. Charlie could discern some sort of activity up the stairs but he wasn't sure what it was. All he could focus on were the blows of the big man who was sitting on his chest, making it difficult to breathe.

Margaret had fled, fueled by pure adrenaline, desperate to find help. Onstage a moment earlier, Shirley Jones had opened the envelope containing the name of the Best Supporting Actor.

"The winner is George Chakiris from *West Side Story*," Jones said as the orchestra began playing "Maria."

"I don't think I'll talk too much," Chakiris said onstage. "I just want to say thank you very, very much."

The orchestra played "Maria" again, and Chakiris walked backstage, toward Margaret. He was grinning from ear to ear as two women holding clipboards greeted him in the wings. They steered him toward the door, where Margaret approached him and held out her hands for the gold statuette. He automatically handed it to her, presuming she was with the Academy.

Margaret turned and ran back down the stairs, raised the Oscar high, and brought it down on Les Wolff's head.

She heard a crack.

The studio executive fell forward, unconscious.

Margaret wondered what had cracked. She examined the statue—there was a red smear on the edge of the base, which she wiped off with her thumb. Otherwise it looked fine.

Charlie pushed Wolff off him.

Margaret turned around to see George Chakiris and two women holding clipboards, all three with their mouths open.

"Here," Margaret said, handing the trophy back to a stunned Chakiris. "These things *are* heavier than they look!"

Within minutes the Santa Monica Police had cordoned off the stairwell. A perimeter had also been established backstage, police tape demarcating the area where Fontaine had landed. The police seemed focused on keeping everything as discreet as possible. They ensured that when Manny Fontaine and Les Wolff were carried out on stretchers, they went through a back door to ambulances parked in a restricted area.

While Charlie's wounds were tended by a medic, Margaret guided a detective to the van where Joe Edmondson, Frankenheimer's sound mixer, had set up shop and recorded her conversations with Fontaine and Wolff. Soon after, Charlie and Margaret found themselves seated in the back of a parked police cruiser.

Night had fallen on Los Angeles. From the back seat, Charlie tried to look in the rearview mirror, but there wasn't enough light for him to see. With her hands on his cheeks, Margaret turned his face toward hers.

"Nothing permanent," she said.

"I think he bruised my rib." He patted his side. "If I hadn't fallen down those stairs, I could've knocked him out."

Margaret smiled. "I'm sure you would've, sweetie."

They turned toward a tap on Margaret's window: Detective Meehan. She tried to roll it down but realized there was no way to do so. Likewise, the door wouldn't open from the inside.

Meehan smiled and opened the door. "One of the officers will be here in a minute to drive you back to the hotel, and we can talk there," he said. "Too many ears around here." He handed Margaret a plastic baggie of ice. "Give this to Charlie," he said. He tried to shut the door but Margaret stopped him.

"My friend was kidnapped!" she exclaimed. "Her name is Sheryl Ann Gold. You should see if she's at Wolff's house."

"Or Fontaine's," Charlie added.

Margaret gave Meehan a description of her friend and her home address. Meehan nodded, tapped the roof of the squad car twice, and gently shoved the door closed as he turned to leave them. But Margaret subtly stopped the door before the latch locked them in. She turned to Charlie.

"They're not going to lift a finger to find Sheryl Ann," she said.

Charlie looked out into the parking lot, which was buzzing with patrolmen, ambulances, and squad cars.

They calmly walked out of the restricted area and, ditching their car, took a back alley to the Georgian Hotel, which was about a ten-minute walk from the Santa Monica Civic Auditorium. Isaiah Street was waiting for them in his suite; he put his finger to his lips when he opened the door and whispered to them that Violet was asleep in the bedroom. Her mom—Margaret's sister—would be there to take her home the next day.

All three of them went out to the balcony, where chairs and

cigarettes awaited and Charlie and Margaret could catch Street up on every last detail of the night. They had to try to figure out where Sheryl Ann was being kept and how to save her. By the time they were done, the dawn light was beginning to illuminate the scenic vista before them.

Street opened his notebook. "I have addresses for both Wolff and Fontaine," he said. "But…" He paused.

"What?" Margaret asked.

"Well, frankly, neither man is dumb enough to stash a kidnapping victim at his house," said Street.

"So where would she be?" Charlie asked.

"Where are those documents?" Street asked. "Still in your purse?"

"Those were taken from me," Margaret said.

"But I have copies," Charlie said.

CHAPTER THIRTY

LOS ANGELES, CALIFORNIA

April 1962

Locals had feared that the shallow canyon known as Chavez Ravine would be choked with traffic for the first game at the brand-new eighteen-million-dollar Dodger Stadium, but the congestion never materialized. In fact, there were roughly thirty-five hundred un-filled seats for the Dodgers' face-off against the Cincinnati Reds.

Joey Tarantula cared not a lick about baseball—he was a boxing fan—but he was on hand with his camera to capture any celebrities in attendance. Henry Fonda, Milton Berle, and John Wayne had all been shuttled in right before the opening pitch at one p.m., and Mickey Rooney jumped up and down in the stands, providing Tarantula and the other shutterbugs with goofy photos.

It was a fancy park, the first one in the U.S. in decades to be constructed with private funds. There were rumors of New York strip steak and lobster thermidor in the Stadium Club, though Tarantula wasn't allowed access to it. But that was okay. The press box on the fifth floor had cigarette girls, not machines, and he was fine with the options of spaghetti or lamb in the press dining room. In fact, he'd had both.

At the top of the seventh inning, the score tied at 2 to 2, Wally Post of the Reds smashed a homer into the parking lot past center field. The enthusiasm in the stadium evaporated—"You can give them a nice park but that don't mean they still ain't bums," one scribe said to another—and Tarantula excused himself. Enough. Everything here was wholesome. In other words, nothing here to sell papers.

He hauled himself out to the parking lot and wedged his frame behind the wheel of his ten-year-old Hudson Hornet. The sight of some Mexican-American vendors selling bootleg Dodgers pennants reminded him that the city of Los Angeles had land-grabbed Chavez Ravine from the laborers and their families who lived here, the city's claims of eminent domain giving way to lying and bullying. Now, *that* had been a scandal.

The public didn't care; the victims were Mexican-Americans, and Angelenos wanted a new stadium for their new team. The snobs at the *Los Angeles Times* looked down on the likes of Tarantula, he thought, not only because of his appearance and coarse manner but also—perhaps primarily—because he worked for a scandal sheet. And yet, where were these would-be Jacob Riises when it came to the men, women, and children ousted from Chavez Ravine? All of the major newspapers had stood behind the Dodger Stadium project, Tarantula recalled with disgust. They fancied themselves speakers of truth to power but they quickly turned on the last holdouts, Manuel and Abrana Arechiga and their daughter Aurora, diligently regurgitating untrue claims pushed by the developers that the Arechigas actually owned many properties throughout the Los Angeles area.

It was all a lie, Tarantula thought as he merged onto the Santa Monica Freeway. A complete hit job. The Arechigas didn't own those other houses; their relatives did. But falsehood flies, and truth comes limping after it, as Jonathan Swift once said. A quote Tarantula knew well because those swift falsehoods were his bread and butter. But in this case, the folks who considered themselves true newspapermen, who sneered and grimaced at Tarantula when their paths crossed at events like this, were the ones who'd led the charge, smearing the poor Arechigas on behalf of the richest Angelenos, afflicting the afflicted, comforting the comfortable. Tarantula was so worked up over the memory, he didn't notice the car that had been tailing him from the moment he left the parking lot.

Other than his bosses, no one knew where Tarantula lived. *Hollywood Nightlife* was owned by USA Media Inc., a subsidiary of Information Technologies Ltd., which itself was owned by a larger conglomerate. Tarantula's abode had been purchased by a shell corporation owned by that bigger entity, incorporated in the Caribbean and run by Rosselli. Paychecks were sent to his work address.

The residents of his apartment complex, built in the 1950s, had no idea who he was. This thought comforted Tarantula every time he parked outside 301 Ocean Avenue, nondescript middle-class housing. The four dozen or so other tenants enjoyed their views of the Pacific Ocean and kept to themselves. An expectation of minding one's own business came with the territory; at least half the tenants were women who earned their livings on their backs, almost always with a studio-boss sugar daddy paying the rent, though sometimes they had to be more entrepreneurial.

As he walked up the stairs to his apartment, Tarantula felt like someone was watching him. He looked behind him, then resumed his climb to the third floor, breaking a sweat as he always did, beginning to gasp for air. He knew that his disgusting appearance was an asset to his desire for anonymity. Folks didn't want to know more about him and made every effort to forget his existence.

He opened the triple locks of the steel-reinforced door and stepped in. The television could be heard from the study. It sounded like religious programming. That was too bad; he should have done his guest the courtesy of at least putting the game on, even if the Reds were up. He peered into the study, made sure that his houseguest was still there, then waddled into the kitchen and grabbed a beer, an ice-cold Olympia, out of the fridge. After making two punctures in the top with a can opener, he plopped himself down on his armchair, took a sip, and nodded off.

Hours later, Tarantula awoke to the sounds of a bang and heavy glass cracking.

The window in his living room, with its panoramic view of the Pacific faintly lit by streetlamps three floors down, revealed no evidence of disturbance. He heard the smashing sound again; it was coming from the study.

He ran in. Sheryl Ann Gold was sitting where he had left her hours before, her hands and feet tied tightly to a chair, a dishrag gagging her. Her eyes were wide open, but she looked confused. That flustered him, since he had assumed she'd been up to something. But she hadn't moved, so there was no apparent way she could have caused the sound that—

Crack!

Tarantula turned to the window overlooking the alley and saw cracks in the glass spreading like a spiderweb. He dropped to the ground. Was someone firing a gun? Throwing rocks? He looked back at Sheryl Ann, who was shaking her head at him: *No, no, no.*

She had been well behaved since the creeps from the church had brought her over. Once Tarantula had told his contact at the church that he thought Charlotte Goode was up to something, it had all happened so fast. After strangling Goode, they watched the house and saw Margaret and Sheryl Ann come and go from her basement apartment and then followed them to the Hollywood sign. And luckily, ever since Sheryl Ann had been taken, she had kept quiet. Didn't act up when allowed to go to the bathroom or eat. He'd told her all she had to do was sit quiet and she'd be released as soon as Charlie and his wife gave back the docu—

Crack!

This time he saw what it was: an enormous black bird flying into the large bay window. It wasn't like when dumb sparrows mistake a clean window for the sky and accidentally kamikaze into it; no, this seemed predatory, intentional. Tarantula scurried over to the huge safe where the tabloid stored the most salacious, exquisitely damaging photographs and receipts, the evidence that kept Hollywood, Manhattan, DC, and Chicago cooperative. Material far worse than what was in the files at work. He had a gun in the safe too, and he began spinning the combination lock: three times to the right to 35, twice to the—

The window shattered as the black bird burst through, sending shards of glass throughout the room.

Sheryl Ann looked away, but pieces of glass hit her arms and face, leaving behind a confetti of small cuts.

Tarantula managed to open the safe. He reached for the gun but failed to grab it before the raven flew at him. He fell on his back and tried to fend it off, and suddenly there was another raven, and another, and another. Sheryl Ann watched, dumbfounded, as a conspiracy of ravens—two dozen or so—dived at Tarantula's face and body, pecking viciously. They left Sheryl Ann alone. Tarantula let out a high-pitched shriek as he tried to bat the birds away. It was such an insane spectacle, Sheryl Ann barely noticed when Isaiah Street appeared outside the window as if by magic, standing on a ledge, clearing the remaining glass away with a handkerchief, then stepping through the frame.

Street looked at Sheryl Ann, then at Tarantula wriggling on the ground as the ravens continued their attack, then back at Sheryl Ann. He held up one finger—*One second*—then ran into the living room. She could hear him opening the front door and others entering the apartment. Her heart pounded. She had no idea how many days she'd been here.

"Sheryl Ann!" yelled Margaret, running to her from the living room. She took the gag out of her friend's mouth. Sheryl Ann tried to speak but her throat was dry.

"Oh, thank God," Sheryl Ann finally said.

A high-pitched whistle emanated from the living room and the ravens began backing off Tarantula's bloodied face and body. They flew obediently into the other room, where Symone LeGrue stood holding deer jerky in one hand, a large cage in the other.

"Good job, Archie," Charlie said to the first bird, which had assumed its rightful place on LeGrue's shoulder. Charlie proceeded into the study, where Street was using a knife on the ropes constraining Sheryl Ann, whom Margaret was consoling.

Charlie looked down at Tarantula's face, which had been pecked to shreds. His bulbous throat was a mess of deep red hash. He was gurgling. Minutes left, max.

Charlie noticed the open safe. He turned to Margaret and Street.

"Why don't you make sure everyone gets home safely," Charlie said. "I'm going to have a look around."

CHAPTER THIRTY-ONE

LOS ANGELES, CALIFORNIA

April 1962

Charlie turned the key in the lock of his Miramar suite but Detective Meehan opened the door from inside.

"We've been waiting for you," the detective said, an irritated expression on his face. "For a day."

Charlie entered the room and looked at his watch: 4:33 a.m. "You've been waiting for us inside our room since yesterday?" he asked.

"We've had a presence in the lobby," Meehan said, walking back to the living room; Margaret was sitting alone on the couch, having returned from Tarantula's before her husband, who'd stayed behind to sweep the place of their fingerprints and look for anything that might prove useful. Street had dropped off Sheryl Ann Gold, then Margaret, then returned to his hotel. "After your Irish exit from the Santa Monica Civic Auditorium."

"We had things to do," Charlie said.

Meehan rolled his eyes, sat down, and asked them to tell him again what had happened at the Oscars, which they did. It took some time because they had to explain events from the night before—Disneyland and the Hollywood sign—though in Margaret's telling, Sheryl Ann escaped with her. There was no need to add the body of Joey Tarantula to their long list of offenses.

"All for these documents?" Meehan said, holding them up after Charlie had produced them from his inside jacket pocket and handed them to him. "Suggesting that...let me see if I have this straight—"

"Suggesting that, led by Wolff, the studios have been holding parties for VIPs at which they pimp out underage girls," Margaret said.

"But why?" Meehan asked. "This town is crawling with young girls with stars in their eyes, eager to make any connection. Why pay for it?"

"The money's for their silence as much as anything else," Margaret said.

"And Wolff was filming it all," Charlie said. "For blackmail."

"You have proof of any of that?" Meehan asked.

"You do," Margaret said. "You have the wireless-mike recording of Wolff, the files we just gave you, Charlotte Goode's murder..."

"We've given you more than enough testimony and evidence to begin investigating these sick parties," Charlie said.

"Did Charlotte ever tell you she'd had any confrontations with anyone?" Meehan asked.

"Like, half the city," Margaret said. "But you must know that, Detective."

"I do," Meehan said. "But Stanley Kubrick didn't kill her for being rude on a red carpet."

"No, probably not," Margaret allowed. "Her coworker, what's his name—"

"Tarantula?" Charlie asked casually, mispronouncing his name on purpose. "The guy Lawford introduced us to that time?"

"'Tah-ran-*too*-lah,'" Meehan corrected him.

"Yeah, him," Margaret said. "That Tarantula guy was furious at her for that. I was in the bathroom and overheard everything."

Meehan wrote that down in his little leather-bound notebook.

He took a sip from the glass of water Margaret had given him and perused his notes from earlier in their conversation.

"So you had help in this little caper of yours," he said. "Janet Leigh did spy work for you and John Frankenheimer's sound guy hooked you up with recording devices."

"And because of him, as Charlie noted," Margaret said, "Santa Monica Police have the tape of Les Wolff confessing to having Chris Powell and Lola Bridgewater murdered to hide this pedophile ring."

Meehan scratched his head. "Where did"—he checked his notes—"where did Charlotte Goode get these documents from anyway?"

"*Hollywood Nightlife,*" Margaret said, exasperated. Was he really this dumb or was he just pretending?

But Meehan didn't ask the natural follow-ups: Why didn't they publish any of it? A huge scandal involving studios, predators, and the wealthy and well-connected—what journalist wouldn't run with such a story? He turned to another page in his notes.

"And, Congressman Marder, you say Peter Lawford and Sammy Davis Jr. can corroborate this trip to Disneyland? What you say you witnessed there?"

Charlie nodded. "Yes, but please be—"

"Discreet, yes, I know," Meehan said, writing down the names. "Okay, well, that's a lot to work on. Thanks for your time." He nodded, stood, hitched up his pants, and exited the room, joining two uniformed officers waiting for him in the hall.

Charlie and Margaret passed out on the bed, fully clothed, utterly spent. It would be dawn in a few hours.

Charlie woke shortly after ten that morning; Margaret was showered and dressed, and a delicious room-service breakfast was waiting for him. The sight of his beaten-up mug in the mirror was something of a shock, but closer inspection suggested there'd be no permanent scars. The stab wounds in his back were still gruesome, but they were healing acceptably, as was his bruised rib. He began brushing his teeth and grooming himself. As he did, from the combination living room/dining room of their spacious suite, he could hear music from the hi-fi system, the soothing sound of Nat King Cole singing "Let There Be Love":

> *Let there be you, let there be me*
> *Let there be oysters under the sea*

A light breeze blew through the room and Charlie remembered meeting Cole at the 1956 convention for Eisenhower. It was a pleasant memory of a simpler time. But then Cole's crooning stopped, and there were voices, a conversation. Charlie wiped his face with a towel and walked out to see what Margaret was listening to.

—but it didn't happen, said one man.

Well, Havana today, said a second. *It's not so simple anymore. It's Iron Curtain, basically.*

Charlie looked at the hi-fi. "Is this the radio?" he asked.

Margaret shook her head and pointed to a record spinning on the turntable. "That's the LP Sinatra gave you."

"Is that…Giancana?" Charlie asked.

Margaret nodded, just as puzzled as Charlie.

It's not for lack of trying, said a third voice.

"Rosselli," said Margaret.

You made it sound a little simpler in Miami, said Rosselli. Charlie looked at Margaret, who shrugged.

We also didn't want your money, said Giancana. *We wanted to do it for our country.*

And we still do, said Rosselli.

"Where did this record come from?" Charlie asked.

They're really on eggshells now, with the missiles, said the third voice. *Don't do it if there's even a chance of fingerprints.*

Quiet, here comes Frank's boy, said Giancana, prompting both Charlie and Margaret to cringe. *What a horrible guy.*

This was followed by the faint voice of George Jacobs: *Gentlemen, dinner will be ready in twenty minutes. Is there anything I can get you until then?*

Another round, said Rosselli.

I'm not staying for dinner, said the third voice.

Whatever you wish, Mr. Maheu, said Jacobs.

A few seconds later, Giancana said, *Fuck it, I'm going to the pool*, and the record went silent.

"Maheu," noted Margaret.

Charlie walked over to the turntable and tried to read the label as it spun. It took him a second to make sense of it: "'Devil…May…Dance…demo.'"

Margaret shrugged again. "It was in the car with all that stuff I brought up," she said.

Charlie said, "Frank told me to listen to it, but I forgot."

"What do you think they were talking about? Some operation in Havana."

"Who *is* Maheu?" Charlie asked. He couldn't shake the idea that he knew him somehow from before this adventure.

"So both the president of the United States and the Mob want Castro dead," Margaret said.

"You wouldn't believe the crazy stuff the CIA has proposed to get rid of him," Charlie said.

"Such as?"

"Honey, you know it's classified," he said, thinking of one CIA plan that involved an exploding cigar, another where special salts dusted onto Castro's boots would cause his iconic beard to fall out. "Crazier than any beach thriller."

"The-U.S.-government-asks-the-Mob-to-whack-Castro preposterous?" she asked.

Charlie thought about it. "That's a good question, given Bob's supposed war on the Mob."

The record began hissing as the needle hit dead-air grooves. "What's on the other side?" Charlie asked. He walked over to the phonograph and flipped the LP, then picked up the blank white cardboard sleeve that had held the record. A glimmer of pink caught his eye; he pulled out a piece of notebook paper, clumsily ripped, on which was written in loopy script:

JACK
WH NA8-1414
FE8-2325 — Georgetown
Plaza — PL5 7600 EL5-4878
Apt- 277 Park
Hyannis — Yachtman hotel Spring 5-4600
Palm Beac TE2-7117 TE3-4622 (Ev. TE3-5761)
EVELYN
1440 Rock Creek Ford Road NW apt 402 TA9-5552
3132 16th st NW #507 AD4-5745 MA4-1011 MA4-9335
HO2-5632
SOB — 362 CA7-0064 x3341
Priv RE7-0064

"What the hell is this?" Charlie asked.

Margaret took it from his hand. "A woman's handwriting," she observed. "Is Jack who I think it is? Yes! That's their old Georgetown number!"

There was a low hum as the needle hit the LP and then a conversation that couldn't have been more different in tone from the previous one.

So when will you be here again, Sam? The weather is so nice. A woman's voice, intimate and intense.

You could have stopped over on your way to Washington, said the man. Giancana. *If it wasn't for me, your boyfriend wouldn't even be in the White House.*

Oh, Sam, said the woman.

"That's Judy" Margaret said. "From Vegas!"

"Holy cannoli," said Charlie.

None of that means I don't miss you, Judy said with longing in her voice.

"Yikes, is she…sleeping with…the president *and* a Mob boss?" Margaret asked.

"And maybe Frank too," Charlie said. "I mean, why was she at the Compound?"

"So the president is having an affair with a woman who is simultaneously having an affair with a Mob boss and a movie star with Mob ties," Margaret said, "while his brother the attorney general is cracking down on organized crime."

"Nice work if you can get it," said Charlie. He pointed to the pink paper. "This must be hers."

"'In front of one's nose,'" Margaret said.

"You think this is what Dad was talking about?" Charlie asked. "Bobby sent us to look into Sinatra and the Mob but that was a decoy? Like the First Army Group? And it was all this other stuff with the Mob that he wanted us to find—that Judy was sleeping with Sinatra, Giancana, and the president? That the CIA contracted the Mob to take out Castro? I mean, it stands to reason that he thought we would discover much more than just Frank slinging highballs with made men."

"And it makes sense that he wouldn't trust Hoover's FBI to tell him what was going on," Margaret said.

"If the president is sharing a mistress with Giancana, there's no chance Hoover doesn't know."

"And Frank meant to give you this record?"

"Only one way for us to find out," said Charlie.

CHAPTER THIRTY-TWO

RANCHO MIRAGE, CALIFORNIA

April 1962

There was no answer at Sinatra's Beverly Hills estate, so Charlie called the Compound in Rancho Mirage. George Jacobs answered and confirmed that his boss was there with some friends but said he couldn't come to the phone.

"He's not doing so hot?" Charlie asked.

"Mr. S. went from being the First Friend to just another greaser from Hoboken," Jacobs said.

"He's still upset," Charlie told Margaret after he hung up.

"About losing the Oscar to 'Moon River'?" Margaret asked.

"No, no, about the Kennedys treating him like a vat of bad moonshine," Charlie said.

Their drive through the unending developments and lush mountains of western Los Angeles, Pomona, Rancho Cucamonga, and San Bernardino took two hours, but they were two hours without mayhem, without interruption, without anyone trying to kill them. The city seemed to stretch beyond any limits other than the mountain ranges, every town blurring into one giant sprawl.

"I've noticed you haven't had a drink," she said.

"It's only been a day," Charlie said, his eyes on the road, though he was happy she'd noticed.

"More than that. The return from Disneyland, the trip to Isaiah's hotel, Frankenheimer's, the Oscars, saving Sheryl Ann." She ticked each one off. "Unless you snuck one when I wasn't looking?"

"No, ma'am," he said.

"That's a lot of stress, to say nothing of how sore your face and back must be," she said.

Charlie nodded. "And rib," he added. She reached over, grabbed his right knee, gave it a squeeze.

"You don't need to hide anything from me," she said.

"I know," he said.

"Your drinking—" she began.

"I know," he said. "I know, but I might need—"

"I'm always here," she said. "I know you can do it."

"It's been one day."

"And that's how we will do it," she said. "One day. Then another. Then another."

The burden of Charlie's weaknesses and Margaret's disapproval didn't vanish in that moment, but it became a task they would finally tackle together.

Most of their time in the car, however, was spent meticulously analyzing every detail of the information they'd gleaned. By the time they arrived in Rancho Mirage, they felt as though they had a decent theory of the case.

"Enough to bluff our way into the actual facts, at any rate," Charlie said. Margaret smiled with anticipation.

They got out of their car; Jacobs answered the front door.

"Mr. S. is in the pool," he said and shook his head. It had not been going well.

Sinatra lay splayed on a raft, his eyes hidden behind gold-accented aviators, his skin a deep bronze. He wore a red short-sleeved shirt, but it was unbuttoned, and his gut protruded over his aqua bathing suit. It was impossible to tell if he was awake.

Charlie and Margaret looked at each other, unsure what to do.

"If he woulda called me to say that it was politically difficult to have me around, I'd've understood," Sinatra suddenly said. "I don't want to hurt him. But he couldn't even bother to pick up the phone."

"Politicians are selfish pricks, Frank," Margaret said. "Take it from the wife of a four-term congressman."

Sinatra laughed. "You got a good one here, Charlie," he said. "Can I get you anything? Coffee? A snack? A drink? It's five o'clock somewhere."

Margaret sat on the edge of a chaise while Charlie took off his shoes and socks, rolled up his pant legs, and stuck his feet in the water.

"It's nice," he told his wife.

"Not as hot as the Jacuzzi, though, I would assume," she said. He grimaced and Sinatra winced. "Oh, Charlie, I'm just kidding," she added. "Frank, Frank—it's fine. Charlie told me the whole story."

"So let me ask you kids, speaking of the whole story," Sinatra said, his face aimed at the beating sun. "What did you tell that little Puritan? Bobby."

Charlie looked at his wife, then back to his host. Sinatra knew that Charlie was there as a spy for Kennedy? How the hell did he know?

"Oh, don't be surprised," Sinatra said. "I put two and two together after your talk with George."

"I'm sorry," Charlie said. "They have my dad at Sing Sing."

"I know," Sinatra said. "So what did you tell him?"

"That you have friends with rough pasts but we didn't see any evidence that you were involved in anything illegal," he said. "And we told him that the president should stay here," Charlie lied, because who wanted to deal with the ire?

"I know a lot of people," Sinatra said. "If the Justice Department were to look into every acquaintance I have who's got dirt under their fingernails, they'd be pretty busy."

"So is that why you gave me that recording?" Charlie asked. "And that pink paper?"

"We assumed that was from Judy's diary," Margaret said. "With all of the president's contact information."

"You were trying to show me that the president's got some dirty fingernails too?" Charlie asked.

"Ain't his fingernails that's the issue," Sinatra said. "The Kennedys should look in the mirror."

"And you want Charlie to hold up the mirror?" Margaret asked. Sinatra smiled.

"So clear something up for us: Who *is* Maheu?" Charlie asked.

"He's just one of these guys," Sinatra said. "Go-betweens. Was FBI, did intelligence during the war, makes a lot more dough as a contractor. Works for that nutball Howard Hughes. Does a ton for the CIA. The Agency got him to ask Rosselli to whack Fidel."

"And you introduced them?" Margaret asked. "You're quite the yenta."

"I met Dulles through Jack at a thing a couple years ago," Sinatra said. "Dulles asked me to introduce Maheu around, I did, and business was done. This was before the Bay of Pigs."

"But aren't you worried about getting in trouble with the law?" Margaret asked.

Sinatra raised his head. "Jack *is* the law," he said.

"So Jack himself asked the CIA to ask the mobsters to kill Castro?" Charlie asked.

Sinatra lifted up his sunglasses, looked at Charlie, then lowered them again. "I thought you did oversight in the House," Sinatra said.

"Kennedy would claim he didn't know about any of this, anyway," Margaret said. "Plausible deniability."

"And Bobby wouldn't necessarily know," Charlie said. "CIA wouldn't tell FBI. Competing agencies, plus everyone hates Hoover. Though Bobby would learn enough to wonder."

"Bingo," said Sinatra. "You're getting warmer."

"So that's what Bobby actually wanted us to investigate," Charlie said.

"Warmer still," said Sinatra.

"Why not stop it?" Margaret asked.

Sinatra cocked his head like a cat contemplating whether to pounce. "What do you want me to do?" he asked. "CIA works for Jack, Momo's a friend, Castro's a tyrant. You want me to stop the president from protecting us from a Commie? That's not my table, Charlie."

"So why do you have a recording of Rosselli, Giancana, and Maheu talking about this all?" Margaret asked.

"Frank wired this whole place, ostensibly in preparation for the president's visit," Charlie recalled. "And got the private recordings pressed into an LP."

"Yep," said Sinatra.

"You know about the files Charlotte Goode gave us, right?" Margaret asked.

"Is that the stuff Manny and Les chased you down for?" Sinatra asked. "About those twisted parties?"

"So you knew about that too?" Margaret asked.

"I know about Charlie taking the boys to that freak show at Disneyland," Sinatra said. "As for Les Wolff, it's been said he likes beautiful women as much as I do, and many of them are on the younger side. But I didn't know any more than that."

"Younger side?" asked Margaret.

"Yeah, some guys like 'em young, what can I tell you," Sinatra said. "I mean, Natalie Wood was a teenager when Bob Wagner married her. Chaplin's wives were kids. Elvis has that young girl squirreled away for him once she's ripe. It's not my thing, as you know, but good Christ, look at *Lolita*!"

"It's reprehensible," said Margaret. "I just don't even remotely understand this. Fifteen-, sixteen-year-olds are children."

"Don't tell me, Mags, I'm with you," Sinatra said. "Tell society."

"What did Peter and Sammy tell you about Disneyland?" Charlie asked.

"Private party on Tom Sawyer's Island," Sinatra said, "young girls. Rich guys. You got in a fight. Saved your niece. That's about it."

"But you say you've heard about Les Wolff and girls on the younger side," Margaret noted. "What had you heard?"

"Just...y'know...that he liked some of these younger girls," Sinatra said a bit defensively. "You see them at parties and restaurants, they could be anywhere from fourteen to twenty-four."

"But you never did anything about it," Margaret said. "A major player in your world serving up children to gluttonous robber barons and you just shake his hand when you see him?"

"Look—I didn't know any of that for a fact—" Sinatra didn't know how to handle what she was throwing at him. Since Ava Gardner, no woman had challenged him. "It was whispers. When Errol Flynn got pinched and tried for statutory rape, even goddamn William F. Buckley joined the—what was it called? The initials were ABCDEF—"

"American Boys' Club for the Defense of Errol Flynn," said Charlie.

"Right. Margaret, you're being ridiculous," Sinatra said, clearly growing irritated. "*I* didn't do any of this crap."

"But that's the whole point, isn't it, Frank?" Margaret said, her voice rising as well. "You're sulking like a teenybopper because JFK wouldn't stay here, and meanwhile you're surrounded by sin and corruption and you expect the world to think you're oblivious to it all! Giancana, Rosselli, Maheu—"

"Margaret," Charlie cautioned.

"—and now you are simultaneously asking me to believe that, one, you didn't know what Les Wolff was up to," she continued, "and, two, that *everyone* knew what Les Wolff was up to *and* all sorts of men like girls—"

"Okay," Sinatra said, "watch your mouth!"

"You deserve your due," Margaret said. "You've done a whole lot for civil rights, Francis, forcing the integration of the Strip in Vegas, the anti-discrimination movie. You've pushed for Black musicians to be treated equally and with respect. But you couldn't stop the Kennedys from blackballing Sammy from the inaugural gala, so I guess how effective you are is an open question—"

"You can fuck right off," Sinatra said, "you have no idea what I've done, the risks I've taken!"

"But," Margaret continued, "given that half the goddamn country is female, including Nancy and Tina, what have you done for women—not only women, damn it; *girls*—who are human chattel in the suite next door?"

"I told you, goddamn it, it's all been rumors! What, do you want me to chase down every bit of gossip I hear? I'm not Jack Anderson! What do you expect me to do? This is Hollywood!"

"You sure do a lot when you see discrimination against Sammy and Nat King Cole!" Margaret said. "And that's great! That's laudable! But what about fifty percent of the population?"

"*What the fuck are you on my dick about?*" Sinatra yelled, boiling like a teakettle.

"My *goddamned niece* was missing," Margaret exploded, "she's a *child* and she had fallen into the underbelly of this city of *wanton sleaze* and you never did a thing to help me, you never lifted a *finger* or even expressed one single sentiment of concern! You just sat there—"

"*Who the holy fuck do you think told Charlotte to get you those files, you dumb cooze?*" Sinatra erupted. "*It was me. I did it!*"

Charlie and Margaret sat stunned, mouths agape, shocked not just that Sinatra had confessed to what they'd theorized might have been the case but that their plan to enrage him into an admission worked. They could barely contain their smiles.

Sinatra, still worked up and in a lather, was almost panting.

He looked at Charlie and Margaret, exhaled, thought about what had just transpired—it was rather out of character for Margaret to yell at anyone—then smiled.

He took a moment to collect himself. He exhaled dramatically.

"You are the smartest fucking broad I have ever met," Sinatra finally said.

Margaret grinned. "To be fair, this was a team effort," she said.

"Look, Frank," said Charlie, "we're just trying to figure out how all the pieces fit in the puzzle here."

"So you told Charlotte to give us this information," Margaret said.

Sinatra took another moment.

"I own a piece of *Hollywood Nightlife*. Dino and me."

"Nothing bad appears about you or the Rat Pack in their pages," Margaret observed. "Which tends to set the tone for all the others."

"Bogie told me once," Sinatra said, "he said, 'You have to remember one thing, Frank, there's only one way that anyone can fight a newspaper, and that's with a newspaper.' I got sick of the garbage smearing me. They called me a Red. They called me a Commie. Punching Lee Mortimer didn't do anything. So I bought a paper. Secretly. We hired away the sleaziest but best slime merchant in town, Tarantula, who hired Charlotte Goode—who lived up to her name—and a staff of thirty or so other talented freelance hacks, and lo and behold, we became the circulation leader. Crazy, I know."

"So you kept a lot of scandal out of the news," Charlie said.

"Kept a lot of lies out of the news," Sinatra corrected him.

"And you also learned a whole bunch of other stuff," Margaret said.

George Jacobs appeared with a new glass of Jack Daniel's on the rocks for his boss. "Do you want me to bring it to you?" he asked. "I don't mind—it's hot."

"Sure, if you don't mind, George, that'd be swell," Sinatra said.

Jacobs—in shorts and a white polo—walked past Charlie, down the stairs, and into the pool to deliver the drink. "You two want anything?" he asked. Margaret looked at her watch; it was just after two p.m.

"What do you have?" Charlie asked.

"Anything you want, Congressman," Jacobs said. "Bourbon, scotch, rye, vodka, gin, tequila, rum, cognac, brandy, liqueurs, beer, white wine, red wine, rosé, and every mixer known to man—orange juice, pineapple juice, cranberry, lemonade, sour, margarita mix, Bloody Mary—"

Charlie peeked at Margaret, who was watching him with interest.

"Just a plain lemonade would be fine," he said. "Margaret?"

"Water would be grand, George," she said.

"And George," Sinatra added. "Bring that present I have for him." He pointed at Charlie.

Sinatra took a sip from his glass, then waited until Jacobs had gone back inside. Margaret looked up to the spectacularly blue sky, completely cloudless, with a lone hawk soaring in the distance.

"I learned some things, yes, although I don't run *Nightlife* anymore," Sinatra said. "Rosselli rewrote the original contract and took it over. There wasn't much I could do about it. Soon the fellas realized that the hacks collected a lot of information that powerful people would pay to keep out of print. The business became much more about what wasn't published. Catch and kill, they call it."

"Do you know about everything they catch?" Charlie asked.

Sinatra took another swig. "No, not at all. Johnny promised to keep me out of it. But I knew enough to try to help you with your niece. I asked Charlotte to look into Itchy Meyer, to look into whatever rumors there were about Les Wolff, to get you whatever they'd compiled on these young girls through the years."

"Was Rosselli sitting on the skinny on Les Wolff? For money?" Margaret asked.

"For money, for power, for real estate, for influence, for favors, for trade, for barter," Sinatra said. "I don't know what Rosselli has on this girl sex ring in terms of proof. I didn't know Wolff killed Powell and Lola to shut them up until Charlotte told me she suspected as much."

"So you knew her," said Charlie.

"We talked on the phone sometimes," he said.

"Who killed her?" Margaret asked.

Sinatra shrugged. "I dunno. Who killed her, who killed Powell, who killed Lola and stuffed her in your trunk? I gotta believe Wolff ordered it all but I don't know if Rosselli did the deed or if those Scientology creeps did it."

He clammed up and nodded as Jacobs reappeared with his re-fill, a water for Margaret, and a lemonade and a manila folder for Charlie. Jacobs handed over the drinks to the couple, but before he could give Charlie the folder, Sinatra stopped him.

"No, bring it to me, along with a smoke, if you got one," he said.

Jacobs waded into the pool again carrying a small round tray that held the new drink and the folder and, from his pocket, a pack of Marlboro Reds. Sinatra lit the cigarette with the gold lighter Jacobs handed him at the precise moment he needed it. He inhaled deeply, then took a gulp of whiskey. Then he lit the folder on fire.

"Mr. S.—" protested Jacobs.

"I got it, George," Sinatra said, holding up the cardboard so as to catch as much of the flame as possible.

"What is that?" asked Charlie.

"The only two remaining photographs and the negative of your very brief moment in the hot tub with Lola," Sinatra said, dropping the destroyed remnants back onto the tray.

"Thank you, Francis," Margaret said.

"Not a thing, Margaret," Sinatra said. "This is a good boy you have here. And now this photo is gone forever."

"That's an incredible gift, Frank," Charlie said. "Thank you."

"No worries, pally," Sinatra said, raising his glass.

"Makes me feel sheepish asking one last favor of you, though."

"Don't," Sinatra said. "Shoot."

"I had a tough reelect in 1960, as you might imagine, with your boy at the top of the ticket," Charlie said. "I was worried, so I did something I normally wouldn't do: I took my dad's advice. I hired a consultant he recommended."

He looked at Margaret, to whom he had finally told the story during their drive. She nodded supportively.

"He was a slippery fella," Charlie said. "I didn't know how slippery until after the election when I had to cash the metaphorical checks he wrote. One of the unions in my district had come through in a big way. They now wanted some favors."

"Right," Sinatra said. "Momo said something about this that night in Vegas."

"It started small—stuff to help workers," Charlie said. "Better workman's comp, oversight on safety regs. Then one night came the ask I dreaded: to pressure the U.S. attorney, who I had helped get the job, to back off on an extortion case."

Sinatra smirked. He could relate. "What did you do?"

"Nothing yet," Charlie said. "I put it off for as long as I could, hoping it would resolve itself."

"That's what I did too," Sinatra said.

"He also drank a lot more," Margaret added. "Which was similarly effective."

Sinatra laughed. "That was also part of my brilliant plan."

Charlie smiled. "And then this all happened and I've been busy. But now that it's over…"

"Right," said Sinatra. "The bill collector still gonna come calling."

"I need you to tell Momo something," Charlie said. "Among the documents in the safe at Tarantula's was a file about him." Sinatra raised his eyebrows. "All sorts of details about all sorts of stuff." Sinatra waited.

"I left it on the ottoman in your living room," Charlie said. "It's his. Tell him if these terms are acceptable, I would like it if we could be square. I don't want to hear from his friends in New York anymore. If the union goes another direction next election, that's fine."

"Got it," Sinatra said. "I shall pass it along."

They sat there for a few minutes as the sun started to duck behind Mount San Jacinto to the west.

"Frank?" Margaret said meekly. "I want to ask you—and I don't want to seem at all unappreciative, but I want to ask…"

"Go ahead, baby doll," said the singer.

"What I don't get is, if you know about all of these crimes, blackmail or murders or the girls or what have you, why didn't—why don't you go to the police?" she asked.

Sinatra looked at her incredulously. "You think the police don't know?" he asked.

"What do you mean?"

"You think that, say, Detective Meehan isn't part of this?" Sinatra asked. "Why do you think he had such a hard-on for you and Lola? If Bobby hadn't vouched for you, you'd be in Alcatraz by now."

"Jesus, really?" Margaret asked. "Meehan?"

Sinatra laughed. "This whole system stinks, girlie. You think the police have no idea about Les Wolff's bobby-soxer parties?"

"They do? But—"

"Come on," Sinatra said. "You think all these powerful men do whatever the fuck they want with whatever girl they want and law enforcement doesn't know? C'mon!"

Sinatra looked at Charlie and Margaret as if he were the serpent in the Garden of Eden. They were worse than naive; they were stupid.

"That's the grand hypocrisy of me being tagged by Bobby as some bad boy because I've stayed friends with some guys from the old neighborhood," Sinatra said. "The fact that gossip kept TP away from here, so instead he went to Bing's, where he shlonged Marilyn. And don't get me started on Cuba!"

Charlie looked at the aging crooner. At first, Sinatra had reminded him of his father at his apex, savvy and charismatic, a man of action and energy who made things happen, someone whom he wanted to impress. But five months into this adventure, Sinatra looked defeated and deflated as he floated in the pool. He still reminded Charlie of his father, but in his later, sadder years, when the weight of all that he had done and accepted was taking its toll whether or not he understood why.

"So the cops are in on it?" Charlie asked. "All of it?"

"Depends what you mean by 'in on it,'" Sinatra said. "Some of them know. Hubbard's group and the Mob helped Les Wolff. But beyond that, I have no details. I don't know who did what and what was illegal and what was just sleazy."

"No details," Margaret said, "just that bad men exist and worse men carry out their orders."

Sinatra raised a glass to her. "Bad men exist and worse men carry out their orders—and the rest of us avert our eyes," he said. "Everyone comes out here to dance with the devil, and the devil may dance. That's what they should have up there on that hill, instead of fucking *Hollywood*."

CHAPTER THIRTY-THREE

NEW YORK CITY

May 1962

Sitting among the other fifteen thousand Democratic fat cats, a freshly coiffed President Kennedy beamed as he was feted on the occasion of his forty-fifth birthday.

Maria Callas sang from *Carmen*. Members of Jerome Robbins's Ballets USA dance company performed. Shirley MacLaine and Jimmy Durante, Harry Belafonte, Bobby Darin. Mike Nichols and Elaine May made the thousand-dollar-a-seat crowd roar by reading fake telegrams, one of which was addressed to a "Mr. Francis X. Kennedy" on the occasion of his forty-fifth wedding anniversary. The punch line—it had been sent by the CIA.

What a thing, to have an intelligence agency mocked for unintelligence, Charlie thought as he and Margaret watched the festivities from backstage. Sinatra's absence from the event was stunning, though no one talked about it.

They had been given this special access by Lawford, who said that his brother-in-law the attorney general wanted to talk while in town.

And now here was Lawford, onstage, presenting the president with his present.

"Mr. President, on this occasion of your birthday, this lovely lady is not only pulchritudinous but punctual," Lawford boomed. "Mr. President…Marilyn Monroe!"

A rowdy applause filled the Garden; a spotlight hit the stage. But Marilyn did not appear.

She was backstage, looking nowhere near able to perform.

Charlie and Margaret were yards away, feeling a mix of sorrow and revulsion. Whether because of pills or booze or both, Marilyn could barely stand. She had literally been sewn into her Jean Louis gown—flesh-colored, festooned with rhinestones—and she was obviously wearing nothing underneath. Her beauty was ethereal but she reeked of desperation.

Lawford returned to the microphone and coughed, embracing the awkwardness. "A woman about whom," he said to laughter, "it truly may be said she needs no introduction. Let me just say—here she is!"

A bass drum solo began and then quickly ended as the spotlight again highlighted only her absence.

"But I'll give her an introduction anyway, Mr. President," Lawford said to more laughter, "because in the history of show business, perhaps there has been no one female who meant so much, who has done more—"

Lawford was surprised by the men and women in the audience applauding before he had cued them to do so; he turned to his left and saw Monroe had strode out and in fact was already almost at the lectern.

"Mr. President!" Lawford quickly said, "the 'late' Marilyn Monroe!"

Sporting an enormous helmet of blond hair and blindingly white teeth, Marilyn slunk to the microphone. For a few seconds it wasn't clear that she knew what to do.

Margaret grabbed Charlie's hand and gripped it tight as if

somehow she could squeeze wherewithal into Marilyn's brain by twisting Charlie's fingers. Soon, however, the starlet began her breathless cooing into the microphone.

"*Haaaa-pee…birth…day…tooo…youuuu,*" she sang. "*Haaaa-pee birthdayyyy…tooo-oooo-oooo yooooouuuu—*"

The crowd ate it up, hooting and grunting as if she were a burlesque dancer at a stag party.

"They think it's sexy," Margaret said to Charlie, "but she's about to pass out."

After the performance, Lawford offered Charlie and Margaret a ride in his limo to a private gathering at the Upper East Side town house of United Artists chairman Arthur Krim.

"We have our own ride," Charlie said. "We'll meet you there."

The van that took them to East Sixty-Ninth Street parked as close to the house as possible. They thanked the driver and walked up the stairs of the enormous brownstone. Margaret gasped as they were led from the reception room to the atrium, decorated in neo–French classical walnut. Krim stood on the patio in the center of the property. Charlie and Margaret looked up to the glass ceiling, which revealed stars in the inky night sky.

Weeks before, Manny Fontaine's dead body had been discovered in a back alley of a Hollywood neighborhood known for homosexual activities. Les Wolff's hospital stay had been publicly attributed to a mild heart attack. As he shook Arthur Krim's hand, Charlie wondered how much the studio chief knew about what had actually happened.

"Good to see you, Congressman," Krim said. "And Mrs. Marder, lovely to have you here. Thank you both so much for helping with *The Manchurian Candidate.* I hope it isn't too controversial when it comes out! John feels very hopeful."

Charlie stole a look at his wife, who was nodding charmingly. She had predicted that Krim would act as if he knew nothing. Whether or not that was the case, he wouldn't behave any other way.

"How's Les?" Margaret asked impulsively.

"Recovering nicely, thank you," Krim said. "I'll tell him you send your best." He smiled broadly. "Bob's upstairs," Krim said, walking to the atrium where Charlie glimpsed Marilyn Monroe.

As she and her husband reached the second floor of the luxurious brownstone, Margaret was stunned by the detailed balustrade, multipaned windows, and gigantic oak arch. Charlie patted her on the back; she had been after him to upgrade to a more spacious town house as the kids got bigger.

"I can always leave politics and become a fixer for the Mob," he whispered. "Or get into show business."

"Please, not show business," she said.

The attorney general sat uncomfortably on a couch ashing a cigar into a dish. Amid the ottomans and fancy sofas stood Addington White pouring drinks at a bar and, in a wheelchair across from Kennedy, Charlie's father, Winston. In a suit and tie.

"Dad!" Charlie said, striding over to his father to hug him. His dad gave his back a weak pat. Winston smelled clean, freshly showered. He was thin but looked much healthier than Charlie would have expected.

"Your dad is a free man," Kennedy said as White handed him a scotch on the rocks. "We appreciate the information you've given us."

"So the whole time, you really wanted to know what the CIA was up to," Margaret said. "'To see what is in front of one's nose needs a constant struggle.' You cared about the Mob, but not Sinatra's relationship to it—only the CIA's."

"I wanted to know anything going on with Mr. Sinatra's less savory friends," said the attorney general.

"Including Judy Campbell?" Charlie said.

"That I would have preferred to have learned before Director Hoover, but I didn't," Kennedy said. "He sat the president down a few weeks ago and told him that the woman who'd been calling on him all over—Palm Beach, Hyannis Port, the White House—had other paramours."

Winston grunted, and Charlie looked at him. It had actually sounded like a chuckle.

"It's okay, Winston, you can knock off your charade," Kennedy said.

Winston couldn't contain his smile. "You son of a bitch," Winston said. "How'd you know?"

"Oh, we'd long suspected that you faked the stroke to avoid answering questions," Kennedy said.

"What the—" Charlie said.

"I was going to tell you, son," Winston said. "I only got sprung earlier today. When I got home, I called you, but no answer. Then I made some other calls and learned that you found out what these hooligans suspected but couldn't prove: that the Kennedy administration is more in bed with the Mob than Frank is. And then, speaking of beds, your brother—"

Kennedy held up his hand. "First off, let's differentiate between the administration and the CIA," he said. "And let's not pretend that you didn't have a hand in connecting the Agency to Giancana yourself. That you and Maheu aren't thick as thieves."

Aha! Charlie thought. *That must be why Maheu seemed familiar.*

"All of this could have been avoided if you'd just cooperated, Winston," Kennedy said. "But you wouldn't."

"Why not just ask us directly for help?" Charlie asked.

"Why not just ask a Republican congressman who's a pain in the ass on the Oversight Committee with a dad who has his own questionable ties to move to Hollywood and spy on a movie star and a gangster?" said White. "To help a president he doesn't support? Jeez, that's a tough one."

"We weren't sure we could trust you," Kennedy said.

"Well, now you know," Charlie said. A couple weeks before, back in Washington, Charlie had given Addington White a debrief of their Los Angeles misadventures, leaving out only a few incriminating details. He was surprised to hear the evident mistrust, which he'd seen no evidence of in DC, expressed so clearly.

"Either way, now you have more leads than you thought you'd have," Margaret added. "I guess there's nothing criminal about Sinatra and his friends partly controlling *Hollywood Nightlife*, but at the very least you should be able to launch an investigation into Les Wolff."

"Not much to investigate," Kennedy said. "He hanged himself earlier today."

An uncomfortable silence hung in the room now as well.

Unspoken went the inescapable conclusion that there would be no follow-up investigation. Powerful forces had once again reached out from the shadows, killed one of their own for self-preservation, and disappeared.

"What about the Church of Scientology?" Margaret asked. "Hubbard?"

"Nothing directly ties Hubbard or the church as an institution to any of this," Kennedy said. "It's a church, so we can't just raid them. Their desire to have celebrity adherents is not evidence of conspiracy. And both witnesses to alleged wrongdoing—Julius and Wolff—are gone. No one has even seen Julius since April."

"Speaking of loose ends," White said, "do you know anything about who might have wanted to kill yet another *Hollywood Nightlife* reporter? His body was found in his home a few weeks ago."

Charlie and Margaret shook their heads no.

"What about all that evidence we gave you of the larger

conspiracy in the studios for these parties? The photos and the receipts?" Charlie asked.

"And the recording of Les Wolff talking about it all?" added Margaret.

"We have the tapes," White said. "We will be reviewing. And looping in the appropriate authorities, LAPD, et cetera."

"What if they're in on it too?" Charlie asked under his breath.

"What's that?" White asked.

"You heard me," said Charlie.

"How's your niece?" Kennedy asked Margaret, tabling the other discussion.

"She's okay," Charlie volunteered after it became clear Margaret wasn't going to respond. "Back in Ohio with her folks."

Winston stood up from his wheelchair, shoved it away, and walked over to the table where a decanter of scotch beckoned. He looked surprisingly limber.

"So what's up with Sinatra?" Winston asked, bemused. "The Irish princes throw the Sicilian jester into the moat?"

Kennedy rolled his eyes at Winston, an opponent whom he could barely control even after he'd imprisoned him.

"We're going to stop that picture he wants to make about the nukes landing on North Carolina," White said, slurring a bit, maybe a bit in the bag. "That script you shared with us."

"Why?" Charlie asked.

"It's classified," White said.

"That's enough, Addington," Kennedy said.

Charlie and Margaret exchanged looks. What on earth?

"So was that Sinatra sending you a message via a screenplay?" Winston asked. "A hint that he's willing to expose truths? Motivated by revenge? Or maybe he's still deep down the same bleeding-heart Commie-symp he's always been?"

Kennedy ignored the question.

"So," Winston said, filling the dead air, "are you going to call off Giancana's hit on Castro?" He smiled, finishing his glass of scotch. He was having fun.

Kennedy didn't respond. White looked down at the ground.

After a second, Kennedy stepped toward Winston. "As you know, that wasn't a Justice Department proposal."

"Surely it would be a war crime, which would be an issue of concern, I would think, for an attorney general," Margaret jumped in. "Western societies don't contract mobsters to kill foreign leaders, even despots."

Winston laughed aloud. "We don't?" he asked, pouring himself another drink. "C'mon, little girl."

Kennedy turned to Charlie, exasperated, as if Charlie had any control of either his father or his wife. "We can't talk about this here," he said.

"Should we talk instead about what the Agency got your brother to sign off on a year ago?" said Winston. "And how you kept the press from reporting on the Alabama National Guardsmen killed in Cuban airspace after that goat-fuck?"

Kennedy frowned at Winston.

"Wait, what?" Charlie asked.

"They didn't declassify that for you, did they, on your Oversight Committee?" Winston said. "Four Alabama Guardsmen were killed during the Bay of Pigs. Castro's even got one of their cadavers on ice as proof of an American invasion."

"The Agency is responsible for any number of fiascos," Kennedy agreed. "Some of these were plans that President Eisenhower signed off on. It's one of the reasons we got rid of Dulles."

"Dick Bissell is your problem, Bobby," Winston said. "Not Dulles."

"Don't I know it," he replied.

"Hoover is just as dangerous," White added.

"It's all a goat-fuck," Kennedy said, "as Winston says."

"Look at you, one of the most powerful men in the world and you're acting as if you're powerless," said Margaret with equal parts disgust and disappointment in her voice. "You fought so hard to get to the White House. Why? How are you different from Nixon? What are you doing with this power?"

From downstairs echoed the bubblegum voice of Marilyn Monroe, followed by deep laughter.

"Are you fighting for women to be seen by your brother as something other than depositories?" Margaret asked, motioning vaguely toward the stairs. "What about civil rights? I voted for your brother. What was it all for? Anything other than power?"

Kennedy sat down on a maroon felt sofa; a table lamp shining on his face deepened the bags under his eyes. He rolled his tongue around in his mouth as if there were something stuck in his molars. Addington White sat down at the edge of the sofa.

"We probably should head downstairs and meet our guest of honor," White said. "Not to mention we need to show the Krims some love." He turned to Margaret. "You really should meet Mathilde Krim. She does cancer research at Cornell. Very impressive woman." Kennedy and White began walking to the door.

"Before you go," Charlie said, "I have to ask…"

Kennedy put his hands on his hips, irritated in anticipation. "Yes?"

"Are you just going to abandon Sinatra?" Charlie asked. "You and your brother? After all he did for you?"

"Abandon?" Kennedy asked.

"You treat him worse than you treat Marilyn," Margaret said.

"He'll be fine," White said.

"You didn't even invite him to this birthday party!" Charlie said.

"He's a big boy," White said.

"What's he going to do?" asked Kennedy. "Become a Republican?" He chuckled; it became a snort. The concept was completely alien. "Endorse Goldwater?"

"Join Ronnie Reagan's crusades against socialized medicine?" White added, joining in the laughter. Kennedy patted his arm and the two walked out of the room giggling. "We'll see you downstairs," White said as he exited. Then he quickly returned: "Obviously, nothing we discussed here leaves this room." He emphasized the point with a grave expression, then left again.

Winston looked at his son and daughter-in-law. He was in better spirits than Charlie had seen him in years.

"I'm going to mingle," he said. "Maybe Miss Monroe needs a dance partner. I haven't had any fun in months!" Winston chuckled, knocked back his drink, and practically bounded out of the room and down the stairs.

Charlie put his arm around his wife. "You okay?" he asked.

"I'm fine," she said. "How do you feel about giving the dirt from Tarantula's vault to those barracudas?"

"Fine," he said. "I feel even better that we kept copies for ourselves for insurance purposes." He held her tight. "And speaking of insurance," he added, subtly caressing her under her bra, where there was a microphone and wire leading to a small device on her lower back. "Testing, one, two."

"I sure hope Isaiah got all that out in the van," Margaret said. "Thank God he's more technologically savvy than us."

"You hearing all this, Isaiah?" Charlie said, knowing his friend wasn't able to respond.

Charlie looked at his gorgeous, brilliant wife and smiled. She kissed him tenderly on the lips. He grabbed her hand and intertwined their fingers as they left the room and began walking down the stairs.

"What's up?" he asked Margaret, repeating Dwight's morning ritual.

"My sense that this is all finally over," she said.

"What's down?" he asked.

"My anxiety," she said.

"What's right?" he asked.

"Very little in this world," she said, "but we can keep trying."

"What's left?" he asked.

"For us to go home," she said.

And so they did.

SOURCES AND ACKNOWLEDGMENTS

This is a work of fiction, but obviously many of the characters and events depicted are real. In addition, some of the dialogue is from actual conversations. Resources from which I drew information, inspiration, and sometimes dialogue include, in alphabetical order:

Bare-Faced Messiah: The True Story of L. Ron Hubbard, by Russell Miller. London: Sphere, 1987.

Breaking My Silence: Confessions of a Rat Pack Party Girl and Sex-Trade Survivor, by Jane McCormick with Patti Wicklund. St. Paul, MN: Rapfire Press, 2007.

The Cinema of John Frankenheimer, by Gerald Pratley. New York: A. S. Barnes, 1969.

The Dark Heart of Hollywood: Glamour, Guns and Gambling Inside the Mafia's Global Empire, by Douglas Thompson. London: Mainstream Publishing, 2013.

Dino: Living High in the Dirty Business of Dreams, by Nick Tosches. New York: Dell, 1992.

Double Cross: The Explosive Inside Story of the Mobster Who Controlled America, by Sam and Chuck Giancana. New York: Warner, 1992.

Frank: The Voice, by James Kaplan. New York: Doubleday, 2010.

Frank Sinatra: A Life in Pictures, edited by Yann-Brice Dherbier. London: Pavilion, 2011.

Frank Sinatra: An American Legend, by Nancy Sinatra. Santa Monica, CA: General Publishing Group, 1998.

Going Clear: Scientology, Hollywood, and the Prison of Belief, by Lawrence Wright. New York: Knopf, 2013.

Handsome Johnny: The Life and Death of Johnny Rosselli, by Lee Server. New York: St. Martin's, 2018.

His Way: The Unauthorized Biography of Frank Sinatra, by Kitty Kelley. New York: Bantam, 1986.

Inside Scientology: The Story of America's Most Secretive Religion, by Janet Reitman. Boston: Houghton Mifflin Harcourt, 2011.

JFK and Sam: The Connection Between the Giancana and Kennedy Assassinations, by Antoinette Giancana, John R. Hughes, D. M. Ozon, and Thomas H. Jobe. Nashville, TN: Cumberland House, 2005.

The Manchurian Candidate, by Greil Marcus. London: British Film Institute, 2002.

Mr. S: My Life with Frank Sinatra, by George Jacobs and William Stadiem. New York: HarperCollins, 2003. (Please note, the offensive songs Dean Martin and Sammy Davis Jr. sing to each other in the book are from here.)

My Story, by Judith Exner as told to Ovid Demaris. London: Circus/Futura, 1977. (Conversations with Sinatra, Kennedy, and Giancana, as well as the Kennedy phone numbers, are taken from this book.)

The Power and the Glitter: The Hollywood-Washington Connection, by Ronald Brownstein. New York: Pantheon, 1990.

Rat Pack Confidential, by Shawn Levy. London: Fourth Estate, 2002. (The Formosa and Giancana transcript is taken from this book.)

Robert Kennedy and His Times, by Arthur M. Schlesinger Jr. New York: Ballantine, 1978.

Sammy: An Autobiography, by Sammy Davis Jr. and Jane and Burt Boyar. New York: Farrar, Straus, and Giroux, 2000.

Sinatra: All or Nothing at All, documentary film by Alex Gibney, produced by Alcon Television Group, Jigsaw Productions, and the Kennedy/Marshall Company, 2015.

Sinatra: Behind the Legend, by J. Randy Taraborrelli. New York: Grand Central Publishing, 2015.

Sinatra and the Jack Pack: The Extraordinary Friendship between Frank Sinatra and John F. Kennedy—Why They Bonded and What Went Wrong, by Michael Sheridan with David Harvey. New York: Skyhorse, 2016.

Sinatra: The Chairman, by James Kaplan. New York: Doubleday, 2015. (The Giancana and Rosselli transcripts are taken from this book.)

Sinatra: The Photographs, by Andrew Howick with a foreword by Barbara Sinatra. New York: Abrams, 2015.

Sinatra on Sinatra, compiled by Guy Yarwood. London: W. H. Allen, 1982.

Tell It to Louella!, by Louella Parsons. New York: Putnam, 1961.

Tippi: A Memoir, by Tippi Hedren. New York: William Morrow, 2016.

What Have They Built You to Do?: The Manchurian Candidate and Cold War America, by Mathew Frye Jacobson and Gaspar González. Minneapolis: University of Minnesota Press, 2006.

Why Me? The Sammy Davis, Jr. Story, by Sammy Davis, Jr. and Jane and Burt Boyar. New York: Farrar, Straus, and Giroux, 1989.

Yes I Can: The Story of Sammy Davis, Jr., by Sammy Davis, Jr. and Jane and Burt Boyar. New York: Farrar, Straus, and Giroux, 1965.

Some other sources include:

Automobile information was offered by David Burge as well as Joe Sheppard in the *Daily Mail* online, "Drive Me to the Moon! One of Five Vintage Italian Cars Given to Members of Frank Sinatra's Rat Pack Emerges for Sale for £300,000," August 13, 2017.

Description of the Tombs came from description of visitation from James Rhem et al., Plaintiffs, v. Benjamin J. Malcolm, Commissioner of Correction for the City of New York, et al., Defendants. No. 70 Civ. 3962. United States District Court, S. D. New York. January 7, 1974.

Palm Springs was described in *Explorer's Guide: Palm Springs and Desert Resorts*, by Christopher Paul Baker, Explorer's Great Destinations 2008. Sinatra's Rancho Mirage compound was covered in *Architectural Digest* in December 1998 and *Palm Springs Life* on November 6, 2014.

Information about the Daisy (yes, I know it was actually founded in 1962, after this book takes place) from martinostimemachine .blogspot.com. As a general note, I took liberties with events that occurred in 1961–1962. "Boys Night Out," which members of the Rat Pack sing in December 1961 within these pages, wasn't released by Sinatra until March 1962. I similarly played with the release dates of *Lolita*, the Jimmy Dean song "PT-109," and so on.

Information about and attitude of John Wayne drawn from a 1974 BBC interview with him and from two UPI stories, "Sinatra Blasted for Writer Choice," March 1960, and "Sinatra vs. 'Big John,'" May 1960.

Dialogue from the Rat Pack show re-created in the book is largely drawn from a 1963 concert, *Live at the Sands*, with additional information from Mary Manning, "Rat Pack Reveled in Vegas; Revered by the World," in *Las Vegas Sun*, May 15, 2008.

The relationship between Ambassador Kennedy and Gloria Swanson is detailed in *The Fitzgeralds and the Kennedys: An American Saga*, by Doris Kearns Goodwin. New York: St. Martin's, 1991.

The January 1962 Los Angeles snowstorm was written about in "Freak Southland Storm Brings Snow, Sleet, Hail," *Los Angeles Times*, January 22, 1962.

The death of attorney Jerry Giesler was covered by the Associated Press, "$800k Estate Left by Giesler," January 20, 1962.

Some of the early days of Scientology were covered in "'Have You Ever Been a Boo-Hoo?'," by James Phelan, *Saturday Evening Post*, March 21, 1964.

"Project Celebrity" information was taken from "Scientology Founder L. Ron Hubbard Offered Rewards for Celebrity Recruits in 1955," by Kirsten Acuna, *Business Insider*, July 19, 2012.

Shirley MacLaine talked about some of the difficulties filming *The Trouble with Harry* here: https://talkfilmsociety.com/columns/beginners -guide-to-alfred-hitchcock-the-trouble-with-harry-1955.

The police poster at the LAPD headquarters was described by Alan Nicholls in News of the Day, *Age*, August 22, 1961. The police bulletin came from https://www.scpr.org/programs/offramp/2017/03

/03/55421/la-city-archive-the-lapd-s-police-bulletin-opens-w/. The death of Officer Riegel is from *Valley Times*, July 3, 1961, https://www.odmp.org/officer/11267-policeman-sidney-riegel.

John Frankenheimer discussed some of his experiences filming *The Manchurian Candidate* for the Criterion Collection.

Some details about filming *The Birds* came from Mark Mancini, "10 Fascinating Facts About *The Birds*," *Mental Floss*, January 4, 2018, and from https://the.hitchcock.zone/wiki/Cinemafantastique_(1980)_The_Making_of_Alfred_Hitchcock%27s_The_Birds. Some dialogue attributed to LeGrue was actually said by bird trainer Ray Berwick in "The Making of Alfred Hitchcock's *The Birds*," by Kyle B. Counts and Steve Rubin in *Cinemafantastique* (Fall 1980).

Some of the dialogue and descriptions about filming *The Manchurian Candidate* in New York came from Don Ross, "Frank Sinatra: 'Decent, Wholesome and Nice Boy,'" *New York Herald Tribune*, February 21, 1962; UPI, "Actor Laurence Harvey Is Helped from the Freezing Waters," February 8, 1962; Earl Wilson, "Midnight Earl," *St. Louis Globe-Democrat*, February 9, 1962.

The description of Toots Shor's restaurant came from John Bainbridge, "Toots's World; Part II—Friendship," *The New Yorker*,

November 18, 1950, as well as https://www.tipsontables.com/toots.html. Details of the *Psycho* shower scene were relayed by Will Hodgkinson, "Secrets of the *Psycho* Shower," *The Guardian*, March 29, 2010; Oliver Lunn, "10 Things You (Probably) Never Knew About the Shower Scene in *Psycho*," *BFI*, December 11, 2017; and Bernard Weinraub, "'Psycho' in Janet Leigh's Psyche," *New York Times*, May 1, 1995.

Lolita actually premiered June 13, 1962, at Loew's State and Murray Hill Theaters in New York. Kate Cameron wrote about it in "'Lolita' On Screen...for Adults Only," *New York Daily News*, June 10, 1962. Some of the Kubrick dialogue was taken from an unpublished interview with the director by novelist and screenwriter Terry Southern; see http://www.archiviokubrick.it/english/words/interviews/1962southern.html.

Operation Northwoods was described in the National Security Archive at the George Washington University at https://nsarchive2.gwu.edu//news/20010430/northwoods.pdf. Other operations described in the book come from various sources, including a memo by Brigadier General William Craig to Brigadier General Edward Lansdale as reprinted in Letters of Note: Possible Actions to Provoke, Harass, or Disrupt Cuba, August 23, 2011; http://www.lettersofnote.com/2011/08/possible-actions-to-provoke-harass-or.html.

Lawford actually delivered the news to Sinatra that President Kennedy wouldn't be staying with him by phone. His thoughts in this novel are taken from his interview with Kitty Kelley for *His Way: The Unauthorized Biography of Frank Sinatra*. The party at Bing's house was taken from Kelley's book, as well as Bill Adler's *Sinatra: The Man and the Myth* (New York: New American Library, 1987) and Donald Spoto's *Marilyn Monroe: The Biography* (New York: HarperCollins, 1993).

Disneyland was described in "Your First Visit to Disneyland," *Long Beach Independent-Press-Telegram*, July 15, 1955. A great map of the park in that era can be found at https://disneyavenue.word press.com/2015/04/10/disneyland-map-evolution-1955-2015/. Christopher Klein wrote about "Disneyland's Disastrous Opening Day" at https://www.history.com/news/disneylands-disastrous-opening-day -60-years-ago. Other thoughts are from Kathy Merlock Jackson and Mark West, *Disneyland and Culture: Essays on Parks and Their Influence*. London: McFarland Books, 2011.

Details about Le Havre during World War II came from Andrew Knapp, "The Destruction and Liberation of Le Havre in Modern Memory," *War in History* 14 (November 2007).

Details about the Hollywood sign came from https://hollywoodsign .org/wp-content/uploads/2018/10/Hollywood-Sign-Brochure-FINAL

_102918.pdf; Rob Owen, "Hooray for the Hollywood Sign Hike," *Pittsburgh Post-Gazette*, January 2016; "Groups Rally to Preserve Historic 'Hollywood' Sign," *Van Nuys News*, January 18, 1973.

Dirty fighting in World War II is described in https://www.scribd.com /doc/33564438/Dirty-Fighting-World-War-2-hand-to-hand-combat -manual.

"The Ugly, Violent Clearing of Chavez Ravine Before It Was Home to the Dodgers" can be read at https://laist.com/2018/10/17 /dodger_stadium_chavez_ravine_battle.php.

The sad story of Marilyn Monroe is detailed by James Spada, "The Man Who Kept Marilyn's Secrets," *Vanity Fair*, May 1991, and James Patterson, *The House of Kennedy*. New York: Little, Brown, 2020. Lawford's introduction of Monroe at the JFK birthday taken verbatim from https://www.youtube.com/watch?v=JHt1_HXN8LI. Additional details about the Kennedy birthday party were gleaned from press accounts at the time in May 1962, including "Good Time Had by All at Million Dollar Party," by Milt Freudenheim, *Chicago Daily News Service*, and "Kennedy Bridges a Gap," by Mary McGrory, *Washington Star*.

Arthur Krim's house was detailed at http://daytoninmanhattan.blogspot .com/2016/01/the-j-harper-poor-mansion-no-33-east.html.

But again, let me underline, this is a work of fiction. My editors are insisting that I tell you I completely invented the song "The Devil May Dance," because they're worried some of the eager Googlers among you might drive yourselves to the brink trying to find it. Don't look for it; it's not real. Neither is the "Cubana" song from the scene on Tom Sawyer's Island, nor the snippet of the Sinatra song Lawford and Charlie hear on their way to Sinatra's compound.

I had great help in writing this book, from the support of my boss, Jeff Zucker, to wonderful edits suggested by dear friends John Berman, Matt Klam, Damon Lindelof, Geoff Shandler, and my little brother, Professor Aaron Hahn Tapper. After making excellent edits and suggestions to much of the first draft, my first editor, Reagan Arthur, left for another publishing house and I was lucky enough to have the talented Judy Clain come and steer the ship through rough seas and to port—I am so grateful to her and her team, including Helen O'Hare and Miya Kumangai, as well as Sabrina Callahan, Pamela Brown, and the whole gang at Little, Brown and, of course, Michael Pietsch of Hachette Book Group, who has been publishing my books for more than twenty years now. CNN's Lauren Pratapas and Anna Beth Jager were immensely helpful and supportive, as always. My lawyer Bob Barnett was a stalwart supporter as always; my agent Jay Sures was supportive while helping *The Hellfire Club* find a home in Hollywood. Most important, of course, I thank my loving parents, my best friend/wife, Jennifer, and my creative, beautiful, amazing children, Alice and Jack, to whom this book is dedicated.

ABOUT THE AUTHOR

Jake Tapper is the author of *The Hellfire Club*, the novel that introduced Charlie and Margaret Marder, as well as *The Outpost*, which became a celebrated film released in 2020. Tapper is an award-winning anchor for CNN, the network he joined in 2013. He lives in Washington, DC, with his wife, daughter, and son.